Megan's Kiss

by

Andre D. Cox

Table of Contents

Part One:

Reflections and

Consequences

Decisions

I look at the letter that is laying on my desk. There's an envelope crumpled next to it, and I'm smiling to myself. I am barely noticing anything else at this time, but in the background, Roger Daltrey is singing. Belting it out is probably a better description. Keith Moon is going hell for leather on the drums, and honestly? It's a bit too loud, but right now I have this rather childish urge to jump up, pick up the Mont Blanc lying next to the envelope, which is looking like a great substitute for a mic, and join in with them. I know the words, absolutely love the song, and I still think I can compete volume-wise, but I refrain. Instead, I reluctantly turn it down a touch, as it really was just a little too loud, and, letting out a huge sigh, I can feel my body relax now that The Who aren't pounding me into submission, but who can resist not listening to "Won't Get Fooled Again" at ridiculous volumes?

It's been three days since I received the verbal offer, and now I have the official one in writing. With my senses now back in the real world, I consider the letter. Firstly, it's not going to redefine my life; I don't need this job. Secondly, financially I'm more than fine, but this job is going to make everything a lot easier. It's the next stage, finally completed, in a decision I made a few weeks ago. I've been waiting for HR to process it, write it, get it signed off and posted, the US Postal Service to deliver it, and here it is, arrived at last.

I lean back in the chair, swinging gently, rocking side-to-side, and humming as an alternative to the impromptu performance still ready to burst out of me. My newly mapped out future with her, my girl, flashing in my imagination before me, and I'm now feeling relaxed and carefree. Just so ridiculously happy. Smiling like a child at Christmas. Damn! I feel like I've just met Santa Claus and he just handed me a winning lottery ticket. In the background, Roger is still belting it out with his fellow band members, and that urge to sing is still awfully tempting. "No one would know," I think, with a quick look around my empty room, considering my neighbors below me. If they did hear me, knowing me, they wouldn't be surprised, and I'm eyeing that microphone that looks like a pen.

A verbal offer is one thing, but there were always those little details that could easily have caused everything to have gone awry, ruining my very carefully mapped out plans. The deal with my previous company, allowing me to start a new position so quickly, might have fallen through, and there were a few people who had made a concerted effort to block my every move. Deals had to be struck, promises agreed, commitments made, and at any point, it all could have crumbled. One decision against me and nothing, nada, zilch, and yet I had still felt optimistic about getting this position, smiling with confidence at every criticism. My experience: excellent. My price: well below market value. I chuckle to myself, I'm very cheap, and I know Philip well. However, my previous employer? That was the unknown.

In the end, after they'd moaned and groaned, after they'd talked with legal and had me double check my contract, as if I hadn't known that they had a good point, they had acquiesced. It's good for them to be associated with this non-profit, and they know it. So, the deal was done. I shouldn't have been too surprised, it's what I do, and over the years they had paid me a lot of money to do it for them. Sure, they didn't want me to go, and they definitely didn't want me to go to a competitor, but that really wasn't the point, was it? I was going. I made sure they couldn't doubt that, and this deal was good for everyone concerned. And for me? For me, it removes any doubts and anxieties that I've been experiencing this past week or so. It's completed, so tonight I'm off to Boston to see *her*, with the good news of our new future.

The closing bars of the song pull me in for a moment, and again I'm temporarily on stage with the band, ready to take a bow; then I play the NBA player with the envelope. I can hear imaginary crowds cheering as I pick it up, crumple it into a ball, aim, and shoot at the wastebasket. And... it's in! Unlike some of the other pieces lying haphazardly around the improvised net, but I'm momentarily pleased with my three-pointer. A smug look still on my face, I lean back in my chair. I look at my Calatrava and check the time. As usual, I pause and admire its beauty, seemingly simple, yet classically elegant. I have no doubt that Nat would have approved of it, and when I purchased it, I believe that's what I was most likely thinking. What would Nat say? Would she approve? The aesthetic: maybe. The cost: not a chance. I chuckle to myself, register the time, and remind myself that I need to be leaving soon.

I can conclude this business on Monday before I drive back to New York to close out all my affairs here. I'll drop off the signed letter to confirm my start date, have a chat with Philip the CEO, and get the lay of the land, so to speak. I'm ready for this now. I've been preparing for this for weeks, and why? For her. I'm doing all this for her – Angie. This dramatic change to my life: quitting my job, leaving the city I've lived in and loved for the past sixteen years, it's all about and all for her. Angie. My girl. To be with her at last, to always be there for her. This, I look at the letter and my packed bags, this is what I want, this is all I want, and I can finally make up for the time we've been apart. So much time lost and so much time wasted. I continue looking around: I will miss this apartment though.

Hell, if I hadn't gotten the job, I would still be moving to Boston. This just keeps me occupied during the quiet moments, those times when we're not together. I just hope that she'll be pleased. I haven't told her directly, but I've implied it. We've discussed the idea of us being together a few times, sort of skirted the subject really, but we've not yet fully committed to it. Well, I'm now committed, I think triumphantly. In my mind, I smash my fist on my desk, but I refrain from such external extravagance. I look again at the pen with a smile, and I realize that R. Daltrey has just turned into R. Plant. Tempting, but I still resist. Oh dear, "Rock and Roll." Bonham's signature drums intro pulls me in, and it's so very tempting, as all the while I'm singing along in my head with Mr. Plant, "...hey, hey, Mother," my foot tapping along with Bonham. I turn away from the pen in an attempt to remove the temptation and stop singing along. There will be no impromptu concert tonight, folks!

My girl occupies my thoughts again, which she has done for the last three months now. We still need to get to know one another better, much better, but we're trying and we're slowly getting there. And later? I'm fairly certain she would love to move here, to New York. I smile. She just loves New York. I visualize the excited girl who wants to do as much in a weekend as is humanly possible, leaving me tired, but exhilarated, barely ready for work the next Monday. But would she leave her aunt and come here to stay with me? That's still an unanswered question. She's still so very young. What am I thinking? She's still so young? She's now old enough for college, and right now? She's currently pregnant, I recall sourly. Anyway, she's unlikely to think it's a good idea, and yes, she is still young, so I, at least for this foreseeable future, am going to go to her.

My change of mood quickly turns my previous optimism into a sudden wave of pessimism, and I find myself once again trying to justify everything, allaying any small doubt in my mind. I'll give her some space. I won't crowd her, but I'll be there for her when she needs me, and we'll see where and how it all goes. I just need to be patient. We've been getting on so well. We are getting on so well, I correct myself with a smile. Well, I think we are. I backtrack a bit, that pessimism still creeping into my outlook. No, we are! I insist with a little more confidence, reassuring myself. I could feel it, our conversations are less formal, less carefully thought out and more freely spoken. I love the moment her eyes, watching me with deep, silent concentration, suddenly light up during a conversation, and how her wide and totally disarming smile welcomes me when we meet. She's calling me Dad now, and my smile widens at the thought. Not all the time, but sometimes. Dad. I just love it when she calls me that. Dad, Dad, Dad, I repeat, feeling the sound of her voice in my head. And soon I'll be a Grandpa, I laugh at the thought. It does sadden me that someone so young, so unprepared is having a child, but I'll help her however I can. Anything. I'm coming, Sweetheart.

I lean forward and quickly scribble my signatures on the required marked places on the contract and place the document in an envelope fished out of my desk drawer. The envelope and signed document disappear into my bulging weekend bag, sitting on the floor beside me. I'm ready for my little girl, ready for this new future.

My mood darkens again slightly and I sigh, my grin disappearing as I am again reminded why I'm going through this dramatic change of life for my daughter and for me. Why? Because so much time has passed, so many years have been wasted. For eighteen years she grew up without me, without her father. All those years going by without me even knowing that she existed, and I would have continued to be ignorant of her existence if she hadn't written to me. That letter, so unexpected, took me very much by surprise. It was short and to the point.

Dear Simon Islane,

My name is Angela Bridgewater. My mother was Adela Bridgewater.

I am your daughter. I know you are my father. My mother never hid this fact, but she never told me your full name or where I could find you. My aunt has at last given me those details, where you currently are, and how to get in contact with you.

I would very much like to meet you. If you feel the same please write back.

I've enclosed some photos of me and Mom.

Yours,

Angie

Receiving that letter had been such a shock. No, it had been two shocks, both hitting deep within me. Adela, dead? And I have a daughter? It was hard to choose between these two monumental pieces of news. Which was the more painful? Being informed in one half of a sentence that the once love of my life is forever gone, or in the other half that she'd had our baby? A girl who, now after eighteen years, was just informing me of her existence. Both still sadden me, but only one still makes me angry.

I hadn't thought of Adela in months, the occasional fleeting regret usually set off by the aftermath of an evening out drinking and a night in bed alone. Reminiscing on those parts of my past always brings pain, though it has softened from the periods of angst and the near-constant agony I experienced in the year or so after she left me.

I have a daughter! The idea, even after three months, is still new and sends a thrill through me. The timing was perfect, or nearly so. I rethink that statement as a wave of anger surfaces. It would have been more perfect eighteen years ago, I remind myself, but given what happened, right now it is perfect.

That was then, and this is now. I have a daughter and she wants to see me. I relax and let the warm feeling envelop me as I smile at the thought. The past is the past, and I'm trying to move forward, live in the here and now, and the now is all about Angie. How Kay must have blanched when Angie asked about me, her intentions of finding me and getting to know me. I can't blame Kay. But eighteen years? I'm lying to myself. Of course, I blame her. My fist clenches at the thought, as breathing slowing I try to keep control. I am still very much angry at her and this whole situation. She could have prevented all this, so yes, I'm still angry with her, the smile disappearing from my face, a cold feeling of regret creeping through me, playing with the anger simmering below. If she'd only told me the truth, I would have been there for Adela and for my daughter.

I get up and pace around the room, primarily in an attempt to cool this mounting anger, but I'm also bored waiting. The music is, for the moment, in the background and has faded into the distance. I'm not tapping my feet, or singing along anymore, as a recurring question comes back to haunt me. Would I? Would I have been there for

Adela? I'm trying not to lie to myself. I'm trying to be honest, but the truth is difficult to discern after so many years. Would I really have put myself in such a position? A position where I may have had to give up the potential life of an NFL player to be with her and our child? The truth? Honestly? I've asked this question of myself so many times: I just don't know. This useless answer is still the best I can do after all these years. What else is there to say? I was 20, immature and stupid, so damn stupid. That's how I see it now, and I wanted to be part of the Game. I needed to be part of it, part of the team. At least, that's what I had thought then. I'd worked for years to be part of it. I'd trained hard, and I'd played hard. I wanted the crowds, the noise, the competition, the glamor. I can still feel the rush as I remember running out onto the field. Throwing a touchdown pass and then listening to the fans screaming, and enjoying the opposition booing. What a rush. I pause for a moment, sucked into that memory. A memory so easily recalled. It had been hard to let it all go. Even when I didn't have a choice after the injury. The camaraderie and even the failures. I wanted everything, even the losses; they were part of the game too. I wanted it all. I wanted to prove I belonged there. I needed to prove it. So, would I have quit? Would I have given all that up if I'd known? I would now, of course. There is no doubt in my mind about it now. Now, the decision is easy, but then? Then, I don't know. These questions keep coming back, haunting me, and I still have no clear answer. There seems to be no answer that says: "I am the truth, you can stop searching."

And Kay? She knew I was alive, and she knew I was working here in Manhattan. She could have told Angie about me at any time. Well, Kay's told her now, I remind myself, and am I surprised she hadn't before? Of course not! She really hated me, and I would assume she still does. She probably believes she's been doing the right thing ever since.

I find that thought somewhat depressing, it reflects on me, her opinion of me, as a person. Did she really hate me so much? Yeah, it's a depressing thought. I continue to wander around my study, aimlessly picking up arbitrary objects and quickly placing them back in an attempt to distract myself, but there is no interruption to these thoughts because they consume me.

We had gotten on so well, I recall so vividly. There were times, many times when she had told me how good I was for Adela. How we made such a great couple, and I'd smiled in agreement, so confident I was of our relationship. Adela and me? It felt fated. That is until my selfish, stupid decision. Deep down I know the truth: I'm not angry at Kay. This I have learned to accept as a truth. This is what it is really all about; I'm angry at myself.

Oh, Adela, my love, why didn't you call me? I loved you so much, and I know you loved me. I would have come running. I would have, could have, helped, I… but the doubt is still there, isn't it? The doubt is always there. Would I really have come running? And I'm still asking myself this question. I've beaten it to death. I still ask it, because I still don't know.

And considering myself back then? I was so shallow, so self-centered. Have I really changed so much? I look back at the person who was me then and I have to ask myself. Have to? I don't know, I do anyway. Was I truly as shallow then as I now believe I must have been? Was it really all about me? Football? The crowds? Adoration? Sometimes I believe it was, it must have been. I remember the pleasure in such detail, but it all seems so trivial now. I can't have changed that much, can I? I'm better now, aren't I? I know I would quit for her now. But then? There is so much doubt, and there is still so much guilt because I just do not know.

I've returned full circle back to my chair. I eye it, shake my head, at it, at everything. I turn away from it, turn back, away, and then I flop back down into it. I'm depressed at this train of thought because I've found that one of the consequences of having my daughter back, is the return of these memories. I've tried to hide from them, keep them suppressed, but now they're back these last three months. Back to haunt me again after all these years. I can't blame her. How can I blame her? It's not her fault. It is most definitely mine. Adela, I'm so sorry, and even more so now you're gone. A sadness hits me at that thought, and I recall our last conversation those many years ago, wrestling with the situation we had created. It was the last time I saw her, and lately, I've been reliving it repeatedly, trying to find some tiny, extra, missing clue to these questions I am endlessly asking of my younger self, as I'm still trying to find the elusive satisfactory answer. Even though I know it's futile, even though I know there's no future in any answer, I still ask the question, and I'm still looking for that answer that I know doesn't exist, as I relive that last day with her over and over again.

We are sitting in her dorm room, the weather hot, the sky cloudless, the air conditioning humming in the background. I'm sweating despite the cold air being pushed into the small room. I'm nervous. I glance at the window and see the sky, blue and inviting, and for a moment I'm thinking: we should be outside, holding hands, eating ice cream, enjoying each other's company, but we're not. We're inside, in here, in her dorm room. Where it's cold and forbidding, the atmosphere oppressive. Where I'm feeling the walls closing in on me, and I'm thinking: I have football practice in thirty minutes. Maybe I can use that as an excuse to leave, just to get out of this claustrophobic room, but I look at her and realize: I can't do that.

She most certainly isn't happy to be here with me, that is so painfully obvious, and I remind myself that she'd rather be outside as well, but probably…probably? No, definitely not with me. Her body language is so negative that she is unable to look me in the eye for more than a fleeting moment. A flick of her eyes towards me for just a second or so and then her head drops and she looks away again. I find that action so depressing. She asked me here, and I wish I hadn't come, and I'm playing with that Football Practice excuse.

"We have to talk about it," she said.

"We have to decide," she insisted.

No decision had been reached last time, and I have to make a decision, tell her what I think. She wants to know, she tells me. Aren't we here to make this decision together? I ask myself, screaming on the inside.

Before the news, we were that perfect college couple. Friends would tell us how lucky we were and how they wished they could have what we had. Our respective families had welcomed each other and told us how good we were for each other, how well we complemented each other. We spent all our spare time together, and there was no one else's company we preferred. We had started to talk about marriage after college: our futures, our careers, our children, in hushed conversations, with cuddling and kisses, touching and holding hands, always together. It was perfect. We thought we were perfect. We knew it!

Then a mistake. I clench my fist at that thought, squeezing my eyes shut hoping it just never happened. It did. A mistake? Is that the best way to describe it? One small act, a life changing event for us. Earth shattering? To us? Yes. A mistake? That just seems like a wrong and inadequate word. How did this happen? Well, that's obvious! Whose fault was it? Who can say? I know that I'm blaming her. She had warned me, and we'd both laughed. At the time did either of us care? Of course not. We'll be okay. It's so unlikely. We've done it before. Why worry? So, how can I blame her? I'm just as culpable.

Then "The Result" came. We were oblivious to the mistake before the results, we were still happy, and even after the self-test came back positive, we were still hopeful. We were still in it together, a couple. Then the doctor confirmed it, and I suggested... and now this! Estranged. Apart. Barely able to talk to one another, to even look at each other in the eyes. And she has such lovely eyes. Dark, barely able to discern her pupils, they dominate her face, seemingly larger than normal, but now they harden or look away with hints of shame and recrimination. I know, because I feel the same, as we each pass blame onto the other. We're uncomfortable in each other's company, yet silently pleading to hold each other, but we keep apart. The silence is so loud, screaming in my mind, I have to break it. There's still a decision to make. Am I, are we, ready for a baby?

"So, have you thought about it? Have you thought about what I said?" Am I pleading? Am I being too detached? I worry my tone is wrong, and I stare at her, hoping for an answer, but unable to gauge her thoughts.

She's just sitting there, looking away into a distance I can't see. She's not registering the question or me. I give her a moment, the silence still loud between us. I'm not sure if she's even heard me. I try again.

"Hey, Ade, are..." She had.

"So, you still think we should get rid of it?" she asks, cutting off my new attempt, her voice tiny and neutral.

I'm not used to hearing this new voice of hers. There's no warmth in it, no love, no laughter. It's not her voice. I tell myself, knowing why. She's still looking down at her hands, twisting her fingers, her body turned slightly, ever so slightly, away from me. I'm looking at her, watching her twist those hands, and I notice that she's been biting her nails. Once beautiful, so carefully groomed, so carefully maintained, they are now bitten to the skin. Now I truly understand, and I'm reminded, that if this is bad for me, this is definitely not going well for her. Those hands, once so lovingly cared for, have reminded me.

A baby? Does she know what she wants? Or is she forcing me to make this difficult decision for her? Thoughts are continually screaming in my mind. She isn't helping here. I thought I was helping her, but she's not giving me anything. I don't know, Ade. Should I? You make the decision for us. Are we ready for a baby? Really? A baby? Us? We're still young, still at college. What does she want to hear from me? I try explaining again.

"Look, Ade, we're young. Perhaps we should finish college first. It will determine our futures. I have a great chance of being picked in next year's draft. A baby's a lot of responsibility for the both of us right now. There's always later..." My voice trails off. Isn't there? Am I ready for a baby? I'm I ready to be a father? Now? Nothing is convincing me I am; that we are.

"So, you thing we should," she hesitates slightly, looks at me fleetingly and then away, back at her hands, "get rid of it?" There's that phrase again, and I wince. I hate that phrase, I really do. I'm sure I can hear a hint of disgust when she says it, and she refuses to use the other word: abortion. I don't like the sound of either wording choice. The words sour my thoughts, and that phrase, completed, is not gone, it still bites into me, lingering between us. It is full of so many connotations. I don't know, maybe it's me, maybe I'm disgusted with myself, but having a baby? Me? Us? Now?

"I think it's for the best," I reply. I don't know if I'm ready. I shout to myself: Are you, Simon? Are you ready? And I look at her: Please just give me a sign of some sort, anything, I beg, but I don't say anything to help her.

"Okay, if you really think so," she says, her voice quiet, lifeless. I haven't helped, have I? I really don't know want she thinks. She looks back up at me and doesn't look away. At last, I sigh. I was finding it hard to talk to her when she kept looking away. Now she's searching my face. For what? I'm not sure. I'm so confused, and she looks so desperate, so depressed, so ready to submit. Ready to quit? This just isn't the Adela I know, this isn't the vibrant, strong willed girl I know and love, and I know why, I think shamefully. Come back to me, Adela. I reach for her, but she leans back just enough and I pause, pulling my hands down to my sides, confused and hurt.

She continues looking at me for a moment, then without warning, turns away and stands up, a graceful motion that took my breath away when I first witnessed it, and it still achieves that effect now, a motion born of the dancer she is. My eyes follow her sway, her natural rhythm, as she glides towards the window. She stands there, silhouetted, no obvious sign of her condition, and I watch, entranced, as she stares outside into what appears to be a better place than in here, into a world I so fervently wish we could be together in. I love her so.

Then, the spell partially broken, I rise, smoothly but with athleticism and power, not the subtle grace of a dancer. She would say, with power and precision. I move towards the window and stand behind her. I can smell the subtle mix of aromas from her hair, her skin, her sweat. Eyes closed, I breath her in, familiar and erotic, wanting to touch her, wanting to hold her, and for a moment remembering a world passed: pleasant, hopeful, an old world, one where we're hopelessly in love, now weeks gone, and I want it back so badly.

I open my eyes, still wishing that world hadn't disappeared, and she's facing me, silently, in this new one, still searching for something that I don't understand, and I'm still in the dark, still confused, so I try again.

"Let's finish school first, then there'll be more time for us and more time for kids," I say with a finality I do not quite believe, but I make the decision. For both of us? For her and for me, I think guiltily, knowing I'm being selfish, and for a moment I hear the roar of the crowds, see the smiles of my teammates, and then that moment is broken. She is so beautiful.

"Okay. I see. I understand," her voice is still neutral, but clearer now, firmer.

Inside I smile, just a small one of hope. She does understand, I believe. I'm so glad that she does. We can go back to being us again.

"I'll see you later, okay?" she asks rhetorically. Of course it's ok, my love. She doesn't look pleased, but she gives me a smile, not one of her radiant, enveloping smiles, but a little taste of a smile nonetheless. I can't expect that radiant smile in these circumstances, but I've still received a smile from her, however small, and there's hope filling me.

Relief starts to wash over me as now I'm believing we'll be okay once we're through all of this. I'm hoping, praying for it to be so. Yes, once we're through all of this, we'll be okay. I know it. I believe it so much. I just have to or my heart will break.

"Yes, of course," I reply with hope, supporting her. Yes, this will soon be behind us, and we'll be together, like before.

"I'll see you tomorrow, Simon. I just need some time alone. I..." she pauses, the tight smile fades, she looks worn out and fatigued, "I have arrangements to make, then I believe everything will be fine."

"I understand. You know where to find me if you need me." I feel a warmth running through with relief. I'm so hopeful now, the encroaching sadness has been somewhat halted, and suddenly being in this room doesn't seem so bad.

"Yes. Yes, I know," she confirms simply, and now she's looking at me with renewed intensely, her brow creases, the blank look is now gone. I still can't read her, but this is preferable to her staring elsewhere. Then suddenly, she leans forward. She wraps her arms inside mine and around my torso, her fingers grabbing my back. It's so quick, so unexpected, that I jump with surprise with the initial contact. The side of her head crushes into my chest, and she squeezes tightly, the warmth of her body spreads over me with the pressure, and I relax with the contact, as it offers a comfort I haven't felt for days.

"Oh, Simon, I love you so very much," and I hear such depths of pain, of anguish, of love, in her voice. I feel it deeply, and I bring my arms up and hold her as if this is the only thing that matters, and I feel that if I let go, I will die, we will die, and that the world will crumble around us, but she's told me that she loves me, and I can hear and feel it in every fiber of my body that she means what she says, and at that moment it is just us, together, and I'm so happy. I feel that I really could cry, but I hold back as I always do, trying to be strong for the both of us.

"I love you too, Ade," I whisper with a tremor that courses through my body. Hugging her tighter, I kiss her on the forehead and squeeze her body gently, grasping her with my hands, and realize I mean it too. I know without any doubt that I mean it, a truth suddenly laid bare in front of me, as if for all these months of being with her, I never fully understood what it truly meant until now. This is the girl for me, there is no doubt in that statement, not anymore, and I've always known it, but here, at last, I realize it to be the truth and then everything crystallizes. If she wants the baby, I'm fine with it. All she has to do is tell me. But this, I believe is better, isn't it? She says so. Now, with our minds made up together on this matter, we can be happier after we're through this. We can make this work, and we'll be much stronger because of it. We'll be together, and we'll have kids later and this, all this, will be a distant memory.

She pulls away, the pressure of her touch disappears, and the cold and the world intrudes again, and looking down at her I see that there are tears in her eyes, but her head quickly turns and she's looking down at the floor and not looking at me at all.

"Later, Si. I'll see you later," she mumbles and then turns, and head still down, she leaves me alone and cold, as I watch her go in that loud silence. She pauses slightly at the door. I hope, and silently pray, that she's going to turn around, that's she going to run back into my arms, but then the door opens, warm air flows in and with a click she is gone, and I stand there alone in her room.

"Adela," I say, quietly, trying to fill the hole left by her absence, and I hear her footsteps fading into the distance.

I never saw her again.

The next day there was a letter posted in the frat house from her, and my heart broke. The envelope had my name handwritten on it. I opened it with tentative hands because deep down I knew it was not going to be happy news. Inside, on ordinary photocopy paper, short but beautifully written with obvious care and love:

My precious, precious Simon, love of my life.

Being with you has been a dream come true, and the last 18 months have been the best of my young life, but I am sorry. I'm so, so sorry. I'm achingly sorry, but I can't stay here, with you or at college, with this decision we've made. So, I have decided that we can't be together, and I can't be with you. I need to move from this life and try and find my way elsewhere to start again with renewed purpose. I'm moving back to live with my sister. She's just received a job offer in another city, in another state. I'm going with her, and there I will try and start again, and attempt to come to terms with my decision. Our decision.

Please don't attempt to find me, and though I know you will try. Please don't!!!

I love you and I will always love you, but I know that I cannot be with you and that there is no future for us anymore.

The Lord be with you.

All my love, yours forever, now forever lost.

Adela xxxx

I haven't cried many times in my life. I'm not the crying type. As a kid, watching the classic movie *Old Yeller* was about it. That's something I've always remembered. It's rather silly really, definitely childish, but for some reason I always recall it, I just do, especially in moments of stress. I was seven or eight, maybe that's why it left such an impression. I still think it's weird. I use it as a fun anecdote from my past to laugh at with friends. To show them that I have a soft side, but somehow, I believe there's more to it.

Then there was the time when I got my preferred college offer, but that was different because then I was crying with joy as I thanked Tim, alone in my room, arms raised with the relief, tears streaming down my face, crying at the heavens and newly promised futures. This is something he never needs to know, the sudden sobering thought comes to me, and I shudder thinking of him knowing this, and then I laugh. It's Tim. He was my best friend, probably still is, it wouldn't really matter. He wouldn't judge me for crying.

And I recall, always with shame and regret, the last time I cried. Much later in life, crying when my parents died. I was abroad on business, where a huge contract was in the balance and I was the one to save it. I did save it, but I didn't get back for the funeral, and the guilt still hangs heavy as does the pain of their passing. Later seeing the photos of the mangled car wreck, an unwanted vision imprinted on my memory. Standing in the cemetery alone, looking at the tombstones side by side, and the disapproving look on my sister's face for not being there, bringing me such shame and tears. I was never able to celebrate that business deal, overwhelmed with guilt from the success of it. The joy I felt at my achievements, juxtaposed with the pain of not being there for them, for her, Jackie, my sister, who needed me so much. I miss her too, recalling, with further guilt, that she died soon after our parents, and we never resolved the issue. We never got to speak, so there's the added guilt there for her. I never told her how much I loved her and I've never cried for her.

I've been strong and confident all my life, dominating the offense, controlling the defense, beating the opposition in sport, at college, and now business. After I read Adela's letter, I broke down, repeating her name over and over again, tears flowing uncontrollably, body clenched so tightly I thought something might break, and I truly hoped something would. I remember wanting to smash everything around me, but I refrained. I just sat there sobbing for the first time in my life, and it didn't feel good. The subsequent drinking didn't help either.

The next day was even worse, awake and sober, fully cognizant of what I had done and the mistake I had made with that terrible decision. I spend hours analyzing the conversation we had in that room. Trying to understand how I missed the obvious, now realizing how much I'd hurt her. Wishing I'd supported her instead of pushing my own selfish agenda on her.

She was right: I did try to find her. I was wrong: there wasn't "always later."

And the decision? Is the word "wrong" appropriate? Is it truly indicative of the scope of my failure? Is it really a good enough, big enough word to describe the impact of what I had done, the pain I had brought to the most important person in my life? And now when

I see my daughter, she continually reminds me of how stupid I had been when I was 20.

I'm now 39; 40 in two months. I'm still single, and possibly not any less stupid, though probably, I'd like to think, a little wiser. I'm definitely more cautious, and hopefully, more mindful of others. I've done well at work. Who am I kidding? I've done great at work, and I still have lots of life and new chances and choices still to go.

Since college, I've had many dates, met some great women, and some pretty so so, and I chuckle, remembering my Match days, but I haven't found another Megan or another Adela, and most certainly not another Natalie: my tall, crazy Artist. I haven't found a life partner. I've not even been close to finding one, surely, but possibly unfairly, defined by my relationships with these extraordinary women. They've set the standard for me and the opportunities have never appeared to come again.

I fish out my wallet and open it, and take out one of the photos of Angie and her mother. My love, Adela, a few years older, now noticeably a woman, changed from the girl I knew, but still recognizable, still beautiful, and my daughter, much younger, a child. Though now grown up, she's still a child to me. They are together, smiling. I will always keep this close to me. I won't forget either ever again. I sit up straight and, putting the wallet back, I chide myself.

"Stop feeling sorry for yourself," I say out loud to break my maudlin mood. I have a chance to redeem myself in both my eyes and my daughter's eyes. Hopefully, in years to come, I can believe that Adela forgives me, even if I can never forgive myself. I look up towards the heavens. She is so sweet, Adela. I tell her, deep down believing, hoping, she can hear me. And Kay too. I remind myself. You have both done such a wonderful job, and I sometimes, just sometimes, think that maybe she was better off without me.

I'm feeling better, as thoughts of Angie sweep aside those painful memories of Adela, at least for the moment. Angie will have her baby soon, she's due sometime in November, and I'll be a grandfather. I'm not even a proper father yet, and soon I'll be a granddad! The thought provokes a chuckle and a groan. A granddad? I can live with that. I'll work hard at both; I won't let you down, Adela. She didn't start college this semester. She told them that she was taking a year out. Now she has nearly a year to prepare, a year to be a mother before the needs of college life swamp her. I may still need to convince her to go. She knows that I will help her, that I'll be there for her, but in a year? In a year with a child, she might change her mind. I know Adela would want her to go, and heaven knows I do, but what little Angie wants is what is important. I'm with her 100 percent. Whatever she decides, I'm there for her. Even if I disagree. I roll my eyes. Even then, I reminded myself, smiling ruefully, the sadness fading as I think of my new future; maybe 99.999 percent, I chuckle.

I lean back and survey my room, the familiar surroundings calming me and I realize I'm missing it and the apartment already, even while I sit here, but I've made the decision. Everything is ready, so next week I need to start sorting out: not being here, not being in New York! At least for the next six months or so. I lean forward and pull a pad from out of the drawer and retrieve the pen lying on my desktop. Ready, I lean back in the chair and start to make a list.

My mind clears and I notice that the music has stopped. I decide to leave it off for the moment. I'll have plenty to listen to it on my trip. I check the time again. I still have plenty of time before I need to leave. I twirl the Mont Blanc that was nearly a microphone through my fingers as I think about my tasks for the coming week. The room is now silent, and the familiar sounds of Manhattan are in the distant background.

Okay, where to start? Jason, Tuesday is usually good. I'll check on the details of her Trust Fund and my Will and Estate as we'd discussed earlier this week. Thoughts of the excellent sushi enjoyed during our last lunch enter my head. I hope I can find as good a place as that in Boston. I'll check with Philip, he'll know.

Okay, Jason, and again I chuckle, do I really need to see you? I'm shaking my head. I don't need to see you at all, I answer myself, but I do enjoy your company. The subtle aroma of fresh sushi is still playing in my memory. He will, as usual, do a great job, as he always has done for me. My skepticism of his legal and financial skills disappeared years ago. He's earned every penny I've paid him and more. I bequeathed a couple of the paintings in the dining room to him, but is that a bit much? Well, I know he likes them, and it's just a gesture. I'm absolutely sure he could easily afford his own, but on the other hand, these, I twist to view the paintings in this room, these are her early works, rare, very hard to find and now very much in demand. So, it is a very, very nice gesture, I correct myself.

Distracted by the paintings I'm now looking at, I remember those days during my MBA. It hadn't been a long relationship. Why had I asked her out anyway? The memory coming back the instant I ask myself the question, and I recall why with a smile of nostalgia.

It had been a dare at a post-graduate party we'd crashed. The night was young, and we were bored. We walked in, the four of us, cocky and confident young grads with a purpose. We surveyed the room, jostling each other as we quickly made decisions about the women and some of the men, and then, there she was. She looked so different. She stood out from the crowd, and we were all impressed, chatting excitedly about her, and we all agreed, laughing amongst ourselves, we had to try. If nothing else to prove to ourselves our manhood, and she was definitely worthy of such an effort. She was tall and elegant in her long gown and high heels, seemingly overdressed for such a party, but she really stood out, catching our attention as exceptional amongst the jeans and t-shirts. She looked so confident, and she had a smile that could either make you soar or bring you crashing down to earth.

My friends: "the Warriors Three," you can guess what they called me, had already experienced the latter. In a flash of that smile, in a turn of a phrase, they had crashed and burned, and we'd only been there 30 minutes or so. They had dared me, had bet amongst themselves on my odds of failure. You have no chance with her. If she's not interested in me, why you? I bet she's a lesbian. Has to be, they laughed. Go on, I dare you. They commented, joked, dared! I was intrigued and really couldn't resist the challenge.

I glided over, parting the room with my confidence, my most winning smile at the ready. She was tall, her build was slim, accentuated by her dress, which flowed over her curves. Her hair fell simply to one side, and I tried to see the color of her eyes as I walked towards her. She watched me as I approached, a smile playing teasingly on her lip, her eyes glued to mine, daring me, calling me over. I arrived oozing confidence. She, however, just ignored my initial advances.

She looked me up and down with hazel eyes, flecked with green. She paused, as if thinking of the appropriate response to my admittedly poor attempt, and then asked, in a beautiful mezzo soprano with a very unexpected English accent, "Mozart, Picasso, or Miles? Who was the most important?" The accent caught my attention immediately, and for a moment I just savored it. Outside of TV and movies, I'd rarely heard it in person. I shivered with delight at hearing it, simultaneously moaning at the proffered question. She looked at me with a truly beguiling smile that she held just over the rim of the champagne glass from which she was slowly and deliberately sipping, daring me to make a fool of myself, confident in her basically correct assessment of me, that making a fool of myself was the act I was most likely to perform next.

"Honestly?" I asked. It was the best I could come up with at that moment, simultaneously distracted by the girl and stymied by her question, based on the sad premise that she was right and that I had no clue on the subject and less of a reasonable response to the question. Mozart, Picasso, or Miles? Are you kidding me? I thought, loudly to myself, trying to keep my composure. Why not the "The Beatles, Stones and Led Zeppelin?" Knowing how impressive I could be on that subject.

"Honestly," she repeated, so very sweetly, her voice husky, and musical. I could imagine Mozart asking her to sing for him, Picasso asking her to pose for him, or Miles naming a song for her. Me? At that moment I had nothing to offer. She slowly sipped as she waited, fingers delicately holding the fluted glass.

"Well, we could discuss this over dinner, if you..." trying the direct do or die approach.

"No," she interrupted gently, "I think I would like your answer now," she laughed. A little twinkle of a laugh, refreshing and infectious. Laughter lines betraying the obviously fun she was having at my expense.

"Now?" I asked, depression setting in, thinking I had nothing, not even one remotely interesting thing to say on this subject.

"Yes. Now, or I'm gone," she laughed again, but now with some finality, waving the glass holding hand in a direction other than here, her eyes firmly fixed on mine, holding my helpless returned stare, daring me.

"Okay," I breathed in. I'm going with the truth, I thought, there really wasn't much I could use to embellish a lie, "I can honestly say that I don't know anything about them outside of the movies and other general stories, and seriously I wouldn't recognize them even if I tripped over them in the street." I winced, that sounded much worse out loud than when I'd formed it in my head, a lot worse. It was supposed to sound funny, sort of geeky, bring some levity, show my fun side. Stupid was the only expression that now came to mind, really stupid, and on hearing myself say it out loud, I didn't find it anywhere close to being funny, so I was fairly sure she couldn't have.

Resigned, I was already imagining the pats on my back in sympathy from my fellow rejected friends.

"Nothing?" she beamed at me, and then, from the flicker of a look away, a glance at her nearly empty glass, a hint of disappointment, a slight shift of her shoulders and I knew she was ready to move on, or away from me at the very least.

"But!" I exclaimed, with not a little internal desperation, thinking furiously.

"Oh, you have a big but?" she said still smiling, her eyes still holding mine steady, but now seemingly recovering her interest, at least in the conversation, if not in me personally.

"Yes, I have a huge but!" I smiled back, letting that wonderfully clichéd line hang in the air a moment, "but, you teach me about Amadeus, Pablo, and Mr. Davis and anyone else you desire for that matter," thinking I had quickly managed, at the very least, to show her that I knew their names, and hopefully convey to her that I'm not a total ignoramus, "and then, I don't know, after five weeks? ask me the question again, and then consider me, and my answer, hopefully," I paused dramatically, "worthy?" I completed with a question as graciously as I could muster in the circumstances, my winning smile returning, desperate and possibly ready to beg.

I was already intrigued by her. I could feel my heart beating faster, the beginnings of the prickling of sweat on my forehead. I was ready for this challenging lady, but I was preparing to go down in flames. I truly wanted to believe that she had, at the very least, a little interest in me. I watched her, hoping, as she pondered my offer.

"Five weeks?" That twinkle of interest was back.

"Just five," I said with hope, feeling I was about to drop to my knees. I wasn't above begging, at least not for the right girl. She'd ensnared me, my heart was hammering with desire and anticipation.

"You've intrigued me, Mr. Islane," she paused, a little dramatically I thought. I got the obvious hint. She knew my name, and she obviously wanted me to know that she knew. She'd known even before I'd started to make a fool of myself, I realized, groaning inside. "But I think...three weeks?" she asked rhetorically, "Oh, we're going to have some fun, you and I, but first, there are some ground rules!" she stated mischievously, grabbing my arm and pulling me close. I breathed in, intoxicated at the closeness and her aroma.

"I can handle ground rules," I smiled inside and out.

Six months and Natalie! I, of course, surprised her, and, to be honest, myself too. I think that it really took only two or so weeks before she realized that I was actually interesting. We got on well immediately, but she held me at arm's length for those two weeks, attempting to test my patience, my resolve. Only two weeks? I would have easily waited longer for her. I'd been so happy to disappoint her initial conclusions, and she was happy to be disappointed. I smiled at that memory. I'd known after two minutes!

And for six months? For six months I enjoyed my first, fully committed relationship since Adela, this was never going to be a quick one or two-night stand. She made sure of that, day one! I never got bored of listening to her talk, and as far as I can tell I didn't bore her, and for those six months I managed to forget about Adela. Okay, I didn't forget about Adela, I correct myself, recalling those occasional days, morose and angry, but she wasn't on my mind 24/7 anymore, and those depressing moments were few and far between when I was with Nat.

Nat pulled me out of the funk I'd been in for nearly two years after Adela had left me, and she introduced me to the world of Art. It was a whirlwind six months, a glorious six months, and I learned so much about Art, Music, and Culture. Jazz? Tim had tried and failed. Classical? Megan had tried and equally failed. Nat? She managed to instill both an understanding in me and more, and with understanding came pleasure and a new-found respect for that "old stuff" that I had such a disdain for before.

By the time Nat had finished with me, I knew the difference between Schubert and Schumann, the Impressionists and the Expressionists, Bebop and Modal, and I could understand that crazy "Scouse" accent. She even introduced me to some interesting Rock, though I never developed her penchant for Progressive Rock. While she did develop in me a different perspective to music, it wasn't just one-way traffic. Rock was my forte, so I was able to introduce her to my world as well. We're talking a girl who loved Radiohead but didn't appreciate Joni Mitchell! Played Dire Straits but didn't listen to the Talking Heads! Yes, I had a major contribution to make there.

I must admit though, if I had heard Blur's "Parklife" a few years earlier, I'd have sung that one on the stage with the band. Every time she played it, I could visualize the band playing it, and once I'd even given her an impromptu show, a veritable tour de force performance, singing that song at a karaoke night. She'd been in fits of laughter at my fake English accent, joining in with me during that infectious chorus.

But the relationship hadn't lasted long; it was just too intense. It was educational, collaborative, and the right kind of crazy, and the amount of time it did last was perfect. There was never that deep blush of love between us, the love I had with Adela and still feel for Megan, but we both obtained what we'd wanted, what we needed, and happily, with only a twinge of regret, we parted as good friends.

I smile at my nostalgia, it really had been such a great and unique time for me, and I was unable to recall such a similar feeling in recent years. We'd played off each other the whole time, but we were just too competitive, and possibly too aggressive - not in a physical or ever in an angry way - but definitely intellectually and emotionally, and sometimes sexually. And, though we enjoyed it, after six months, we were both thoroughly exhausted. Neither of us would let up, and so it had to end. I was disappointed, but not totally surprised when she ended it. We stayed very good friends, and I can't and never will be able to thank her enough. During those six months, the painful episodes of my life faded into the background: Megan, Adela, and my injury all took a backseat, and I was able to move on.

I stare at one of Nat's paintings across the room, its swirls of color reminding me of happier times and a life changing education and an intense unique passion, the like of which I have never encountered since. I smile wistfully, remembering: what a time that had been, and sigh with fading reminiscence at the painting. Megan gets this one. The memory of her easily coming back to the now. This painting always reminds me of when she allowed me to confront and conquer one of my fears.

I think of my two best friends from high school. Tim and Megan will be happy with what I have left them, it's not too much, but it'll help them, and I think I owe them something of my good fortune, and thus my fortune, I laughed, and anyway they're my best friends so it's another good gesture.

Oh, dear! Aren't I a bit young to be thinking about death and Wills, but then I recall the reason I'm doing this: Angie! This was all being done to ensure that whatever may happen to me now, tomorrow, in ten years, that she'll be okay, that her child, my grandchild, will never want for any necessity.

Oh, how my mind is wandering, and aren't I being just a little bit morbid and just a tiny bit maudlin? Shaking my head with a smile. The past, my past can do that, but I'm happy because I have a future. A new, purposeful future, I tell myself, and I know I'm ready for the change and I know that I mean it. Yes! I'm ready to leave Manhattan for Boston. I'm ready to move on for Angie.

And Megan? Last Wednesday's events come flooding back to me, my mind still racing as I'm enjoying the painting I'm still staring at – from one love to another. I see that Nat understood that story more than I had realized when she painted this beautiful, powerful piece of art. How can I doubt that she understood my memories associated with it? As it invokes everything, and more associated that moment. They recall Megan and my love for her, and then seeing her, that night was...

She looked fantastic, her hair was pulled back into a ponytail showing all her face, and she seemed... just the same! I hadn't seen her in a couple of years, and I swear she really looked the same. I hadn't seen her looking like that since before her marriage: her eyes wide and alive, a confidence lost for many years, now returned. She was wearing a form hugging, dark burgundy dress. It looked black at first in the darkness, but then it showed sensuous colors that flicked in and out under the street lights. She'd kept herself in good shape. Her dress pulled in, extenuating those curves of her; she was never thin, and I ran my eyes up and down her body, heat building up in me, as I watched her hips swaying to the beat of her walk. Her heels looked uncomfortably high, but she seemed to have no issues walking in them, although I winced at the thought, and when she was there in front of me, she reminded me, because after so many years I had completely forgotten what she can sometimes do to me, so desirable, so unintentionally sexy: I wanted her, and the picture was completed, all pulled together by a necklace with a single pearl at her throat, and those forgotten passions returned to haunt me, and my next decision concerning her.

I knew then, that the intervening years had dulled my memory with other women and other relationships, but as I watched her, as she came towards me, her walk familiar, yet even sexier, her bearing now so much more mature and so grown up and confident. She appeared so different, and yet the same. I recognized so many subtle aspects about her that I've known for so many years, but I was also seeing a new woman.

And she is an actress! I really couldn't believe how good she was on stage. It was so pleasantly surprising to witness: she was so powerful. Initially it was a little weird, like watching two people at once, a sort of schizophrenic act, the woman she was playing and the woman I know in juxtaposition, but after a while her performance won out and she, for the most part, as every now and then my mind flittered back to the girl I knew, became the portrayed character.

She'd never pursued her career while married, so I never had the chance to see her acting. With her husband traveling, moving around the country every few months, she had no opportunity to pursue this great love of hers, but seeing her now? I can honestly say I was very impressed with her performance. I think I'll donate some money to her troupe. I don't think Jason will object if I up my non-profit quota a bit.

How she had talked and talked. I laugh at the memory, she had obviously needed to unburden herself after another shitty relationship, and I was happy to be there for her, but I am truly glad that I was able to unburden myself as well, that I got a chance to tell her about Tim. Though there's no denying that was an awkward moment. I had no idea how she was going to react to that news, but all things being considered, it didn't go too badly. I wasn't too sure how I was going to react to the news myself. I still desired her, desire her, but it was the right decision. We'll see where that all goes. I laugh again as I recall her confused look and her nearly incoherent responses. In retrospect I was possibly a little harsh when telling her, it was hard for me too though, but we'll see. I still believe it was the right thing to do.

My mood sours again for a moment as I remember my true feelings for her, and how they don't coincide with her feelings for me. I know she doesn't feel the same way about me as I feel about her, I remind myself again, still trying to convince myself otherwise. Of course, the reality is that I've known this for many years, and I close my eyes and contain and control the painful thoughts, and slowly, very slowly, they fade away but don't disappear. On seeing her, even the new, more confident her, my memories were strengthening, and it took all my will power not to grab her, kiss her passionately and tell her how much I still loved her. That would have been truly foolhardy and stupid. We had our time, and I had messed it up.

But Tim! Our mutual friend. I've made this decision and am going to follow it through as best I can. I've thought it through, and I've reconciled it with my own emotions, my own desires, and I believe that Megan and Tim could work. If nothing else she should try. I might even get the opportunity to be Best Man for the first time. My eyes light up at that thought, images for a speech already forming. The distraction doesn't last long. I've always known, deep down, even before Tim told me that he had wanted to ask her out, that he wanted so much more out of their relationship. It was so obvious, even then, but like me, he valued her friendship. Like me? Much more so than me. I should have told her years ago, I've known for years how he felt, but then she met Peter, and then she married the asshole. I roll my eyes, and give a small shake of my head, as I feel a tinge of bitterness towards a man I barely knew but truly despise for what he'd done to her, my dear friend.

She seems to have recovered well, but when she mentioned him I could see the pain in her eyes and hear it in her voice as she continued talking about him. And poor heartbroken Tim? Tim had been distraught when she had gotten married. He'd tried to hide it, but it was so obvious. To me anyway. He hadn't lasted long at the wedding, making some sort of lame excuse, he'd left early and I could see he was in pain. I wanted to help him, but he wasn't listening, and let's be honest, I wasn't feeling too good about the whole thing anyway, even though I was with Liz. Yeah, it was hard to talk to him. I not sure he even knows why she got divorced. I haven't talked to him since, and I know he hasn't spoken to her. I tried to get in touch with him, but it was so difficult talking with him after the wedding. I really tried, but he just didn't seem interested. I should have tried harder. Of course, he wasn't interested! He was in pain, I reprimand myself. He was my best friend! I should have tried a lot harder. Maybe I was being a little selfish, even though I knew how he felt about her. I still loved her too, and when she'd left Peter, I thought, I hoped, I prayed that we could try again. Get to know each other more intimately now since we knew each other so well. An old flame, still friends. I knew I could do better, that I could try harder, that we could try again, I kept telling myself. I had been kidding myself, just nostalgic, wishful thinking.

We have a great friendship, and I treasure it so much. I understand that now, but I still have to remind myself, again and again, that she just doesn't think of me that way. We tried, it didn't work, and it hurts, but I can honestly say I can live with it. I suddenly smile to myself, with a snort. Well, I can now, now that I have Angie. With Angie in the picture, everything else seems easy, sometimes irrelevant, definitely secondary.

I'm back in Manhattan next week, so I'll call and see her again as I promised that night. We'll meet up after her show, and I will tell her everything else. Honesty can be so contagious. I'm smiling and feeling good about myself. And I have to see Tim. I need to tell him to follow his dreams, take a chance with her and just go for it. I jot both points down, I don't really need to, but I like the gesture. Seeing it in writing reinforces the thought, and I feel like I'm doing something selfless, something worthwhile, for my friends.

With this new positive outlook, I look across my desk and see the letter propped up against some books. My last loose end before I go? I lean forward, fingers tapping the desk in deep thought. There's a decision to be made here, I fruitlessly tell myself. Reaching forward slowly and deliberately, I pick up the letter I'd written to Angie in a moment of despair a few weeks back. That wasn't a good day. It wasn't a good few days, I correct myself, wincing at the memory, but smiling since we are past it now. I fish into the envelope and pull it out. I read a few lines, not really concentrating: the rest is so easily recalled. Yes, they really weren't very good days at all, the memory still strong in me.

Since then, I've told myself, promised myself, that I will not hold back on any of the truth with her again. I will never lie to her, she deserves better than that! But when "That Topic" had come up that afternoon…I felt a tightening in my stomach at the memory of it. I was unprepared. I always knew it would have to come up at some point, but here it was, earlier, rather than later. Much too soon, I now realize, and I had thought I was ready for it. I had most certainly thought about it many times, coming up with various responses to this inevitable question. I really thought I was prepared. I was wrong. Prepared? I wasn't even close to being prepared for it, but I didn't realize how bad it would be, how bad I would be.

A moment's silence in the conversation and I am enjoying the peace. Surrounding us is the buzz of a distant murmuring, as can always be expected in this small but busy restaurant. We've had a nice meal, laughed together, and shared some secrets from our pasts, and we're getting to know each other a little bit more. I'm feeling content and relaxed. It's not too noisy here, I'm thinking with relaxed thoughts as I flow with the surrounding buzz, and the food is very good. I like the place. I enjoy the moment, looking around at the decor, running the food's tastes and textures through my head. Yes, it was very good, I confirm to myself, satisfied.

I look at my daughter in this comfortable silence, and she's looking at me, head slightly tilted to the side, eyes slightly scrunched. She's studying me. I'm reminded of her mother, and I get the feeling that she wants to say something, but she doesn't quite know how to put it. There's a certain posture and look that her mother had, and I believe I can see it now. If she's anything like her mother, it shouldn't be too long, I tell myself, and I wait, expecting something soon, but too relaxed to worry about it.

I've enjoyed the evening and currently don't feel the pressure that I sometimes do to impress or to occupy the silent spaces, so I sit content to wait in this quiet and relaxed moment.

"Why did you leave Mom?" she says, and she's looking at me, eyes wide, expecting something.

And there it is. The calm is broken, and a tension enters me almost immediately. She's broached that subject, and I should be prepared for it, I really should, but I'm not. I had thought I was prepared for it, and now, suddenly, I don't know what to say. I'm speechless. It's amazing how quickly my mood has changed.

My mind, just seconds ago relaxed, is now racing, searching for an appropriate response to a question I've anticipated her asking since before we met, but now all those prepared responses seem inadequate. I try being a little cagey, try to feel my way carefully through the situation, improvise a reply where, hopefully, I won't appear to be so bad. I made a mistake, a terrible mistake with Adela, I don't want to make the same with my daughter.

"Well," I begin with a confidence I don't really feel, "I didn't leave her, she left me," and the moment I say it I know I've already made another mistake. It sounds honest, and it isn't actually a lie, but the connotations imply otherwise. I've removed all the context, and so it most certainly doesn't tell the whole truth, and I know that I'm not being honest with her or myself.

"Don't be facetious!" she replies quickly, with a hint of contempt, her eyes flashing, staring at me, daring me to say something else stupid. She is angry now.

There is no easy way out for me, there never was, I tell myself. There is only the truth and the repercussions that may come with it, and though I'm looking at her, focused on her, inside I close my eyes and resign myself to this truth.

"She left me," I say with a quiet, honest caution, and her look hardens, lips tightening, and she's staring at me, daring me to say something else stupid, and I continue, "because I couldn't see past myself and my own desires. It was the worst decision of my life. I put myself before her," my voice drops further, "and before you, and have regretted it ever since," my voice shakes as my shame is palpable; I can feel the heat rising to my face. I'm staring at her, but I want to look away, ashamed. For weeks I've been trying to show that I'm a good person, a good father, despite what I'd done to her and to her mother, but now it all appears to be undone in a moment.

"So, you did want to get rid of me?" That phrase again. It digs deep into me, and now I recognized the contempt in it, the same as her mother had, but this time I know it for what it is. How can I explain such a thing to her? She's just made the same decision as her mother had.

"Angie, I…" I try to explain.

"No!" She cuts me off short, and then abruptly gets up, the chair tipping backwards, crashing to the floor, the noise resounding through the room. She just stares at me ignoring the noise ringing off the walls, and ignoring my shame on full display in my reddened face. Then turning, she leaves without a backward glance. People are staring at me as I sit there in my disgrace, and I'm staring at a closed door, trying to ignore the increase in the ambient noise surrounding me.

If the long drive home from Boston was painful, the next few days are agony for me. Angie usually called or texted me on the Monday after our weekend visits, but not this time. Monday, nothing! All day at work, my mobile beside me, all hopes unfulfilled.

And by Tuesday night? I'm frantic, berating myself over and over again, the conversation continuously running in my head. Each hour I'm concocting a better response. I want to call her, but I know I can't. It's now out of my hands. There's a bottle of wine, nearly finished, beside me, and I stare at the monitor on my desk, her last words running in my head, repeating over and over again, I can't forget even as I try.

I realize that I need to explain to her about me. I need her to understand about Adela and me. I need her to understand that she is safe with me, to know that her future is and will always be safe with me. I need her to know that I'm not a bad guy, that I wasn't a bad guy even then. I was a young, stupid man who made a terrible decision. There is nothing I can say to remedy what has already happened or what I did or why. I'm not going to try to justify those past actions. There are no words I could use to do so. This is my shame and I've accepted it, but she needs to know that I truly believe we have a future together, that I have something, a lot, to offer her and that I will never again leave her. So, I decide to write it down. I collect my thoughts. I need the cathartic experience of putting it to paper, so I type.

It takes me most of the night, even though it isn't even that long, and another bottle of wine, whose taste I barely notice, though I feel its effect. I print it out and hold it, then consider tearing it up. I sip the wine and then read it and re-read it, and I'm still feeling such deep-rooted shame, and I'm tired, a little drunk, and a lot worse for wear. I fall asleep on the sofa.

Wednesday morning finds me cramped and sore and still tired. I didn't have a good night's sleep, and though I'm not hungover, I'm definitely feeling the effects of a heavy night's drinking not supplemented with any food. Gathering myself and sitting up, I find the letter is still in my hand. I look at it with disdain for a moment, recalling last night: my actions, my emotions. I open it up, smoothing the crinkled edges. Through blurry eyes, I read it again and again and again. My shame returning as regret floods my thoughts until I am fully awake and cognizant of why. Head down, I slowly raise from the sofa, and with anger building in each step, I make my way over to my desk. I stand at my desk, staring at the computer screen, with fists pressed into the desk's surface as I'm fighting for control, and I think of the letter now in front of me, and the circumstances of its creation. Anger? Rage? What's the point of either? I berate myself as I bring myself under control and start to stop feeling sorry for myself. I made a bad play, I scold myself. I need to be positive, live with it, and move on. There's always another play. Or nearly always, I remind myself, and place it in an envelope and sign her name on the front. I prop it up on the desk against some books. My anger has now subsided and I assure myself that I will send it if we can't get past this. No more lies and no more anger! I'm still feeling pretty awful, and a long, hot, thought-filled shower doesn't really help much, but I'm at least calm when I exit the bathroom.

Half way through dressing, I decide that I'm not going into the office today. I'm depressed and I'm moody, and during the last couple of days I've moped around the office and have already pissed off a lot of people that I work with, people I like. So, I elect to work from home. Surprisingly, I actually get some constructive work done. Talking to clients, people I don't know, or barely know, with no personal ties, is easier than I initially expected, and to be honest, positively distracting, and Renée, my assistant? She handles everything else, as she usually does, with an efficiency I find borders on the uncanny.

That evening, I'm feeling a little better, just a little, not so frantic, not so self-deprecating, and I'm glad that there's no more anger. I've also decided to forgo more alcohol. A Mozart piano concerto is playing in the background, and amidst all of this, I'm reminded of my desire to learn to play the piano. I happily remember an impromptu recital Nat gave me once when we sneaked into the college music hall one night. What she played I cannot recall, mixing Classical with improvised Pop, tinged with Jazz, as I'd sat on the bench next to her mesmerized. I still remember the desire of wanting to be able to perform such myself. A dry chuckle escapes my throat, yes, I'd love to play, but I still haven't actually made the effort to learn that skill.

With Mozart's music as good company I browse a book, but I'm not really reading it; Joyce is not a good choice when in this mood, a book I'd started reading a few weeks ago. It's a great book, but I'm thinking, given my mood, I'd rather be reading the flow and rhythms of something like Hesse's *Siddhartha*, its inherent beauty and rhythmic prose possibly a more apt balm for my troubled soul.

Then my mobile rings and my world stops, as does the music and my breath. I'm mentally crossing my fingers, hoping, praying that it's Angie. The caller id answers my prayer; I am relieved but still worried, but I appear to be breathing again. My persistent pessimism is getting the better of me and I'm visualizing an Adela-like "don't bother looking for me" rerun of that painful past episode, the one that caused all this, the one where I hear the phone click cutting me off again, and then I have to post last night's letter tomorrow morning, in sorrow and in pain, but none of that is going to stop me answering the phone.

"Hi, Angie?" A vision, where Kay is on the line again, momentarily materializes.

"Hi," Angie replies, her voice soft and quiet, and I don't hear any anger, even in that simple single word.

"Hi," I reply not knowing what else to say. I'd already decided to let her take the lead, control the conversation.

"I'm sorry I haven't called since the weekend," she pauses, her voice still, but clear, "and I'm sorry I left you so abruptly. I was taken unawares at my reaction, and honestly? Now I've thought about it, I'm not too sure what I expected from you. Will you forgive me?" How can I not?

"Of course, Sweetheart. I will always forgive you." How could I not?

"Thanks, Dad," my eyes close and I brighten somewhat at the word, "I just needed some time to think things through, to be alone with my thoughts, and sort things out."

"That's okay, Darling, I understand."

"Dad, I do understand what happened," she rushes, "I know how Mom felt and I know it's as much her own fault as it is yours, maybe more so."

"My decision made..."

"Please, let me finish," she interrupts, and I can hear that she has prepared this and needs to continue quickly, without losing her thread. My heart is bursting for her, and all I want to do is hold her tight and tell her everything will be alright, "I've had a few days to think about this, and I've had Auntie Kay screaming at me, but more importantly, reminding me that she may not like you, but she understands me. She understands that I need to get to know you, that I need to be with you. She understands that it's not about her and me, but you and me. I love you, Dad, but I don't really know you at all. Sometimes when we're talking I see Simon, a stranger, and sometimes I see Dad."

"I love you too, Sweetheart, and I do understand. It takes time."

"And I know that, Dad. I'm not going anywhere. I not going to hide because we disagree, but sometimes I'll..." She stops abruptly and I hear the heaving and broken breathing that indicates that she is crying, and it hurts me so, tugging deeply into my chest.

"Please, don't cry, Angie," my heart is tearing and I can feel my own tears coming. "I never want to hurt you. I never wanted to hurt your mother. I feel terrible." The sound of her sobbing is causing me to start hating myself again. I can't believe what I've done, I most certainly didn't want to do it, and yet, somehow, I have done it.

"Dad, I am not sad, I'm happy," she sniffs down the phone, and a jolt of surprise and hope runs through me.

"Sorry?"

"Thinking of Mom sometimes just makes me cry, and thinking of you and the missed years sometimes makes me cry, but I'm not sad," and I can hear the lightness in her tone.

"I think I understand," and I'm so relieved, and I feel the tension, that has been building up and gripping me these last few days flow and fade away, and my whole body relaxes. I sink back into the chair and start to enjoy the moment.

"I'm happy we found each other. I'm so glad I now have a dad, and I'm looking forward to getting to really know you better. I really am." The lightness in her voice lightens my soul.

"And I you, Sweetheart."

"I have to go, Auntie Kay is looking at me rather severely," she laughs.

"Well, we can't have that now, can we," and I smile for what seems the first time in days.

"When are you coming up next?"

"I can't do this coming weekend," Oh, I sorely wish I could. I run through possible scenarios, but all are failing, due to my current commitments, "but I'll be up the next," as I remind myself to cancel one meeting I know of that weekend. I pause a moment, still wondering if we are okay, there's still that persistent pessimism, and there's still the skepticism due to the shame that will stay with me for a while, "if that's okay?"

"Of course, it's okay, dummy. I love you. Bye, Dad," and I can hear that she's already off to whatever she wants to do next. "I'll call later in the week."

"Bye. I love you too, Sweetheart," and then she's gone, and I feel a lot better.

It was at that moment, after she'd forgiven me, the phone still in my hand, the piano and orchestra fading back in, but now over the tiny speaker, that I realized what I truly had to lose and what I needed to do. It was at that moment I made the decision, relaxed now, after days of anguish and angst, fully contented at those just passed moments, that I decided to leave all of this. Move to Boston to be with her, my daughter, the only person who matters to me and who needs me. The next day I handed in my notice.

I jump in surprise, back to the present, as the buzzing against my chest reminds me it's time to leave. I flip the phone out of my jacket pocket, look at the alarm, checking the time that I already know, and turn the alarm off. I twirl the phone in my hand and pocket it in one smooth practiced motion. I don't need to be reminded again, I tell myself, my bags are packed and I'm ready to leave now.

I look at the letter still in my other hand, still unread, and I carefully place it back in the envelope and put it back into its previous position, propped up against the books. I pause, just for a moment, still looking at it, the memory of its creation continuing to haunt me, a question still unanswered and again distracting me. Should I read it again? Just to reminded myself? As if I really need reminding! No. I'm sure I can recall most of it by heart. I don't need it, I realize, I can tell her myself now. She's given me this second chance, and I'm not letting it go to waste.

I now know, and now understand what's next for me, with these recent events now ingrained in my memory. We still have a long way to go, we still have a lot to learn about each other, but the letter, this letter, I don't need that, it's served its purpose. This is the only way, and now I can tell her myself.

I lean forward, pick it up and stare at it for a moment, still unsure, still undecided, and I lean back in my chair and start rocking again, considering. Should I keep it, or should I throw it away? Keep it. Throw it away. The opposing thoughts running backwards and forwards in my head. I turn it around in my hands a couple of times, deliberating, and then the rocking stops, I'm resolved. I tear it in half, quickly crumple it and throw it at the waste basket, but no points this time as it misses. I don't really register the fact at first, as I'm already making my way to the front door. I've picked up my weekend bag in one hand and keys in the other, and my mind is already moving to this journey I've thought about for days now. I'm out of here, and I'll clear that up later, I tell myself. I'm already closing the door behind me, not prepared to go back now. Such a gesture, I chuckle and shake my head, there's still a copy on the computer.

I pull out of the garage and it's raining, absolutely chucking it down; "cats and dogs" comes to mind, a favorite expression of Nat's. Where do the British get their expressions? Why cats and dogs? The image pulls a chuckle out of me. The Stones are playing in the background and keeping me good company, and I'm back in the college band again.

Driving out of New York City is no worse than usual, though right now it's exacerbated by the rain and the cracking of lightning, lighting up the dark horizon, causing Van Gogh's masterpiece at MOMA to come to mind, the quaint townscape replaced by the gorgeous brutality of the New York skyline. But this weather, the drive out of New York, neither point is bothering me, not even putting the tiniest dent in my current happy demeanor. I can easily handle a few hours of this, if at the end I get to be with my daughter. I have Mick, he's not bad company for the trip to Boston, rain or shine, and I'm still smiling to myself, a wide grin I just can't seem to remove, and why should I?

The congas of "Sympathy for the Devil" grab my attention and there, in my imagination, is Tim playing one of the world's greatest bass lines, in one of the Stone's greatest songs, though admittedly he's looking more like a frantic Flea than the stoic Bill Wyman. And there's me, strutting up and down the stage, bare chest puffed out, an impression of Mick Jagger nearly complete. "Please allow me to introduce myself..." I hit the first lines exactly in time with Mr. Jagger. New York City Friday night traffic, a deluge with cracking lightning and thunder in the distance, and the Stones for company, my daughter waiting at the end of it; the drive out is really not so bad.

The quiet rumble of tires on tarmac and the metronome clicking of the wipers are not nearly enough to disturb my listening pleasure as the guitar riff, coupled with the crackling sound of the harp, catches my attention, and Mick and the band have me hooked again. "... Midnight Rambler ..." I sing out loud, adding my bass baritone to the chorus, enjoying the pleasures of a band at its peak: '65 to '72, before I was even born, and let's be honest they were pretty good outside of their peak. I haven't listened to the Stones for a while, it suddenly dawns on me, and they quickly reminded me why they are still my favorite band.

Both my school and college bands played cover versions of some of their most popular songs. We played them with a manic energy and exuberance worthy of the band themselves, but this one was a particular favorite and always fun on stage. Peter had that riff down pat, and every bass line Tim ever played for us sounded great, and me? I would parade around the stage chest bare, affecting Mick, flirting with any and all the girls close to the stage.

Stones or Beatles? I laughed at the thought, seeing the young me and then imagining the older me still playing the front man, and for a moment I think, how stupid, but then again, I remind myself, the Stones are still touring and still pulling in the crowds, and my laughter continues. The Beatles? No chance, no contest. I was, without a shadow of a doubt, a Stones man, I snorted as my good humor continued unabated. That was one of those subjects that Nat and I always disagreed on. I would counter that she's probably biased, given that she's Scouse, but then, sneakily, as she put it, I would additionally annoy Ms. Stones, by reminding her that her surname wasn't Beatles, so maybe her family tree was telling her something that she didn't want to admit?

The traffic is thinning a bit now, but the weather is still terrible, who needs to be driving in this if they don't have to? But for me, it's not an option and not a big deal. I'm feeling young again, ridiculously carefree and I'm continuously smiling. I'm nice and comfortable in my car, feeling positive about myself and my future for the first time, in what now seems years, and I have the Stones here with me as company. There are no complaints from me right now as I thread my way through the traffic and away from Manhattan.

Does Angie know the Stones? I ask myself suddenly, her mother loved them. I realize, with surprise, that I have never brought them up. "I'm a Mon...key..." I join in again loudly and who cares? No one can hear me here. Her music education is about to begin, I promise myself. Then I remind myself that her mother was a huge fan, so it's highly likely she does know them, and finger tapping, I see her laughing as she watches my rendition of "Monkey Man."

The music and miles slowly, very slowly, roll on. "You can't always get what you want…" I'm singing along with Mick and his school choir, tapping the steering wheel and nodding in time with the beat, and so very pleased with myself that I can still remember the nuances, and as the track is coming to an end, "You get what you need…" I think before Mick does, I hope so, I agree ruefully. I'm ready to at least try this time. I'm now wondering which track is next up in the mix, and nod approvingly as another band and fan favorite, "Brown Sugar," starts. I am thoroughly enjoying this drive despite the terrible weather.

My mind flits between the process of driving and singing, and it suddenly comes to my attention that I'm driving pretty slowly. Peering out through the wipers and the rivulets of rain flowing down the windscreen, I realize that I've been following the same car for the last few minutes. I'm fairly sure it's the same car, unless I'm driving behind another slow Audi. It appears to be the same car as when this track now coming to its end had begun. This weather is admittedly terrible, but why is this guy driving so slowly? I glance at the speedometer. 23 mph? Seriously? Okay, the weather is bad, but 23 miles per hour bad? I'm not going to use my horn, I decide, though it's very tempting. I'm frowning and shaking my head because I am very much considering using that horn, but, finger poised, I tell myself how annoying it is when others do it. How I've previously shouted, in my head: Why? What's the point? So, I decide not to, but still, he really is driving slowly and making it so very tempting, and I consciously move my finger away; it sorely desires to press the button.

I pull out carefully looking for oncoming traffic, there are no car lights visible, nothing ahead, the way forward is dark. Let's get past this car. He, or maybe she, is holding up my meeting with my girl. I'm now distracted from the music, my attention fully occupied with moving past this ridiculously slow driver to continue my journey apace. I look in the rear-view mirror, and the lights tell me that there are a few cars building up behind me. In the distance, I believe I can hear a car horn, and I smile to myself, in a rather self-congratulatory way and put my foot down to overtake this unbearably slow car. The acceleration pushes me gently back into the seat, the rapidly building pressure is exhilarating, and my smile continues.

Jagger is in my ear, my new future is ahead of me, and the lights of New York are fading behind me. New York. I'm not done with you yet. My daughter is waiting for me, so you'll have to wait, but I'll be back, I promise, we'll be back here soon. My life and my future are looking good, very good, as I effortlessly pass the Audi.

Drive carefully

"Excuse me, sir, but are you the gentleman who called emergency services for an ambulance?"

Jim looked up and there, darkly shrouded in a waterproof cowl, stood an officer. His voice was deep and calm, and his hood was up; Jim subconsciously checked the air condition surrounding him, taking a quickly glance at the sky; it had stopped raining.

He refocused on the officer now before him. It's about time, he thought. It's been over an hour, but I've waited patiently, in anguish. I've watched as officers have talked to the other witnesses, and I've waited. I've watched and I've wondered. Every time they appeared to be finished with one of them, I've wondered: when are they going to get to me? I witnessed it all. I was right there, his car was next to mine when it happened, I watched as it rolled, I watched...

Tension rose as the pain of memory grabbed him in a strangle hold, and he tried not to think about what he'd seen. At last, someone is here to talk to me, and he hoped, prayed, that unburdening the event would help because this internal monologue was not helping him. His thoughts kept going around and around, re-playing that terrible event vividly in his mind.

I should have phoned my wife, he realized and reprimanded himself that in all this time he had failed to do so, but he had been so preoccupied with his pain.

He'd watched in pain as the ambulance had taken the injured man away a while ago now, but it wasn't a physical pain, and he himself had incurred no injuries. It was a mental pain, a pain derived from a horrific vision etched deep into the very depths of his soul, as if imprinted in his DNA, and he feared it would never leave him.

He had witnessed the accident, and now the memory came back unbidden. He had stooped over the injured man and had tried, unsuccessfully, to help him, as blood pooled everywhere. He looked at his own shoes and could see the dark stain of the man's blood on them. He remembered the pain carved into the man's face, unable to talk, but reaching with his eyes. I can't stop seeing those eyes, he thought, deep anguish washing over him. His eyes stung at the thought, and his stomach clenched with pain.

It felt like hours now that he'd been watching. He had watched as the members of the other vehicle in the accident were gathered up in a group, seated, unhurt, surrounded by other officers and emergency service people. He couldn't make out their faces, but he could see them turning to each other, probably for comfort in that mêlée of authority.

He had watched as the other witnesses had given their statements. Waving their arms, pointing and gesticulating at objects and people to make their various points, and now his wait was finally over. Finally, someone had come to talk to him.

At least the rain had stopped, he thought, well at least for the moment, looking at the sky and seeing the gathering rain clouds, gray against a black sky, highlighted by the city in the distance, the pin-pricks of light creating the skyline of the city he knew so well.

When the police had arrived, it had still been raining, not as badly as it had been during the accident, but still a steady drizzle of rain with only a light wind, and so he'd sat in his car dripping wet, water pooling on the floor, alone with his thoughts. The dark water reflected what little available light there was, reminding him of the blood. His hands had been clenched tight and his eyes glaring wide as he had tried not to cry, as he had tried to expunge the memory; neither had worked, so he had sat in the pool of water crying, watching as more emergency services vehicles arrived announcing themselves with flashing lights.

The lights were still here, but at least the rain was gone, and he'd left the confines of the car for the outside, with just a spray of moisture in the air. Breathing in deeply he noticed that the air was crisp and had a fresh green smell, so noticeable in its contrast to the smell of his city. The surfaces glistened with reflections upon reflections: red and yellow and blue on black, of moon light, head lamps, and spinning emergency lights.

Now, at last, it seemed his wait was over, and he was asking himself. Am I ready? Now just a little unsure of himself. Now just a little self-conscious, worried he might not be able to control himself, worried he might break down in front of these strangers. He was still disorientated, his senses still reeling with the shock of the sight of those injuries sustained by the man in the car.

They've come to me, but am I ready to unburden, to recall in speech that which I have just witnessed with these eyes? He focused his eyes and there in front of him, the officer still stood, his waterproof cape reflecting light, his face dark, hidden in the folds of the hood, as the bright lights backlit his form. He stood quietly, large and imposing, obviously waiting for Jim to respond, but he appeared patient, not rushing the witness.

Jim gathered himself. He wanted to run, to hide somewhere, but he also wanted to unburden himself, recount the story, exorcize it, let it out and shut the doors and windows of his mind so it would never return.

"Oh, yes, Officer, err, yes, I..." Nodding quickly, in small jerking motions, his voice came out tiny and nervous. He tried to make out some features in the dark recess of the officer's hood, his facial details concealed, barely discernible. Calm yourself, calm yourself, he kept repeating to himself, as his heart fluttered, beating so loudly he thought he could hear it.

"I'm sorry it has taken so long to get back to you, sir. May I please take a statement from you?" the dark visage asked, politely and calmly.

He wanted to ask the office to put the hood down, but he couldn't find the courage. It had all been used up in the flurry of the storm and chaos of the accident.

"Yes, of course, I've been waiting for you. You asked me to wait after you took my details. When you arrived, earlier, a while back. Of course, I'm ready now, please ask your questions," he was babbling, feeling nervousness rising within his stomach, spreading out with the onset of returned panic. Was this the officer? He asked himself, or was it another? He tried, as his mind started wandering, with nervousness, away from the original question.

"Now, sir, just relax," the dark visage asked patiently. I'm trying, thought Jim, I just can't, I can't, I can't, he found himself repeating, as the increased tension gripped his body, the experience playing over and over again in his mind, the wait had allowed the events to become the focal point of his thoughts, and they were painful and unrelenting. He closed his eyes, momentarily, to allow himself to think through the panic.

"Yes, of course, I'll try." He took in a deep breath, listening to the air vibrating through his nose. In, out. In, out. He started to relax, concentrating on the moment and he forced himself not to look at the carnage to his left. The wheels of the upturned car sticking out from behind the officer, which only reminded him, again, of the terrible event. The lights spinning in their rainbows of color which continued to be disorienting.

"Are you okay, sir?" the officer sounded concerned.

Jim rapidly blinked, bringing himself back to the moment. He still felt awkward, and breathing deeply, he realized that he was starting to relax in the man's company, at least a bit. As long as I don't look over there, he thought, where blood was pooled, black on black on the tarmac. Once again, his mind wandered, and he thought of his shoes, blood stained and ruined. He couldn't actually see the blood from where he was, but he knew it was there. He had seen it crawling away from the injured man, whose body was now gone, but whose image remained in his memory, the scene constantly reminding. In, out. In, out.

"Yes, officer, carry on, please. I'm okay now. I think I'm ready," he smiled weakly at the sheen of the reflected lights coming off the cape, and at the unseen face, dark and hidden, behind the glare of lights, bright and strobing. Sort of ready, he thought to himself.

"So, sir, could you please tell me what you witnessed?" he asked, his tone still patient.

In, out. In, out. Jim's shoulders rose and his chest filled out as he took another deep calming breath, "Yes. Just a moment, please, okay?" he exhaled slowly. Then pausing for a moment, gathering his thoughts, his eyes closed, he allowed himself to remember, the incident coming back in more detail than he liked. "I was driving slowly because of the rain, and this Mercedes overtook me," he quickly started.

So simple and yet that's what happened he thought, gaining some relief by just making the statement, and he momentarily gained some composure and returned his gaze to the wheels behind the officer, as he continued.

"He, the injured man, obviously didn't see the car coming towards us on the opposite side, on his side. I didn't notice it either, not at first, not until the accident was actually happening. It seemed to all happen in slow motion, and the weather was so bad, the visibility just wasn't very good at all. The car seemed to have come out of nowhere." I'm babbling, he thought, did the office get all that? Was it too much, too quickly! Why doesn't he remove that hood?

"So, you didn't notice the car coming towards you?" The office interjected, with a calmness Jim really wished he could have too. For a second Jim felt panic, he was suddenly worried. He'd remembered that he hadn't been wearing his proper glasses, so had the visibility really been that bad? Panic started rising. It's not that I can't see out of them. It had been pouring down, his windshield wipers were working furiously to allow him to peer through the deluge, but how did he not see the car coming towards them? How could he have not noticed it? The officer waited quietly for him to continue. It's just that…and then it came to him, previous forgotten, but now recalled. Previously hidden behind a sequence of events of turmoil and of pain, but now returned, the image fully formed in his mind.

"They had had no lights on!" he blurted out. He stared in the direction of the young people sitting with the other officers, but he couldn't actually make out any details due to the glare of the lights, only the shadows telling him that they were still there. "Oh dear, I remember now, officer, their car headlamps were not on," he stammered. How could he have forgotten that? He felt embarrassed at the thought.

"You claim their car headlamps were off sir, is that correct?" the officer prompted. Jim paused a moment in thought, he felt pressured, as he started to realize the implications of what he had just said, but the memory had returned, fully visualized, fully recalled, there was no doubt in his mind now. They had had no lights on. They had appeared to have come out of nowhere. No headlamps? How stupid! Anger suddenly filled him at the thought, both of the fact, and his lapse in memory.

"Yes, officer, I'm sure of it," he stated firmly. He stared again at the group. "The Mercedes had overtaken me." Such a nice Mercedes, he had thought, suddenly distracted, recalling the time he had taken one out for a test drive, unable to actually afford one, a whim, a dare, a passion. He refocused. Then it had swerved.

"It had started to swerve away. The Mercedes that is. It swerved away from me, and I had wondered why. I turned to look ahead and I could just make out a car coming towards us, without lights on, just an outline of black. I was braking and could only watch as it happened to the side of me, there was nothing I could do. Nothing," he stared at the officer for a moment, stricken, who just waited, and he continued. "His car, the man's, slid into the road's side fencing, avoiding them and then it rolled over a few times. They had just slid straight, then skidded into..." The aftermath scene returned to haunt him, interrupting him. "Oh, it was terrible, I couldn't believe my eyes. There was just nothing I could do as I brought my car to a stop." His anger had slowed and panic had fully risen back to the surface due to the awful memory.

"Okay, thank you, sir, that's very good," interrupted the office gently, "let's take it back a bit. So, was the car driver speeding, was he possibly driving recklessly as he overtook you?"

"Well, yes, no. I'm not too sure. Definitely not recklessly. He didn't appear to be speeding as he passed me. I must have been doing about 30-35," he paused slightly wondering if that would have been regarded as too slow on the highway, he'd been driving carefully, maybe even slower than that, possibly too slowly. A couple of cars had sounded their horns when they had passed him earlier. Maybe one of the other witnesses had mentioned it to the officer? "It was raining so hard and the visibility was really quite bad," he looked at the dark, hidden visage of the officer, unable to get a feel for what the officer was thinking. I must have said that ten times, he thought. Have I said that several times? Why is he asking me? It was their fault. It was. It… He calmed for a moment. The man's just doing his job. Just tell him what you know, and then you'll be able to go home soon and leave this place. The thought flowed through him, and gave him some comfort.

The officer continued, "So the driver overtook you and swerved to avoid the oncoming car, which, you say, had no lights on." His hood turned slightly towards the car crashed into the side, its front buckled in, the driver's door still open. "Then the car rolled a few times, with the driver crashing through the window. Yes?"

"Yes, yes, oh god," he felt the panic rising again, "it was awful, the car slid, aquaplaned?" he looked at the officer expectantly, and then nervously continued, "Yes, it slid, skidded, and then the car just twisted and turned over and over and over. Oh my god, it was terrible. He just flew out through the window screen, after the car hit the barrier." And the fright of that memory, and what was to come, took hold of him, and he started to cry again.

"It's okay, sir. Take your time. We'll be finished with this soon. We just require a few more details." He waited for Jim to stop sobbing. After a short moment as the sobbing subsided, Jim felt relaxed enough to continue and looked up again, at the invisible, dark visage.

"I'm so sorry, officer," he offered, holding back further tears.

"That's okay, sir, just relax and try not to worry yourself."

"Okay. Sorry, yes. I think I can continue. What else would you like to know?"

"So, after witnessing the accident, you stopped your car, and?" Waiting for Jim to fill in the details.

"Well, yes, my car stopped a little further down the road, as had a couple of others behind me, and I ran back towards the crashed Mercedes and the driver, to see if I could help. It was terrible, there was blood everywhere, as I said, the driver had been thrown from his car. I don't think he could have been wearing a seatbelt, but he was still alive. He stared at me blinking, gurgling blood, unable to speak, and his arm? It was terrible. His arm..." but he couldn't bring himself to talk about it. The image was seared into his memory. It was so clear, in such detail, and ever present in his thoughts. It filled his mind. "They had had no lights on." The anger had returned, and looking over he noticed that the group, from that lightless car, were being escorted away, arms behind their backs, heads bowed. Good, he thought, and looked at the office and then it occurred to him.

"You knew though, didn't you?" he asked, a little annoyed.

"We just need your witness statement of the events, sir." He couldn't see any sort of reaction in the barely outlined face hidden in the hooded shadow. I should have asked him to remove that hood, he thought, lowering his gaze, knowing he never could have.

"You knew," he said quietly to himself.

"So, you then called emergency services?" The policeman asked, apparently ignoring the statement and its implied accusation.

"Oh," Jim refocused on answering the officer's questions, "yes officer, immediately after I reached the man," he paused, and swallowed, as anxiety came flooding back. "There was nothing else

I could do. He was in such pain, and there was nothing I could do. I tried, I wanted to, but..." what else is there to say? I couldn't help him. He wanted to scream. I couldn't help him. The image bit into him, as did guilt, because there was nothing he could do to help the poor man. There was such pain in his eyes, and Jim couldn't do anything to help.

"Okay, sir, thank you for your help. We may be in touch later." The officer was quiet for a moment and then turned to go, apparently finished with Jim.

"Is he ok?" The officer paused and turned to him. "The man? Is he ok? He looked terrible, I mean..." he started to heave again at the thought of the terrible injuries he'd seen and the pain in the man's face. Oh my god! there was so much blood and his arm was barely hanging on.

The officer had decided to wait a while longer. He can probably see I'm obviously in distress, and the thought brought a little calm to his turmoiled mind.

"The EMTs will do everything they can, as will the hospital staff," he responded in the same calm, sonorous voice.

"Oh god, it was so terrible. I just can't get the image out of my head. He was still alive and he appeared to be in so much pain, such terrible pain. I could see it in his eyes!" he wailed, as the force of the memory fully hit him, and he cupped his head in his hands hoping he could hide the vision.

"Sir, are you going to be okay to drive home?"

"What?" Jim looked up, perplexed.

"Are you okay, sir? To drive home?"

"Yes, I'm sure I am, I will be," trying to regain some composure, "I just need a few more minutes."

"We can arrange a car for you." Jim noticed a slight change in the pitch of his voice, the officer now appeared to be actually concerned.

"No, thanks, it really is okay," Jim pulled himself up, straightened his shoulders and breathed in deeply. "Yes, I'll be okay, officer, in a minute or so. Thank you." He closed his eyes for a moment and let the night air and faint misting of water refresh him, the rhythms of the surrounding sounds soothe him. It had started raining again, and he could just make out the pitter-patter against the background noise. He looked up and studied the clouds, wondering how much rain was going to fall, and the sound washed over him, and he wished the rain would, could, just wash the memory away. Away, away, away.

I have to get home, what am I going to say to Philippa? Oh, God, will this vision ever go away, and the tightness inside started to build again. He prayed: "Please, Lord, help me?" and then, "And please help that man?"

Philippa, he reminded himself quickly and pulled out his phone and dialed his wife. The officer hadn't moved and was still watching, waiting.

"Hi, darling."

"I'm sorry I'm late," he wanted to cry. He wanted her to hold him and tell him that everything was going to be fine.

"There's been a car accident," she's going to worry, but what else can I say.

"No, not me."

"No, really, I'm fine," oh I wish I were.

"Yes, truly."

"Ok? Not really, but I'm not injured or anything," not on the outside.

"Yes. I'll be home soon."

"No, I'm really okay. I'll explain when I get home."

"I love you too, darling, very much." He put the phone away and felt the tears returning, but he took in a deep breath to gather his composure, to stop this crying.

"Hi, excuse me, officer?" The officer was still standing in front of him, but he had turned in the other direction. He turned back in a controlled manner that aggravated the nervous Jim.

"Yes, sir?" as now did his voice.

"May I leave now?" I have to get out of here. I have to go home. All he wanted to do was be with his wife.

"Of course, sir, we have your details?" Jim wasn't sure if it was a question, but he nodded as an answer anyway. "We may be in touch very soon and may possibly require another statement from you. If that is okay?" Jim nodded again. "Then, yes, you may leave. Have a good evening and drive carefully." The hooded man turned and left Jim, who watched the man return to the pulsing lights and moving shadows.

He surveyed the scene of crashed cars, parked cars, and people: witnesses, police, fireman, others, CSI? It was like a scene from a TV show or from a movie, but it was more of a nightmare. Flashing emergency lights distorted the view. A memory so harrowing it brought tears to his eyes and created fear in his heart. A constant wave of unwanted noise hummed in the background. He walked towards his car, eyeing the crowd of onlookers he was going to have to walk through. Head down, keep walking, don't look, he thought to himself, but glad he was at last leaving, telling himself that the memory would fade over time, but knowing it would never be gone. Philippa, I'll be home soon. Drive carefully? As if I was going to drive any other way, he thought to himself.

The show must go on

Megan sat in the hospital waiting room, waiting in sad anticipation for further news, news she did not want to hear. Head bowed, shoulders slumped, she kept squeezing her hands together, digging her nails into her palms trying to let the pain control her, distract her, stop her from screaming out loud. Every now and then she could be heard talking to herself, muttering. She was praying. Please let him live, please let him live. Then she'd realize that she was again talking out loud, and she'd look up, barely moving her head, as her eyes scanned for anyone noticing her, whilst she wondered if anyone was watching her or had heard her, suddenly self-conscious of her grief and her quiet muttering, feeling she was now rendered bare for all around to see. After another moment, she would slowly gaze around the room: white, clean, impersonal, and then she would consider and realize that others here might be going through a similar situation, some maybe even worse. Possibly a husband, or a wife, or maybe someone's child, and then she felt embarrassment at her own relatively small pain. But the thought of this news, her news, her pain and shock, wouldn't go away. So, head bowed, she kept digging her nails into her palms to control herself, not hard enough to cut, but enough to produce enough physical pain to keep the mental anguish at bay.

She breathed in deeply and wrinkled her nose, as the antiseptic smell of the room imposed itself on her, disappearing and reasserting itself onto her senses as her mind flitted from past and present and this coming new future, a future without her friend. Never to laugh, to cry, never to, well, anything at all with him again, she concluded. She was saddened by the prospect that all that would remain would be memories, and imperfect ones at that. A future of missed moments, a past never to be recaptured, and old lies never to be corrected.

She knew it was going to happen soon. She knew that all her current prayers would come to naught. Soon, someone would come – a doctor, possibly a nurse, she thought, no, a doctor. It's always a doctor. Yes, a doctor would come and deliver the terrible, unwanted news, and then it would all be over. But it wouldn't, would it? But he would be gone, her dear friend, still. Please don't leave me, she begged, knowing the end was near. So, she prayed for him, and she hoped.

Distracted by a noise, she looked up and surveyed the room again, the source didn't reveal itself to her, the noise still reverberating around. The room was half empty, it had been fuller earlier, she felt, or had it? She was barely conscious of her surroundings. She would notice something or someone briefly, but then it would fade and disappear to be forgotten, easily replaced by this terrible knowledge, and again she would become completely oblivious to all around her, her emotions overwhelming most of her coherent thoughts, but not this simple one, this terrible one: Simon is dying. The doctors are certain that he is not going to survive the night, and all my praying will not help. But what else can I do? And she continued to pray.

She'd been given some brief and incomprehensible explanations by three different specialists with equally incomprehensible specializations, each, apparently, performing different tasks in an effort to save Simon's life. They had all failed. That is what they'd implied in so many words. They were all surprised he'd even survived the crash, but survive the night? Of that, they had told her, all in agreement, there was very little chance.

He had briefly regained consciousness, and they had ushered her into the room. He lay there, his head swathed in bandages, but she easily recognized him, his eyes looking at her with concern, he even tried to force a smile. Megan was taken aback for a moment - he appeared to be missing an arm. She felt a huge wave of tears welling up from deep within, but she controlled herself, for him, for her friend, knowing they would return later. Head held fixed, his gaze holding hers, she walked over slowly, with as much control as she could muster, with each step feeling she might fall. Upon reaching him she stood and stared for a moment before taking the seat beside the bed. The weight of nervousness off her legs brought some relief as she sat beside him, and she held his hand and watched him as he quietly struggled to communicate, unable to form words, his eyes gently wild. He had gripped her hand weakly, and then with a small, sweet smile, he had faded back into unconsciousness. She felt his hand go limp in hers, which caused her to shout for the nurse, as panic rose up in her. Then, in a small moment of clarity, she'd calmed somewhat as the machines told her that he was still alive. The nurse ushered her out, though she had tried to insist that she wanted to stay with him, and then later she had been informed that it was unlikely that Simon would regain consciousness. The doctors' eyes looked worried and upset at having to give her the news. In the short time she was with him, those last moments, she had said nothing, unable to speak to him for fear of her emotions bursting out.

"We have done all we can," they had told her.

"We have to wait and see," they reiterated.

"We're surprised he made it here," they emphasized.

"His injuries were so very extensive," they explained.

And so, she sat with hands sore and heart heavy, her mind in turmoil, the tears temporarily stopped, the pain ever present. Waiting.

She had thought the worst when she'd received the call from the hospital. The Wilde Troupe, as they called themselves, had just completed that evening's show, and she was sitting happily in the dressing room after another successful performance. She was staring at herself in the dressing room mirror with the quiet admiration of art well-performed and well-received. The bright dressing room lights highlighted the sheen of sweat, due to both the exertions of the play and the exhilaration of the moment. Outside her room, the boisterous noise of her fellow actors reflected that same mood.

She'd wiped her face of the makeup, but not the huge grin that she just couldn't remove, and she'd found herself laughing at her own joy.

What a night! Her thoughts, but not her mood, interrupted, she'd checked her messages as a distracting alert was flashing on the phone. Congratulations from fans? She'd thought.

The expectations of joy turned to disbelief, and that disbelief quickly turned to grief. A quick drink with the other happy, but now confused, actors was cancelled, as was the removal of the rest of her makeup, and with a few mumbled words, a hasty change of clothes, she'd hurried out of the theater and into the first available taxi.

The taxi took forever. Why is New York City traffic so bad, so slow, so congested, when you are in a hurry? She had questioned herself, and not for the first time, but with more urgency than she'd ever previously known. Frequent glances at her watch didn't speed things up, and time appeared to slow whilst she sat there unable to do anything but wait. She'd occupied herself with wiping the rest of the makeup from face, as she glanced out of the window, checking for streets signs and familiar spots, all in a vain attempt to calculate how much longer the journey was going to take. When at last she did arrive, her nerves frayed, her imagination running riot, it was even worse than she had imagined.

She'd been surprised to learn that she was one of Simon's primary contacts; the other being his lawyer whom she'd never met and didn't know, but he'd been there, waiting, when she had arrived.

"Hi, Megan," a small, well-dressed man, red bearded and bespectacled and who, as far as she could recall, she didn't know, had greeted her. She was a little confused and wracked her brains trying to place where she may have met him because he obviously recognized her. "My name is Jason Doherty. I'm a friend of Simon and his lawyer," he'd stated in a voice that offered no help in recognition either. He'd thrust out his hand, and she'd just stared at it, confused for a moment, her thoughts jumbling, and then registering the action she gave the proffered hand a tentative shake.

"Hi, Jason?" she asked in a small voice, having barely registered his introduction, and he'd nodded in confirmation. She coughed, "His lawyer?" she repeated, a little louder, her mind attempting to catch up with the situation.

"Yes, his lawyer and his friend," he repeated, though he sounded patient and Megan quickly attempted to pull her thoughts together.

"Simon? Please? Tell me what's happening? Is he still alive?" there was an edge of hysteria in her voice, suddenly realizing that she didn't necessarily want an answer to this last question, as the worst-case scenarios started playing in her mind.

"How much did they tell you?" He looked at her concerned, but his voice was controlled and calm and his demeanor appeared very professional. Detached, that would have been the word I would use, she thought, but she was more concerned with Simon's situation than the lawyer's manners, and his attitude was quickly put behind her. She took in a deep breath to control herself, but her mind was still racing.

"I was informed that he'd been in some sort of car accident? Very bad. Not much else," she said, trying to remember any other details, realizing that she hadn't checked at what time the message had even come in. "And I'm…we're," she quickly corrected herself, "his primary contacts?" This surprising piece of information still niggling her.

"Yes, we are. I've been here a while now," his response matched his manner.

"When did it happen?" she interjected quickly, wondering what she had done to offend this person, a stranger that she had, literally, just met.

"The accident," he continued unperturbed, "happened around 8:30. Well, that's approximately when he arrived at the hospital." He appeared to be running calculations in his head, muttering a bit. "I was called around, 8:45, arrived about 9:00, 9:15." He noticed her surprised look. "I'd been working late at the office, just about to leave. It's only a 10, maybe, 15 minutes' drive from there."

"Oh, okay," sorry for interrupting his flow. Two hours ago, she thought, I was on stage experiencing one of my finest moments, and my friend was dying. "I was unavailable," she reported simply, not really a justification, but it was all she could offer. Her small voice, implied an apology, knowing that she couldn't have, but feeling that she should have, been here earlier.

"Anyway, I believe he's just come out of the operating theater, and he's not yet regained consciousness." So, he's still alive, she sighed with renewed hope.

"He's alive? Can I see him?" There was desperation in her rising voice, and with the tragic event confirmed she started to feel herself unraveling, but again she fought for control, measuring her breathing and tempering her thoughts. Then it all crystalized. I must see him, I have to see him.

"Yes, of course. We should ask. I'll call a nurse." He turned, started to walk away, then stopped and turned back to her.

"Do you know where I can find his daughter?"

"His daughter?" she asked, surprised at such a question, still annoyed with his tone. "He doesn't have a daughter."

"I believe he does," he stated with surety.

"Sorry, really? Are you sure?" A daughter?

"Yes, I can assure you that he does," and that professional manner, which held a touch of disdain, returned, and she winced, wishing she had never asked, wondering again what she had done to this man, this stranger, to illicit such a response, "we had recently discussed some matters concerning her, but he hadn't, as yet, given me any details of her whereabouts." Simon has a daughter. How can he have a daughter?

"His daughter?" she repeated, in a high pitch squeal, and immediately felt embarrassed, her eyes momentarily flitting around the room then returning to face him, confused, still unable to absorb this new information. "No, I don't know where she is. I had no idea she even existed. How can that be? I've known him for years," that hysterical edge had returned to her voice. She stared at the lawyer in disbelief, "since high school. He has a daughter?" Jason could see her confusion, watching her as she tried to put this new knowledge in place. "We were best friends. He never told me. When? Why?" Jason couldn't answer that question, but he felt he could clear up the incongruity, and hopefully calm this rather agitated lady.

"As far as I know, even Simon didn't know until very recently, three maybe four months ago now. He came to me a week or so ago," he briefly paused, his professional instincts quickly realizing that he couldn't give her any details of the private meeting, "and we chatted about her. He was, I believe, driving out to see her this evening."

"Oh my god! He has a daughter," she said as much to herself, rather than the lawyer in front of her. Ignoring the details proffered by him, she was still stunned by the news.

"Look, I'll go and get the nurse," Jason said, a little embarrassed at the unfolding situation. He'd noticed her lack of attention to any additional information he had to offer on the subject, as she was lost in her own thoughts on the news. So, he went off to find a nurse, leaving her in her disbelief and distress, which he was actually finding a little stressful himself, something he really didn't need given the current circumstances.

With Jason gone and Megan now alone, she wandered over to an empty area of the room and sat down. She used the space and silence to gather her thoughts, calm herself, and to think through the information she'd just received.

She hadn't been in contact with Simon, for what, nearly two years? Not until just recently. She recalled that they had chatted after her divorce, both reminiscing on days past. School. College. The Band. Those times now long gone, held so close in memory, so distant in nostalgia. He'd helped her through that last traumatic experience, listening as only a good friend could, not interrupting, offering advice positive and personal, which would, of course, be ignored, but which was much needed and had helped. Yes, it truly had helped at the time. That time, her divorce, had not been a good time, and she'd realized that most of their friends were his friends, and she'd lost contact with hers. That was just over two years ago. Then a week or so ago he'd contacted her, completely out of the blue and much welcomed. He'd come to the theater to see The Play, and afterwards they'd, no, she had chatted and chatted and chatted, she reminded herself.

I just don't remember him mentioning a daughter, she thought. Had I even given him the chance to? She felt a pang of guilt. It had been so good to talk with someone, even more so him. Just to be allowed to talk, and to let all her bottled emotions pour out. The last few months had been consumed by her off-Broadway play. The months prior to that, the bitterness of another separation. We were going to meet up this coming week again. We were going to talk about so many things, he said so. The thought brought pain, as tears came unbidden to her eyes. Holding them back didn't work, so she let them flow, with her hands holding a sodden handkerchief to her face and her body shaking, a mass of tension and sorrow, her wet palms now sore, her guilt heavy on her soul.

A close rustling caught her attention. She looked up to see that Jason had returned with a nurse.

"Apparently, Simon has regained consciousness," he told Megan, rather stoically. She gave him a quizzical look, wondering at his reaction to her, still unable to fathom it. She'd understood that this wasn't the best of times to meet someone, but she would have expected at least something comforting from the man, not this... disdain!

"He's conscious?" rhetorically, a glimmer of hope surfacing, repeated Megan, "Is he okay now?" but the look on their faces didn't offer any signs of renewed hope. "Please, take me to him. Please. I must see him. I need to see him," she had pleaded, finding herself unable to stop weeping. The nurse nodded, her face nearly as unreadable as the lawyer's as she escorted them to Simon's room.

"Excuse me," Megan looked up, returning to the present, in front of her a doctor, one she had previously had a conversation with, but she was unable to place her particular specialization. The lady was looking at her notes, and then looked back and down at Megan, she continued, "Mrs. Seaman?"

"It's Ms." The response still automatic since leaving Peter, and again wishing she hadn't taken his name, as she equally still chastised herself for not reverting back to her maiden name. Those bitter memories added more fuel to her already pain leaden thoughts.

"Sorry, Ms. Seaman," the doctor corrected, her voice was soft and gentle, and Megan feared the worse.

Was it now? She felt further guilt as she realized she was hoping that it was, and for this to be all over so she could leave this antiseptic and friendless place, go home and cry, alone and quietly, or loudly, or however she chose, but in peace and solitude away from here, in the security of her home.

"I'm sorry to have to inform you that Mr. Islane has passed away," she said quietly, with care and compassion. Megan stared at the doctor, who was looking sympathetically back at her, "the injuries were very extensive, and there was little we could do. He never regained consciousness again."

"Thank you," Megan mumbled, unable to find any other appropriate response as she screamed inside.

"We just need you to fill out some paper work. If you'll accompany me, I'll take you to a nurse who will help you complete the required documents," her voice soft and soothing.

Megan stared at the doctor, as she still screamed silently. Are any documents appropriate in these circumstances? the voice in her head asked. The doctor was still talking, and Megan didn't know how much she'd missed, so she stared at the lady's mouth to concentrate on what she was saying.

"...I believe there was also a Mr.," she referred to her notes again, and quickly looked up, "Doherty?" Megan noticed that she pronounced his name as spelled, that is, incorrectly.

"Yes, his lawyer," deciding not to correct the lady. Why should I care how she pronounces that pompous man's name? She thought with a small guilty satisfaction, "he should be back here in a moment. He went to the restroom." She'd momentarily forgotten about him. How long had he been gone? After introductions, barely a word had passed between them. He didn't appear to be the talkative type, for which, at this moment, she was grateful, and for some reason, which she couldn't fathom, and given the circumstances, didn't have time to address properly, he appeared to dislike her, even though he didn't know her, or his manner gave her that impression. She looked around not quite sure where the restrooms were, then noticed that the doctor had turned her head to see Jason hurrying over.

"That's him, there, coming over now," she pointed him out, as he walked over in a slightly rushed, but dignified, manner.

"Oh, yes, thank you, we'll just wait for him."

"Hi, sorry, any updates on Simon's condition?" he panted, a little out of breath. Jason's head turned to each in sequence waiting for a response from either to his general query. Megan decided to keep quiet, staring blankly at the man she was disliking more with each moment. She didn't have the energy or desire to tell him, and so let the doctor do it.

"I was just informing, Mrs.," she looked at Megan and smiled thinly, "Ms. Seaman, that Mr. Islane has just passed away." She paused to let the news sink in. The lawyer nodded to acknowledge it. He'd guessed as much when he had seen the doctor with Megan, her bearing sober, her demeanor controlled. Unlike Megan, whose every emotion radiated out, the pain now obvious in her eyes.

"If you will come with me and Ms. Seaman, you can both finish the paperwork that needs to be completed," and she turned towards the nurse's desk.

"No problem," said Jason, wishing to be away as quickly as possible, realizing that his originally planned quiet tomorrow at the office, was now going to be full with sorting out Simon's Will and Estate.

Hospital paperwork completed, Megan and Jason stood outside, a distance between them as they thought through the traumatic experience, which dominated their every thought, the other, for the moment, forgotten. There was a light drizzle in the air, but it smelled fresh compared to the constant nasal assault inside. Megan breathed in, slowly, deeply, as her mind started to refocus on the now. The cool fresh air felt good and comforting after the oppressive atmosphere of the hospital. Her tears for the time were being held at bay, with a control she'd learned from the separation with her former husband. She still had that feeling of deep melancholy but was at least glad to be free of the smell, glad that, for the moment, the internal screaming had at last stopped.

Jason, turned his head, slightly to see her, and considered her: she is beautiful, striking skin tone, dark penetrating eyes, really rather pretty; though she's not really my type, he quickly interjected, but I can see why Simon liked her. Yes, I can, he mused.

"May I give you a lift anywhere?" he asked her. It was an automatic question given the circumstances, but now that he'd asked, he hoped he didn't have to or at least hoped that she lived close to the direction in which he was heading. Under the circumstances, it would be difficult to take back his rather rushed offer, wherever she lived.

Megan looked at him, blankly, for a moment, the offer rather unexpected. He watched her and waited. He was in a hurry to get away, but he was used to being patient and though he wanted to, he wasn't going to hurry her needlessly.

"No, no, it's all right," she rushed out, as the question registered, and an association of distaste emerged. Right now, she didn't wish to be with anyone, and she really didn't wish to be with him. "I'm not far from here," she lied, "I'll walk." Jason glanced up at the sky checking the weather, and then back at her with a slightly quizzical look on his face. A light spray of water was already starting to fall from the sky, blown around in the stiff breeze.

"No, it's fine, I'll really be okay," she said, feeling far from okay, and at the moment doubting she ever would be again, definitely desirous of solitude, and definitely not wishing to be with this offish man with terrible manners. She wondered for a moment if she was being just a little too sensitive, then she recalled his tone throughout the past few hours and dismissed the idea.

"Okay, I'll leave you then," he said with an internal sigh of relief, thinking that he'd been in this situation a few times before, knowing that some people, after such news, just wanted to be alone, which suited him fine. He didn't particularly like being with others, with strangers, in these or many other circumstances.

He fished in his inside jacket pocket and pulled out a small wallet. He knew Simon well, they were college buddies. Jason didn't really have many friends, but he realized that Simon may have been the closest one he had. They had had a great and profitable working relationship, and he already missed the big guy. The suddenness of his death had given Jason no time for the acceptance of it, no time for heartfelt goodbyes. He'd sat and stared at his friend, in that short time they'd been alone in the hospital room. He hadn't said anything, couldn't think of anything to say, not out loud, so he'd just looked at him and silently prayed. He hadn't cried or shouted, and when the expected news had finally arrived, he'd just wanted to leave, but Megan had been there, so he'd stayed to be polite. I want to be with my son, he'd thought, feeling the grief building up, but keeping it internalized, controlled, and waited for and left with her. Rushes of emotions just weren't his style, but he felt being polite was in order here. Later, at home, he would open up a bottle of wine and toast Simon, his friend, his best friend, with a few glasses. Possibly reminisce with the whole bottle, but he also knew he was going to be living with this at work for the next few weeks. Simon's estate wasn't huge, but it was substantial enough, and he had to find the daughter, Angie. Megan appeared, genuinely, to know nothing of her. Let's just hope Simon had left some more details of her whereabouts. It shouldn't be that difficult, he reassured himself.

"Here's my card," he said, pulling one out of his wallet and handing it over to her. "I will be in touch within the next few days, but if you have any questions concerning his estate or his affairs, just call me."

"Yes, of course, yes, I'll call if I need to," she said pocketing the card without a glance, asking herself why she would want to call him, and not particularly looking forward to his call later by any means.

Jason thought about shaking hands or possibly a sympathetic hug. An image formed quickly in his mind, of an extended hug, close and slightly erotic. He thought better of it and just turned abruptly and walk off into the night.

She watched him leave, surprised at his reactions, not even a goodbye, she thought. He's not really a well-mannered person, is he? wondering if he really was a friend of Simon's. Maybe just his lawyer, who probably needs a friend and some lessons in good manners, and she shook her head slowly, sad at the thought, but too tired to be angry, and really thankful for the solitude, and of at last being alone with her thoughts and sorrow. She listened as the sound of his car disappeared into the general background noise of NYC and watched as its tail lights faded into the general glow that is Manhattan. Then, following slowly on foot, she left the hospital grounds, alone and deeply melancholy.

Standing on the pavement, the light rain felt clean and refreshing and she lifted her chin up to catch the moisture, enjoying the moment, her mind for a short time free of painful thoughts, but only for a short time. Her thoughts contained memories, and new painful memories were never far away. In the solitude and cool rain, she started to relax, but the memories soon returned, oppressive. Her tears, held back for a few minutes, started to fall, merging with the rain. With head bowed, not wanting to notice or be noticed, she looked up and down the road, registering people, traffic and getting her bearings. Then she straightened herself, pulled her coat tightly around her and started to walk in the direction of the subway. She watched an oncoming lit taxi for a moment and changed her mind about the subway, and soon she was whisked away towards home.

The apartment was, as always, empty. There was no one here, no one to talk to. What had yesterday been comforting and familiar, now felt cold and uninviting. The solitude was imposing, and the silence loud with the distant sounds of traffic and NYC outside. And inside? Everything normally ignored was now an assault on her senses: the humming fridge, the tapping of feet in the above apartment, the edge of the hollow sound of someone in the stairwell, a closed door, banging – all aggravated her, though they would normally have been unnoticed.

The sound of the door clicking shut behind her returned her to some semblance of normalcy, and she let those noises fade to the normal background.

"Alone," she whispered. Closing her eyes momentarily to enjoy the peace. Alone? I could phone Tim, she thought. It'd be nice to talk to someone who would understand. His name, which had been absent for so long, was now in the forefront of her thoughts, and then she remembered why, recalling the conversation earlier that week with Simon. I'm not ready to confront him yet, she realized, I want to, but I can't, not now! She hadn't fully processed that piece of information and knew she needed more time, and Simon's death overpowered all else at this moment, but she realized that she must be the one to tell him. Tim needs to know about Simon, I'll write to him tomorrow, but not right now, she decided, the pain returning. Alone's fine.

Throwing her handbag to the floor and kicking off her shoes, she left the items where they fell, so unlike her usual self, and she moved into the living room not giving them a second thought. She looked around, but nothing really registered, it was the same as she had left it. There really wasn't anything new or out of the ordinary to address the current state of her consciousness. She dumped herself on the sofa and sat there: upright, knees together, in a stiff posture, staring at the blank TV, the remote in front of her on her coffee table. Minutes passed. She sat staring, unmoving, undisturbed, with just the background noise of Manhattan, the subjects of her thoughts coming and going, everything quickly forgotten, except the persistent memory of the harrowing and painful evening. After a while, and even though the memory remained, she finally started to relax. Exhaustion, both physical and mental, started to take over her body and mind. She thought about a drink, then thought better of it, mainly because she was unwilling to move from her current repose. So, she sat motionless and let the pain recede with time and inaction, the turmoil in her mind slowly fading.

After a time, she felt herself doze in and out of light sleep. Then in a moment of resolute clarity, suddenly, to no one in particular, and the world in general, she announced, "I'm tired, and I'm going to bed," her voice loud in the surrounding silence. There was a positive finality to her voice, to make, no force, the point, though there was no one else to hear. This personal silence, this stillness, was oppressive and comforting at the same time, but she knew she needed to step away from it.

"I have a play tomorrow," she told the world and no one in particular, the cliché coming unbidden, "and The Show must go on."

A mini wake

The drive home had been relaxing, and Jason was glad to be out of Manhattan and out of New York City. He loved the city. He'd lived there with Sarah for nearly five years before moving upstate. After they'd separated, he hadn't returned; he hadn't wanted the hassle of moving again. He didn't need the noise and was glad to live away from the hustle and bustle. The commute was easy enough. The drive gave him time to think, and the quiet kept him calm and sane. He was single again, but he still had no desire to move back to New York City and its boundless energy, and its noisy and dirty environment. Though he was interested in returning to the dating game, he hadn't really made the effort since Sarah. When he thought about it honestly, he wasn't ready for it either. Simon's sudden death made him realize life was passing him by: he'd done nothing since she'd left him.

He breathed in the cool air, feeling it in his lungs. He was a little damp from having left the side window slightly open to allow the cool, wet breeze to clear his thoughts. The events of the evening were still troubling his mind, and every now and then a little flash of guilt intruded into his thoughts as he considered his treatment of Megan. He could not understand why he had treated her so formally, so badly, he'd finally admitted to himself.

During the quiet, thoughtful drive home, he'd finally understood something he had desperately tried to deny: he found her attractive, and he didn't want to. It somehow felt as if he was dishonoring Simon in some way he just couldn't articulate, and yet he knew that this wasn't the true reason for his actions towards her, and so the unanswered point kept coming back to plague him. It wasn't helping that he was getting home much later than he had intended and that his son would already be in bed when he arrived. He hated missing saying goodnight to his little boy. Timmy would be going back to his mother's place tomorrow, and it would be another two weeks before he would see him again. Both thoughts depressed him. There was no way his ex would allow him another day with his son, and there was no way he was going to ask since he had no desire to see the pleasure on her face when she said no. Sarah was strict and not very considerate of Jason's needs. The divorce had not been pleasant, though he'd witnessed worse, a lot worse, but on certain aspects he'd been adamant, and it had not gone as much in her favor as she would have liked. She still very much resented his stance during the divorce and the outcomes and allocations of possessions and wealth. However, she had been given custody of their son in a moment of weakness, which he now regarded as stupidity, and he had quickly acquiesced. Seeing the pain in her eyes, the pain of someone he still loved, he'd wanted it all to end, since the divorce had also started to affect their son. In that moment of weakness, he'd forgotten – he'd forgotten what she really could be like. He'd witnessed it on numerous occasions with others. This was Sarah, and this time it was his turn, now that she had her chance, and she only allowed Jason as much time with his son as the courts had dictated. She had never been much of a forgiving person, and their relationship continued to exist only because of Timmy, and only then when she absolutely had to have Jason's approval. No, she definitely is not a forgiving person, he reminded himself sadly, but she was and is a good mother. He had to admit that he was still in love with her too, and that, coupled with the separation and divorce, still brought him waves of depressed thoughts. His mind continually replayed these thoughts and now those of the death of his friend and client. This led again to his memory of being at the hospital and how he had treated Megan, and the guilt pervaded his thoughts. The peace he normally accrued from the drive home now eluded him.

He stood outside for a moment, still and contemplative, before entering his house. It loomed up in front of him, dark against the gray, cloudy sky, panes of light indicating the presence of occupancy – the babysitter in the living room. His son's bedroom window was dark, as was to be expected at this time. Eyes closed, body relaxed, the whisper of the windblown rain lightly brushing over him, cleansing and clearing his thoughts, he attempted to calm his mind. His open coat flapped in the gentle breeze, a slight, though not uncomfortable, chill running though the thinner fabric of his trouser legs.

Again, he asked himself: why? Why had he treated Megan so disdainfully? Why had he been so unprofessional? He felt guilty for not maintaining the standards he had set himself over the years, and again the thoughts and questions remained unanswered. He stood there, hoping for an answer, waiting for a level of relaxation to come.

He didn't want to appear agitated in front of the babysitter, so he let the gentle, cool breeze refresh him.

After a moment, feeling like he was back in control, he opened his eyes, stared at the front door, and gathered himself and his still roiling emotions. He knew that even though internally he was still on edge, conflicted and still emotionally attuned to Simon's death, externally he looked calm and composed. It was a trick that over the years he had learned from work. It was never good if he allowed his clients to know how he truly felt, and though sometimes he let his guard down, it was extremely rare, so the action had become very much a habit. He knew he acted as such in social settings as well as work ones, but that didn't really bother him. So, hands jammed into his coat pocket, he shook off the malaise and the rain and trudged towards his front door. He paused, letting his hand rest on the handle. I miss my son, he reminded himself, and then pushed himself forward.

He entered the house. The familiar living room opened before him and there, as expected, was the babysitter. She was curled on the sofa staring at him as he walked in, a book held forgotten in her hand. Her dark brown hair was pulled back in a ponytail, and though he couldn't see it, he knew it fell all the way down the length of her back, and as always, he marveled at the sharp contrast of her gray-blue eyes with her hair.

"Hello, Mr. Doherty," her smile wide, her look bright. It took him by surprise, as a feeling of warmth flowed through him in response. Yes, he liked the girl, but there was nothing much else to think about it.

She's young, too young, he thought, though admittedly pretty. A sophomore at NYU, he sometimes fantasized about her coming on to him, but God forbid he would even actually, in reality, even hint at such a thing or do anything untoward! She was great with Timmy and always appeared happy. No, perky would be a more suitable term. Surprisingly, her perkiness never annoyed him, though that quality in others usually did, and now that smile, after the trauma of this evening, and the guilt still gnawing at him, was unexpectedly pleasurable. This unexpected reaction to her smile threw him off-balance internally just a little, but he quickly controlled his external demeanor.

"Hello, Sheila. I'm sorry for the delay. Sorry I'm so late. Is everything okay? Did Timothy behave himself?" He asked with a smile and hint of warmth he hadn't offered to Megan.

"Yes, sir, he was very good, but he missed you at bed time," there was a touch of sadness in her voice and he winced inside, guilt and regret mingling.

"And I missed him," he smiled thinly back at her, not wanting to go into any detail about an evening he'd rather forget, as he tried to show a side of himself which just didn't exist at the moment, hoping it conveyed to her that all was okay.

She sprung up from the sofa, walking away from him and over to her backpack lying opposite the door he'd just entered, and stowed her book away. He watched her, admiring her but telling himself that she was a bit thin for his tastes. And Timmy has a crush on her, he reminded himself with a little laugh. She is very sweet though, he confessed, the edge of a fantasy returning. She turned, hefting the bag onto her shoulder, flicking her bag into position behind her. She was in a hurry to go, which was hardly surprising given how late it now was.

"Thank you again, Sheila." Just a harmless fantasy he reminded himself, glad that she always dressed appropriately when she came over, though hoping that maybe she'd wear something less formal, attire he'd seen her wear socially.

"No problem, Mr. Doherty." The smile hadn't left her face, and given his last few hours, he was grateful for the open, happy expression the girl always brought. Walking towards her, he pulled out his wallet and paid her with an extra-large tip. For the inconvenience the evening's events had imposed on her and on me, he sighed.

"Thank you, Mr. Doherty, thank you very much." The smile was radiant, the gratitude appeared genuine. He actually felt pleased with himself from her response.

"You get home safely," he smiled back. Thoughts of the evening's event still very present in his mind. She lived not far from here, a quiet neighborhood, and he wasn't really that worried, but a little concern crossed his mind. As he watched her, he imagined her moving close to him, touching him as she brushed his cheek with her lips, pushing her body against his. It didn't happen. There was no real temptation for him, but the fantasies came and went and, he knew they would return, but that they'd also always remain fantasies.

"Don't worry, Mr. Doherty, I'll be okay," and smiling she turned, open the door, turned back and waved at him and left. As he watched her swaying hips, he could still feel the imagined lips on his cheek, and he unconsciously raised his hand to wipe his face. Looking at the tips of his fingers, he expected them to be damp. The fantasy faded as he watched her enter her car, and he waited for a moment as he heard her car start up, followed by the tires crunching on the drive way, and he continued to watch as the sound of tires and motor faded into the distance.

A sense of relief flowed through his exhausted mind. He was alone now and free of any company. A hint of the fantasy remained, as he turned away and reentered his house, and he pondered the evening's events. Why had he treated Megan so unprofessionally? It returned to his thoughts unbidden, unanswered. He stifled a yawn. I should really go to bed, he told himself, feeling the weariness creeping up on him, but his mind was active and though he felt tired he knew that sleep could still easily be a few hours away, and he had no desire to lie there waiting for it to occur. He knew that the evening's events would be playing on his mind and that sleep would not be coming for a while yet.

He turned abruptly, and left the room. Slowly climbed the stairs, his steps soft, and sneaked quietly into his son's room, trying not to wake his boy, wincing at each audible creak. Soft light entered the room, showing his son splayed out asleep on the bed, his eyes closed, his breathing soft with comforting regularity. He watched and listened to his son for a moment, and thought of Simon and Angie, and the thought of never having seen his son grow up crossed his mind. Never having seen the only person that truly mattered to him! The thought brought pain and some regret, and he promised himself more time with his boy. However strict his ex-wife was with visitation, many missed moments were due to his work. I must try harder, he admonished himself. I will try harder. He turned away leaving his son undisturbed, quietly closing the door behind him and returning to the living room.

Simon's death had bothered him far more than he'd shown when he was in the hospital. He'd put on a brave face in front of the doctors and Megan. Strangers! Outside of business he was rarely very good with strangers. Though she was rather attractive, he mused, quickly quelling the thought with a "but not my type." He'd known that Simon had still loved her, and he could see why. I treated her so badly, and I don't know why. He was glad he didn't have to explain it to Simon, and having thought that, he felt even more guilt.

He'd met Simon at college as a freshman, where they had both taken Introduction to Programming. Both had looked out of place in the class; Simon was tall, large, muscular and handsome with sandy blond hair and piecing blue eyes. He just looked so out of place there, and there weren't many other athletes in this class. And Jason?

There weren't that many redheads on the course, either. His large, curly hairdo, which dominated his boyish looks, would later be reduced to something more fashionable and less noticeable, as would the large and noticeably dated glasses that he wore, but not in his first few freshman months at college, still young and impressionable, and not a little ignorant of this new life ahead of him.

They had ended up in the same study group, and he still remembered the looks on each and every face when they'd been given "The Sportsman," but Simon had been surprisingly very good at the subject. Surprisingly, since they all knew that he'd received a full scholarship for Football. Jason soon acknowledged his prejudice. He had worked hard for his place here and had received a partial scholarship, but he would still carry a sizable debt when he graduated, plus any loans required for graduate school, and so he had a disdain for anyone with scholarships other than academic. Simon dissuaded him from that notion, maybe not completely, but enough for him to be a little more open-minded on the matter.

Simon appeared to have no prejudices. He got on with everyone: jocks, geeks, loners, girls – especially girls. Everyone seemed to know him. It helped, of course, that he was on the football team. It helped that he always seemed to be smiling. It helped that he could hold a group's attention with wit and snappy repartee. Jason was envious, as were many of their peers, but Simon invariably won over nearly everyone he encountered. It was rare to hear anything remotely negative said about the guy. That was annoying until you were in his company and held captive under his sway.

In the study group, Simon had been helpful and friendly. He was very knowledgeable on the subject, and he appeared to relish in teaching it, showing the group particular solutions to homework assignments. He enjoyed explaining subtleties, but he also took pleasure in listening and absorbing the answers others had to offer too. He never hurried, and he never appeared flustered at a lack of understanding. He would listen carefully, rarely interrupting, and help when he could. It was such a surprise, so incongruent to everyone's expectations, and everyone benefited, including Simon who appeared to get a great deal of pleasure out of it. It was many years later when Jason finally found out why, over a bottle of wine far away from college. Well, I've now met the other infamous love of his life, and now I'll possibly see this Tim fellow. The coincidence of the name wasn't lost on him.

It had been over a bottle of wine that he'd heard with such deep regret about the only two women he'd known Simon to have taken seriously. It was one of the first times, and most certainly the first significant time, that Simon had opened up to him, and Jason regarded it as the pivotal point when their friendship became close, becoming an actual friendship, even though they'd known each other for so many years, first at college and then later after he had become Simon's financial advisor. He remembered his response to a stray comment concerning Simon's latest failed relationship.

"You've broken up with Jane already?" I had asked, possibly too loudly, though definitely a little shocked. Simon had been dating Jane for a couple of months now, and he had seemed very enthusiastic about her at first. I'd even met her briefly, which was rare. So, I'd assumed that there was likely to be some longevity to the relationship. I was hoping for it, but it appeared I was wrong in that assumption. We were having a drink after work, in a bar close to my office, prior to a reservation at a particularly good restaurant. Simon looked at me, his hands cupping the wine, his face a little flushed from the first bottle. Maybe we've already had too much to drink, I mused staring at my glass. It was, however, a very nice wine and a very good restaurant. He took another sip, savoring the flavors, considering his response. I took a sip, waiting.

"Yes." Yep! Surprise, surprise, all that for a little yes.

"Yes, and?" I wasn't letting him off the hook that easily.

"Yes! yes! yes!" he flashed at me, and inwardly I blanched, taking a mental step back. Okay, that was just a little unexpected. He sounded uncharacteristically annoyed. "It just didn't work out. As usual," he continued. There was that sound of inevitability in his response, and I felt its weight and thought it so sad. Then he went quiet, staring at the glass cupped in his hands, obviously thinking again. After a few seconds of what seemed an awkward silence, I thought I'd better change the subject, and with a couple of fairly banal ideas rushing in my mind, I was about to start another conversation when he continued.

"There was Adela," he quietly stated. He hadn't looked up at me, but I could hear the depth of sorrow in his voice. I nodded at the mention of her name, thoughts of college returning. I'd met her a few times, and though we weren't really friends then, I remembered thinking that Simon was genuinely happy when he'd been with her. Then one day she was just gone and no reasons ever came forward. I never could find out why. It had been a surprise to us all, shrouded in mystery unanswered. After she'd gone, being around Simon had been depressing. He hadn't coped well. He'd missed a few games and classes, and rumor had it that he'd nearly quit school. I recalled a visit from his mother, very quiet, and a much gossiped about hair-raising "chat" with the coach. Then nothing! He had disappeared from campus for a week, and after his return, he'd refocused on his classes and football and never mentioned her again.

He was still very social, one of the "in" people to be with, but he never seemed to laugh or joke as much. He was just a little bit more serious. And Adela? Her name never came up, or if someone did mention her, there was an uncomfortable silence, we'd all look at one another, and then he would quickly change the subject, nervously laughing off the matter. I hadn't heard a word on the subject for years, until now.

Simon continued, still staring into his glass, "You know since Adela left me I just haven't been able to find the right girl." I wasn't too sure if he was talking to me or just himself.

"Simon, that was 11 or 12 years ago, you..." Simon looked up at me and stopped me with a gentle shake of his head, his eyes full of sorrow.

"Jason, I've truly loved only two women in my life, they both left me," his eyes bore into mine holding my full attention. "One is still my best friend but married, and the other just up and left: me, college, and her friends." There was such sadness in his voice, and I started to feel it. It made me think of my own love, wondering how I'd feel if I lost her, my wife, my companion, the mother of my little boy, she and the jewel of my life. I was lucky. "She just disappeared, and it was all my fault. I tried to find her. I tried to do the right thing. I was very young, and I was very stupid, and I didn't try hard enough."

"I'm not too sure I understand," I replied a little confused because this was a long time ago.

"You've heard me mention Megan?"

"Yeah, the girl from high school. She played in your band?" Megan? Adela? I was becoming more confused.

"Yes, she did," he paused a moment, "Megan." He said the name quietly with such a mixture of regret, melancholy, and love. "We dated for just a couple of months or so in my junior year of high school. She was so cool, she didn't even know it, and I thought I'd hit the jackpot!" He smiled as he remembered her. "When we broke up, it seemed okay at the time. We were young, and for all the enjoyment we were having, we just didn't take it, or each other, that seriously.

We got lazy. No! I was young and lazy, it was so easy for me to get girls then." And that has changed? I thought to myself, happy I'd found mine, but still a little envious of his history at college and since, but I said nothing and continued to listen. "I took it, her, for granted. She'd had a crush on me. She had chased after me." Well, she's not the only one, my envy still rummaging around in my head as I watched him, listened to him, in silence and quiet fascination. "I barely knew her before, and then she'd joined my band just to get to know me. It was easy fun, but I really liked her – a lot – even in those short few months. I was hoping it was us just getting to know each other. Then she broke up with me. I just laughed it off at the time, saying I felt the same, but later I realized I didn't. I had a whole year to get to know her so much better than when we had dated, and then I just wanted her more." Simon stopped for a moment, taking a large sip from the glass. I looked on, taking it all in, witnessing Simon opening up for the first time, but wondering where he was now going with this reminiscing. I really wanted to know, so I waited and listened patiently.

"We got on so much better as friends, and the more I got to know her, the better our friendship became and the more I realized my initial mistake. Maybe I was growing up," he gave a dry humorless laugh and shrugged his shoulders with a small quick smile, "but she would joke about, "that time" and "when we dated," and I knew I'd lost her. Then I met Adela. I'd been in college for a couple of years and had floated through one relationship and the next, just having a good time, nothing serious in the slightest." Jason could hear the distaste when he used the word "relationship," and recalling, with a little jealousy that had never fully gone away, Simon's reputation. "No one could compare to Megan. I met some girls who were prettier, even some more interesting girls. I had girls flinging themselves at me, and I loved every moment of it," that caused a little wry smile to return, "but the chemistry wasn't the same, none of them clicked, not like it had with Megan. There was just something about her that the others didn't have. She came and visited me a few times, and each time it reminded me of what I really wanted. Though I said nothing to her. I couldn't. I flirted a bit, but that came to nothing, so I said nothing. None of the other relationships lasted, and I really didn't care, not really, not until Adela. Oh God, Adela! I thought she was just going to be another short fling, I was so wrong. And all those mistakes I had made with Megan, I was determined not to make with her. But no, could I even do that? No. I just ended up making even worse ones." He's looking angry, I thought, but then I knew why.

"She left you," I added, searching for some reply, trying to help. Simon directed that angry glance at me, it quickly disappeared and softened. He shook his head, and smiled a tight, forced smile back at me, his eyes showing his continuing sorrow.

"Do you know why she left me?" He whispered. He wasn't looking at me when he asked, I'm not too sure he was looking at anything.

"No," aware that it might be a rhetorical question, but I answered anyway. I was starting to feel a little uncomfortable at the personal nature of the conversation. This was such new territory with this old college buddy and now client of mine, but I was being pulled in with a fascination at this new knowledge and Simon opening up to me.

"It doesn't matter. She left me and college, and I never saw her again."

"I'm sorry," was all I could come up with. I couldn't think of anything else to say, but I knew Simon was about to say something possibly quite important, but then he changed his mind. I was tempted to ask, but do I know Simon well enough to ask? I asked myself.

"I looked for her, but her sister told me that she'd," he paused, and the faraway look returned for a moment, "moved, and that I shouldn't bother looking. Though I still tried for a week or so without any success. I then returned to college and football." Another gulp of wine, he straightened his back, pulled back his shoulders and was suddenly back to the old Simon. I watched the sudden transformation, as his wry smile returned, and I thought at that moment that this level of intimacy with Simon may never happen again, though I was thankfully wrong.

Jason stood at the wine fridge, the cool air enveloping him, clearing his thoughts as he turned his mind to pondering his selection, searching for an appropriate bottle for this moment. Definitely red, a bold Italian I think. He pulled a Barolo out, staring at the label, recalling flavors from a previous bottle, and he knew Simon would approve, though he also knew that he wasn't going to let it come to room temperature or let it breathe as it should before it was half-finished, and he chuckled as he visualized Simon's disapproving look at his treatment of such a fine wine, and then he smiled, as he knew Simon would have laughed and taken a glass anyway without any qualms.

Sipping the wine without really tasting it, Jason recalled how the beginning of his friendship with Simon was finally strengthened a few years later, when the love of his life, Sarah, had left him, and Simon had offered one of his spare rooms to him. Jason had initially declined, but then over the next few months as divorce issues had escalated and Jason had had no time to find a new place, Simon had insisted, and he had moved in.

While he was there, Simon had listened as Jason had poured out his pain, relived his mistakes and questioned his divorce strategy and his one true worry: losing access to his son. His friend had listened quietly and attentively giving advice when needed. Oh, how he missed Simon.

Now, seated at his desk with a refilled wine glass, he leaned back in his chair and turned the on the TV. He flipped to one of the sports channels, watched and listened to the commentary without concentration, sipping the wine, savoring the tannins and the fruits and spices inherent in the drink, pushing it around his mouth, before swallowing, a mostly unconscious act, his mind elsewhere. He felt a deep sadness. Just a few weeks ago he'd been chatting with Simon over lunch, a bonus before their next regular monthly business lunch, which was due the following week. He had been surprised, but he was glad to be out of the office. They'd gone for sushi at one of the better places. A place that Simon knew Jason loved, where they sat at the bar being personally served by one of the chefs, the place buzzing but not too noisy, dark brown wood and white linens giving it, I suppose, he thought, a traditional Japanese ambience. As they enjoyed the delicious sushi, they chatted about general unmemorable topics. Then Simon seemed to get to his point, the reason they were here.

"Jason. The reason I called for lunch," as a piece of sushi was placed in front of them by the chef, "apart from the excellent sushi," he exclaimed, they both smiled broadly. "I want to draw up my Will."

"Your Will?" Jason replied. Surprised that someone so easy going and single would even consider such a thing at his age. Of course, I have one, but I have a son's future to consider.

"Yes, my Will, and I wish to create a managed fund for my daughter."

"Daughter?" Jason coughed, spluttered, and nearly choked, alarmed at this new information. "You have a daughter?" he repeated as he coughed to clear his throat and thoughts, now believing that he must have heard incorrectly.

Simon just smiled, "Yes, I have an 18-year old daughter."

"Since when?" The shock still in his voice. A little loud for the quiet restaurant, a few patrons looked over with disapproval at the noisy disturbance.

"Well I suppose since 18 years ago," he laughed.

Jason quickly did the math.

"Adela's?"

"Adela's."

He didn't want to say it, but it just came out. "Are you sure she's yours?" Shit, he thought, the moment the words passed his lips.

"Yes." Simon didn't react, he just popped another piece of sushi into his mouth. Jason decided to join him, closing his eyes, enjoying the clean, slightly tangy flavor of the fresh fish and the subtly sweet, vinegary taste of the complementing rice, and then a compliment given to the chef with an audible grunt and a quick nod.

"I'm sure," Simon continued with a humorous snort.

"She was pregnant when she quit college?" he blurted out, as understanding suddenly came to him.

"Yes."

"So, what happened?" the Simon he knew would never have left her alone. At worst he would have paid child support, been there to help. He'd seen Simon with his son Timmy. The guy positively loves kids, and he had certainly loved Adela.

"She was pregnant with our child, my daughter, but I didn't know that she'd kept the child, Angela. Her sister had told me that Adela had had an abortion. I should have known she wouldn't. I had wanted her to, but I should have known. We'd discussed it, Adela and I, and I'd thought we'd come to a mutual decision. I was wrong," he paused fleetingly, a faraway look taking his gaze away from me, then quickly returning to the present. "Anyway, when I realized my mistake, it was too late. I had no idea where she was to confirm or deny. I never knew. It's so obvious now." He stopped again, staring at the next piece on offer, and at that moment, he was back in the present. Jason knew how much he must regret this. Eighteen years! Jason thought. What if I hadn't known Timmy for eighteen years? What if Sarah had just left me when she'd gotten pregnant, never told me, and I'd never seen Timmy grow up? The thought made him shudder.

"Well, I'm here to help. Whatever I can do," Jason offered, but feeling a little helpless, "I will do." The age-old Adela conundrum was answered after all these years.

"There is nothing I regret more, nothing," he said, voice, eyes distant, seemingly ignoring Jason for the moment.

"I'm so sorry," Jason replied quietly, the sushi for the moment forgotten.

"Anyway," suddenly, brightly, returning to the present, "the past is the past and passed, and I need to make up for lost time. I have a daughter who needs a father. And you have some work to do for all that money I've given you." There was a smile on his face, the old Simon, the Simon he knew, was now back.

Jason smiled as he reminisced, shaking his head slightly at the memory. Then he took a large sip from his glass, again savoring the bold red flavors, floral and tannic, which were now starting to open up and impose on his thoughts, and he held the glass to his nose and breathed in deeply, enjoying the complex bouquet and sighed. Yes, Simon would have most certainly approved, as he quaffed a large mouthful.

Later, after a bit too much great sushi and feeling just a bit bloated, they went back to Jason's office and started drawing up the details. I was supposed to finalize and outline the financial plan with him next week on his return from Boston. The events of the evening resurfaced with a sting of pain. I need to find his girl, he thought with resolution, as part of his job as well as a personal choice, for his friend. He knew that even if Simon had left no details, it wouldn't be difficult. First thing tomorrow.

He picked up the bottle, perused the label, poured himself another healthy portion and sank back in his chair. I'll arrange entrance to his apartment and also get the agency on it if I need to, but tomorrow! He swished the wine in the glass, letting in air, brought it to his nose and again breathed in deeply, extracting the layers of pleasure that great wines bring. Then he took another healthy gulp from the glass, part of his mind enjoying the wine, the other occupied with thoughts of tomorrow. Yes, tomorrow we'll find her, but tonight I'll drink to an old friend. The phrase sounded right, and he felt a tear falling on his cheek. I'll get a little drunk and remember some great times.

He got up, taking the bottle off the table, and glass in hand, he moved towards the more comfortable sofa, and while still standing he poured more wine into his glass. Thoughts of Megan and his ill-mannered attitude returned to bother him.

He placed the bottle on the coffee table and flopped onto the sofa, guilt overcoming him. He noticed the hint of warmth left by Sheila. The memory of his actions earlier in the evening wouldn't leave him. He hadn't been professional, he thought, realizing that that wouldn't have been a good enough excuse either. He was being detached, acting like a professional, and yet he knew we wasn't. His actions this evening were a quandary, and worse, he still couldn't determine why. Well, it's done, and I won't do it again, he promised himself, feeling a little ashamed. He sat up straight and lifted his glass.

"Simon, forgive me, I'm better than that, you of all people believed that, believed in me. I'm sorry, she deserved better from me, I'll do better next time, I promise. Goodbye, old friend. Slàinte!"

Terrible news

Angela was curled up on the couch, a haze of disappointment enveloping her. She was alone, feeling a little depressed and sorry for herself, and exhibiting one of her bad habits: sucking her thumb. Now she didn't regard it as a bad habit as such, but as a child, she had been reminded not to do it. She believed others thought of it as a bad habit, and so she never confided this habit to anyone, and she never did it in company. She had, however, researched it on the Internet and had found out that many people who aren't children still do it, and she knew her aunt must know too. Her aunt would sometimes check in on her at night, and she must have seen her niece asleep, thumb in mouth. Though her aunt, unlike her mother, never asked her to stop doing it, never told her that she should have grown out of it, never told her only babies do it. In fact, Auntie Kay never mentioned it. Regardless, she knew there was a social stigma, so apart from waking up and finding the comfort of it in her mouth, these days she rarely did it consciously.

She hadn't been doing it that much at all until recently, but now, having decided to wait at least one year before starting college because of the coming baby, she found herself doing it more often than not. It was relaxing, comforting, familiar, but today she was doing it because she was alone and disappointed and feeling a little sorry for herself, and she really felt that she needed the comfort it offered.

Ads were on TV again, and she had no idea what it was she'd been watching a mere minute or so ago. She flipped the channel, again, angrily digging her fingers into the remote when it didn't respond promptly to her touch, as if the object was the cause of her current mood, the thumb on her other hand still firmly in her mouth. She'd been watching TV all day, except for short trips to the bathroom or fiddling about in the kitchen for lunch or a drink. A dirty bowl and spoon, the remnants of her last visit, lay on the coffee table in front of her next to her iPad, which she was using for occasional web browsing. A half-drunk mug of what had been hot cocoa was surrounded by the foil from a bar of chocolate she had eaten, and not the first today. She knew that she had to tidy up before her aunt returned from work, but her annoyance was winning over the knowledge of her aunt's usual response to such messes. So, she just kept on flipping channels amid the accumulating mess she was making. What a waste of a day, she thought, curling back up on the sofa watching something, nothing. Why doesn't he call me? She had expected to hear from her dad last night, but he hadn't called or turned up, and not even yet today, which was now disappearing and evening was coming fast. Today's plans have been a complete and utter bust, she thought, pouting with righteous anger. She felt the annoyance rising and again she quelled it. It's not worth getting angry over now, she tried to convince herself. Yet, she still was. I was angry last night. I was angry this morning. It's all a bit late now, it's just so futile, last night has gone and today is nearly over. Wasted. The mess on the table reminded her of that. Anger? It isn't worth it, and yet her anger and disappointment remained. We were supposed to be going out and having fun, she thought regretfully. Getting to know one another just a little bit more, and she had wanted to see a movie: the latest Linklater.

She picked up her phone and checked again for messages or a text or a missed call. Again. There was, of course, no reason to expect anything, since the phone had been on her person all day, and no sound or ringing or vibrating had occurred since the last time she'd checked, ten minutes ago. She'd been hoping he was going to call, so she'd waited. Continually disappointed as the morning went by, followed by the afternoon and the onset of depression, her anger increasing, slow and simmering with annoyance, not with rage, but the calculated thoughts of what she was going to say during their next conversation. Which was, at this moment, a monologue of whys, as she could think of no justification for his actions, so he was going to have to take everything she was going to throw at him!

She heard the door opening, and the moment and time coalesced. Oh, it's that time already, she thought. She looked at the clock on the DVR, which confirmed what she had now just surmised: Auntie Kay had returned from work. She continued watching the TV with half her attention, knowing what was coming next, her thumb removed from its place of comfort, already missed.

"Angie?" shouted Auntie Kay from the kitchen, Angie recognized the tone. She had expected that tone, and she still winced, "you're supposed to clean up in the kitchen after you have used it," her aunt continued. Angie was already off the sofa and with the bowl, spoon, mug, and chocolate wrapper in her hand, and headed towards the kitchen.

Her aunt stood there in a classic pose of righteous indignation. Her legs apart, hands on her hips, and on her face, a frown of disapproval. Thoughts of her father, for the moment forgotten, Angela was of two minds, to laugh at the predicted pose or to affect a correct contrite attitude. She correctly chose the latter, having previously tried the former to disastrous effect, and the vision of extra chores keeping her in check.

"Sorry, Auntie. Sorry. I'll do it now." She kissed her aunt on the proffered cheek and smiled warmly as her aunt smiled back, her anger revealed for what it really was: fake, but effective.

"And prepare me a nice cup of tea while you're at it, would you," she smiled back echoing the good mood she appeared to be in, "please?"

"Yes, of course, it'll just be a few minutes." She smiled as her aunt left the room, near dancing as she was leaving the kitchen, an indication that she'd had a good day at work.

"What are you watching?" came a shout from the living room.

"Not much, Auntie. Just stuff," she shouted back, as on tiptoes she reached to pull the tea chest from the cupboard.

"What! All day?" exclaimed her aunt, Angie's eye brows raised in embarrassment, glad her aunt was in the other room. Moving to the sink, she realized she had no idea what was on, trying to remember as she filled the kettle at the faucet.

"My original plans didn't happen. I was hoping to go out." Auntie Kay knew with whom, and Angie didn't want to mention him. Things always turned sour when his name came up. Her aunt never wanted to hear it, even though she'd accepted it, and Angie didn't need the hassle it invariably brought out of her.

"Oh." Angie heard in the distance, watching the kettle boil, having quickly cleaned up the small, tiny, barely worth mentioning, mess.

Where was he? Where's Dad? She thought, the disappointment returning as she waited, and not for the first time that day. He is usually punctual, and the few times he has had to cancel, he has called me. Dad. She was starting to get used to calling him that. I know he loves hearing it, she mused. His face always lights up with a bigger smile when I say it. Sometimes it's just a little tweak of the lips, the corners slightly upturned, and then there are those huge grins. I must admit I still see him as Simon most of the time, not a stranger anymore, but still not close enough for a dad, a real dad, and sometimes I see him as the man who left Mom, she thought, her mood souring slightly. But he's trying hard, and I like him, she thought firmly, and she knew that this was the truth, her mood lightening, and she smiled.

They'd been seeing each other now for a few months, and for the last few weeks, she'd visited him in New York. Oh my God! New York! I love New York. A smile lit up her face at the memory. I thought it was pretty cool when I was there visiting campuses, but he's shown me so much more. Museums, SoHo, the village where he lived – what an apartment! She looked down and was reminded, her mood souring again. She patted her belly. If it wasn't for the baby, she would be studying at Columbia now, living there in New York. Her future was still a little uncertain, but she knew that she was going to have a baby, she was going to be a single mother, and there was no chance the father was going to be involved, but Simon had hinted that if she wanted to she could move to Manhattan. He had told her he would help her in any way he could. They could work out a mutual arrangement. Mutual? She thought, he really means one that will make me happy.

But then there was Auntie Kay. She loved her aunt more than anyone, including her dad. I'm not hurting Auntie Kay, not even for him. I don't think I can move to New York yet, and she stroked her belly, and I'll need help with my child. Is he going to ready to be a granddad? More than just a granddad? I know he believes he can, but knowing and doing are not the same thing, she thought. He's not even called me to tell me where he is and why he didn't come for his visit. How can I trust him? She hated that thought because she really wanted to trust him, believing he could still be a father and soon a grandfather, but his absence and lack of communication were causing previous doubts to resurface.

A few minutes later Angie walked in with the tea. Her aunt was dozing, and Angie looked down at her with love in her eyes, studying the familiar curves and lines on her aunt's face. Was there anyone she was more familiar with? The answer was obvious. She placed the cup and saucer carefully on the coffee table. She looks so peaceful, and I love her so much. She started unconsciously rubbing her belly again, knowing that this woman would always be there for her, and would help her through the difficult months to come. Angie touched her aunt's shoulder and gently shook. Her aunt woke with a start.

"Oh my, did I doze off? I'm a little tired is all. Thank you, darling, just what I needed," her voice quiet as she was still in the light grip of slumber. Kay leaned forward and slowly with the deliberate care of someone still not fully awake, but trying to become so, picked up the teacup and saucer from the table, "Ah, a nice cup of tea," she murmured, then looked up to thank her niece with a smile. The girl was looking away. She was staring at the TV stricken, her fists clenched, her body rigid.

"No! No! No!" she shouted, and Kay could hear the anguish in her niece's voice. Her still sleepy mind only just registering the surrounding sounds.

"Angie, what's wrong?" she asked, focusing on her niece. She turned to look at the screen, in the direction of the girl's gaze, and there was Simon's picture on the screen, larger than life.

"No, please, no," her niece's voice was quieter, but the pain was still evident. Simon on the TV? Kay concentrated on what was being said, now fully awake. It was the news, and it didn't appear to be good.

Angie suddenly quickly turned and grabbed the remote from the table, then turned up the volume. Too loud for Kay's taste, but she ignored that fact. There were tears streaming down her niece's face, sorrow and anger mixed, flashing as the news unfolded. Some drunk college kids had been driving without their lights on in the torrential rain last night. A frat-house dare or something, causing a fatal accident. Apparently, one of the students was the son of a New England Senator, which was why it was actually newsworthy here. Simon had been the driver in the oncoming vehicle, he'd been driving up to Boston from New York and had died of his injuries in the hospital, in an emergency ward in New York City.

Angie was distraught. The sobbing wouldn't stop, and Kay didn't know what to say to her. Her feelings about Simon were well known to Angie, and they rarely talked about him. She still hadn't forgiven him for what he'd done to her sister, but she also knew, and had admitted to herself against all arguments attempted, that he was a good influence on Angie, and she had been witnessing the positive effect this relationship was having on her niece over the past few weeks, especially with regard to the baby. She'd watched her niece change from an embarrassed teenager to a woman embracing her future in a positive manner. Kay had cried with happiness when Angie had come prancing in one evening, flushed with the excitement the day had brought her. They never talked about her time with Simon, as Kay couldn't broach the subject without getting angry, but she was overjoyed at the positive transformation that seeing Simon was making on her little girl. But this news, this terrible accident, she wouldn't wish such a tragedy on him or anyone.

"Oh, Angie, baby, I'm so sorry." She stood up, trembling slightly, her niece's pain already filling her, and the girl clung tightly to her, her nails digging through the fabric of Kay's sweater. Kay winced slightly, but took the small pain, holding her.

"Auntie, it's not fair. It's just not fair. I've lost my dad, and I only just found him," she wailed into her aunt's chest. Kay pulled her closer and held her more tightly. Stroking her hair and talking in a soothing voice trying to calm her, knowing that she couldn't.

"I'm so sorry, sweetheart. I'm so sorry," she whispered, unable to think of anything else to say. They were just getting to know one another. I know he was trying hard, and I know he was good for her. What will this do to her? She remembered having to console her when she was still a little girl. First during her mother's illness, and then a few months later after her mother had died. Kay's thoughts tightened at both the memory of losing her sister and best friend and having to comfort her little niece. Trying hard to explain the inexplicable. Trying to comfort a little girl who had no idea why such a thing should happen, when Kay herself had no clue either.

"It's me, isn't it? There was Mom, then this stupid pregnancy and no college, and now Dad," she squeezed Kay's arm digging her fingers in further. Key winced again at the sudden pain, but she bore it with a grimace, knowing she could take more if she had to. Then Angie relaxed in her hold, sobbing gently. "I'm being punished!"

"Now don't you say that. Don't!" There were tears of anger in her voice. "It's not your fault, you hear me, not your fault at all. It's just life, it happens. You mustn't think such thoughts. Never! It's not you!" She felt her heart breaking all over again, and she squeezed Angie gently.

"But why me?" She looked up, tears streaking her face, staring into her aunt's eyes, as if searching for an answer. Kay was also crying, and she had no satisfactory answer. "Why?" Angie repeated, and Kay knew she couldn't explain because she herself didn't know.

"It just is, my sweet. They're with the Lord now, as we all shall be some day. It's painful for us here, but one day we will be with them, we will all be together." Angie's belief wasn't as strong as her Auntie Kay's, and even though she believed, she was hurting so badly and just wanted to know why. She wanted a reason, a proper one. It just wasn't good enough, but she knew that her aunt didn't have the answers. Who actually does?

Kay felt such guilt. Simon was dead. Didn't she once wish him so, those many years ago? She recalled, unbidden, her last conversation with Simon. Now Angie was seeing her father, she'd recalled the memory in more and more detail with bitterness and regret, and she was there again, as she held her niece tightly, and the guilt flooded though her, mingled with her niece's pain. She was still in two minds, guilt or innocence, concerning her decisions and that conversation.

From the caller id I know who it is, and I gesture towards my sister. She's been lying on the sofa distraught, but on hearing the phone she sits upright, rigid, holding her control as much as she can, and now she's frantically waving at me to answer it. I really don't want to.

"It's Simon," I confirm her assumption. I walk back to her, the phone still ringing, and hand it to her. She stares at me, then at the object in my hand, and then back to me. She waves me, and it, away, as if the object is poisonousness or somehow deadly. The look on her face showing both disgust and fear as she shrinks away from it, and me. Over the past few days her emotions concerning him have swayed between love and an awful bitterness I've never seen before but recognize as hate, and that's what I see now, and it hurts me so much.

"I'm not here," she spits out, again staring at the phone with brittle distaste, backing into the sofa as far as she possibly can.

"He needs to know," I say as gently as possible, hoping she'll acquiesce, the phone angled towards her, and inside I'm screaming:

I don't want to speak to him either. She starts to cry, and I know I'm going to have to talk to him.

"He doesn't want the baby. I do. End of story," she whispers, though her tone is emphatic. She stares at me, wide eyed and scared, and I know she's committed to her course, as am I, but I try one more time, pushing the phone towards her. She stops shrinking away, and she doesn't look at the object anymore, just continues to stare at me, her answer obvious.

"But if you're going to keep it..." The phone is still ringing, and she doesn't appear to notice anymore, just me and the phone I am holding has her complete focus.

"Tell him I had the abortion he wanted. Tell him I don't want to talk to him. Tell him that I don't want to see him again, ever!" Then crying, she jumps up and hurriedly leaves the room and me with the ringing phone. I pause for another ring and then brace myself to answer it.

"Hello?" I really don't want to speak to him, but she's my sister, and this needs to be resolved. Now.

"Hi, Adela? It's Simon," I can hear the concern in his voice, and I can visualize his worried look. I know he cares for Adela. I know he loves her, but so do I, I tell myself, determined to keep my sister safe. Hoping, wanting, to see her smiling face that has been lost these past few days.

"Hi, Simon, it's Kay," I reply, my voice neutral, in opposition to the turmoil in my head.

"Oh. Hi, Kay. How are you? May I speak with Adela? Is she available?" I can hear the desperation in his voice, but I'm not going to be swayed. He doesn't want the baby. Let's just get this over and done with. I have packing to do.

"She's not here," I lie. I really want to tell him the truth, but he wants an abortion, and such an idea is disgusting to me. It is totally against my principles. My sister doesn't want one either, and she doesn't want to see him, that's all I need to know. If he'd wanted the baby, I would have tried to convince Adela otherwise, but I was finding it very hard to even talk to him at this moment. I breathe in deeply, trying to relax and keep my calm.

"I just want to talk with her, please," the desperation in his voice is increasing, and I really feel for him, but the facts haven't changed. He wants an abortion, and my sister does not, and she doesn't want to see him. These thoughts keep repeating in my head.

"I'm sorry, but she's unavailable, not here," I reply, keeping all my emotions from my voice, hoping that he's not hearing the feelings roiling inside of me, and praying that he's not hearing the lies.

"I've tried her mobile, but she appears to have disconnected it." I collect myself. This has to stop. I have to end this before I crack, letting it all out. I don't want to hurt him, but she's all that matters to me, so this will probably hurt him. I just hope I can live with the lie.

"Simon, please listen. I'm just going to say this once," I pause, allowing him a moment to absorb the point, "She had the abortion you wanted," the guilt immediately hits me with this proffered lie, but she is my sister and my only family and we have to look out for each other, I remind myself, "and she's moved away. She doesn't want to see you. She doesn't want to speak to you. She doesn't want anything more to do with you. Do you understand?"

"Yes, but..."

"Do you understand?" I repeat, more forcefully. I really need this conversation to finish. I am so close to breaking, to telling him the truth, to betraying my sister.

"Yes, I understand," his reply is small and resigned. So quiet I can barely hear it, but I can, and I can also hear the anguish in his voice, but I stay firm, for her, my sister, my family.

"Please, don't call again." I close my eyes and remind myself that we'll be in Boston soon, the job offer has already been accepted. Adela can stay with me for as long as she wishes. I'll help bring up the baby if she needs me to. He need never know. The guilt claws in me, gripping me, clutching me, and I know it will always be there. It will never let go.

"Kay, I just want to talk to her, I need to explain," he sounds desperate, but I'm resolute. He wants an abortion. I've had my say, and I've at last come to terms with my lie.

"I think you've already done enough damage to my sister. Please just leave her alone; it's what she wants. You know this," my voice softens as I feel for him.

"I know, and I'm so sorry."

"So is she, Simon, so is she, and so am I. Goodbye." And without waiting for a response, I end the call, tears gently falling, still ashamed at having told the lie, but determined to protect her, my little sister, from all and everyone.

Kay gave a small prayer for them both and realized, believed, and took some comfort in the fact that they would now be together. They'd loved each other so very much. Kay knew that. Other than Angie, Adela had never loved anyone as much as she'd loved Simon. She looked down at her niece, still sobbing into her chest, and she held her tighter, feeling her heavy breathing, rising up and down, trembling limbs unable to control the emotions this terrible news had brought to her. Such a lot to go through for one so young, she pondered, and Kay wanted to cry with her, feeling the tears coming again. Then she turned to her faith again and prays. Oh Lord, please help my little girl.

Kay woke early the next morning. During the night she'd had a dreamless but good sleep. However, now that she was awake, she instantly recalled the events of the previous evening and the suffering of her niece. She lay in bed for a few moments, comfortable and warm, but full of doubts, wondering if she would be able to be strong enough for Angie, knowing she would have to be.

"Lying here is doing no good," she told herself, and she hauled herself wearily out of bed, realizing that tiredness was still upon her. The morning chill immediately surrounded her, and she wrapped herself tightly in her dressing gown. This morning is not going to be any better, but I have to try and help her. Her footsteps soft as she made her way to Angie's room, she paused at the door, enjoying a quiet moment for a few seconds, and preparing herself for the day ahead. Right now, only my sweet child matters, she told herself, knowing that this trauma would last a while. Pulling her shoulders back, her focus fully on her darling niece, she gently knocked on the door.

"Angie?" she said quietly, her ear close to the door, with her hand waiting on the handle, she could feel the thumping of her heart in the stillness surrounding her.

"Angie, darling, are you okay?" Kay waited for few seconds. Hearing nothing, she pushed open the door carefully and peered in. Her niece was lying curled up on her bed, still clothed, crying softly, thumb in mouth, and not looking towards Kay, as if she hadn't heard or didn't care; Kay assumed the latter. The room was dark, the curtains drawn shut, the light of a glorious sunny morning in such contrast to the last few days, hidden behind them, a tiny shaft of light creeping in. She considered, but quickly decided not to turn on the lights. She walked in softly towards the bed and sat on the edge, looking down with worry at her niece.

Kay listened to Angie's light breathing and gentle heaving of sobs, as the young girl finally stirred and looked up at her aunt. Kay couldn't think of anything to say, not anything that could help. Angie said nothing either, as she looked at her aunt for a moment and then slowly lowered herself back into her previous listless position: knees up against her growing belly, thumb back in her mouth, her right hand dangling over the edge of the bed, as she continued gently crying. Kay stroked the arm of her baby with the tips of her fingers, afraid she might break something if her touch were too firm, her heart breaking with her niece's pain.

"You'll be okay, my sweet. I'm here for you," she managed to say, as she continued looking down at her niece, feeling her own tears arising, as the pain became unbearable. Wondering when, if ever, it would be ok. She stopped stroking Angie.

"I'll be back in a minute, my sweet," her voice rough with emotion and pending tears, and she rose quickly, and quietly left the room.

The feeling of helplessness was weighing heavily on her, so much more so than the last time, so many years ago now, when her sister, Angie's mother, had died. The much younger Angie had been distraught and unable to understand. Looking back, it seemed so much easier then. Maybe because they were in grief together, the pain shared equally. Maybe because the illness made the death less sudden. She looked at the door and considered returning, as the guilt of leaving came upon her. She paused, organizing her thoughts. I need to sort out work first, leaving this day, my time, for her. So, she reluctantly turned away from the door. With each step towards the kitchen and the phone, she wanted to rush back and comfort her girl.

She called the restaurant and told them that she was ill and unable to come in today and gave instructions, quietly praying that they wouldn't ruin her reputation without her influence and touches to ensure that everything leaving the kitchen was to her satisfaction. I'll call again tomorrow, telling herself that this may be a few days. For a few moments, she stood in her kitchen, suddenly hit with exhaustion. She slumped down on a stool for a minute as tears and anguish hit her, rising up quickly. She allowed herself to cry softly, not wanting Angie to hear her. She didn't want to move. It felt quiet and safe and easy, but soon she forced herself back to her responsibilities.

"She's my girl, my little angel, I need to help her," she scolded herself, and she clenched her fists in anger, though only momentarily. Then holding her breath for a moment, she relaxed. Wiping the tears from her eyes and breathing deeply, she felt a semblance of control.

"This is not about me," she reminded herself, and then, refocused, she hauled herself off the stool. Everything aches. I'm getting too old for this, she thought, as a familiar pain ran through her at the sudden motion. She felt what seemed to be aches in every muscle and heard creaks in every bone, but now resolved she returned to her kitchen to help her distraught girl. Here in my kitchen, I am the queen, she thought as she decided what she needed to do first. She made some hot, sweet cocoa, blending it with a touch of cinnamon, just the way Angie liked it and returned to Angie's room.

Kay placed the mug on her niece's bedside table and sat on the bed beside her. She looked down at the distraught girl, so delicate and vulnerable, and for a moment Kay started to have doubts about the Lord's plan. Lord, why does my baby have to go through all of this again? But her belief was strong and she answered herself. It's the Lord's plan and not for me to question. However, if looking at her niece was, even just for a moment, shaking her faith, she realized she would need to be extra strong for the girl and the baby. Her faith returned just as quickly as it wavered, and she thanked her Lord for the gift of a surrogate daughter, and the faith she had always had for Him. Her faith renewed, and now fully resolute, she leaned towards her niece, and gently stroked her hair. Angie turned towards her aunt and stared up at her, red eyes filled with helplessness.

"How you are, darling?" Kay asked with concern written on her face. Her tone was soothing and her feelings hopeful, but she knew the answer.

"Not too good, Auntie, not good. It hurts so much," her tiny voice sounded so desperate, so sad. Angie had stopped crying, but anguish was etched in every line on her face, her body was rigid with tension, and Kay felt it might just snap with the strain.

"Here's a nice mug of cocoa. Hot, sweet, just how you like it. Drink it up and get some warmth in you. It'll help a bit." I don't know if it will, but I have to be positive, I have to be strong for her. I'm so sorry my poppet, and inside she knew she could crumble at any minute. Angie slowly rose and sat up. Her head bowed, she reached out and brought the mug to her chest with both hands. She stared into it, as if it held some inner secret, some solution to all this horror. Kay watched in anguish, transfixed by both her own and her niece's pain. Angie slowly turned her head and wiping the tears from her face, faced her aunt, the mug still held close to her. She looked at her aunt, wide eyed and questioning, and Kay prayed to the Lord for further guidance.

"I'll be staying with you today, and we're going to get through this together. Me and you."

"Thank you, Auntie." Her voice was tiny and so sad, but soon she took some sips from the mug, and as her aunt had told her, it was hot and sweet. The peaceful moment was suddenly broken by the sound of the phone ringing downstairs. They both looked away from each other, then back questioning, then Angie shook her head slightly, and Kay reassured her, understanding.

"I'll get it." Not really wishing to leave her niece, "I'll be back in a moment my dear," and she headed downstairs to answer the phone, not really wishing to answer or to talk to anyone but her niece in this moment of pain. She immediately noticed from the caller id that it was a New York City number. I suppose it's something to do with Simon's death, probably the police, she quickly surmised, due to the unlikelihood of anyone in New York calling here, and she didn't generally believe in coincidences. She took a deep breath and exhaled slowly, which helped to calm her somewhat, and she answered the phone.

"Hi, Kay speaking."

"Hello, my name is Jason Doherty, I'm trying to get in contact with Angela," the man on the phone paused, "Angela Bridgewater?" he sounded a little unsure. "Can you help me?"

"Who are you? And why are you looking for her?" came out rather more aggressively than she intended, and Kay instantly regretted her tone.

"I'm so sorry to have to bring this up," and he paused. She already knew what was coming, but she waited for the stranger to continue. "I don't know if you know, but there has been some terrible news concerning her father. Has anyone else been in contact with you?"

"No one has, but we already know, it was on the news last night," she was trying to be more amenable, but knew she was failing. The voice on the other end of the line, however, wasn't reacting, and she was grateful for it.

"I'm so very sorry you had to receive the news in such a manner. I am a friend of Simon's, and I'm also his lawyer and the executor of his estate."

"Oh."

"Is it possible for me to speak with Angela?"

"She's not available right now. As you might expect, she is not taking Simon's passing very well," she realizes that her anger was causing her to be aggressive, but given what had happened and the state of her niece, she couldn't really be at all bothered to control it, "I wouldn't recommend you talking with her right now, and she doesn't really want to speak to anyone. Later would be better," much later, she thought, but she knows this has to be done. "How about early next week?"

"Thank you, early next week is fine. I will call on Monday? If that's okay?"

"That'll be fine. I will inform her."

"May I ask to whom I am talking?"

"I'm her aunt and her guardian. My name is Kaitlin Bridgewater."

"Thank you, Ms. Bridgewater. I'm so sorry for her loss," he sounded awkward but sincere, "he was a good friend." The moment continued with an unwelcome silence, and she was preparing to finish the conversation and get back to her niece and help with her pain.

"There are also funeral arrangements that need to be made," he suddenly continued, sounding a little rushed.

"Not now, please. Just call on Monday. Okay? Goodbye, Mr. Doherty."

"Thank you, goodbye."

Kay looked up the stairs, thinking of her niece, wondering what she would say to her, how to explain, knowing she will need to before the lawyer calls next week. Ah, fried chicken, rice and peas, with a side of ackee and salt fish – Angie's favorites – and I have the whole weekend. She made her way to the kitchen, unable to face her niece for the moment, to take small comfort in cooking.

It's all worthwhile, regardless

Tim sat back exasperated. Hadn't any of the class produced even a reasonable attempt at the set homework? Leaning the chair back, he let the music wash over him, his foot tapping to the cool sounds of early Miles, his fingers making imaginary runs with the bass-line he knew so well. It relaxed him a bit, but a look at the time told him he needed to continue marking homework. He was only halfway through marking the class's papers and hadn't seen a decent response to the set question yet. He looked at his monitor, and the coursework software confirmed that he wasn't quite halfway through yet. It was close, but he still sighed at the slight difference. A committed agnostic, he prayed. It was always depressing having to explain the actual answers when no one seemed to understand the original problems given. Blank faces staring back at him, then face down, and furiously typing away or writing notes as he spoke, before returning their gazes back, eager, but again blank. Then after class was over, he would start to doubt his teaching skills, questioning his methods and relationship with his students, the previous year's good results already forgotten.

Well, not all of the students, he reminded himself, and his eyes rolled as the thought came to him without any surprise. He was sure that Darren's work, once he got to it, would be much more than adequate. I can see the smug look on the boy's face, whilst I'm explaining the answers to the rest of the class. I most certainly am not going to allow that young lad to explain an answer to the class again! He'd let him do so once before, and the resultant charade still sent shivers down his spine. There was absolutely no doubt that it had been a mistake. He'd been happy to let a student explain the answer, the idea being that the others may realize that it was well within their grasp. He'd thought it was a good idea, and in principle he still did, but not in this case. That the kid was talented, there was no doubt, and by the time classes were finished he would probably know more on the subject than Tim did himself. This, of course, was an exaggeration, and Tim smiled. Dr. Tim PhD is being modest, he told himself. And he was; he was very good at the subject, having recently published some thought-provoking research that had garnered some excellent responses in the academic forums. Darren was a natural, and genuinely loved computers and programming, but he also had a huge streak of arrogance that Tim was finding hard to cope with and which the rest of the class seemed to resent. Neither seemed to bother Darren. Tim remembered, with embarrassment, the tears Darren had been able to produce from one of the other pupils. A girl had unwittingly asked for further explanation of an admittedly easy point. Darren, chest puffed out, had been unforgiving in his contempt and barbed reply. It was two weeks before the girl returned to class, and Tim had had to endure an interrogation from both the school head and her parents.

Pain flared in Tim's back, abruptly bringing his thoughts back to the moment. He stood up, stretched, grimaced, stretched again, and then relaxed. Then he closed his eyes momentarily, as he let Miles and the music take control of his senses, issues of homework for the moment forgotten. I really have to change that chair, he thought, wincing, not for the first time and probably not for the last. It wasn't a comfortable chair. It had been cheap. It looked like an office chair but really wasn't. It was okay for short stints, very short ones, but after a few hours. Oh dear! Just painful. He twisted at the waist to alleviate the tightness. It worked as expected, and for a moment he felt better. Coffee, he thought. It was still a little early for dinner. It was still bright outside, and shafts of natural light filtering through lessened the need for any artificial lights.

He made his way to the kitchen. As he walked towards it, the letters on the stand next to the front door caught his attention. He'd picked them up when entering the apartment block, but when he'd entered his apartment, his thoughts had been interrupted, the letters forgotten, as he was distracted by the ringing phone. He had barely riffled through them and had just dropped them on the stand. He stopped now to examine them further. The distraction was welcome, and thoughts of coffee and marking papers moved out of his thoughts as he wandered across to the front door, eyes glued on the small pile. He picked up the letters. Immediately recognizing a couple of bills, he shuffled through them and then tossed the rest of the pile into the waste basket for recycling. Nothing to relieve the monotony of the coming evening, so like yesterday, the day before, so like last week, and last month.

He then noticed a small letter had fallen to the side, beside the basket, the red of the envelope merging somewhat with the red of his carpet, barely noticeable at a distance, more so close up. He stared at it for a moment, something unexpected in a life of unspectacular predictability. Picking it up he quickly opened it, since personal letters were rare, and he was intrigued. It's not Christmas or my birthday, he thought and read with anticipation of something unforeseen in his admittedly mundane life:

My Dear Tim

I hope this letter finds you well, or as well as can be expected. I don't know the best way or an easy way of saying this, but it is with a great and terrible sorrow that I have to tell you that Simon, our good friend, recently passed away...

Simon? Passed away? Tim stopped, numb, and read from the beginning again, not quite understanding what he'd just read. It wasn't until the third time he'd re-read the sentence, that it fully sank in. Simon dead? Everything tensed and he trembled. Unable to hold the letter still, and with tears welling in his eyes, the letters on the page blurred, and his fists clenched on the paper. How can that be? Even after rereading, it still didn't make sense, though he understood exactly what he'd read. He wiped the wetness away, steadied himself, and read on.

Simon had been in a road accident last Thursday, dying after briefly regaining consciousness. A funeral was being arranged; he could expect an invitation soon. It then caught his attention that the letter was handwritten, not printed. Momentarily distracted from his pain and intrigued, he scanned to the bottom to discover the sender. It was Megan; he should have recognized her writing. The letter only concerned the accident and contained no personal details. Oh, Megan, I'm so sorry, he thought, feeling deeply for her as memories flooded back, and he realized how much this would have hurt her, as it certainly was hurting him, and this knowledge caused his own pain to flare as he knew hers was even greater. They'd all been best friends late into high school, through college and after, but over the last few years, jobs, partners, and life, separated by cities and time, had seen them gradually drift apart. But the memories? The memories were still there. And the love? The love for both of them, different in their own way, was just as powerful. How could he have let them go? He knew though. The now childish reason with Megan, but Simon? He had no excuses, and now he would never be able to connect with him again. Tears spilled down his cheeks as much for his friend, now gone, as for the own personal loss that this news gave him. He stumbled in tears to the sofa, sat down, and kicked out at the coffee table. Pain flared in his foot, causing a grunt and a grimace, and no satisfaction from the futile gesture. The letter, held limply in his hand, was for the moment forgotten, unlike the news bringing forward memories, long buried but not forgotten. Simon's dead, he needlessly reminded himself, but the single thought wouldn't leave him, and he felt dismayed and drained.

He recalled the last few times that he'd seen his friend. Once, a few weeks after Megan's wedding. They had barely spoken at the wedding. I hadn't spoken much to anyone, I'd made excuses and left early, he reminded himself. So, he'd been surprised and glad when the caller id had shown Simon's name, and he had been thrilled to chat again with one of his best friends and get a chance to apologize for his boorish behavior. They'd met up for a drink after work, downtown in the financial district, a busy street full of bankers and the noisy exuberance of after work. People unwinding with food and beer served on long tables, the weather still amenable to such outdoor activities. Simon had been similarly enthusiastic and chatty, barely audible over a background noise that Tim found imposing and annoying, but which Simon appeared to revel in, as he competed with his fellow workers over the ever-increasing volumes. The anticipation Tim had originally felt soon faded, and he quickly found the whole meeting a little oppressive. The noise was overbearing as it ground into his being, and he found himself fighting to hear and fighting to concentrate. He wanted to be here, here with Simon his friend, but he also found that being with this childhood friend soon invoked thoughts of their mutual friend and her wedding, which still wore heavily on his mind. Try as he might, the oppressive bustle and noise wouldn't allow him to shake the thoughts, the memory so undesired. Yes, he was happy to see Simon, watching him in his element, jousting with the people around, many he obviously knew, though such knowledge appeared irrelevant to him as he appeared to jest with friends and strangers alike. Within what seemed an eternity but was only an hour or so, Tim couldn't handle it any longer, and he concocted an excuse to cut the meeting short. The disappointment in his friend's eyes nearly caused him to change his mind, especially after a suggestion to move elsewhere, but now all that was in his mind was the sight of Megan, all in white, saying "I do." This image burdened him, and would not leave him, and he committed himself to his decision.

They pulled out phones to arrange a later meeting at a place more conducive to conversation and reminiscing. His friend's suggestions were obviously thoughtful of Tim's discomfort, but their schedules had been busy. Tim had some school workshops, and Simon had some business trips abroad. They parted with promises and smiles and every intention of meeting up later that summer, but truth be told he was still feeling depressed. Thoughts of the wedding, returned renewed, and had taken everything out of him. Megan was now married, and little else seemed to matter. Childishly, he later realized and regretted, he had ignored Simon's calls, using the excuse that he would call later. Maybe next week, he'd kept telling himself, I just need a little time. However, he never did call his friend. Prevaricating over phoning or replying, long self-dialogs of what he would say and how he would apologize, the weeks turned to months and he never called back. Simon tried. Though his calls, intermittent over those months, had finally stopped, and now he was gone. Guilt flooded into him because now he would never be able to catch up with, chat and laugh with, reminisce with, his best friend. Now, he could never apologize for his selfish behavior, and the guilt hung heavy over him.

I must phone Megan, she'll need a friend, and even more guilt overwhelmed him. He hadn't spoken with her for years. He tried once, calling her when he'd found out that she'd separated from Peter. She hadn't answered, and he hadn't tried again, leaving a brief, incoherent message, his own pain making excuses for him. Tomorrow I'll call, he promised himself, then realized that he didn't have her number, last had on a lost phone many months ago. He scanned the letter hopefully, and upon turning it over found what he needed. Yes, tomorrow I'll call, and we'll chat. With that resolution, he relaxed and fell back into the comfort of his sofa.

I have papers to mark, he reminded himself, and halfheartedly prized himself from the sofa, returning to his uncomfortable desk chair and his students' homework, coffee now long forgotten. He forced himself to concentrate on the work despite the news, as it was important to him.

Surprisingly, Darren's homework was not the best, and he momentarily felt pleased on behalf of his students Sandra and Philip. And himself? Maybe his teachings were sinking in, maybe it is all worthwhile. It's certainly most important to try. The thought brought a small smile to his face, and then he remembered with a warm glow his lessons tutoring Simon, recalling when Simon, usually confident in doing whatever he put his mind and body to had, completely out of the blue, approached him for a favor.

"Tim? Tim? Wait up." I know who it is, immediately, not a voice I wouldn't recognize, and I pause before turning around. My arm snakes out to stop Nick, I miss him as he moves out of range, and he hasn't noticed I've stopped and he is walking and chatting, oblivious to the change in our current circumstances.

"Nick?" I ask loud enough, I hope, to get his attention, though I really don't want to have to shout. I look around with a furtive stare, hoping he'll hear me and stop, worrying who might notice if I have to raise my voice. Luckily, he stops. He turns around slowly and looks at me waiting. His neutral look betrays nothing, though I'm not that bothered, it's a phase he's been going through lately. "I'll catch up with you a little later, it's probably some band stuff. I shouldn't be too long." He looks behind me and I assume, from his eye roll and the single raised eyebrow, that he now recognizes Simon. He focuses back to me, shaking his head slightly with a small shrug and that neutral look, which he believes makes him appear cool, has returned. I'm not too sure that "cool" is quite the word I would use to describe that look, but it keeps him happy.

"Okay, Tim, but please turn up soon. Don't be late – we're off in," he lifts his arm, forcing the sleeve back with a twist and looks at his watch, "15 minutes?" He asks rhetorically, and not a little sarcastically. I can see the Mickey Mouse hands, and I wince inside. He has a new watch again! Last week it was flower hands or something similar. He does realize that there are proper watches out there, doesn't he? I laugh to myself. Of course, he knows, that was the point.

"Yeah, no problem, I wouldn't miss it for the world." Yeah, right, I am thinking, still trying to remember why I had decided to accept the invitation. The last quiz night was so boring. Nine people had turned up and we had had a decision to make: four teams of two, or two teams of four, plus the arranger and organizer: Mr. Question Master. We'd stood there, a small crowd in a large room, and spent at least ten minutes deciding, going over and over and over again the pros and cons of either configuration. The former had won out. That, however, hadn't solved the boring problem, but they were my friends, and they wanted to try again, and I knew I wouldn't, couldn't, refuse them. This time the invite was posted on the school's public board, coupled with more effort to cajole others to join us. Well, even if tonight is as boring as the last time, I sigh, I know they'll try again and, of course, I know I'll be there with them, and I can do nothing else but smile at the whole situation.

"Great, see you later." I watch Nick still playing with his watch as he turns to leave, and then as he nearly knocks over someone as he moves off. I could see it coming, though I'm not too sure if I could have warned either of them in time. It all happened rather quickly. Books go flying, as do certain unkind epithets, followed by a profuse number of apologies. All attempts at looking cool are now gone, as he tries to quieten the girl down while he separates his books from hers now lying scattered on the floor. I laugh quietly to myself, knowing how long he's been concocting ways to try to introduce himself to this particular victim of his clumsiness. Locked behind secret meetings, we'd discussed, planned, and in our minds, executed the perfect pickup lines with various pretty and inaccessible girls from around the school. The more inaccessible, the more elaborate the method. This one, not previously conceived, would surely be added. I shake my head with a smile, turning away so as not to get involved with this minor fracas and Nick's latest embarrassment.

"Tim, thanks for waiting." Simon was breathing a little heavily, which I must admit is a surprise for me. Usually, he's relaxed and cool, he'll generally wait for me to catch up with him, or if really required, he will nonchalantly stroll over in his own sweet time, while I stand there waiting. It was a nice change of circumstances, which I'm actually feeling rather pleased about, and I'm suddenly intrigued by the change of status. He's looking around as he approaches me, gauging the area, the people.

"Let's get out of here, I need to talk in private." Is that distaste I'm hearing? No, I believe he's annoyed at something, but not me I hope. What could I have done? My intrigue, coupled with my usual pessimism, is now starting to turn into worry.

"Yes. Of course," I reply hesitantly. He's already steering me away and, given his strength, that's pretty hard to resist without a major effort on my part. I let him lead. We wander in silence for a minute or two, through the thinning crowds in the school corridors where students are making their own way out and home. Outside it's overcast but warm, and other students are still milling around in clumps of friends at the end of the school day.

Simon continues walking us further away from the crowds, towards an empty bench on the edge of the car park. It's relatively quiet here, the spaces are mostly empty since many students have already gone home. Across the carpark, I can see my geek squad milling around on the other side knowing that I'd be joining them in a moment, but this whole anxious Simon thing is starting to play on my mind.

"Simon, what's up?" I ask, the silence doing its job of coaxing the question out of me, impatient for him to start, and to get to the point.

"You're good at math and science aren't you?" he stares at me in an intense way, giving me the impression that he's weighing up my response to a question he obviously knows the answer to.

"I suppose so," I offer casually, knowing I am a lot better than him. Why should he care? I ask myself. As far as I know, he's never had any interest in either subject.

"I mean Megan says you're good." What the hell was he doing asking Megan about my science skills? "She says you tutored her." Ahh? Okay? and I'm now starting to see where this is going. I'm going to have a little fun at his expense, I admit to myself, and a warm feeling flows through me.

"Yes?" I bait him, feeling a little cocky, my confidence returning.

"Yes, you're good, or yes, you tutored her?" Is that an attempt at levity I hear in his voice? Is he trying to gain control of the situation? He wants something from me. I'm sorry, Simon, it's me who has the cards here. He seems a little embarrassed to ask me directly, I deduce, and rather too happily, I have to admit to myself. Mr. Quarterback, Mr. Oh So Confident Singer in the Band was embarrassed to ask for my help. I'd been in the band for a couple of months, and I accept that we're still not exactly friends, given our own opposing social groups: jocks and geeks, and ne'er the twain shall meet outside of the band, excepting Megan of course, but... he continues, as I'm internally gloating. I can see him taking a deep breath, and he looks me in the eye with that unwavering gaze of his. You're confident, but still a little wary, I think, but you're obviously determined. I back down a bit and wait for the anticipated request.

"I really need you to tutor me." There now, that wasn't that difficult, was it? I'm maybe too satisfied with how this is going, but I have to admit, I can't help it. I'm doing all I can to not actually smile right now. There's a big huge grin just dying to come out.

"In?" as if I didn't know.

"Math, science and computers."

"Science?" and I just can't help it, reveling in the small amount of power I'm currently enjoying. When you've been beaten up and trodden on as much as I have, you take what small pleasures you can get, when at last they turn up. I wasn't going to abuse it, just enjoy it.

"Err," he's fumbling for the correct term, I can see it, but I just watch, until at last his memory helps him, "Physics!" he says emphatically as if he's made a major achievement.

"You'd like me to tutor you in math, physics and computer science?" I confirm, correcting him, just a little too smugly I realize, but I can't resist.

"Yes," he says with relief, presumably due to me finally understanding his request.

"You do understand what that would entail?"

"I think so." That's better. It looks like he's back to the brevity of his normal self. It's the Simon I'm used to, and honestly, it's the Simon I prefer.

"Look, I've got to go now," I say, looking at my friends across the car park, where the group is definitely, and thankfully, looking like more than eight people, I quickly and surprisingly notice. I register them in the periphery of my sight, as one or two of them are waving me to come over. "We can discuss it after band practice tomorrow evening," I say, returning my attention to him, "if that's okay?"

"Yeah, yeah. Just think about it, please." Please? I smile inside, it's a warm fuzzy feeling and I like the idea. I had really enjoyed tutoring Megan last year when her math marks had started to drop.

She'd never be a mathematician, she hated the subject, but she brought up her grades to what she needed and should breeze through her SAT's next year, with a little more help from me, I muse, enjoying the idea, and deep down hoping that she is going to want more of my help. That's going to be easy, but with Simon, he's a year above us, and I'll be using stuff I'm already studying in my spare time, though I have to admit that this personally and intellectually is going to be a lot more fun! Still, I'd take Megan over Simon any day. I'd take Megan over anyone.

"Look, Simon, as I said, I just need to discuss some details and lay some ground rules with you."

"Great, so you will?" He's staring at me for an answer, but I'm distracted by my people behind him.

"Tomorrow, Simon, tomorrow." I look at my group, still frantically waving, presumably on the basis that they think I haven't noticed five or six people dancing in the middle car park, arms gesticulating for me to come over. I give a small wave to let them know, and then I stand up and look down at him. "Look, I really have to go." He says nothing, grunts slightly and rises, and suddenly I'm looking up. He looks at me for a second, as if trying to discern my decision by reading my face.

"Okay. Later, Tim." And without waiting for a reply, leaves in the opposite direction to that which I'm about to take.

That evening had turned out better than I had expected, better than any of us had expected. Nick had somehow convinced his accident victim and a couple of her friends to come along. Maybe that tactic should be added to our imaginary pickup methods? And some other girls from our year had also turned up, and a couple of them were on my team, after an animated argument as to who would be on whose team.

Without a doubt, the quiz night had been a lot more enjoyable than the previous one, though that had not really been too difficult a task to achieve. The close proximity of team members Linda and Jo, thigh against thigh, accidentally touching hands, shoulders rubbing and that little bit of flirting, had added a lot more spice into the mix. We had agreed to keep the team for the next event, having come a close second, losing on a tiebreaker. We were pretty happy with ourselves, and I recalled with pleasure the goodbye hugging.

When I got home, flushed with a thoroughly entertaining evening, Simon's request returned to intrigue me. Tutoring would be good for me when I applied to college. I had to make sure my teachers knew, I reminded myself, but it also gave me the opportunity to concentrate on topics I'd been looking at but not studying in earnest. I knew I was going to do it.

Initially, tutoring Simon had been great, he was an enthusiastic and quick learner. He listened and applied himself, which made me feel good about myself, and we progressed though the syllabus quickly. But after about a month, the ground rules turned into more like guidelines to him. It started with turning up an hour or so late for sessions, then not at all, leaving me waiting, frustrated, and to be honest, feeling pretty stupid and disappointed. After a couple of no-shows, I'd had enough, so I decided to confront him when he did bother to turn up next.

He'd let himself into my house with his usual confidence, I watched as he dumped his backpack on the floor and then himself in his usual chair. He was actually on time, which was something, but he made no apology for the last missed sessions. I hadn't really expected one, knowing him, but I had hoped he would surprise me.

"Hi, Tim, I'm here, and I'm raring to go," he smiled at me, and he looked like he was in a very good mood. He obviously hadn't noticed that I was not. A hello, his trademark smile, no apology, and now he was waiting for me to start his next lesson. All very well and good, but not this time, buddy, not yet.

"Simon?" I kept my voice as neutral as possible.

"Yeah, Tim, what's up?" He looked up at me ready to study, though wearily, as he now seemed to have recognized the changed tone in my normal voice and probably the determined look on my face.

"Why's the band so good?" and for a high school band, we were pretty good.

"The band?" he asked perplexed, one eyebrow raised, presumably not expecting this train of conversation or questioning, when there was math to be studied. "Well, we practice at lot," he continued as if stating the obvious to an idiot. Once a week on Thursday, and if we have a gig, a couple of times on the weekends to get the set right, I remind myself. We like to put on a show, and we want two things: for everyone to have a good time, and for us not to look stupid, and so far, we've been pretty successful.

"So, if I decided to stop turning up, what would you do?"

"Seriously?" he joked quizzically, as if it was even remotely possible I didn't know the answer. "I'd..." the response froze in his mouth. I could, at last, see the light of understanding. He could be very quick when he wanted to be. I'd discovered that over the last few weeks, which made him missing sessions all the more infuriating. "This is about the tutoring?" he concluded quickly and accurately.

"Yes, it's about tutoring," I concurred, trying to give the impression of a little sternness, as I recalled a teacher's tone from classes past.

"And me not turning up?" he smiled thinly at me with a slight shrug of his shoulders.

"In a sense. It's more to do with the ground rules we agreed upon, and that you now seem to have ignored." He stopped smiling, which was at least something, and he was looking properly contrite.

"Sorry?" he asked hopefully.

"Sorry?" I mimicked, "Sorry: I'm going to follow the ground rules, or sorry, just sorry?" It comes out a little loud, I was letting my anger get the better of me, and I quickly brought it under control. I was annoyed, but it also was not worth getting angry about.

"Hey, Tim, I get it, I..." he was a little flustered, but his tone was still even, which actually annoyed me even more.

I interrupted him. "No, I don't think you do," my tone was more even. I was now better controlled, but I was still very irritated.

"No, Tim, I really..."

"Simon, let me finish," he wasn't getting out of this except on my terms. "When we started, you put in the work, and I could see that you were making good progress. I don't know, maybe you got bored or cocky or both, but you started missing sessions, and I was sitting here waiting alone, on my own," I emphasized. "No, hold on a moment and don't interrupt," as his mouth started to open. He shut it quickly. "After a while, I stopped waiting around, but I was always here at the beginning of each tutorial just in case."

"Look, man, I'm really sorry," and he sounded it, but that wasn't good enough.

I ignored the interruption. "I really enjoy teaching you. You're pretty good when you put your mind to it, and it's good for me too, but I've had enough of sitting around, waiting for you to decide if you want to turn up and when you want to turn up. I canceled evenings with friends for you, and then you didn't even bother to turn up. Well, I've had enough to of it," I held my hand up to stop another potential interruption, "I guarantee that if you stick at this, if we finish what we've started, you'll get into pretty much any college you apply to, but I also guarantee that the tutoring stops right now if you don't re-agree to the ground rules. I'm happy to discuss them if you think you need to change them, but if you miss another session without telling me beforehand, we're done."

"What if I'm ill or something?" he asked with slightly jovial air, and I knew he was our Simon again. It was a good point, but this attempt at humor and the point itself, though not lost on me, I still regarded as irrelevant.

"I'll consider the circumstances if you happen to be in hospital or something similar." I paused and waited. Outside of the band and these studies, that was maybe the longest thing I'd ever said to him in one go. It was most certainly the only time I'd ever exhibited any anger towards him. I wasn't too sure what to expect as a response, but I had said my piece and I was happy with my stance, I said to myself, not a little pleased with my confidence.

"Okay."

"Okay?" I wasn't expecting that, not even a hint of a disagreement? A pithy comeback?

"Yeah, okay, you're right. There's no need to discuss it anymore. I'll stick to the original ground rules. I'll turn up and I'll study."

"Just like that?"

"Yep."

"We're not done yet," I replied, taking the edge out of his confident acquiescence.

"We're not?" his shoulders dropped slightly, and he let out an audible, and I would say rather theatrical, sigh. He waited.

"Nope, we're not. You miss more than two more sessions, without good reason, and I mean a really good reason," I smiled thinly, "and that's it, terminated. No more. We're done." I knew I was slightly overdoing it, but...

"That's not in the original ground rules," he beamed broadly at me.

"No, it's not." So, why was he smiling? I asked myself.

"Okay. Fine."

"Fine?"

"Tim, I get it. I miss two sessions and, assuming I'm not dying, you're likely to cancel the tutorials." He sat back in the chair, apparently happy. "But I'm not going to miss anymore anyway."

"None?"

"None."

"None at all, not even the occasional one?"

"Not even one of those. None. Not one," he confirmed emphatically.

"Not even one of those "some lovely girl wants your attention", occasions?" I smiled unable to resist teasing him.

"Not even one of those," he beamed back with understanding, "they'll just have to wait," he was enjoying himself. I think I can change that, I thought mischievously.

"Okay then, where were we?" I asked ready to dampen his enjoyment.

"Calculus and derivatives," he smiled in return, apparently ready to go.

And he didn't miss even one, I was always proud of that about him, Tim recalled, as he felt the tears coming again. They became the best of friends. Simon had killed his SATs and took his APs in Calculus and Computer Science. He'd received a full sports scholarship and studied Economics at the college of his choice. I was as happy for him as he was, and why not? I'd helped him, and gained a friend, a really good friend. Then, after he'd been seriously injured and couldn't compete again, he went on to do an MBA and then off to Wall Street to make piles of cash. I believe it benefited me too. All that tutoring helped get me into MIT, later a doctorate and finally into teaching. My marks were very good, just like most applying there, at one of the most prestigious colleges in the world, but my essay and recommendations, I was told, helped considerably. People like Simon, Susan, Philip, and, yes, even Darren, they make it worthwhile. It wasn't enough that I enjoyed teaching, which I truly do.

It is their successes that really make it worthwhile, he thought with pride of his pupil's successes and achievements, and Simon had really been the first and most successful, and he had achieved so much.

The Stones! He thought to himself how the association of Mick and Simon were indelibly fused together in his subconscious. He walked over to his Flac player. He easily found the band's playlist of his favorite songs and put them to play on shuffle. He turned away and stopped. He held himself stock still, holding his breath to control the flow of further tears. Oh, Simon, I'm so sorry, as the pain of the memory returned.

The sound of congas told him that "Sympathy for the Devil" had just started. How appropriate, he thought, at last breathing and relaxing to the music and its associated memories. He then walked over to his old bass, sitting on its stand unused these many months, and he picked it up. He mused over it, turning it over in his hands, quickly checking the tuning, its familiar feel bringing back memories of the band and practices and the gigs and the fun they'd all had. He returned to the sofa, bass in hand and sat back down. As he joined in, the members of their old band, The Glasshouse, were with him and with the Stones. Megan stoic behind the keyboards, adding musical color and depth, allowing Peter the freedom a solo guitarist sometimes needs, especially when playing music that has two guitarists, and Karl: what a drummer, so solid in time and feel. He's now a session player. We were lucky to have someone that good at school, he thought fondly, as his fingers automatically played the right notes and found himself effortlessly playing along in perfect time with the Keith Richards' line. He's a guitarist, he remembered, but what a bass line! It's a guitarist's bass line, but it's still great. No extra fills and no elaborating, just what Keith intended, and now there's Simon, strutting up and down the stage shadowing Mick, or is Mick shadowing him? He's flirting with the girls, coaxing and cajoling the crowd to join in.

I know Simon would have approved, and he knew this deep within, as his tears joined in.

Part Two: Old friends and introspections

Long time, no see

"Tim?" He froze for a moment, feeling the cold tingle of memory at the sound of her voice, and though he'd been in touch with her briefly last week, he hadn't heard her voice for years. His memories had caused it to morph over time, and now? Recognition is instant, but the feelings are still there, still playing with all his senses, more so since they have now been awakened, forewarned, by the short phone call. He turned towards the sound of his name, slowly, towards the familiar voice, and with a flutter of trepidation building in him, he tried to keep himself in check. In this instant, he knew how much he had missed her, as the intervening years shrink into months, days, hours, seconds and then expand back into years, so many years, disappearing into this moment. Last week's conversation had been brief and embarrassing. He hadn't known what to say, his nervousness consuming him as the conversation faltered. He had wanted to tell her how happy he was to speak with her, but that hadn't happened. In the end, it was just a "Hello, how are you? It's so sad. Are you ok?" And then "We'll catch up at the funeral," and the call was over. Now I see her, and I have a million questions to ask. I want to converse about all those things that we should have discussed on the phone, but we're not here to reminisce, we're not here to celebrate, we're here to mourn. So, he holds all his questions, all the passion and desire for her deep inside, torn between his love for her, which has returned as if the intervening years had never existed, and which has seemingly never diminished, and the love and respect and pain of loss for their friend Simon, who is now gone. She's here, he thought with a sigh, all doubt now superfluous as she walked towards him, and all else fades into the background. Of course, I knew she was going to be here, he rationalized, where else would she be? I guess I just had some doubts about it. My hopes have grown so high, I thought that I was ready, but now I realize that I'm still not fully prepared for this moment. His mind was in turmoil as wave upon wave of thoughts and old memories and long held feelings crashed through his head. He felt dazed as his eyes were glued to her approaching movement. I've thought about it since before replying to the formal invitation, since before the all too brief call, since the letter with the terrible news. I've played this meeting in my mind in its various guises, all invariably ending with us hugging and kissing and holding hands like some crazy soap opera. It was all crazy, and he knew it, and yet still the thoughts and fantasies kept returning in his mind's eye.

She'd sent the letters, she'd probably arranged and prepared the whole event, but you never know, he'd thought, a trip, a prior engagement, an excuse; he had even thought of a few himself. There were always any number of reasons for someone to not turn up. Those hadn't happened, and there she was in front of him as if no time had passed – except Simon was dead. They were all here: friends from school, from college, from work, but no family, not even a close cousin. No family except his daughter, a girl Tim had never met, had never even seen a picture of, though he had known her mother. She is the last of his direct family. I must meet her, he thought, determined, then his mind returned to the woman approaching and he waited, nerves on edge, useless thoughts crossing his mind, and he flicked his tongue over his teeth. Yes, I did brush this morning, still wanting to check his breath, but he knew he was just panicking at meeting her.

"Hi, Tim." She was now close to him, and he shivered with a quiet delight as he made out the familiar details in her face. The freckles around her nose, brown eyes so dark they merged with her pupils, smile so broad, still showing perfectly white teeth contrasting with her full lips and light coffee skin. She looks the same, as beautiful and enchanting as I remember. No, better, she's matured into a woman. Even more beautiful, even more enchanting. Or is my memory playing tricks? Nostalgia enhancing the past, details lost, but now renewed with the present. It didn't matter, he thought, she looks, she is... He searched for the right word, and it easily came to him, that simple word that describes all you could ever want: perfection. And there she was, all he had ever wanted, still the same after all these years. His ideal woman, here before him in the flesh.

"Hi, Megan." The call came back to haunt him, and he stood there composing his thoughts, for the moment transfixed. What else was there to say after all these years? Should I tell you how much I still love you? How much I've missed you? How beautiful you look? How just talking with you brought pleasure. His eyes quickly flicked over her, admiring her dress, appropriately black and shimmering, stylish yet simple, hugging her form in a perfect fit. A single string pearl necklace contrasting with both her skin and her dress, and high heels, which to him looked extremely uncomfortable, but which he knew she had no problems with, and all too soon and yet not soon enough, she's standing before him for the first time in years. For the past few days, he'd practiced for this meeting with appropriate conversation until he knew exactly what to say and how to say it, and yet now, all he could say was: Hi, Megan?

"Don't I get a hug?" she asked. And though her smile broadened, her eyes showed the pain of the occasion, and he felt his insides give way. Simon was dead, and he had missed her so. His emotions were conflicting at every level.

"Of course, you get a hug," he laughed nervously, but before he could move she'd already stepped in, wrapped her arms around him, her head pushing into his shoulder. His arms came up and gently surrounded her, and he held her, his mind in turmoil. He recognized her musk, even over the subtle scent she was wearing, and he gently breathed in, trying to not be obvious about it, his eyes closed, his memory taking him back to a similar moment, as it resurfaced in him with this action. It only lasted a moment, as she disengaged, and stepped back from him, still holding his arm and looking up at him. Her smile remained, disarming him, but the moment? Already fading. He could still feel her presence on his hands, the pressure against his body and the tickling of her hair that had touched his chin.

Through her smile he could now see the pain in her eyes, reminding him why he was here.

"I'm so glad you made it," she said and her smile faded with a serious, sad look replacing it. Oh, how he felt the loss of that smile deeply. "I've been crying every day since I was told the news in the hospital," she confessed sadly, and she looked away momentarily, obviously hurting with the memory, and he wanted to hold her tight and tell her it was all okay, but he just stood there and waited.

"Yes, it was a shock," was all that came out and he felt hypocritical because his next thought was, and yet it means I get to see you. Simon's dead. The thought returning, and all the melancholy and pain associated with it, juxtaposed with the feelings of joy at his renewed acquaintance because he was with her.

"Oh, Tim, I can't believe he's gone," and the pain in her voice reached through him mingling with his own, and he could see her eyes glistening with such sorrow, and she buried her head in his shoulder again. His arms enfolded her, trying to keep the world and its pain away. He knew he couldn't succeed, it was already too late, but at the very least he wanted to try. Simon was dead. How long would it take to erase that pain?

They stood there for a few seconds, though for Tim it seemed an age as he breathed with her, her heart beating with his heart, the rhythm soothing him, her aroma bringing back memories painful though greatly received. She pulled back, carefully wiping the tears from her eyes with her index finger. This moment? A picture now etched into his memory. Then she gave a small smile.

"So, Timmy," she said knowingly, lightening the mood. Arghhh! I hate it when she calls me that, but he couldn't help but smile that she'd remembered, reminding him that even through all the missed years, that they were still close friends. "What have you been doing with yourself?" What indeed?

"Still teaching, still single," his gaze flicking away for a fleeting second, embarrassed that he had nothing else to offer at this moment. Mourning a friend. Still loving you, he thought, now more than ever, as his memories of her continued to build within him. "Nothing much has changed. Except..." he paused and she nodded slowly, knowing exactly what he meant. A memory then returned, suddenly, and he looked at her unadorned wedding ring finger still slightly impressed with the missing rings. "I'm sorry to hear about you and Peter." No, I'm not sorry, half in guilt and half pleasure, and he knew that she knew he wasn't, and that he couldn't feel bad about it at all, yet he did feel for her.

"It was a while ago. He was an asshole. I'm over it," she rasped. Her reply was delivered with obvious distaste, and the look in her eyes told him the subject was closed.

Tim looked at her with a worried look, which even after all these years she recognized, and her steely resolve softened.

"I'm okay, Tim. Truly. We had a few good years. I knew what he was like, but thought he would be different with me, and for a while it was good. For a while," and she tapered off. Tim knew the story and quickly flicked his gaze around the room to see if Shelly was here. She wasn't, and there was no reason why she should be. She hadn't been a friend or lover of Simon's, and she'd betrayed her best friend, his best friend: Megan.

"No serious relationships since then?" he asked suddenly hoping that he wasn't sounding too hopeful himself, as he realized how much he desired there not to be, and yet how long ago had he last been in contact with her? Years. He had spoken with her only a few times after her wedding. It had broken his heart to watch her say her vows. The radiant smile on her face, the beautiful dress, her eyes transfixed on her new husband. He'd made some excuse about having to mark papers, some school event, something inane, most certainly a lie, and he'd left early. They'd met up a couple of times after. Chatted a few times over the phone, once when he'd tried to apologize – that hadn't been good – and then she'd moved out of state when her new husband's job had required it, and Tim had tried to move on.

"No, nothing serious right now, actually nothing at all," she said wistfully, "but I'm back on the stage." Her eyes brightening, as did his hope.

"Really?"

"Yes, my second Off Broadway production. I'm back in Manhattan. Peter gave me that apartment as part of the settlement," she nearly spat out his name, and Tim decided to let it drop, at least for now. "I'd been renting it out for year or so as the previous lease ran out, but now since I'm working here, I moved in a few months ago. It's really nice," her face relaxed, and he watched the hard edges fade.

While she was speaking, questions ran though his mind: So, what's the play? Tell me about it. Who do you play? Can I come and see it? Can I come and see you? His enthusiasm running riot. Slow down, he told himself, pleased with the opportunity just to be in her company, even given the circumstances. She was speaking and he'd missed part of the conversation.

"... Look. I've got to go. We'll have more time to chat after the funeral, and sort stuff out and talk at the reception, but not right now," she quickly glanced around, and then back at him, "Later." The words reached him, and he fumbled for a response, but it was too late. She'd turned away and was gone, and that brief moment was gone now too, already a fading memory. Oh, but he was so glad that they'd been together, glad to be able to rekindle those memories of her. Simon's dead, he thought again, fighting the two opposing emotions, as he watched her greeting new arrivals, reminding himself why they were all here. Oh, Simon, I could really do with someone to talk to.

He wandered off to the side, lost in reverie. His thoughts were still conflicted, between the joy of seeing her and pain of the occasion.

"Hi, Tim." He jerked out of his contemplation and turned towards the voice, easily recognizing it after all these years, watching with happy anticipation as two men walked towards him.

"Peter. Karl. Long time, no see."

I've missed you too

Megan was busy. There was so much to do, and being occupied and distracted helped her. She wanted to be busy, needed to be busy. She tried to speak to everyone, making sure that they were okay, that they knew where to go, what was happening and in what order. Did you bring a car? Do you need a lift? Is it possible for you take so-and-so? She knew that if she stopped she would start to cry again. Busy was good, she kept repeating to herself, and every now and then, during a short quiet moment, she would look over at Tim to see if he was okay. He was. Currently, he was deep in animated conversation, chatting with the old band members. Jamie should be here soon, she thought, as she watched the guys chatting, smiling, reminiscing, presumably about the band. Even though Tim had taken his place, he and Jamie had gotten on so well after his wrist had healed. He'd asked, and Tim had started to give him lessons. I do so miss those days, she recollected, and looking at Tim, now distracted from her current task, she recalled her last conversation with Simon, just a few weeks ago.

I rush into my changing room, eager to leave and see my friend. He'll be outside waiting for me. Warmth runs through me at the thought. The play is finished and a number of generous applauses have been completed, and all I could think was that I was ready to go, now! I couldn't wait to get off the stage. I change as quickly as I can, and just as quickly I leave the theatre and my fellow actors and friends, and there, as I expect, is Simon waiting for me. I hurry towards him and though I can't see his face, after all these years and even at this distance, I recognize him. My heart starts beating just a little faster, with trepidation as much as anticipation, as I approach him. There's no hurry, but I walk in a rather rushed, unladylike manner, as quickly as my heels will allow me. I watch him as I approach, fully focused upon the anticipation of seeing him, being with him. It has been such a long time, too long, and a hint of regret momentarily dampens my good spirits. He's wearing a large, dark coat into which his hands are jammed, his shoulders are slightly slumped, and he appears to be looking at nothing in particular, seemingly oblivious to his surroundings. He most certainly isn't reacting to the activity around him, which still buzzes with the after-theatre crowd, readying themselves to head to the busier parts of town, or maybe just head home. I continue towards him, wondering when he will see me, shivering in anticipation. I haven't seen him in such a long while, and I smile happily at the change in that status. As I get closer to him, still unnoticed, the details start to emerge, there's enough detail to confirm that I wasn't mistaken, but most prominent in my mind is that I can now see that his hair is longer than I remember. He used to hate his hair below his neck line, and I recall him joking about men with long hair, told with his usual humor but also a touch of disdain. How times change, and I hold myself back from laughing. His hunched posture gives the impression of someone who is tired to their bones. I hope it wasn't the play. Oh dear, I suddenly think, it surely wasn't me in the play. I laugh to myself, a little too self-consciously, I realize. Lines of justification start rattling around my head. "Come on, I wasn't that bad!" "I thought we were rather good!" "Well, the audience appeared to like it." All pointless – I'm just being paranoid, I tell myself, and I laugh it off.

I watch as he turns slightly. He is now facing me, but as far as I can tell from his reaction, or rather lack of it, he still hasn't seen me. For a few tottering steps as I continue, still rushing as quickly as my shoes will allow, I want to laugh, to keep my nerves at bay. He hasn't registered my approach at all. He appears to be looking right at me, but there's no reaction, and I laugh, my mood light, my feelings growing warmer within me. Then his hand goes up, and he's waving at me, and as I'm getting closer I can make out the smile appearing on his face, and increasing details that fully confirm that this is my friend. The inward heat now rushes right through me, I smile back as his posture straightens and his imposing size fills the space and my mind.

We hug, exchanging friendly pecks on the cheek, and hold on to each other for a prolonged moment, both needing the warmth, comfort, and closeness of the other person. He pulls away first, a large boyish grin on his face, his cheeks flushed. The smile sparks nostalgia in me; I've missed him so, I tell myself again, and I feel all bubbly and childish in the anticipation of the rest of the evening, now that he's here with me.

"Hi, Megan," and he lets out a deep sigh, "I really enjoyed that." And I wonder if he means the hug or the play. I know now how much

I needed that hug as the warmth slips away, the contact fading, and I already miss it.

"The play?" I ask, hedging my bets.

"Yes," he seems surprised, an eyebrow slightly raised, "it was good, you were good. Very good," and I can hear the enthusiasm in his voice. I feel a little blush surfacing on my cheeks at the compliment. I'm usually used to them. I've always enjoyed getting them, even if I'm not too sure if the giver means it, but from him, just now, it seems, I think, just for a moment, it truly seems so sincere, so genuine. I wonder if he can see me blushing? Oh, Simon, I've missed you so, the thought battering me with its truth. But he's here now, and the pleasure of the moment is contained in my enduring smile.

"Let's go eat," I say, slipping my arm in his and immediately enjoying the touch and closeness again as I steer him down the street to a cozy place I know just off Times Square that usually gets missed by the tourists.

The conversation is very one-sided. I talk, he listens. I talk about my late marriage. Then I talk about the divorce, which still seems very recent to me, and then the return to acting. I'm talking a lot, and he's listening. I'm sure he's heard a lot of this before, so I apologize, but he's fine. He just smiles and asks me to continue, and he listens to whatever I say, with just a few words and gestures that signal his interest, never interrupting the flow of my near monologue. So, I continue talking, and he listens.

I hadn't really spoken to anyone about my personal life since I'd broken it off with my last long-term relationship, Jeremy, and so Simon receives all the tension that's been building up in me these last few months. There has only been the play, and the odd bottle of wine or two, as my outlet. But tonight, he is here with me – my dear friend – and he listens as I chatter on.

As the evening continues, the wine runs out and we agree to buy another bottle. For a while, at last, I'm silent, flushed and heady with the alcohol and content within myself for the first time in months. During the lull, I give myself a moment to fully take in my friend in front of me. He's still so damned attractive, I remind myself, staring into those brilliant blue eyes. He's looking back at me with that familiar smile of his, and I finally feel as relaxed as he has appeared all evening. It's so comforting. Thank you, I mouth to him, and his smile broadens, and he gives me a slow, knowing nod as confirmation, but he says nothing, and I am so grateful he is here. These days, only the theater is keeping me sane, with The Play keeping me busy. But once the applause has died down, the audiences are gone, and the lights are out, reality returns to remind me of my current status in the world. Alone. With Jeremy now out of my life, I've been lonely, very glad to be rid of him, but still lonely and sad. So, everyday it's back to the theater, where only the stage seems to hold any concrete meaning, any purpose. Once there and on the stage, I'm a different person, and I don't just mean the character I'm playing. The outside world and its problems disappear, and I'm free from that world. I'm not really me. The thought brings a small emotional conflict, and I return my attention back to my friend. I really should have called Simon ages ago. I look at my wine, and I feel a little sad. I'm playing with it to distract me from regrets. He's reminded me of something important that I'd forgotten these past few months: I like being me.

"I have several confessions to make," he says quietly, breaking the silence. He speaks at last, I think, as he pulls me out of my reverie. I look up and stare at him silently, as I continue to sip the wine, which I momentarily realize I'm preferring to the previous bottle, "but tonight, I think, I'll give you one that has plagued me for many years."

"How many is many years?" I ask with a smile. I'm relaxed and in a very peaceful place, swirling the wine in the glass, and thoroughly enjoying this moment and Simon's company. He's allowed me to get so much off my chest, so many thoughts out in the open. I really haven't felt this good in anyone's company since I'd left Jeremy. The asshole! I quickly add, as I always do when thoughts of our relationship momentarily return to the fore, but this is quickly quashed given my current mood, and my attention is back with this new intrigue and my friend.

"From way back at school," he says with a tight smile, waiting again. His gaze is a little more intense, as if he is gauging my response.

"Oh, from way back at school? Now that was a while ago," my reply jovial, the wine and my mood keeping their hold on me, now relaxed, away from past thoughts, and enjoying this moment.

"Yes, it was," and there's a momentary flicker of nostalgia in his gaze, and then he returns to me, "but this is something that I've always wished I'd told you, but felt I couldn't. But now..." He stops for a moment and seems to consider something. A secret from school? I'm looking forward to this.

"You didn't two-time me, did you?" I offer with humor, knowing he didn't, but bring back an old running joke of ours.

"Oh, no," his chuckle starts but is quickly cut off. What is he thinking? It dawns on me that he's taking this very seriously. "Nothing like that. But something that I now feel very guilty about." I notice that there is no amusement in his voice or in his mood; he really is being extremely serious, and this is something very important to him. I react to his mood, my smile fading.

"Really?" my curiosity is piqued. "And you still feel guilty about it?"

"In some respect probably more so now than then," he's still looking at me trying to gauge my reaction. I sit up straight and give him my full attention; the wine is temporarily forgotten, though it's effect is still playing on me.

"Ok, I'm all yours," I say, and on saying think I may have been unintentionally a little theatric. We've had a bit to drink, and I'm still not really fully matching his seriousness. He sighs, takes in a deep breath, and I wait silently.

"It's about Tim." Tim? That catches my attention, and I can see him relaxing as if just saying the name has unburdened him of a great weight.

"Tim?" I murmur, the mention of his name, unexpected, surprising me, bringing a wave of memories and emotions A name that contains a history, a whole piece of my past that's been locked away for far too long, merely peeked at over the last few years. The name of a person I hurt so badly and miss so much. That guilt has stopped me doing what I should have done years ago. Tim.

"I've always wondered if you knew," he continues a little more fluidly now, "but somehow I'm now sure, somehow I'm convinced, that you still don't." Tim? What should I know about him that I've never known? I probably know him as well as anyone. What could Simon be alluding to? What does he know? They're guys, and best friends, so I'm not surprised, but my mind starts reaching at all the extreme possibilities that I wouldn't possibly know, that they may have discussed. Is he married? And he didn't tell me. No, he said past. Is he gay? I know we did kiss once, but that might possibly explain why he never asked me out on a date, a real date. On the other hand, I know he's dated other girls, but that is not necessarily a reliable indicator. But if it's a secret? He never told me or gave any hint. Then again why should he? On the other hand, we were best friends, so why wouldn't he? Simon pauses, staring at me. I know he's gathering his thoughts. Mine are all over the place. He said he felt guilty about it. What can he possibly have to say about Tim that he would feel guilty about? I decide to wait patiently, my mind running through possibilities, still trying to anticipate whatever he might say, but not actually coming up with any answers.

"He loves you. He's always loved you," he says, a little rushed. Ok, that was unexpected. I feel taken aback, and I'm staring at him, though I wish to look away. It was hard. He'd obviously prepared himself for this, but it was hard.

"And I love him," I reply quickly, rushed, in an automatic response, attempting to deflect that which I really have understood but which am not sure I want to accept. I need time to process this information, this revelation.

"You know what I mean," he says abruptly, and his eyes bore into me with a slightly disapproving look, a look I know, a look I love and I hate.

"Yes, I do," I look away for a brief moment, contrite as always with that tone and that particular look. He relaxes, but I still feel a little guilty about my response, but I'm also feeling a bit desperate.

"And?"

"And what? He was my best friend," I say defensively, still trying to absorb this information, this bombshell, "is my best friend," and the feelings of the guilt and of missing him are not pleasant.

"And?" He's not letting up. He's not giving me time to think through it, work on it, to over think my response. I need to pause a moment. I'm already on the verge of panic.

"And what? What else is there?" I'm trying my best to keep my voice down in public. I'm feeling very much on the defensive as I'm trying to digest what he's just implied, and I'm really trying to find some space to think. "Look, I never thought of him that way." I never thought he thought of me that way, is more like it. There were no hints. He never flirted with me, just that one fantastic dance, one memorable kiss, after which he ignored me for a couple of weeks. I thought I had overstepped the line, our line. I'd accepted the status quo, the friendship. That was good enough for me. We were, are, were friends, best friends. Oh, I miss him so much, and the thought pains me with the truth of it.

"Why do you believe he does?" I ask quickly, as I feel I'm being backed into a corner, and I look away. Yes, ask him a question and buy yourself some time, I tell myself in panic. I pick up the wine glass, and take a large gulp from it, trying to assess the situation. I gain a few more seconds for my possible responses. He answers me.

"Well, I'd already guessed, even at school, it always seemed obvious, but he did tell me," he recalls, his voice calm, which, given the circumstances, I'm finding a little unnerving.

"You'd already guessed? It was obvious? What? He told you? When?" I'm still confused, and I know I'm slightly inebriated. My mind is racing as fast as it can, and it's not putting this information together fast enough. Another gulp and a pour from the bottle. My hand is shaking, but I manage it without a spill. I carefully place the bottle down on the table, and I'm gripping the glass with both hands, trying not to shake, as well as trying not to break the glass.

"He came to visit me at college one weekend," Simon started. I return my gaze to him and listen, trying to relax. His gaze hasn't wavered since he threw this little secret at me, "We were drunk, well he was. Well, I may have been a little. Though I'm not too sure he was used to drinking in those days," he muses. Seriously get to the point, I'm shouting in my head, "There was beer in the frat house fridge, the other guys were all out elsewhere, it was just him and me," Yes, yes, yes, I get it, and... "So, we'd ordered some fried chicken and we were having one of those school days reminiscences. What did you regret? That sort of thing. That was one of his, the main one, hardly surprising really. It was a while ago," for a few seconds he has a faraway look and then he smiles, quickly returning his attention back to me. I can't hold back.

"You've known since college? Why are you telling me now?" I plead with him, my voice raised in the general hush of the restaurant. I'm wishing he hadn't told me at all, as I'm reviewing whole scenes from my past, as I'm trying to process this information. Past events and conversations start to coalesce into something different, taking on whole new meanings, and guilt ensues as I reassess them in this new light. I really don't need more guilt when it comes to Tim. Simon

184

is looking at me intently and I assume, I'm hoping, he's considering his answer because at this moment I'm at a complete loss for words. He picks up his glass, looks carefully at the wine, sips, and even through all this, I can see him enjoying the flavors. Then he places the glass on the table, carefully pours more wine into his glass, with no shaking that I can notice. I feel like I am about to scream, and he finally returns his full attention back to me. He's being very patient, and I'm getting annoyed, very annoyed!

"Think about it for a while," he says to me with concern and consideration, and that's just no help at all. "I'm off to Boston this weekend. When I return we'll talk again." He smiles and takes a big gulp from the glass, then refills both our glasses with his very steady hands, emptying the bottle.

"Oh, thanks," I start sarcastically. Very annoyed? Extremely annoyed, and then the final statement registers; Boston? "Boston? You're going to Boston?" I'm surprised and confused and frustrated. Everything's coming thick and fast, and I'm really having a challenge keeping up with him. He's still so calm, and my previous calm, my previous contentment, is gone.

"I'm leaving Manhattan. I've had enough of banking. Heck, I have more than enough money and income from properties and investments to retire on anyway. I've, hopefully, got a consulting position in Boston at a non-profit, where I'll be starting in about a month, if all goes to plan. I'm driving up there this weekend," he pauses, appears to rethink what he is about to say, and continues, "to sort a few things out." I'm suddenly convinced he was about to say something else, something important, but he changed his mind, why did he change his mind? Was it one of those confessions he'd mentioned earlier? I'm still confused, and I still haven't caught up with him.

"Next week? Sort out what? Next month? You're leaving New York next month?" I ask, my voice rises with each question, as I'm increasingly frustrated and bewildered.

"Look, we'll talk next week," he reassures me, with a quiet calming tone. "We'll talk about Tim. We'll talk about Boston. We'll talk about," he pauses, and there's that look again, "things, the past, everything. It's a little late now, we've had a bit to drink. Probably a little too much, and you have a lot to process," he proffers with a small smile. You think! "So, next week will be fine, and we'll be sober," he emphasizes with a smile, "I'll be back next week, and we'll continue our conversation then. I promise."

But that was their last conversation. When next week came, they hadn't been able to talk about it. Megan saw him later that week, but he'd been unable to talk at all. He'd been in such pain, and he'd tried to keep that promise, but he had no coherent words to offer her, and so he'd never had the opportunity to tell her about his daughter. She looked over at Angie and pondered her history. It must have been at college, she thought, running the rough calculations in her head. There was that girl he'd been dating for a quite a while, she thought with a hint of jealousy, reminding herself that she sometimes wished that she and Simon could have had a better relationship, thinking back on the short one they'd had, but it had just not worked. The girl had left college mid-semester. What was the girl's name?

"Megan?" She turned at the sound of her name heard over the hubbub of surrounding conversations, her mind now refocused on the moment.

"Yes?" Jason was now standing next to her, his posture was a little stiff, she noticed, but he had a warm smile, and she was grateful for his help. His manner and attitude over the past couple of days had been in complete contrast to that terrible night nearly a week ago.

"We need to move off to the church?" She looked at her watch, and then back up at him with a forced smile.

"Oh, thank you, Jason, yes of course. I'll get everyone moving." Occupied again, her previous train of thought was, at least for the moment, forgotten.

"Hi, everyone. Hello. Excuse me," she said, her voice raised and projecting across the room. A hush filled the room, with only a few lingering conversations persisting.

"We need to leave now to go to the church," her voice was strong, showing no signs of the pain she still felt, but now, busy again, she was able to focus on the required tasks at hand.

"Can we all start moving, please?" she continued, and the murmuring sound of returned conversation and people shifting and shuffling gave affirmation to the request. "Does anyone need a lift to the church?" she shouted as people started making their way to the front door.

You can't what?

Tears were streaming down her face as she was helped down from the podium to retake her seat, and even though she'd practiced the speech many times, her speech had not gone as planned. She'd used her skill at learning scripts, honing her memory with practiced techniques, and before the day had started, she had believed that she could have given her speech by heart. A beautifully written script, from deep within her, worthy of her friend. It had moved her, and she was proud of it, but in the moment it was required, before the mourners, before her friends, she'd forgotten most of it. Even with the text right there in front of her, her memory failed, her composure failed. She had lost her place in the text and stumbled through the eulogy in tears, incoherent even to herself, and she dreaded to think what others had heard. She knew what she had wanted to say, but she could barely recall what she had actually said. Jason, his lawyer, who had been there with her at the hospital, who had kindly and surprisingly offered to help her with arrangements, had stepped up and saved her. He'd waited for an appropriate moment, and moved from his seat and up to her in a calm manner. She hadn't even noticed until he was beside her and taking her arm, gently leading her away, helping her down and seating her. Then he had quickly returned to the lectern to continue the proceedings. He was now talking. He was saying something, but she couldn't concentrate on his words through her haze, her thoughts still tumbling this way and that, the embarrassment still persisting, and there was Simon in the center of them all, and in that, surprisingly, she found some respite. She recalled one of their happiest moments, the one they laughed about the most, and she clung to this memory. With her head still bowed, unable to look at and not wanting to register the surrounding crowd, she managed a small smile and wiped the tears from her eyes. Oh, my dear Simon, we were so young, so devil may care, so happy. Those were indeed the good old days. It seems such a long time ago. She thought about when she'd first meet him, a moment in time they'd laughed about many times over the years; it had been such fun.

"I dare you."

"What?"

"I dare you. Go on, ask him out."

"No way! Why would I do that?"

"Well, you like him, don't you? You never stop talking about him. So, ask him out."

"Well, you know..."

"Oh, come on, I bet he says yes."

"But what if he says no!"

"Seriously, he'll say yes, I'll bet my life on it?"

"Yes, your life, how's that important? What about my credibility?" We laugh together, and then we both look back across the cafeteria at our unsuspecting person of interest. He's seated at a table chatting with some of the other jocks, and he's pretty much the center of attention. They're all focused on him as he talks, weaving a spell, keeping them bound to his every word. I'd been in his company a few times, and I knew how charismatic he was. He knew how to play a crowd to his advantage, but from what I could tell, he never used that to any other benefit, though he obviously enjoyed doing it. He was definitely one of the jocks and on the school football team, but he never appeared to look down at the non-jocks: the "geeks" or us common folk, I chuckle to myself, and I had never heard Tim say anything specific about him good or bad, I realize. I am, however, a little worried that Tim may take issue with him if we dated, me and one of those jocks. I like the idea of him, and I definitely like the look of him. Oh, he is definitely hot! Big broad shoulders, tall, short blond hair, and seriously blue eyes. What's not to like?

"So, are you going to do it or not?" Shelly asks mischievously. "Or should I do it for you?"

"You better not!" A momentary fear enters my mind. She definitely would, I remind myself, I know Shelly.

"It'll be easy, I could hint at your interest, all subtle like," she giggles, and twisting slightly, peers over at him, then quickly returns her attention back to me.

"You? Subtle?" I exclaim jokingly.

"I can do subtle!" Mock surprise hiding behind her laughing smile.

"Shell, you can do a lot of things, but subtle does not come to mind." She gives me a look of indignation, and we both laugh again, the sounds infectious.

"I can do subtle," she repeats, and puffs up, her shoulders square, hand pressed against her chest as if she's about to deliver a line from play, a drama requiring all seriousness, but her voice hasn't got quite the conviction it had before, and I have to suppress a chuckle.

"You think I should?" The idea is appealing, and it has been on my mind for weeks now. I look over again, but then I quickly return my eyes back to Shelly. I don't want him noticing me looking. Or do I? The impish thought comes to mind. If he would notice me, a little flirting might resolve my problem, but he's always surrounded by jocks and often so many other girls; I have some very stiff competition.

"Yes, of course, I think you should. What have I been saying for the last ten minutes?" mimicking my voice.

"Debs will be pissed!"

"Debbie's been pissed ever since he broke up with her; she shouldn't have been two-timing him."

"I wouldn't two-time him," I say wistfully, my thoughts faraway for a fleeting moment. Then I remember that Shelly had once shown an interest.

"And Debbie wouldn't be the only jealous one, now would she? Why not you anymore?"

"Not interested now. I have my eye on someone else."

"Jamie!" We chorus together and laugh. Faces from surrounding tables look over, with the disapproval of being disturbed, but also wanting to know what's going on that is so funny, but we don't care and have no intention of letting anyone in on our playful banter. We lean in closer to continue our conspiracy. The other faces return to their own business, and we continue with our own conversation, our voices again low.

"How are you going to catch Jamie?" I ask, trying to steer the conversation's direction away from me to my nosy friend.

"Sorry? Have we finished with Simon? I don't think so!" Shelly states, determined not to be sidetracked from her current and greatest project. Getting me a boyfriend! "Jamie? My problem, no problem. Let's get on back to your problem," she says, dismissing the subject.

"Anyway," she continues, "why are we having this conversation? You're never going to actually ask him. But I have a plan," there's a triumphant look in her eyes, as if she'd had this idea all along, all of this just preamble to get to this, the real point.

"You have a plan? Miss Not-So-Subtle has a plan, presumably Not-So-Subtle," and I roll my eyes, but Shelly just smiles.

"The band," she says with an assured finality.

"The band?" I repeat, confused.

"Yes, the band," she repeats, giving me a smug look, as if that statement says all that I need to know.

"Ok, I'm missing something somewhere," still confused.

"This is what happens when you don't keep up-to-date with current events. You lose your edge," her condescension is reaching whole new levels, "You lose your advantage. You start looking foolish in front of others." Shelly waits, reveling in her superior knowledge on this matter. Such occasions rarely happen, so I assume she is going to enjoy this for the moment.

"Ok, ok, tell me about this Band idea," I say, mimicking Shelly.

"Well, you know that Simon's in a band?"

"Yeah, Greenhouse, or something."

"The Glasshouse," she corrects me with an exaggerated sigh.

"Yes, err, The Glasshouse, and?" I'm now a little embarrassed that I've volunteered an incorrect name, but I'm starting to be intrigued by the direction Shelly is taking the conversation, though I have no idea where it's actually going.

"Well, Damon quit." Damon quit and? I think, really starting to believe I'm missing something, no, I know I'm missing something. And there's Shelly looking at me as if everything I need to know has been given to me, but I still feel in the dark. Truth be told, I'd only seen the band a couple of times. They were ok, and Simon was okay at singing, and actually a pretty good front man, but my preference for music is Classical and Jazz. I love listening to Rock and can dance with the best on R&B, but I really am not that bothered about playing either.

Okay, I'll bite, "Damon quit," I repeat, still none the wiser.

"Oh come on, you know. Damon, the keyboard player, he quit."

"And?"

"And they'll need a new keyboard player." Her voice is rising, as she fails to understand this unusually dumb version of her best friend. Surrounding faces look over at us again. She ignores them with a sniff and a quick look of contempt, and then it's all smiles back at me.

"They need a keyboard player. You play keyboard," she lowers her voice and enunciates her words as if to a five-year-old.

"Piano," I correct her, "but yes, I get what you saying," I reply, now fully intrigued. The idea has at last filtered through and is now playing in my mind, including a vision of me on the stage in a band with adoring fans, not actually an unpleasant idea.

"They're having auditions, but what if you just went up to him and told him that you'd like to play in the band?"

"And why would he specifically want me if I asked?" Shelly is now staring at me with utter disbelief, and I realize that she is now at the end of her tether, looking at me and shaking her head.

"Oh my God, Megan. You can be a bit dense sometimes," she says suddenly. "Because you're a woman," Shelly hisses, "it'll be cool for the band, dummy! Arghhhh!!!"

"Oh!" Obvious really.

"Yes! Oh!" Shelly slowly shakes her head. I know what she is thinking: my friend, so bright yet sometimes so stupid. She will be enjoying this, and won't let me forget too soon. I smile at the idea. It's Shelly, we'll still have a lot laughs over it, even if it is at my expense.

Shelly had been right, I made my offer, auditions were cancelled, and by the end of the week, I was the latest member of Glasshouse! And Simon asked me out on a date after the second gig and a lot of flirting from me. We dated for about three months, and we had a lot of fun. We enjoyed each other's company, but it just didn't click. Actually, I knew within a month or so that it wasn't working. We really weren't a very good couple. It just took us a few more months to realize it and come out with it. I didn't want to hurt him, and he didn't want to hurt me, I assumed, but we really liked each other. I found the courage and broke up with him, asking to keep our friendship, and once the obligations of a relationship had been removed, our friendship blossomed.

Those were great times, she thought, as in the distance Jason continued talking. Megan was miles away in her own thoughts, not registering what Jason saying, but thinking of Simon and those best of times. The camping trip – was that the best time we had together? she asked herself remembering just the two of them and the wilderness, out in the woods. I so didn't want to go. Out in the woods? Sleeping in a tent? All weekend? Apparently, yes, he'd enthused. I couldn't find anything appealing about the idea, but he kept on insisting. It'll be great. It's something new, something different. Just the two of us. So, I acquiesced and thought why not? And then I tried to come up with something positive about the trip to keep my lack of enthusiasm from taking over.

It hadn't been as scary as I thought it would be from my imagination full of the exaggerations of too many horror movies. The first morning, holding hands as we were wandering through the woods, I admired the shafts of light that were filtering through the trees, enjoying the contrasts of light and shade, the woodland colors, and the silence, so different from at home, in town. No cars, no continuous background chatter. It was the middle of the day, and all I could hear was the wind and the birds and the crunch of our feet. I could even hear myself breathing, and when I closed my eyes, I could feel the thumping of my heart in this slightly frightening but new and glorious wilderness. And the smell: flowers and trees and leaves, it was so clean and fresh. I was enchanted. Then we found the pool nestled against a small rocky hill, from which flowed a small waterfall, cascading with reflected sunlight into the pool, creating the only visible disturbance. It looked like it had been created in a fairytale. I just couldn't believe it.

"Let's go for a swim?" excitement rushing through me as the last of those apprehensive visions dissipated thanks to this picturesque scene lying before me.

"Really?" he replied, giving the glistening pool a dubious glance.

"Oh, come on," I said, still enthused, and I was already taking my clothes off.

"Someone might see us," and I thought, now isn't that uncharacteristically shy? This is a guy who struts around on the stage like Mick Jagger in front of hundreds of people, and he's worried someone might see us swimming! He's not getting out of this that easily.

"Oh, really, Si. There's no one here but us," I begged, looking around to check, just in case, but my enthusiasm was building to a peak, and there was no way I was letting this go. I was already down to my knickers and bra, and I tugged his arm in the pool's direction.

"I don't know," he stated, staring at it with distaste. "It looks a bit cold." Cold? A bit cold? Who cares about that? And looking at him, I realize he was genuinely scared, and for the life of me I couldn't see why. The scene was so picture perfect, it was created for us to frolic around in, and that's what I want to do, so what was his problem?

"Oh, come on, Si, it will be great." Tugging at him again, though this was rather ineffective given his size and strength, he resisted me without any real effort.

"No, I don't think so," he said pulling away, easily disengaging my grip, stepping back away from me, eyeing the pool with that look of fear and suspicion.

"You're serious?" now I was annoyed, "you're not going to join me. Why not? it'll be fun!"

"For you," he whispers. I barely hear him, but I do hear him. My nostrils flare. I felt little angry at him.

"What do you mean? For me?" I wasn't going to stamp my foot, but at that moment I felt like I might stamp on his.

"Look, Megan, I'm sorry, but I'd rather not." He seemed to think that was the end of it. I most certainly did not.

"You'd rather not what? Have fun with me?" Simon looked at me and paused, obviously thinking what to say next, but he was quiet. "Ok, Simon, what's the problem here? I know you're not shy," I looked back at the pool and then back to him, "and look, it's so beautiful," and I held his arm and pressed my face against his shoulder, eyes holding his, trying to entice him. I'm now determined that I want to swim and that I want him there with me.

"I can't swim," he replied in a small, quiet, and rather embarrassed voice.

"You can't swim?" I'd heard what he'd said, but I repeated it without really realizing. He can't swim. As it started to register, a look of surprise must have been plastered all over my face. I didn't know anyone at school who couldn't swim, and he's so athletic, that it really was a surprise.

"No, I can't," his voice louder, his eyes were down and he raised them and looks directly at me searching my face, and then shrugged slightly, "I never learned how to as a kid. I tried once, but I couldn't stay afloat. I sank like a stone. I always managed to avoid learning after that."

"Really?"

"Yep."

"So, you really can't swim?"

"Nope."

"That's it? You can't swim?" I shouted laughing. "Well, let's learn," and I'm tugging at his t-shirt attempting to pull it off. I step back and look at him, step toward him and, on tiptoes, I kiss him on the lips, "I'm going to teach you," I tell him softly.

She smiled at the memory. And she had taught him. For all his initial ambivalence, he'd been a quick and enthusiastic learner. Months later he'd tried to teach her to ski. She had not been as quick and enthusiastic a learner. She grimaced at that memory with an ironic chuckle. There were a lot of good memories, she thought to herself, and I'm so glad for them. We were all so close then, in those last couple of years in high school. Tim and Simon became such good friends, so different yet so complementary. That had been so important for Tim, and so important to me too, she reminded herself. She glanced over at him with deep affection. She loved Tim; he was her best friend, but before he'd joined the band he'd been mostly solitary and inward, apart from when he was with her. She told her friends how funny he was, and they would just return a blank look of surprise. She told them how interesting he was, and they would just ignore the statement as if she were discussing something so improbable they couldn't see the point of a reply. No one she knew understood him. At school, he would hang out with the geeks, and before meeting Simon, he was bullied. It was difficult for both of them. She'd wanted to get some of the football players she knew to help him, but he refused her, or anyone's help, and he refused to back down or tell his parents or teachers. Like a man? Like an idiot more likely, she thought, but she loved him and respected his stupid decision. He was one of the few black kids at the school in a predominantly white area and the only one not on a sports team. Even his younger brother was a star as a freshman, and later a sophomore, on the soccer team. She'd remembered that as a high school freshman Tim had tried some sports and though he'd wanted to, he just couldn't physically compete; he was a late grower. So, he'd dropped out of the school sports scene, and a growth spurt in his final two years of school had been too late. It hadn't bothered him though. He preferred to study, and he preferred his computer, and he definitely preferred to play his guitar, and then later his bass, but he only played alone or with her. He loved playing with her, and she had to admit she loved it when they played together. There were moments when they found the groove, then all personal problems, all outside issues, the whole world, just disappeared. When he played, he was a different person, and she was the only one who really saw it.

So, when Jamie got injured, she knew it was an opportunity not to be missed. She wanted others to see what she was she saw in Tim. She thought it through and came up with the idea of getting him in the band. She taped some sessions and played them to the other band members, and their approval had been unanimous. She'd thought he'd be annoyed with her about those practice demos she'd secretly recorded, but he never brought them up. She knew he knew about them, but he never mentioned them. And when he was on stage, it was amazing. She smiled as she remembered how it was more than even she'd expected, and it wasn't just that he was confident or a more assured, he was a new person. Simon had coached and cajoled, and a whole new side to Tim had emerged. The old Tim was still there, but a different side of him appeared when the band got together and the music started. In the end though, she realized it was Simon who had gotten the better of the deal.

Simon was bright, not Tim bright, but bright, and lazy! Ok, maybe not lazy, he put 100 percent into everything he did, but he was fun-loving, and primarily preoccupied with anything not associated with academia. School was one big holiday for him: endless girls, endless gigs, endless games. Then his early test results had come through. He'd been distraught when those mock SATs had been received, and his parents had been extremely unhappy too, threatening to punish him: no car, no money, no band. They wanted him in college, and he needed to study and learn the required subjects quickly, he'd confided with her. She'd offered to help with English coursework and exam skills, but math and science wasn't really her thing. But it was Tim's, she'd told him. And without Tim, Simon would never have gotten into a good college. Tim tutored him through math, physics, and computer science, and he got his scores up so that he could get the scholarship at his college of choice.

Tim was a great teacher. Is a great teacher. He just loved teaching, and by the end of his last semester studying with Tim, prior to talking his exams, Tim had told her that Simon could have joined the geeks. They were inseparable after that, even if they didn't socialize in the same circles at school. Her attention returned to the present as silence intruded on her thoughts, the lawyer having now finished his speech. Movement caught her attention in her periphery, and she turned to see Tim carefully rising, a solemn look on his face. He pulled some papers from his jacket pocket and slowly, head held stiff and high, walked to the stage, shaking Jason's hand as they passed. They leaned towards each other and exchanged some private words. Jason gripped Tim's arm, and Tim appeared to nod in reply. Then they separated, and soon Tim was standing at the lectern, looking over the crowd, face as sad as she'd ever seen it, pain etched into it. She could still read him so well from the memories that stayed with her, coming to the forefront unasked for, but there when required. She knew him so well still. That he was nervous, was obvious to her and hardly surprising, but also, through all that pain she could see a calm steeled by determination.

"Before I start my speech, I'd like to play a song." She could hear the deep sadness in his voice. Over the speaker system, "Monkey Man" came on, accompanied by a muttering flowing through the crowd, there were chuckling and nods of approval from high school and college friends alike. Anyone who had seen Simon perform would have appreciated this gesture, recalling him strutting around the stage, Jagger-like, teasing the audience, proclaiming himself the title. The returned silence amongst those in the church was palpable as the music played, fading with a memory of the artist on stage having had his moment in the spotlight, a moment they all had shared, but now would never be repeated. Tim stood there, leaning on the lectern as if he'd been born to it. He let his gaze wander over the mourners, stopping briefly at Megan and then he continued on, turning his head towards Angie, pausing momentarily. He let the silence hang there for a few more seconds, not focusing on anything or anyone in particular, and the silence became organic.

"Simon," he paused, he still wasn't quite ready, visibly pulling himself to together, as he tried to compose himself. He looked up momentarily, the quick sight of the mourners flashing in his mind, before returning his eyes and concentration to the paper before him and the sad task at hand.

"Simon was my best friend..."

Tim's speech brought further tears to Megan's eyes, not least because he'd also been crying whilst he gave it. However, unlike her, he hadn't lost his way and even through the tears, he'd been articulate, funny when needed, and poignant when required. He had painted a picture of two boys who were such opposites, but when together, best friends, each enriching and filling out a part of each other's life the other didn't know he had. They had truly needed each other, and the mutual impact they had on each other had defined their futures. She knew this better than anyone. She knew it to be true as she'd been an intimate part of it. Her life had been enriched when they had become friends. The reaction of the mourners was hushed and appreciative, continuing for many moments after he had finished talking. He stood there, eyes glistening, holding their attention; everyone had been moved. Simon would have approved, she thought. I most certainly did. And for a while at least, the pain was held at bay.

He's mine!

Tim had wanted to rush over to Megan and help her, but he'd been frozen to his seat. He felt every moment with her, was embarrassed with her, was crying with her. He even felt as if everyone in the crowd were looking at him, as if he was up there too. But he couldn't move. He didn't know what he could do, so he sat there, staring, in a silent pain that held him in stasis, trying to think through the situation. If he could somehow help, without being obtrusive, without adding to her pain or humiliation. She would see him as her savior. The lawyer had done what was required, however. His timing was perfect. A silence had descended as Megan struggled with her next phrase, everyone waiting to see what she was going to say next, but not the lawyer. He'd acted, he'd done what Tim wanted to do, but couldn't. He was up there beside her, and before anyone else could register what was happening, he'd helped her down from the pulpit and escorted her to her seat. Tim, like everyone else, just watched, feeling Megan's pain, empathizing with what she was going through. They all knew that she had been there when her best friend had died. Then she'd arranged everything for today, and even before she'd started her speech, through all the help and smiles, the pain was so obvious to anyone who looked at her, etched deeply into her face. Tim looked at her, hurting with her. Her head was bowed, tears falling onto her lap, hands clasping the crumpled paper of her eulogy. The lawyer was now talking, but Tim wasn't really listening. He fumbled in his pocket, worried, and felt the papers. Still there, he thought. Of course it's still there! It was there five minutes ago, and yet it was the third or fourth time he'd checked. Megan had asked him to say a few words, and of course he couldn't refuse her, and anyway, he wanted to say something. He felt honored being asked. He needed to say something, and he needed to apologize to Simon. Not an out loud apology, but one expressed internally, and as he spoke he'd be speaking to Simon as much as he would be speaking to the crowd before him. "Monkey Man," that's what I'm going to play, he reminded himself. Simon always said he'd have that played at his funeral. He had possibly been joking, but it now it sounded so very apropos; his gathered friends will understand. Memories of Simon washed through Tim, as in the distance the unregistered words of the lawyer continued. His memories were as deeply felt as their first meeting in high school. Meeting Simon was a major turning point in my life, he recalled, the moments still vivid in his thoughts, details coming back to him as if the events had occurred just yesterday. It was a Monday or Tuesday out on the playground, definitely early on in the week, he told himself, and as the lawyer's voice droned on in the background, he let himself relive that moment.

I'm scared. Jeremy doesn't like me and I know that whatever I say to him, however I reply to his coming barbed comments, he is going to hit me: hard! and probably many times. It isn't the first time, and unless one of us graduates tomorrow, assuming that was even possible, I can assume that it's not going to be the last time either. This has been going on for a couple of years now, and for the life of me, I cannot recall any reason why Jeremy dislikes me so much. Of course, from what I can figure out and from his general reputation, I know that he needs no excuse. This is amusing for him. He's mean, small-minded, and a bully, and as usual, here I wait for the expected beating, running excuses through my mind. What I'm going to have to tell my parents, and the disappointment on their faces, first for lying, and second for not sticking up for myself – again!

"Hi, Jerry." I don't recognize the voice behind me. I'm really too afraid to turn away. I feel rooted to the spot, and it's all I can do to keep my focus on Jeremy and his cohorts. "Dude, what's happening?" Continues the voice that I try to but just can't place. The look on Jeremy's face tells me that Jeremy knows the owner of the voice. Hell, the guy even called him Jerry, and he only lets his friends call him that. I'd learnt that particular fact the hard way.

"Not your problem, Simon." Simon? Simon? Simon Islane? Definitely not Simon Froome. "Jerry" would have beat the shit out of him! I knew Simon Islane only from his reputation – everyone knows him – and Froomy was a fellow geek. Must be another Simon. I don't know of any others, but it can't be Islane. He's on the football team and in 11th grade, a year above me. The girls love him, the boys respect him, and us geeks? We wish we could be like him, though we are fine with being geeks, of course. We like being geeks. We just don't like being picked on; we don't like how we are treated, but damn it, we aren't changing for these Neanderthals! I turn and look behind me. It is Islane. Megan's ex!

"Hi! Tim, isn't it?" he asks me, though I feel the question is more for my benefit than his. He knows me? How does he know me? I try and think it through, Megan obviously knows him well, but we've definitely never met, but it really has to be because of her. Maybe she pointed me out. Though that still doesn't explain why he should be interested in me at this very moment. Jeremy coughs, rather loudly, presumably annoyed at being ignored, and I return my attention to him.

"Tim? You're mine. Ignore him," Jerry says, in an aggressive tone, though it now lacks his usual swagger and his original confidence.

"Tim?" I regain some control of my limbs and turn to look at Simon again. Envy creeps in. He really is good looking. Jealousy, just for a moment, overrides my fear. Yeah, good looking, even I can tell that, and enough girls have already confirmed the opinion, including Megan, and my level of jealousy moves up a notch, and that cute blonde hair of his isn't helping. However, the creeping envy is temporary and has not supplanted my current fear, and it is all I can do to stop shaking from the unwanted, and now prolonged wait for my inevitable beating.

"Err, yes, hi, yes, it's Tim." I manage weakly. Come on, Tim, I berate myself, get some back-bone. Not today, not at this moment, I conclude miserably, and rather quickly.

They are now standing together, side by side, Simon's very relaxed; he's a big guy, and quite imposing. Jeremy, not a small person himself, is now looking a little unsure of himself, switching his attention between us, trying to gauge how far he should or even could push Simon. He then stares at me with a scathing look. I think he's going to try something, and I wince in anticipation.

"Yeah, it's Tim," Jeremy repeats sarcastically, turning his attention back to Simon. "Look, Simon, I've got this." Jeremy sounds a little nervous. There's a scuffling noise. I turn around and notice that Jeremy's two friends, those large, scruffy, really badly dressed cohorts, have now moved back slightly, their body language giving the impression that they aren't really involved in any of this, and I'm still wishing very much that I wasn't either.

"I know. I know. It's just that I need him." I whirl back in Simon's direction. What? He needs me? For what? My feelings are now a mixture of fear and inquisitiveness. What the hell does Islane want with me? My fear starts to increase as my imagination takes over. Simon is not really known for being a bully, on the other hand, he has been known for some serious, though admittedly funny, pranks, but then again, not very nice if you're one of the recipients. Those had been a while ago, and though I'd never been privy to one, some of my friends had. But he's not a bully. I keep telling myself this. And let's be honest, I caution myself, still trying to weigh up what is actually happening here, he isn't known for sticking up for us, the geeks. And then there's the added and very personal fact that he dated my best friend for a while, though she'd never introduced us. Then again, I reminded myself, to be totally honest, it was my jealousy at that particular relationship that was the real reason we hadn't met. No matter, I'm thinking frantically, I'm meeting him now, as my attention turns back to my current predicament. He may even save me from a beating, temporarily perhaps, and that would be very nice. My mind is racing as the adrenalin flows.

"You need him?" Jerry asks a little perplexed. His slow mind appears to be having problems with the idea. Probably any idea outside of his self-centered ego, I think, as an inner smile forms and bravely edges its way through my lapsing fear, now that it seems that Simon may have saved me from another beating from this jerk. I want to laugh as I watch him trying to make sense of the statement. I don't though, I'm not that stupid. That would immediately cause Jerry to pummel me, regardless of Simon's request, so I keep my silence and wait.

"Yep," Simon states simply. Silence follows as if Jerry expects an explanation. Simon, however, doesn't feel the need to explain, and Jeremy isn't that patient.

"You gonna tell me why?"

"Nope, but I really do need him, and preferably, no definitely, in one piece." He smiles a friendly grin, which shows his confidence in that he is going to get his way.

"Ok, ok, you can have him," Jerry acquiesces, but he turns to me and says, "Don't think this is over, Timmy." He pushes me, presumably to make his point, turns and stomps away. His goons follow in his wake, and I can hear the silence as they leave, unlike their usually, noisy, boisterous, buddy-thumping exits.

I breathe a sigh of relief, look at Simon and give a tight, nervous smile.

"Err, you need me?"

"I need a bass player," he smiles. It seems that simple short statements are his forte.

"You need a bass player?" I repeat inanely, still confused.

"Megan says you can play bass," he states patiently, ignoring my confused question. "So, I'd like you to come and play bass in my band," he says it slowly as if speaking to a foreigner or someone with limited intelligence. I'm starting to feel he's thinking more in terms of the latter. I stare at him for a moment; my nerves are still settling, the adrenaline rush dissipating, as I now realize that I'm not going to get pummeled into a sobbing mass and that the guy before me genuinely wants my help. I take a deep breath and think through the original question. Simon has a band called The Glasshouse. Megan plays keyboard for them. The name, I recall, something originally to do with the crowd throwing stuff at them, which had happened at their first few gigs. I can't remember what they were called prior to that. Their current bass player is Jamie. He's pretty good for a rocker, but can't slap for shit. Anyway, far from stopping fans throwing things, the change of name seems to positively encourage the action in the crowd. And Megan plays keyboard for them, that simple thought keeps playing in my head.

"What happened to Jamie?" I ask my wits now returned.

"He fractured his wrist during the last match." Oh, of course! I remember. Okay, maybe my wits aren't entirely returned. Jamie had been taken off the field during the second quarter after he'd fallen badly trying to catch the ball. I wince as I recalled the event. It had looked painful when it occurred. I remember the look on his face when it happened and cringe a little in sympathetic pain.

"Anyway, he's going to be unavailable for several months, and I need a bassist, and Megan tells me you're pretty good." He stares at me daring me to contradict the fact. Megan told him. That makes sense. She is one of the few people who actually knows how well I play, and she says I'm quite good? She never said that to my face when we jammed together though. How come she didn't ask me? Then it dawned on me, she just did. Why else was Simon here? I look at Simon, not a little jealous: tall, broad shouldered, good looks, really good looks, annoyingly so. Strong athletic jaw, wide welcoming smile, which never seems to have wavered throughout this whole encounter. Charming and jock all over. Yep, I'm really starting to dislike him. On the other hand, he and Megan have stopped dating, so I won't necessarily want to bash his head in with my bass every time we play. I'm still likely to be a bit jealous though. A bit?

"We're holding auditions Thursday night, and the few guys who are coming are really not that good. Megan says you're pretty good, she tells me that she's played with you before. I trust Megan, so I'm asking you to attend the audition. We have a gig next week, so I need someone who's good right away or I have to cancel, and I really don't want to cancel," Wow! Well, okay, I think to myself, sounds great.

"I'm not too sure. I'm into Jazz and R&B mostly," I reply, feigning an offhandedness I don't feel. Sounds like a great idea! My heart is racing. Yeah! Can't wait!

"But can you play Rock?" he insists, pretty much ignoring me. "Could you stand in for Jamie in just over a week?" Of course, I could. I thought contemptuously. I could wipe the floor with him. A week's a little tight, but I start running some of their stuff through my head, remembering nights with Megan when we worked on what she needed when preparing for a gig. We'd actually worked on some pieces last week. I was surprised at the request, as I knew she knew the pieces. It was all very impromptu, but she asked, no, she insisted, begged, so how could I refuse? I couldn't. Most of it is pretty easy, and some of their more popular covers I've known for years. Deep down, past my snobby Jazz and R&B exterior, I enjoyed playing much of that stuff. Those 60's and 70's Brits produced some incredible basslines.

"Yes, I think I could." Think? I'm laughing for joy inside. But I decide that I'll try and play it cool. Yep! a little cool was in order here. I don't want to look too eager, though very eager I am. On the other hand, I definitely don't want him to think I have no interest in it, and the thought returns: it means I can spend more time with Megan! The smile may have crept into the external world.

"Well, think of it this way," he appears confident that he already has me, which of course he does, but he isn't supposed to know that yet, "if you join the band, then people like Jerry are not going to be coming after you." He looks at me, the smile still playing across his lips, is telling me that he knows that he has me hooked. He does have a very good point and he seems genuinely nice, a point which Megan has made a few times about him, even since she'd stopped dating him. I knew they were still good friends, but I can still see a bass, mine, embedded in a skull, his, and I return his smile.

"I'll think about it." If he had me before, he absolutely has me now. Yes, that really is an excellent point. More Megan and no Jerry! I let both thoughts run through my head a few times. Better stick with Jeremy though, I think soberly. His name is not worth taking any risks.

"You do that. Then turn up Thursday at 5:00 in the small gym." The confident smile is still there. It is pissing me off but, as I remind myself again, he's made a really, really good point. And there's Megan. I know I'll be there, and he does too, damn it!

He doesn't wait for an answer, he turns and leaves. "See you Thursday." He calls back. In my mind, I can still see his smile.

I manage to avoid Jeremy for the next few days and spend the next few evenings working on some of the band's pieces using a couple of recordings of their rehearsal sessions that Megan has given me on a cassette tape. Though the lines are pretty easy and they are effective, I find them too easy and soon fairly boring, so I add some flurries or chromaticism for color and to make them more interesting for me. I resist adding slap, that's bound to come later, I smile to myself: Flea slaps.

I own an old, beaten up but excellent MIJ Fender Precision bass, classic sunburst, with much of the color worn off, showing the natural wood. I'd bought in a garage sale nearly two years ago with a small Fender Bass Amp. A few months prior to that I'd heard Stanley Clarke playing with Return to Forever for the first time on the radio. I had been playing guitar, so I would usually have my attention focused on the guitarist, and thought the guitarist was pretty good. Al DiMiola pretty good? He's brilliant. But it was the bass lines that had really caught my ear. After that, I started to listen to all things bass, and I started saving my money. A few months later, I was dragged out by my mom to go shopping with her, when I found it. It really looked like a totally beaten up excuse for a bass, but it was an absurdly low price, and I could afford it. I had to try it out. I wasn't expecting to be able to afford a decent instrument for another two or three months, and definitely not a Fender. The thing looked like shit, especially since it had no pickup in it, beside it yes, but not in it, but apart from that, it was actually pretty solid. It had a straight neck, no warps, and the tuners were good. My guitar knowledge told me these were good signs. Bass, guitar, same difference. It did need the pickup installed though. I didn't even haggle, there seemed no point, so I just bought it right away. When I got it home, first thing I discovered was it needed new pickups. It took me a couple more months to save the money, but I bought a replacement set. The amp was fine.

After about a year of playing just about everything – Jazz, R&B, Funk and Reggae, old and new Rock, I told Megan. We are best friends and neighbors, but I'd kept it a secret even from her. It turned out she already knew because my sister has a big mouth, and hadn't kept it a secret! We've been friends since forever, and truth be told, I'm madly in love with her, as only teenage boys can love. Of course, I can't tell her about that, and anyway she's invariably dating one of the jocks. They look down on all of my crowd: The Geek Squad. Megan is smart and funny, and she enjoys the company of what we in the geek squad call The Bimbos. The guys, my guys, all know how I feel about her, and I know how most of them felt about some of the others girls. We call them The Bimbos, but what we really mean is "The girls we want to be with but have no chance getting." We talk about them privately and wishfully. We all liked them all in some way, comparing and reasoning their pros and cons, arguing why we like them. Who, at this moment, we like best, and why we should date them, and why they should date us, and then justifying why we don't. Megan plays piano very well. She's been classically trained, and now she's the keyboard player in Simon's band. But when she plays with me, we play Jazz, I remind myself.

It's Wednesday evening, and Megan has come over to check on me. She sits behind my keyboard, her hair's in a long cane-roll, she has a large smile, dark brown penetrating eyes, her full lips and...I'm finding it hard to concentrate on anything but her.

"Are you ready to Rock and Roll?" she shouts theatrically. I bring myself back to the task at hand. She brings her hands down from what appears an excessive height and thumps out a loud set of rock chords, with massive amounts of reverb on an organ patch. I wince as it reverberates around the room, and I am sure I can hear my bones rattling. She laughs.

"And that was the opening to what?" I ask, strapping on my bass and tonking the strings as a riposte with a Pete Townsend style whirlwind action.

"Okay, let's play," she beams at me, and I move back to my more usual John Entwistle posture to accompany her.

We run though the band's complete repertoire, which isn't that much and is really not that difficult, but I enjoy playing it, especially the Rolling Stones and Beatles numbers. Playing their stuff is so much fun, and I rediscovered my love for this music and my respect for these musicians after getting lost in the last few years of playing Jazz and R&B. I'd forgotten that Bill Wyman really is a great bassist, and I just can't get enough of "Sympathy for the Devil." It's worth joining the band just to play that, even if the line wasn't actually created by Wyman himself, but the legendary Richards. All that trivia I once spent hours looking up comes to mind.

"You should nail the audition, no problem. Jamie is going to be so worried," she gushes, as she comes out from behind the keyboards, and sits on my bed beside me. I still have my bass strapped on and the thrill of playing is still coursing through me. I can feel her thigh against mine, as she leans against me, and I freeze as my senses are concentrated at that spot. I fiddle with the bass for distraction, all other thoughts have dissipated, as I feel her touch running through my whole body.

"Jamie can crank out a nice Blues," I say, as an attempt to get back to the evening's and the conversation's point, "he can put in a solid bass line to a song, sort of produce the correct line to a cover and that's about it! Fairly sure he couldn't read a cover for shit though." I'm afraid to look at her directly. It isn't always like this with her, but sometimes, just sometimes, I just can't control it. Her every motion feels like it's enticing me, and she can just overwhelm my senses: sight, smell, touch, sound. They all become subservient to her. Usually, I have no problems, but every now and then, she captivates me. Now is one of those moments. I've been ensnared, and I feel like squirming, but I hold it together on the outside.

"Feeling cocky, are we?" She asks playfully. I feel a little crestfallen. I thought I sounded confident, not cocky. Like Simon. Cocky? Cocky is not really me, not with her!

"No, sorry, you're right, it just..." I look at her, I'm sure I have puppy dog eyes.

"Seriously?" she interrupts and lightly pushes her shoulder into mine knocking me off balance, "I was joking. You're all over those lines, much better than Jamie. Seriously better." The compliment feels good, and I start to relax. "Why do you think I got Simon to ask you?"

"Thanks?" is all I can manage. She has that effect on me. I'm just lucky she's never taken advantage of it.

"Look, just play like that tomorrow night, and you'll easily nail the audition." She tosses her hair, her locks wave around her head, "then you'll be able to see me more often." I blush, distracted again, cough and pretend to adjust the strings on my bass.

"Yes, that would be nice," I answer feebly.

"Yes, it would," she replies softly, and for a moment she seems far away, and my heart does a double take, and before I can react, she leaps up of the bed.

"Anyway, I've got to go," she continues brightly, back to her normal self, as she makes her way to the bedroom door and pauses. "I'll catch you tomorrow in class. Bye." And then she's gone, and the pressure on my thigh is fading, but the memory remains strong and enticing.

"Bye, Megan," I say to the closing door. Not for the first time, I'm thinking I should have told her how I feel about her and the answer as always is the same. We're friends, best friends, how can I? I mope around feeling crestfallen and start to tinker on the bass. There's a lackluster feel to my playing mirroring the feeling of inadequacy in my mind. After a few minutes of going, well, nowhere. I stop, place the bass on its stand and prepare for bed. Lying there, listening to the nightly sounds outside, and the muffled sound of the TV downstairs, I drift off: my thoughts are only of her.

I enter the small gym, now an audition room, with my bass on my back, and my amp gripped in my hand. I pause at the entrance and take in the room, the venue, and the competition. In front of me, at the opposite end of the room, there is a makeshift stage: drums, a Stratocaster leaning on an amp, and a mic stand with a mic, but no keyboards. That means no Megan. A couple of guys are chatting on the stage. Peter, their guitarist, is in Simon's year. I've seen him around. The other guy I've also seen around school, but I don't know him at all. I assume he's the drummer since he's holding a couple of sticks in one of his hands. In the hallway, there are others milling around, but I only count four bassists. Two of the guys appear to know each other.

I quickly scan the guys with their instruments. I recognize one as being in the same year as Simon, a year above me. He owns a nice looking, new Ibanez 5-string. I've played the 4-string version at the Guitar Center in town, or at least a similar one, there are lots of model numbers in the Ibanez series, and it's hard to keep track of which is which, but they are nice basses nonetheless. He also has a very nice, new looking Ampeg amp, though it looks pretty heavy, and I decided that I wouldn't want to drag it around for gigs. Of course, I couldn't afford one either. The idea of roadies comes to mind. That'd be nice to have. Yes, if I could actually afford that amp and some roadies to go with it, I smile to myself, noticing the look on the reddened faces of the two guys with him: his roadies. They probably had to help him drag that amp in from the car. One is still eyeing the amp with distaste, and then the stage, and probably realizing that his work is not yet done. They'll also have to remove it; I laugh to myself. The two bassists who seem to know one another are jamming, swapping licks, laughing and nodding at each other as they appreciate each other's playing. One has a cool looking violin bass, just like Paul McCartney's, and the other has a black Jazz bass, but it's left handed. I laugh at the irony. Like Mr. Ibanez, theirs all look shiny and new and out of my price range. Now, don't get me wrong. I have nothing against new basses. It's just that mine isn't. It's old, really old looking, any shine disappeared years ago, and it was cheap!

The fourth guy is looking right at me, his bass is still in its case, held in his hand, his amp behind him. He's waving at me and starts walking towards me. Intrigued, I wander to an appropriately empty space, my little island, and watch him as he angles over to intercept me. I haul my bass off my back and unzip it from its protective cocoon. I want to feel like I belong here, but suddenly I wish I wasn't here, as my natural nervousness with strangers starts to set in. I realize that apart from Megan, Mom and Dad, my younger brother and little sister – my biggest fan – nobody has really heard me play. Number four duly arrives, and he stands there before me, case still in his hands, eyes firmly on me.

"Hi! Tim, isn't it?" the stranger asks, and he's looking at me intently. He knows me? "You probably don't remember me, but we were in class together in 5th grade. I'm Tom."

Tom? "Tom Stevens?" I ask, as memory, sort of, recalls the face, and I'm now interested. Though my stranger guard is still up, even though he isn't really a stranger anymore.

"Yes!" He seems genuinely surprised that I remember him. His dad used to work with my dad in the factory before it closed. Though, apart from some birthday parties, we weren't really that close.

"When did you move back here?" My nervousness starts to dissipate with the conversation and I find comfort in a feeling of actually knowing someone here.

"Last year. We spent a few years in Ohio and a few in Kansas. Dad moved back here last year."

"I haven't seen you in any classes. Have I?" asking myself, how did I miss him?

"No, you haven't. I missed a year, so I'm a year behind now."

"Oh, I'm sorry." I feel a little embarrassed for him having to admit being behind.

"No, it's not what it sounds like, I was hospitalized for six months," he has a big smile on his face, so I'm assuming he's not bothered by it, so why should I be?

"Really?"

"Yeah, car accident. That's when I started to play bass guitar, and yours looks fantastic, where did you find it? You been playing long? It's awesome!" His eyes just light up looking at it.

"Really, I thought it looked, well, old!" I am so surprised at his response, and I'm now genuinely pleased.

"Yeah, it does," he confirms with admiration and enthusiasm. "That's the point, that's the new craze. Old looking basses. These days you have to pay more to get that look." I must admit he really does look envious. I look at my instrument and see it with a whole new level of respect.

"Can I try it?" he asks nervously, carefully setting his case on the ground, his gaze barely wavering from my bass.

"Yes, of course," I say politely, now a little worried about handing my newfound treasure to a stranger. He takes it, turning it over as he looks at it lovingly. His eyes researching each nook and cranny, he taps the pickup and twiddles the knobs. His fingers lightly stroke the neck, and he runs them down the body. He looks at me with what looks like a touch of embarrassment. I smile back, I realize that he genuinely approves of my old music partner, and I am pleased with it and myself: it being cool makes me look cool. He flips the instrument into playing position, digs into his jean pockets, and pulls out a plectrum. He quickly checks the tuning, and finding that there's no need as it's already in tune, and he proceeds to thump out a blues line. There are some great plectrum bass players, but I'm a finger style player, and my snobbishness gets the better of me as I wince at the sight of a plectrum being used on my bass, but he isn't bad. He produces a nice even tone and his timing seems pretty good, but I smile to myself knowingly: I can do better. Hell, I can do better with a plectrum. However, I have to admit, it looks kind of cool, and I decide that I really need to add some plectrum style to my playing repertoire, especially since I'm hoping to be playing some hard rock. I was a guitarist, and I still play guitar pretty well, so it's not that I can't play with a plectrum, just a bit of a snob is all. Price of being a geek, I laugh to myself.

After a few minutes watching him, I start to feel a bit left out, and I now want my bass back, but I wait patiently for him to finish his playing. I know that I'd be annoyed if someone just stopped me in the middle of playing, so I wait and listen, enjoying the familiar chords, admiring the personal touches. He finishes his blues with a flourish, thumping out a final chord across all the strings, then listens to the dying sound and sighs. He looks at me and smiles a little apologetically, and then shrugs his shoulders as if he's a little embarrassed at his final extravagance.

"You're pretty good," I assure him, and I can see him visibly relax at the compliment.

"Thanks," he replies nervously, not totally convinced, but still enough for a smile to appear. "Just having a bit of fun. It really is a very nice bass." He strokes the neck again, gives it a twirl and hands it back.

"Thanks," I am not too sure what else to say, and I still hadn't fully come to terms with how cool my bass is, but having watched him play, I'm now eager to play myself, show off a bit, let him see my chops.

"Yo! guys?" Comes a shout from the makeshift stage. I look up, as do the others. "Who wants to play first?" The drummer is seated, the guitarist strapped, and there's Simon, speaking into the mic, and ready to sing. I check the tuning of my lovely old lady again.

I decide to go last so I can check out the competition, so to speak. They're not bad, but I think I'm better, and I did have an ace in the hole with Megan. I already knew everything Simon and his band were likely to throw at us.

At last, it's my turn to go on the stage, and my nerves start to fray. All my confidence, there just a few moments ago, is now ebbing away with each step it takes to get to the stage. By the time I arrive, which seems to take forever, my legs feel like jelly and I want to throw up. Mr. 5-String Ibanez, with the heavy amp now plugged in, has kindly allowed us to use his beast. Well, actually, Simon insisted. I distract myself with twiddling knobs and a lot of deep breaths.

"Whenever you're ready," I hear from behind.

"Sorry," I turn around, and there's Simon and the band waiting for me, and not patiently.

"I said when you're ready," he's calm, has a smile on his face, and I assume he knows how I feel, but probably can't empathize with it. The idea brings an inner smile, and that helps me relax a bit.

"What would you like us to play?" I'm sure I hear a touch of sarcasm in his touch, probably more than a touch now I think about it.

"You choose," after all, it's their gig, and anyway, they really couldn't play what I would like to play.

"Really?" Simon's raises an eyebrow, his smile doesn't waver, and the drummer and guitarist are looking at each other grinning with anticipation.

"Monkey Man?" Simon asks the guys.

"Monkey Man," replies the guitarist. The drummer just nods, still smiling.

"Can you play "Monkey Man" by the Rolling Stones?" he asks me.

"Yeah, I can do that," and I know I can, and I'm starting to feel good about being here.

The drummer counts us in.

Tom can't stop gushing about my performance, and the band members appear to also agree with him. I'm very pleased but a little embarrassed. I'm not really used to receiving compliments from strangers. From family, sometimes, rarely from Megan, and a lot from my little sister, jumping up and down and clapping with glee! But deep down, and with only a little humility, I have to admit I rocked! The other bassists all congratulate me and take it well when Simon announces the band's new bassist: me!

Simon asked me to stay a while longer, so I'm waiting for him to finish chatting with the other band members. My bass is packed away, and I'm sitting on a rather uncomfortable gym seat, feet out, hands clasped behind my head. I'm listening to the first track of the first King Crimson album, a brutally loud rock track with a phenomenal bassline, mind blowing drums, crazy lyrics and Fripp on guitar, it's just awesome, and it keeps me in a rocker's mood, and from a distance I watch the animated group on the stage, waiting. I am feeling pretty good about myself and my playing. It has been a long time since anyone outside of family has praised me for anything. Even when I had got good, no, even when I got great marks, there was no praise. That was just expected of me, I was told, as far back as I can remember. So, tonight had made me feel special. They had made me a band member, and I was happy to wait. At last, the guitarist and drummer start packing up the drums, and as I'm watching, I'm running through the audition again in my head, and my respect for these guys has moved to a whole new level, especially the drummer. The guitarist is better than I was. I could probably have played most of what he did, but not with quite the same feel. The drummer was exceptional, and playing with him was a pleasure in its own right. I'd love to play some jazz with him! It most certainly would beat having to use my cheap beatbox. I watch them leave, and they wave at me with smiles. Then they're suddenly gone, leaving Simon and me alone. Simon wanders over, and I turn my music off and remove my headphones as he approaches.

"Okay, Tim, I'm impressed. I know the other band members are as well. You play that well at the gig, and you're a keeper."

"What about Jamie?" I liked the idea of being a band member, but injury or not, Jamie should be able to defend his position in the band. Did he really mean keeper?

"Not your problem," he answered succinctly.

"But he's going to hear about it," I persist, feeling a little embarrassed that I have his position and he's not here.

"I'm sure he is, but then again he has already approved you."

"What? What do you mean? Already approved me?"

"He's already approved you." He repeats with a smirk on his lips.

"I'm not too sure he even knows who I am," realizing I wasn't too sure if I'd recognize him if he walked in now.

"He does, and he likes your playing. Actually, he loves your playing." I'm finding the conversation a little confusing. This guy obviously knows something I don't. Something doesn't add up or I'm missing a point, or possibly both!

"How? I never met him, and he's never heard me play." I am caught completely off guard, trying to make sense of a conversation that seems to make no sense to me at all, but looking at Simon, I know he knows and he's very much enjoying my confusion, and I take a quick glance around the room, expecting Jamie to come and confirm my confusion.

"Well, actually he has. Megan played us some demos."

"What demos?" Demos? What has she done?

"Look, don't take it out on her. I sort of forced her into it. I asked her to convince me, us, of your worth before the auditions. She was convinced you could do it. Us? Let's just say we were a little more skeptical."

"Before the auditions? You knew before and you still held them?" now I'm feeling a little annoyed.

"Look there's no doubting your skill. Jamie loved your playing. You should have seen him! He said he should probably be taking lessons from you. He was really impressed. You saw how the others reacted after your set. Even I have to say you're pretty good." Oh, thanks. I let the compliment slide.

"So, why hold the auditions if I'm so good?" I ask sarcastically.

"Because we needed to know you could play in a band. In our band."

"Of course..." I stop, rerun what he's just said, and consider. My automatic response is quickly shelved. I can see that he knows that I now understand.

"Look, it's one thing to sit at home playing with yourself," he chuckles, and I join in with him, "but playing with others offers a whole new dynamic. We were very impressed, and you passed."

"Thanks." He had a point. "I suppose you have a point."

"And of course, now you'll have to do it in front of a few hundred paying fans. Who'll probably be throwing stuff," he smiles broadly at me as if he knows something I don't.

"There is that I suppose," I smile back. I'm looking forward to it in some sort of masochistic way. I could already see myself on the stage, my imagination taking flight. I'll be like John Entwistle or Bill Wyman, not jumping around but stoic, holding the sound together, producing cool bass lines that people will never forget. I'm the new member of The Glasshouse! I bask in the thought with pleasure.

"Oh, and just one other point?" He interjects, whilst I am reveling in the glow of my new achievement.

"Yes?"

"Sometimes less is more." What?

"Excuse me, what?"

"We really love your playing, but sometimes a simple line can be more effective than some running up and down the frets, no?" I'm now a bit crestfallen, that critique was unexpected.

"I'm sorry. I just wanted. It was just," I can't find a reply, I thought they liked my playing, maybe I was wrong, and misinterpreted what they had said, what he meant. My playing is obviously not as good as I was originally led to believe. I start to feel that this wasn't a good decision. Maybe I'm really not as good as I thought I was, I keep telling myself.

"Tim, don't get me wrong, we love your playing, but sometimes just dial it down a bit, you don't always have to be playing at 100 miles an hour." He's still smiling. I try to absorb what he's just said, and realize, he's right. Furthermore, I remind myself, I've said it about other bass players, and I've criticized them for the same.

"Yes, I suppose you're right," I offer morosely. I'm still feeling a little dejected, but the more I run the idea through my head, the more I agree with his point.

"Just think about it. We love your playing. Keep it up, but just dial it down once in a while, okay?"

"Yeah, no, thanks, it's a good point, I will, I won't disappoint."

Simon gives a fully hearty laugh, which would have been infectious if I wasn't feeling a little sorry for myself.

"Seriously man, relax, there's no chance of that." I watch him as he continues to laugh for a moment. His humor is so infectious, it appears to come from out of his core. I'm sold on every level, and I'm already adjusting lines in my mind, thinking of where to dial it down. Yep! he definitely has a good point, I have to agree. I was getting a little carried away.

"Look, Tim, I'm sure you'll always be a geek, but now you're in with us. Seriously, people are going to want to be your friend. Enjoy it, you'll thank me later."

"I'm not too sure about that," comes out, as a wave of my natural skepticism engulfs me.

"Trust me, I know these things."

"Really?" I am still one of the geeks. I'm looking forward to being in the band, but the geeks, those guys, they're still my friends. On the other hand, I get to see more of Megan. I give out a short snort of a laugh.

"What's so funny?"

"Nothing, just looking forward to being in the band."

"You're damn right," and his face has opened up with another beaming smile.

Tim sighed at the happy memory, a memory overlaid with the sadness of the moment, a moment so pivotal that it had changed all their lives profoundly: he, Simon, Megan, and the other band members, shaping the course of their futures. He looked over at Angie. In some respect she reminded him of a young Megan, the similar coffee skin of mixed race children, her hair also braided, running long behind her back, but her eyes? Angie had her father's eyes. That penetrating blue, which in this case, contrasted so beautifully with her skin, and whereas he always remembers Megan with a smile or laughing, he hadn't seen Angie smile, though that was hardly surprising given these circumstances. He could see, he could feel, the distance between her and her neighboring mourners. She was alone here. He had felt alone so many times, and in some respects, he felt alone now, with Simon gone, but he knew he had Megan and friends here. Angie's loneliness was different, more profound, and watching her was painful. He felt for the girl, though he didn't know her, seeing himself in her predicament. None of us know her, most of us didn't even know she existed until today. I must speak with her, even help her if I can. She's Simon's daughter, and I must, no I will, do everything in my power to make sure she's okay. I know Megan will help. He felt better at the thought and the loneliness faded. Turning to the front, he relaxed and at last started to listen to what Jason had to say. I'm next he realized.

What am I doing here?

Angela was not enjoying the funeral. Okay, I know I'm not supposed to be enjoying myself. They've just buried my father. It's a sad occasion, but...but who are these people? She felt her insides screaming the question at them again and again, but the answer was still the same. I don't know anyone here, just that lawyer, whose name I can't even remember. She looked at him across the room, standing alone, but not lonely, watching, as she was watching everyone else, but unlike her, he looked comfortable in his own space. He appeared to be enjoying his solitude in this endless sea of chatter and strangers. Angie sighed out loud. What the hell, no one at this moment seems to even notice I'm here, though that will soon change she realized with regret. I really wish I could feel as calm as he looks, but I just can't be like that, not here with these strangers.

Initially, before the ceremony, it had been easy. Boring, but easy. There had been polite condolences, all that was required were some sad looks: easily and genuinely achieved. A nod and a thank you were just as easy. The second part in the church had been even easier. As expected, everyone was solemn, some even crying, but everyone kept to themselves, chatting quietly in small clusters, and no one bothered me that much. All so very easy, even having to listen to those interminable speeches. Tedious, but easy. They had given some nice, pretty speeches appropriate to the sad occasion. It annoyed me, more than it should have. Ok, he's a nice guy, a good friend, but what about as a father? Not one word about him leaving my mother, leaving his daughter. He wasn't perfect!

The thoughts kept running through her head, and she felt guilty at thinking them, she knew and understood the circumstances, but she was still angry at him for leaving her, though she knew he wasn't the only one to blame, and since they'd found each other, she never doubted that he had been trying very hard to make up for their lost time. During those few short months spent together, they had been trying to get to know one another and were making progress, but these strangers reminded her that there was so much about her dad she didn't know. And now? Hardly their fault, but now? She would never get the chance to know him, not as well as they had, and this hurt so deeply. She felt she was being punished, and kept asking God: Why? But here they pretty much ignored her, each coping with their own grief. She sat there quietly, acknowledging others when required, but rarely required to say anything of note, which suited her just fine. Then, it was over. Her father buried beside his mother, father, and younger sister.

I had another aunt, she had thought to herself, a little disappointed, because of her close relationship with Auntie Kay. Simon had barely mentioned her, just once mentioning that he had had a sister who had died. There was a history there that she would never know. Any real conversation about his family had never come up. She'd thought there would be time for that later, so she never pressured him into talking about them, and now she realized how little she knew of his family, and then it dawned on her: Auntie Kay is all I have. She felt the baby kick inside her as if in response to this thought. And you, of course, little one. Her hand moved protectively to her belly. They'll all be coming back to his apartment, no, my apartment, she reminded herself. I should have taken that woman up on her offer, she realized. The lawyer had said that she was happy to hold it at her place. Damn! I should have accepted. They're all going to traipse in there, chat amongst themselves, and confront me with more condolences and well wishing, but with no real conversation. I won't be able to leave and be alone with my grief until they've all gone, however long that's going to take.

She was exasperatingly correct. She sat in her new apartment waiting politely, nodding appropriately with the proper expression for all to see, whilst she really wished everyone would leave. Please! Leave Now! kept running through her head, even before they'd all finished arriving, not in ten minutes, not in half an hour, now! She didn't know anyone. They're strangers. They aren't my friends. Auntie Kay wasn't even here. She had begged her aunt to come, but she wasn't surprised that she didn't want to and hadn't come. She'd still had to ask since she didn't want to be here alone. There was no one to talk to, to have an actual conversation with, to unburden her thoughts with. The train journey here had been interminable, she'd processed this decision to come here, alone, the whole way, and now she was doubting it even more: the decision to come her, but she had, and that decision wasn't looking any better now. Dad's lawyer had been the first to arrive, just minutes after her driver had dropped her off, followed by the woman who'd fallen apart during her speech, accompanied by some friends. The lawyer had been a bit stiff but very polite, and he'd tried to make sure she was comfortable, though he hardly looked comfortable himself. He'd barely spoken to her and hadn't attempted any sort of real conversation with her. He had pottered around for a while, made phone calls, and after a few others had arrived, he'd left her to her own devices, presumably satisfied that his job was done. No one has said more than a few words to me, she thought sadly and found that thought depressing her more than she expected it to. They seemed barely able to string a proper sentence together: How are you? Ok? Such a terrible thing. Then that was usually followed by some condolences: I'm so sorry for your loss. He was a good friend. We're going to miss him. And each time with a tight smile and a nod, she kept thinking, I'm regretting that decision, I should have stayed at home. I thought it would be like this, I knew it was going to be like this, but… but I'm sure that this funeral is even more depressing than it should be. Everyone looks embarrassed when they talk to me. After they say their short obligatory words, they rush away as quickly as possible. She wanted to laugh at that because it seemed so comic, the sort of thing she'd seen in the movies. But it didn't make her laugh, it just made her feel depressed at the thought that it was going to continue until they'd all gone home. I want to go home, she sighed, ignoring for the moment that this was her new home. She knew she really meant back with her aunt, back in Boston, back in her room. She started to feel the tears. I'm not going to cry, she thought resolutely, not in front of them! There was contempt in her thoughts for them, these strangers, and she quickly quelled it, annoyed with herself for thinking like that. That's not me, and they're only trying, just so badly! It was such a bad decision, she thought her thoughts saddened by it all. It was tiring her out. They're just trying...

She exhaled loudly at the returning thought, shaking her head ever so slightly, to keep awake from this boredom, and suddenly in front of her was the woman, the one who'd made the offer to hold this reception at her place. Oh, I can't remember her name! She had given that incoherent speech at the church, through the tears and sobbing. I know that she'd at least tried, but it had been so embarrassing watching her. She introduced herself, but I just can't remember her name. Angie felt a little guilty at this, and then she realized that she couldn't recall any of their names, not even the lawyer's. She was tired and everything was moving too fast. The lady, whose name she just couldn't remember no matter how hard she tried, sat down beside her. She looked so sad.

"Hello," she muttered.

"How are you? Err are you... is everything..." she started stuttering words incomprehensibly, leaving little space for Angie to even reply.

"I..." she tried. Angie, just smiled, looking at her with fake concentration, thinking that at least she was trying to start a conversation, which is more than can be said of others here.

"I... I..." then she started to cry, just like during her eulogy. What am I supposed to do?

The woman sat there for a few minutes crying until she excused herself and hurried away without a backward glance. Angie had little time to process this as soon after, another complete stranger came over, and the process continued. Angie kept wondering, why am I even here? How many people are going to continue this charade?

Was that all of them? She thought, several guests later. She sat with her head bowed, tired beyond anything she had previously known. Her neck had a cramp and her back was starting to ache. She stretched and twisted on her seat, attempting to relieve the cramp, thought about standing up, but changed her mind when she considered that might bring more unwanted attention to herself. I need to get away. Would anyone notice? I could just nip into the bedroom for some quiet and solitude. She realized that this was a stupid question. Of course, they would notice. But did it matter? She didn't know them and would possibly never see any of them again. I've got to go, she decided. She shifted in the chair and started to pull herself up to go and hide when an unexpected shadow fell over her.

"Hi, Angela?" the voice brought her back into the room, and she fell back into the sofa again, as a veil of irritation started to creep into her mind. She brought it under control and looked up. Another person has decided to confront me, she thought bitterly, thoughts of leaving put on hold, at least for the moment. Her eyes wandering fleetingly towards the door and exit from this monotony, and then back to her new company.

"Yes?" I'm so tired of this, she thought with a huge internal sigh, and yet here we go again. She recognized him from the church, remembering his acknowledgement of her. He'd cried during his speech, but unlike the lady, whose name she'd still forgotten, he had been coherent. She recalled that he had also managed to be funny and moving at the same time. He was a close high school friend of Dad's. Then she recalled something Dad said to her. If this is Tim, the name flashing in her memory, that would mean the lady was...? Oh, what was her name? It still eluded her.

"Hi, my name's Timothy." Yes, it was Tim, she thought, relieved that she'd remembered, and actually finding a hint of pleasure at this achievement. He was a very close friend of Simon's. Well, aren't all of you that. Giving your nice speeches for him, for yourselves, she thought regretfully, as she settled back into her previous pattern of thought. He was my father, and you are all his friends. I barely knew him, and I don't know any of you. I wanted to know him, and you all did. He was my father, how's that fair? The tears pricked her eyes, but she was resolute: I'm not going to cry.

"Pleased to meet you, Timothy," she said stiffly. You can go now, Timothy. You've made your obligatory introduction. Yes, he was a nice man. Yes, he was your best friend. No, I didn't know him well. From school? How nice. College? Great. Now please just leave me be, and please... don't start crying...

"Tim is fine. Megan told me about you," Megan? Megan! She nearly screamed to herself. At last! "I just wanted to see if you're okay." Really? Am I ok? Please? Not another person wishing I'm okay, thought Angie with more than a hint of sarcasm, of course I'm not okay! Are you! No! Then why should I be!

"Yes. I'm fine," she replied politely, but with a noticeable hint of disdain. Seriously? Of course I'm not fine. Why would I be fine? My father, who deserted me and my mother before I was born, is dead. I met him a few months ago. I barely knew him, and now I'm here at his funeral. Here with you stupid lot asking me all these inane questions! Am I fine? Oh, and by the way did you not notice that I'm 18, I'm not married, and I'm pregnant! She refocused expecting him to now leave as the others had, but Tim didn't go. She watched him, realizing he was actually going to stay and probably try to continue having a conversation. Why are you staying? She thought in horror, not wishing to have any sort of conversation with him or any of these strangers. He sat down beside her. However, he'd gotten his positioning completely wrong and partially sat on her thigh.

"Oh sorry, oh I'm so, so sorry! Just so incredibly clumsy as usual," he smiled sheepishly at her. She shifted out of his way, and he continued to smile back. What am I doing here? She asked herself for the umpteenth time, I barely knew Dad. He was my father and I barely knew him, and she looked around, nor anyone else here. She looked at Tim, he was still fussing and obviously embarrassed. He looked at her apologetically. There was no pity in his look. No look of awkward obligation, just that, to be honest, funny look of embarrassment, and for the first time since the day started, she felt herself relaxing with someone, and as she did so, all the emotions she'd been bottling up were released. The tears started to well up, and she started sobbing. She wanted to stop, but she couldn't; she felt so alone in this crowd, and it hit her, hard. She missed him, and he was gone, forever.

"Dad, I'm so sorry."

Tim had decided now was the time to speak to Angela. He'd noticed that most people had said their invariably short condolences, and he wanted to have some time to have a talk with her, get to know her, and hopefully, put himself in a position to help her if she needed it. He owed Simon at least that much. It hadn't started to well, she appeared to be very aloof, but he was determined to stay, try harder, though the butterflies pounding around inside his chest were seriously urging him to leave. Not yet! He scolded himself. He decided to sit, and then virtually sat on the poor girl. Embarrassment rose up immediately, and he started fussing about his clumsiness, as a way to hide it. Thinking to himself, God! I can't do anything right? I nearly crushed her leg. I mean she's pregnant, how clumsy can a person be? He looked at her and smiled his apology. Not such a good start, Tim, was it? He wanted to roll his eyes or just apologize and run, but he continued to smile his embarrassment at her. She looked at him and smiled thinly back as a reply, and then she just burst into tears. What should I do now? He thought, caught off balance, again! She leaned on him and pushed her head into his shoulder sobbing.

"Dad, I'm so sorry," she kept repeating into his jacket.

"It'll be okay," he replied, having no idea if it would be, but it was all he could think of, and he wrapped his arm around her and held her gently, hoping that it really would be okay. She pushed deeper into his shoulder for comfort and security, and he could feel her heartbeat as well as his own. With the girl crying gently in his arms, Tim relaxed. The sobbing continued in silence, just the erratic heavy breathing rising and falling and hearts beating to remind him of her state and his, so he held her tightly, feeling the world might stop spinning if he let her go, his heart tearing at her loss, and his loss, his friend. People looked over with sympathetic looks but said nothing. A few others walked by with a look of sympathetic embarrassment. They all knew who she was, though no one knew her. A few had tried to talk to her, but they hadn't been able to think of anything to say to the previously unknown, illegitimate daughter whose father, their friend, had passed away in such sudden and tragic circumstances. What was there to say? Tim noticed Megan looking over. She smiled at him, her eyes bright with a comforting message, and nodded knowingly. Tim smiled back, thankful for the acknowledgment and gaining confidence from the proffered smile.

"Angela?" He tried. She raised her head, her eyes red from crying, and she tried a little smile. You're not going to go, are you? Please don't leave me, not now, not alone with them? She pleaded silently.

"It's Angie," she replied meekly, hopefully, a small smile willing him to stay.

"Angie," he confirmed firmly, and he smiled back broadly, with warmth and friendliness, his eyes fixed on hers. "If you wish, I can tell you about your father, at least what I know. I knew him since high school." She stared back at Tim and considered his offer but didn't reply.

"Or we could talk about the weather?" he tried humorously, a thin, weak but hopeful smile on his lips, eyes gently pleading.

She gave a vigorous nod, wiping tears away with the back of her hand. "About my father. That sounds fine," her voice gaining confidence. "Though if you wish, you can talk about the weather?" They both laughed a little tentatively.

Tim proceeded to talk about his best friend to his best friend's daughter. He could see her relaxing as he spoke. The lines and edge in her look had now softened and disappeared, and as he kept on talking, he also relaxed. It was as if he could feel Simon's forgiveness, forgiving him for acting as he had. Tim realized that his friend would have forgiven him anything, well, anything except a missed band rehearsal or a gig. He smiled at the thought. Simon would have told him that there was nothing to forgive, would have laughed at the whole situation and waved it off as trivial, but for Tim, he felt that he had at least earned it, even if it was not required, and that he could, at last, forgive himself.

As Tim talked about her father, weaving stories and anecdotes, with an unabashed enthusiasm, he added color and texture and depth to the person she'd just started to get to know. Angie learned about her father in a new light, in a way her mother would have known him: young, carefree, fun and caring, and she now understood why her mother had never said a bad thing about him, why thoughts of him always brought tears to her eyes, and she understood aspects of her mother she'd never known before. She also started to see him through the eyes of a friend, facets of his personality she'd just started to glimpse over the past few months.

Angie burst out laughing, and Tim laughed with her. Several people looked over in their direction, wondering, presumably, why the seated couple were making such a happy sound, and a loud one at that, during such a solemn occasion. Tim continued with the anecdotes, his hands waving in the air to emphasize parts of the tale he was spinning, and they continued to laugh, oblivious to the rest in the room.

Megan watched Tim with Angela and felt so proud of him. She had seen Angela sitting on her own, nodding along to the short conversations as people introduced themselves, gave their condolences, and then quickly moved on leaving the girl alone. She had wanted to comfort Angela. She had wanted Angela to feel comfortable here in her new home with strangers. She had wanted to get to know the daughter of one of her best friends and a man she loved so dearly, seeing in Angela a girl she might have had with him if things had turned out differently. She really wanted to know the girl. And she had wandered over to the seated girl, ready to help her, ready to ensure she was comfortable, ready to know her and show the girl that she could count on her, one of Simon's friends, as a new friend. She had introduced herself and Angela had looked at her, red eyed, but not crying, a determined look that held depths of sorrow that mirrored Megan's own. She'd said hello and offered her obligatory condolences in a rather stiff manner to the seated, sad looking girl. Then she'd carefully sat beside her, their eyes locked in the moment, ready to open up as a potential friend, but then, so unlike her normal self, she couldn't continue the conversation, suddenly finding herself dismissing as inappropriate anything that came into her head. Over-analyzing phrases as the eyes continued to stare, mirroring her own pain. She was barely able to think any coherent thoughts as the memory of Simon's death returned foremost to her thoughts. Everything coalesced: the accident, the death, the funeral, the lost daughter, the pain of these last few days. All so new to her that she just couldn't come up with anything to say that didn't seem inappropriate or trite. She tried, and all that came out was an incoherent noise, which reminded her of the embarrassment of the church, and she knew now what the others she had just criticized had experienced.

So Megan had sat next to Angela for a moment that seemed an eternity in quiet embarrassment, as the girl waited patiently for her to continue some form of conversation, to say something of note, but nothing came out worth saying, and she felt the tears coming and then she had burst out crying, and it was all she could do to politely excuse herself, and she'd walked off without a backward glance.

She had felt such a deep shame, things she could have said, should have said, now came to mind, but she knew she had missed the opportunity. She'd looked around for the comfort of Tim. Maybe she could explain to him, but he'd been ensconced in another conversation, and she hadn't wanted to join in there, exposing others to her revived pain and having to deal with sympathetic nods. So, alone with her thoughts and pain, she'd refilled her drink and stood there sipping it, trying to hide her head behind the glass.

A little while later, as a sense of calmness started to return, she had watched as Tim had gone over to Angie, and as she watched, she felt nervous for her shy friend. She winced when she saw him sit on the girl, and then became a little envious moments later when they seemed to be getting on so well. That feeling quickly fell away to the pride she now felt. Her feelings for him were complex and further complicated by the knowledge Simon had given her. So, standing alone behind her glass of wine, she watched him, her sorrow receding with the pride and love she felt for him as she continued to watch him from afar.

Then, Tim stopped, turned, and was suddenly looking at her. His hand frantically gesturing for her to come over. His face was aglow, and Angela was looking at him flushed and smiling. She really didn't want to go, but Tim continued waving, and she realized she had no option but to do so, and maybe she could make up for her earlier mishap. Taking a deep breath and a quick gulp from the glass, she gathered herself and walked over towards the couple.

"Angie, this is Megan, my, and your dad's, best friend," Tim introduced her when she'd arrived. Standing, looking down at the seated pair, Megan gave a brief nod and smiled at Angie, hopefully with apologetic intent. Angie's returned smile appeared thin and cold. Not a true smile, Megan thought, but she understood why.

"We've met," Angie sniffed, her response seemed so frigid, and Megan felt embarrassed and ashamed, but knew she had to accept it. Tim, still smiling, didn't seem to even notice.

"Anyway, Angie, this is Megan," he said emphasizing the name, "you know. She's the girl from the band," he put in humorously.

"You mean?" Angie and Tim looked at each other and burst out laughing. Megan felt annoyance and started to consider her leaving options and a possible barbed comment, but it all quickly evaporated as she watched them laughing together, finding happiness in this terrible time.

"Sorry, Megan," he apologized a few seconds later, a smile on his face, as he wiped a laughing tear from his cheek. "I've just been telling Angie about 'the' end of term gig." From the emphasis on "the" Megan knew which gig and what story Tim had told. She initially felt like she wanted to curl up into a small ball or quietly crawl away. Then the notion of possibly knocking the smile off Tim's face also came to mind, but the look on Angie's face said everything. Staring at Tim, flushed with excitement and happiness, current cares and worries gone, the girl was radiant. The look reminded her of Simon, and she knew that Tim had done a good thing here, so Megan, swallowing any inappropriate pride, chuckled and joined in with her version of the story, putting in the parts Tim had conveniently left out.

"Thanks, Tim," Megan's face flushed with joy, and she hugged Tim's arm, realizing that she felt relaxed for the first time since Simon had died.

"Err, you're welcome?" Tim wasn't too sure what he'd done, but Megan looked happy, so he was happy, and he quietly relished her touch.

"I've been so down in the dumps for the past few weeks," there was an openness to her voice, which Tim hadn't heard for a long time, and it filled him with pleasure. Megan was now relaxed and smiling. Tim, holding her hand on his arm, feeling her now so close again was elated, and they continued to talk.

Angie moved away from the couple. She could see that there was something special between them and felt a twinge of jealousy as she watched Tim's body language with Megan, wishing some man felt the same way about her. She thought it so obvious how he must feel about Megan, but looking at them, she could see the conflict in Megan's eyes and body. You need to tell her Tim, she thought. She felt her belly and silently talked to her child. He hadn't been such a person, she thought to her child, she would never hear from him again, she thought sadly of her baby's father. The conversation with Tim and Megan had calmed and relaxed her and had been a moment's delight in a joyless day, the tensions of the last few days fading away into the background. She retrieved a soda and returned to the now empty sofa and sat alone watching people. She realized that she was now comfortable in the company of these strangers. Most people had departed, others were scattered around in small groups chatting privately, and she was happy with the solitude.

"Is everything ok." She jumped out of her quiet musing, her thoughts far away, at home in Boston. She hadn't noticed his approach. She stared at him for a moment, and his name suddenly flashed in her head: Jason.

"Jason? Isn't it." He nodded with a quick smile. "Yes, I'm fine, thank you for asking."

"I've got to go." He quickly glanced at her belly. "I have a son to drive back to that I'd like to see before the day finishes." He gave a quick shrug as a way of apologizing. Angie smiled back. "I just wanted to see make sure that you're ok."

"I am Jason, thanks."

He turned to the couple talking in the corner, "Tim seems quite the character?" he says returning his attention to her, wishing he could, knowing he couldn't have produced such a lovely response in such sad and painful circumstances.

"Yes, he is." She too looked over at them. "They both are."

"Yes, they are." He was pleased and a little envious of his friend, but also happy that he'd met them. He knew how highly Simon had thought of them, and was glad to have been able to help Megan, after their first meeting.

"Are you heading back to Boston soon?"

"I'm not too sure when, but yes, I think I'll be going back soon, but I don't know how soon, when, I don't know," she tried realizing she had no idea.

"But you're ok for Thursday?" he reminded her.

"Oh yes, Thursday." She'd forgotten. "Yeah, I'll still be here." I think.

"You have my card. You know. If you need to call me beforehand."

"Yeah, I do, but Thursday should be fine. I'll call if there's some sort of problem."

"Great. Then we'll meet Thursday. You know. To finalize the legal stuff." He didn't want to say "Simon's Will. Estate", he couldn't. The thoughts of his friends death, the funeral, now, had come flooding back with unexpected intensity, in the days since he'd immersed himself in the professional side of sorting out many of the legal issues outstanding.

"Yeah. Ok." She understood.

"Goodbye Angie. It was a pleasure getting to know you. I'll see you soon."

"Bye Jason, and thanks for your help."

"Bye." He quickly turned, and walked away. She could feel his shyness, and smiled. He seems nice enough, and been very helpful with the funeral arrangements. Dad, you had some good friends.

She happily said her final farewells, with even a little regret when Megan and Tim left, and she watched the last few people leave her new home. Now alone, she breathed easily. The sadness was still there, but its full force had been blunted by the friendship offered and greatly received from Tim and Megan, and a peacefulness she hadn't felt since before the pregnancy settled on her. She knew to whom she wanted to speak now.

"Hello?" just the sound brought pleasure, and a warm glow flowed through her.

"Hi, Auntie," she answered with a smile.

"Hello, Sweetie, is everything okay?" her voice brightened with the recognition.

"Yeah, yeah, it is," and it was, she knew that now, and her smile widened for a moment with the peace she was now feeling. Then the thought of a question unasked these many months came to her mind, and she hesitated for a moment, the smile gone, her reasons for calling receding as the desire for this knowledge became an overriding need. She considered it carefully, and politeness and tact won out.

"Auntie, I need to ask you a question?" There was a tentativeness born of worry as she prepared to ask this question that had been on her mind these past few months, and the potential of the pain it could bring them both.

"You need to ask me something? Of course, darling, go ahead. You can ask me anything, you should know that," her aunt stated.

"Why did you so hate my dad so much?" she blurted out, and even as the words were leaving her mouth she was now wishing she hadn't asked, but she still, desperately, wanted to know.

"Oh, darling. Sweetie," her aunt paused, and doubts flooded Angie, thinking that maybe she had crossed a line, but the need to know was so strong in her after all the emotions of the funeral.

"Please. Why?" I'm begging. Maybe I shouldn't have asked. It's not fair, I know she loved Mom, but I need to know. I love her so much, and yet she hated my father so much.

"I didn't," there was a quick pause, "I never hated Simon. It's just that.. I met him a few times, and we actually got on very well." She could hear the continuing hesitation in her aunt's voice.

"But you were so against me seeing him. I don't understand. We had such terrible arguments, and you were so angry," she stated, more confused now. She felt her aunt was not being totally honest, she understood why, but she wanted, needed the truth here, now.

"My dear. I just didn't want you to get hurt. I didn't want him to hurt you as he had hurt my little sister," and there it was, the bitterness returning to her voice.

"There wasn't anything between you guys, was there?" She asked, fishing, but then regretting asking it immediately, knowing that Auntie Kay would be shocked at such a question, but Angie's thoughts were roiling in her mind. She just wanted, had to know. That's all there was to it; what was the truth here?

Kay was shocked at hearing such a thing from her niece, but she knew that Angie would have been living with this question for months now. I just need to be honest, she told herself, but still hesitated, realizing that she wasn't too sure herself any more: but her and Simon?

"Oh, lord no, nothing like that. How could you think such a thing? No, he was very charming, very sweet and a lot of fun, then, and I've always been sure that he loved Adela, but in the end, despite his love for her, he was selfish and he hurt her so deeply," she felt the anger rising. It still came so easily, even after all these years, but she stopped it and considered what her niece was asking and why. She thought back pass the pain to earlier memoires, and she remembered and was honest about him for the first time in years, because regardless of her own personal thoughts of him, she was certain of one thing. "Darling, they loved each other very much, and they were very good together, until..." She stopped. The pain and anger returned, quickly rising again.

"Until me?" And Kay could hear the self-incrimination in Angie's voice.

"It's not your fault," she responded a little too forcefully, her anger still there. "He left her alone. He left my little sister to bring you up alone. I just couldn't forgive him." I've never forgiven him, and I should have. The guilt returned, and she knew it was partially her own fault when she'd told him what Adela had asked of her. And how could she resist? Adela had been so hurt, so angry with him. He'd wanted an abortion! How could he tell her to have an abortion? It wasn't his decision!

"But he was my dad." And he didn't want you, thought Kay, but she couldn't say it, the thoughts of him still angering her, the guilt she'd tried these many years to suppress, to confess away, enhancing the anger, and the worry, the worry that maybe Angie already knew, that maybe Simon had told her everything, including her own shame in the act. She knew he would feel guilty about it, especially after the conversation when Angie had walked out on him.

What had Angie said? That Simon would keep nothing from her. His guilt had been so profound that he'd promised her the truth and to give it regardless of how he would be portrayed, that he'd never lie to her. How can I do any less?

"I know, Sweetie, but I didn't want him to hurt you as he'd hurt her." Was that even my choice? Yes, she's my daughter. It's my job to protect her, even from her father.

"She never really recovered, did she?"

"No, she didn't. I'm so sorry. I realized too late, I should have done something sooner, I could have, but he hurt her so badly."

"But she loved him?"

"Yes, she did sweetheart. She loved him to her last breath. You are the only person she loved more. I'm so sorry," and she was, but neither this nor all her confessions could remove the guilt that she felt and that she would always feel.

Angie could hear the regret in Auntie Kay's voice. I could never blame you, she thought, everyone made mistakes in this situation, out of love for another. It's so sad that the best people in my life had to go through this when it could so easily have been avoided. C'est la vie, she thought mournfully.

"Oh, Auntie, you don't have to be sorry. How can I ever thank you enough? What could I say and do to express how much I appreciate what you did for Mom and for me? And the love I have for you that is so deep," then she had a thought, "I've been lucky, I've had two great mothers. Yes, I lost my mom, but I gained another just as good." She could hear her aunt weeping.

"Oh, thank you, Sweetie, that means so much to me," she paused, sniffing back tears as she tried to gain her composure, the anger slipping away to grief. "I know how much you loved your mom, and she thought the world of you, and you are the best of her in every way."

"And you mean a lot to me, you mean everything to me."

"You are the daughter I never had, and I'm so proud of you, I'll always be proud of you, and I know your mother would be."

"I'll be back next weekend. I have to see the lawyer on Thursday, drop in and see some friends who are studying here, and I should arrange to see my new doctor."

"Are you sure you want to stay in New York?"

"I don't know. I'm not too sure. I want to stay here, but…" but I already miss you, she thought, a small ache of loss already settling, "but I'm not too sure it's going to be possible. I'll know in a few days." Do I want to live here? Alone? I'll chat with the lawyer first.

"Well, I can't wait until you get back. I'll have some rice and peas waiting for you." The thought of her favorite meal ran through Angie's mind. Her aunt was an excellent cook. She ran her own small restaurant, which was doing nicely. Rice and peas with chicken curry is my favorite, she mused, remembering the complex West Indian flavors and textures. Dry rice with kidney beans and fried chicken in that hot spicy sauce. Of course, her aunt knew that was something she was going to miss if she was staying here.

"Maybe I'll come up Friday," she laughed.

"You do that darling, but I'll be out on Friday night," she offered lightly.

"Out?"

"Yes, I have a date," Angie wanted to laugh out loud at the enthusiasm in her aunt's voice.

"What? You have a date? Oh, that's great! You can tell me all about it when I see you."

"I don't think so," her aunt laughed.

"Okay," that's so fantastic, I'm so pleased, "I'll call again tomorrow. See you soon."

"Lots of love, Sweetie."

Megan was content, at least for the moment. The pain and anguish were still there, but they were now distanced. She wandered out onto the balcony, where she found that the night air was cool and the slight breeze was refreshing in contrast to the warm and slightly cloying atmosphere of the apartment. Outside, the view of Manhattan was dark and backlit in front of her, as her eyes adjusted to the night. It's so beautiful, she mused staring at the buildings looming high into the night sky, as rivulets of lights ran through the streets at their feet. Shall I make this my new home? I'll know soon enough. I think I'll sleep out here tonight.

That night she had the first good night's sleep in ages, under the New York sky.

Part Three: Love

Dinner? At your place?

"Come 'round for dinner?" I ask him before he hangs up.

"Dinner at your place?" he hesitates, "I don't think that's a particularly good idea." I can hear the doubt in his voice, and I know why.

"Please, come around for dinner?" I ask, there's a hint of pleading in my voice, emphasizing my intent, but the reality is I'm not being fair, I'm testing him, teasing him. And honestly? The pleading's sort of fake. I don't have to plead, not even a little. He'll be here. I'm just wondering when he'll know it.

"You really want me to come around for dinner? At your place?" In my mind, I can see him working through the problem, eyes roving, tight lipped. He's possibly even questioning my sanity, but at the same time, he's trying to work out a response to my request, knowing there is only one response, and he does not like it. So, he's really trying to find that elusive alternative. It doesn't exist, I tell myself with a little chuckle and a tiny bit of guilt, but that's not going to stop me.

"Yes, this weekend, instead of us going out to some nice, swanky restaurant, come over here, and I'll cook dinner for you."

"It doesn't have to be a swanky one." Was that a little desperation? I can see the smile that goes with that response, and I return a smile at the thought, and at the fact that he's still trying to discover that alternative, non-existent response to my request.

"I know that, but..." I leave that thought hanging and I wait.

"But that's what you want?" he asks, and I know he's ready to acquiesce.

"Yep," sorry Dad, but there's only one answer.

"Me? Over for dinner? At your place?" he appears to be having problems putting full sentences together. I stifle a laugh. I know he wants to say, at Kay's place? but he refrains.

"Yep, here."

"Okay."

"Okay?"

"Yes, okay. I'll come over for dinner." I feel like dancing, but I'm worried he'll hear it on the other end of the line.

"When are you coming up?" I ask brightly, not yet letting him off the hook.

"I'll leave early Friday evening, I should be there around 8:00 pm?" He doesn't sound that happy, and I continue to stifle my laughter.

"8:00 is perfect," though I must admit that I'm a little disappointed he gave in so quickly, but I suppose he had to at some point, and I was enjoying it and hoped he'd hold out a little longer.

"Should I bring anything?" I can still hear the doubt and worry in his voice. I know he doesn't want to come here, but he said yes, and he's passed my little, admittedly childish, test. I feel a touch guilty at putting him through this, but I just can't resist, and I really do want to cook for him.

"Well, there's usually no alcohol here, so if you'd like some wine you'll need to bring your own, though I'd recommend beer. I'm doing West Indian. Wine works, but beer's better." Then I remembered, "I'm also going to make dessert, so that sweet wine of yours wouldn't go amiss." The memory of those intoxicating flavors come flooding back, and my mouth starts to salivate as I lick my lips at the memory. Only a small sip, I remind myself. I can hear him taking in a deep breath. Here it comes.

"Okay," he pauses, I wait, "should I bring anything for Kay?" he rushes out.

"Anything for Kay?" I ask him, dragging it out just a little more, enjoying my game, relishing the moment.

"Yes," he sighs, "should I bring anything for your aunt," his tone, his speech, are all back to normal, he's fully accepted the request. I can hear the resignation in his voice, and I must admit that I'm a little pleased with myself.

"Oh, she won't be here. She'll be away, off at some cooking seminar in Jamaica. I'm mad, not stupid," I say finally letting him in on my little prank.

"She won't be there?" I laugh at the sound of relief on the other end of the line.

"Nope."

"Okay," and he laughs back, deep and hearty, "you got me there, I was worried."

"Worried? You were petrified." I laugh again, loudly, fully, and uncontrollably.

"Just a little bit," he concurs, joining in with me.

Angie watched the sunrise, a forlorn smile on her face as she remembered her little game. It was a good meal she remembered, and a tear escaped as she is reminded of a future without him.

Immortalized in oil

Natalie sat staring at the painting she had been working on for the past few weeks, her drink momentarily forgotten beside her. The man depicted on the canvas was her husband Andy, not recognizable as such, but it definitely was him amongst the color and form, the shapes and structures that defined the fledgling painting. Soon, however, he would be gone, erased from this canvas. She would have known it was him, and he would too, but she knew she would have had to explain it to others. Sometimes she would, sometimes not. That was one of the natures of her art, there was nothing necessarily obvious about some of her subject matter unless you knew. Sometimes it was quite blatant, other times subtle, and that was the point, not knowing and knowing brought different experiences to viewing her work. Tonight, she would start to rework the surface, removing whole sections, adjusting the theme, changing the context. Tonight, at least at this moment, here on this canvas, Andy would be gone, replaced with another image. That didn't bother her, she'd done that many times before, starting a painting with one idea only for that particular train of thought to grow and morph into something different, something new. However, this time the new vision had been forced upon her. This time she'd felt compelled, overwhelming any previous artistic vision. It had come from a place never before experienced, and this made her both sad and happy. She would never explain this one to anyone. Andy would know, but no one else would understand, besides possibly the owner. This was to be a gift to a girl who has lost her father too soon. She continued to stare at the canvas. Her hand reached out, and without looking she picked up the glass beside her. She took a sip from the drink without really tasting the liquor, now fully immersed in the vision forming in her mind's eye. The base premise was the same; the previous ideas wouldn't need much of a change, a shift in an idea here, a new form there. The original foundations and ideas were still the pillars upon which the painting would be constructed. This she knew and understood, but the context had changed: Simon had died. He had been a very close friend, for a while a lover, and still dearly loved. His death created a profound change, how could it not? And so, the subject of the painting had changed as did its relationship to the whole. On the one hand, she felt a great, overwhelming sadness; on the other hand, the effect of Simon's untimely death was a form of artistic elation at the anticipation of newfound inspiration as it dared her to reach further within herself and her art.

After Andy had told her the news, his voice twisted with the pain he knew he was bringing to her, she'd barely reacted. On the surface, all he saw was a slight nod of acknowledgement and a tight smile as she fought to control her outward emotions. He knew, however, that inside her everything was in turmoil. The vacant look on her face for a few seconds after the news told him so much after being with someone as open as Natalie for so many years. After he'd told her, he watched as she paused and then slowly stood up, taking in a few deep calming breaths. Then he too had stood up, standing close but not too close, waiting for the inevitably calm response – calm on the outside that is.

She hugged him and kissed him lightly but with a passion to which he'd quickly and easily responded. She hugged him more tightly for a second, and then quickly separating, she'd thanked him. She'd told him that she loved him, and she did, more so now than through the years they'd dated, even more than when they had gotten married, getting to know each other with so much more intimacy and the shared experience of having a daughter together. All this he knew because she was so open, so honest. And then she'd moved in towards him and hugged him again tightly, as if she was squeezing her love into him and trying to squeeze his love into herself. She held him close for another moment, and her body spoke of infinite love and pain. Then she pulled back and gazed at him, and thanked him again for his precious love. He could hear her voice starting to break, despite the control she was exhibiting, and then she picked up the glass with her drink, flicked him a quick glance and a tight smile, turned, and without a backward glance left the room. He knew her so well. He knew better than to try and console her, at least for now. He knew that solitude was what she wanted, and her art would be what she needed, so he had hugged her and kissed her in that silence when she needed it, and when she was ready, he'd let her go.

Natalie wandered over to her daughter's room, stood at the foot of the bed and watched her little girl sleeping. So far away from the cares of the world, she thought. I really wish I was asleep now. She wanted to curl up beside the child, feeling the warmth of her daughter's body, the rising and falling as she breathed, her heartbeat ticking gently, together with hers. The pain of the news was building in her, continuously assaulting her thoughts, fanning her emotions, but it was also growing a seed of creativity within her, and she turned away from her sleeping girl, happy that she didn't have to explain anything to such a young child, hoping that her daughter would never have to experience something so painful, yet knowing that at some time she would likely need to because such is life. I have to go, she thought, I have work to do, forcing herself to move, because, honestly? Deep down? She wanted to stay in this moment. At the door she turned back sighing, blew her daughter a kiss and then left, leaving the door slightly ajar, as her little girl liked.

In the corridor, she could hear the noise of knives and pots and pans in the kitchen. She looked at the closed kitchen door, knowing Andy was in there worried about her, but giving her the space she needed to work through her emotions, and she knew he would still be there when she was ready. He'll be in there concocting something special for me when I return to him later. So, she turned away from the kitchen door hiding her husband, and slowly, with deliberately controlled steps, took the stairs to the basement and entered her studio.

She switched the light on and surveyed the large basement room, nearly the size of a whole floor of the house. Large canvases of her work occupied huge easels, as they waited for their journey to one of three art galleries that displayed her work or to be picked up by some private collector. Most had already been sold, but there were a few on the walls, personal ones, pieces that had something about them separating them from her other work. All her work had special meaning for her, but sometimes a particular work would etch itself on her emotions. She would have had no issues selling any of them, but she was also in no particular hurry to sell them. Maybe a crazy enough offer would do it, or a very personal request, but she hadn't offered them to any gallery or collector. Every now and then a collector would come and view her work and ask about these pieces, and slowly they would go, later to be replenished with others. A few were works in progress, requiring either additional inspiration or just the concentration and attention necessary to complete them, or at least put them into a state where she could say "no more, they are done." Some were already in that state, but she wasn't quite ready to admit that to herself. And then there was the one she was currently working on. She stepped into the room, the door closing with a slight click behind her as she headed towards that canvas.

This was her room. Andy rarely came in here unless he was sitting for her, and unless a lightning bolt of inspiration suddenly struck, she rarely came down here at night. She had a lovely, beautiful daughter with whom she wanted to be with most of the time and a husband whom she loved deeply and dearly, and who, after all these years was still great company and a considerate and passionate lover, and still a spontaneous romantic. There were moments, however, and this was one of them, when she wanted and needed to be alone, away from other souls, just she and her imagination to be expressed in her art.

She sat in front of the painting, her current work-in-progress, placing her drink on the stool beside her. Her emotions were starting to overcome her, and she could feel the tears welling up. Just let it go, she thought, there's no one here to feel embarrassed in front of, no one here to try and explain anything to, no one to console you or tell you everything is going to be all right. She knew that! Right now, she wanted to feel the pain, work through it, savor it, until it diminished in its own time. So, she sat there on her work stool and let the tears come.

Memories of Simon came to the fore. College and six months, six incredible months. They had been so special, and Simon had been so amazing. What a student he'd been, what a friend, and what a lover! He had been open to anything and everything she had to offer; learning, absorbing, questioning, experimenting, loving. Arguing. She laughed through the tears, the Stones? Really? Over the Beatles? The thought brought a smile to her face, and she shook her head at the audacious thought. When the subject had first come up, she'd argued with disbelief and incredulity, unable to understand how he could even consider such a travesty of a concept. Simon knew both bands very well, most certainly better than she, as someone who played both on stage. She sometimes thought that he knew the words to every one of their songs. He would always sing along and he never appeared to fumble for the words. At first, she'd thought he was joking, trying to get a rise out of her, but he'd been very persuasive and argued passionately in favor of the Stones, and she'd understood why he'd said it and why he believed it. She could see it in his argument, see it in his passion. It was a good argument, but not that good: she still disagreed.

She remembered the passion he'd had for music, especially Rock, and for sports, especially football. American Football, she corrected herself, and winced as she always did at the alternative: soccer, the word that had to be used here in this country to describe The Beautiful Game. She could see both Simon and Andy laughing at her on that point. She shook her head slowly: They would have gotten on so well. She sighed at the thought of two of her three favorite men. Only one left, she thought with a deep heavy sorry. She missed Dad, gone these many years now, and she would miss Simon. But Andy was her rock, the father of her child. We should have another soon, and she knew she'd been selfish asking him to wait. I know he wants another, and he's been waiting patiently for me to be ready, and she thought of her daughter and knew she was finally, definitely ready. But, snapping back to the moment, tonight is about Simon.

The painting stood before her, enticing her, reaching into her demanding her attention, but not yet, she told herself, and her thoughts returned to her friend, the inspiration for her art at this moment. Such an expansive love of life, at least until he started working as a trader or salesman or whatever he actually did there in the corporate banking world. She grimaced at the thought. There was no doubt he enjoyed his job. He would tell her how he loved the rush, the pressure, but there was never the same passion for it that he had for other things. He always talked about what it did for him, but not what it was for him. There seemed to be no personal context, no passion, the word driving her current thoughts. There was no love in it, she thought with finality. It was like a drug high, something he took, but it never actually gave back anything to him. No, that's not strictly true, she thought, smiling again, he made a lot of money doing it. Alternatively, get him on to the subjects of music or sports, and the difference was profound. Here was passion fueled by knowledge as much as by emotion, each complementing and enhancing the other. That's what she'd seen in him those many years ago. His face would light up. He would become so animated, his normally short sentences extended into diatribes of cogent arguments, and he would just talk and talk. They used to talk and argue endlessly on the subtleties of a bands' songs, players' significances, albums' influences, but he could also listen, even though at the time it might appear he wasn't. He would absorb anything thrown at him, and if it interested him, it would fall on fertile ground and be used for his own benefit later.

Those had been such great times, and even after their romantic relationship had ended, he'd been such a good friend. Then college had ended, and careers had taken off for both of them in diametrically opposed directions. The time between meetings started to extend, and they saw much less of each other. Text messages on the holidays and phone calls on birthdays, the odd corporate charity event, and that was pretty much it. Until a few months ago.

What a surprise that had been, when he'd turned up at her exhibition preview in Boston – with his daughter! He could have just told her, but that was Simon, he wanted to, needed to surprise her. A daughter? Now that was a real surprise. She knew immediately that the girl was Adela's daughter when he'd introduced her. She could see the resemblance from the photos she'd seen of the girl from college. It was one of the reasons she'd broken up with him. She shook her head at the hit of jealousy, which always, even now, accompanied this thought: Adela and Megan. The intellectual competitiveness she could cope with, but in the end, she knew she couldn't compete with them. These were the two people he just couldn't seem to let go of; he still kept them so very close to his heart, closer than she had ever been, and she loved and resented them and him for it. They were his soft spot, his vulnerability, his passion redirected. Misdirected?

She wasn't at all surprised that he was still single, but the look on his face when he was with Angie reminded her of his old passion again, now coupled with the love he'd had for the other two girls. Now more mature, it seemed like the old younger Simon.

I can't believe what I'm seeing. His hair is longer, but there's no mistaking those broad shoulders and that walk, athletic, powerful and so controlled. And there's that smile. He's staring at me as he walks towards me, and I must admit, I'm turned on as memory imposes. He's still hot.

I turn away from the couple I'm talking to with a quick apology.

"I'm sorry, I'll be back in a moment," I say, virtually to the wind, as I'm watching him. I'm returning his smile with a huge one of my own; this is such an unexpected pleasure.

"Simon!" I nearly shout, "What are you doing here?" I can barely contain myself as he's standing there in front of me.

"Nat. I thought I'd just drop in and say Hi," he smiles at me, and I'm shaking my head, in my head. So typically Simon, but what a wonderful surprise. Though I do notice that his date looks a bit young. At first, I barely notice her. I'm just so glad to see him, as my eyes quickly flick away from her.

"It's been a while. Years, how many?" I can't be bothered to count, "Years. How are you? Still earning piles and piles of cash in The City?" I laugh.

"Nice seeing you too, Nat," he beams back, oblivious to my sarcasm – he knows me. I just love that smile.

"Likewise. It really is great. What are you up to? Come on, quick, quick, I've got lots of other guests who also want my attention," I gush. I'm so excited. I love surprises.

"I'd like to introduce you to Angie, my daughter," he says with a nonchalance just like the old days. Ok, there are surprises, and then there are Surprises. I pause, falter, pause and shut up for a second, as my brain runs through this news a few times. I turn away from one surprise and look a bit more closely at the other. My brief glance at his date had missed the now obvious. Blue eyes, long cane-roll, gorgeous caramel skin. I instantly think how it is lighter than her mother's because I'm guessing and I'm calculating and I know who her mother is.

"Adela's daughter?" He doesn't flinch, she does, and I see the pain in her eyes and I know. "I'm sorry," I should keep my mouth shut sometimes, I really should.

"Hi, Angie, I'm Natalie," I say in a quieter, more controlled, and pleasant manner. Most certainly more pleasant than if she had been his date. I was a little jealous, though I shouldn't be: I have Andy.

"Hello, Ms. Stones. I'm pleased to meet you," she replies in a small polite voice, obviously a little embarrassed. And then, "I just love your work, you're amazing," she enthuses, and her blue eyes light up, and she smiles, and I can see Simon in her too.

"Ms. Stones? Seriously. Call me Natalie, and welcome to my exhibition," I smile back, and he's staring at her, and his pride and happiness are so obvious.

Natalie started to cry again. I was so happy for him, she thought. He was so happy being with her. The tears flowed as she remembered just being in his presence. He was always smiling, and oh my god, he was always so considerate. She smiled again. He

276

should have been English. He was always such a gentleman, such a romantic, just like in those old movies. Cary Grant came to mind, the American who could easily be mistaken for an English gentleman.

She had asked him her test question again three weeks after the initial challenge, but she didn't really need the answer, and she couldn't have cared less, really. The true test was in the first meeting; he'd passed that with flying colors. It was a question that Dad had once asked her, though he'd had said Ellington instead of Miles, Beethoven instead of Mozart, Rembrandt instead of Picasso, but she was a huge Miles fan, and given what she knew of his history, she preferred the use of Miles in this particular debate, so she'd decided to update the question to her own preferences: Dad would have understood. She could see the similarities between her and Dad's Ellington vs Miles and her and Simon's Stones vs Beatles debate, and she laughed through her tears, remembering the two men so important to her, now both deceased. Dad would have approved of Simon, she thought, and not for the first time. But they had never met, her father's death had been the impetus for her to leave the country when an offer of study had been made to move away from her home in England and get away from the painful memories of familiar surroundings and constant reminders of her father's passing.

She rose from the stool and went over to her computer. The music choice was easy. The album's name matches my mood, she thought as she remembered him introducing her to the beauty of Joni Mitchell.

"That 'Rite of Spring' is amazing," he extolls with exuberance, as if it was a piece of news no one else had ever surmised. His face is flushed with excitement and happiness as we walk out of the campus concert hall towards his dorm. My friend has company, so I'm staying at his place tonight, though it's not an excuse I really need. The thought thrills me. I enjoy making love with him, and I'm definitely in the mood for a good shag tonight.

"There is nothing in 20th century music better than Stravinsky at his best," I offer, pleased with tonight's rendition of Stravinsky's masterpiece, happy with the anticipation of the evening to come.

"Stravinsky? What about Shostakovich? You're always going on about him. I thought Shostakovich was your favorite 20th century composer, and have you forgotten the great Miles Davis?" He looks at me with that cheeky little smile, and I know he's trying to wind me up. It was sort of working, I can only smile back. I'm in a good mood, but right now there's only sex on my mind when I look at him. However, as much as I try, I just can't let the statement lie. He knew that when he said it.

"What Miles brought to 20th century popular and classical music can never be overstated. His influence pervades so much after him," I offer, and decide not to get into or involved in that argument right now because I really want to get laid tonight. But..."but 'Rite of Spring' is a masterpiece. Shostakovich has his moments, and so many of them," he's smiling broadly, but I don't fall for it and decide to go on my own offensive. "But what do you bring to the table, my Sporting Hunk?" I stop and pull him towards me.

"Ahh, there's a challenge?" he breathes in my ear, and pushes me back a little, looking at me with a wink and a smile to emphasize his point. "I have just the thing," and his smile broadens and his arm snakes around my waist and lowers, pulling me towards him, his hand caressing my bum, his leg pushed into my crotch. We kiss, oblivious to anyone else around us. It's strong and quick, just a taste, our lips pressed hard. A quick flick of the tongue as a taster. I pull away, eager to get back to his dorm. I hug his arm close and lead him towards the building, hurrying him up. He fakes an effort to come with me, laughing.

We enter his dorm room, which as usual is very tidy, far tidier than mine, but then again, I paint and draw in mine, and my flat mate's a slob, which I know is just an excuse, but it's the one I use. He walks straight in, ignoring me for the moment, and I close the door as he wanders over to his hi-fi system.

"It's always bothered me that your rock music tastes are so," he pauses, I'm not too sure if it's for effect, or just to find the right word, "British."

"Too British?" I exclaim for effect, and I realize he's not ready for bed yet. I have to accept this annoyance, but we'll have plenty of time later.

"The Beatles. The Who. Led Zeppelin. All that progressive rock stuff as well. All so seriously British." Yes, Genesis, King Crimson, I continue. Oh yes, we're really good, aren't we? I think to myself with pride, but not wishing to start down that particular argument right now or I'm never going to get him to refocus on other pleasures tonight.

"I like other stuff," I say, now a little on the defensive, "and those are pretty good and important bands," I state the obvious, smiling, and he knows it, but I know we're about to have some music fun, the teaching roles now reversed: I'm about to be educated. "And the Stones, you forgot the Rolling Stones," I state in a little, deliberately girlish, sweet voice.

"Yes, very British," he answers patiently, ignoring my provocation.

"You love the Stones as well. In fact, your tastes are very British," I state a little too defensively.

"I can't deny that, but where's Steely Dan, and where's Joni? You have huge holes in your Rock repertoire," and he stares at me, daring me to contradict him.

"I wouldn't say huge," I counter, knowing his tastes here in this field are more extensive than mine, "You like Steely Dan? I've never heard you play them." Testing him, not quite believing he likes them, surprised that they, with their Jazz-tinged tones, have even been mentioned. I love the band, but I must admit to being surprised that he does too.

"Love Steely Dan, they're one of my friend Tim's favorite bands." We both messed up there, yet Dan had never come up, presumably because we thought we knew each other's tastes better than we actually did. That Tim of his sounds interesting. He's been mentioned before, and I know Simon thinks highly of him, but I don't know that much about him.

"The bass player? I haven't met him yet."

"You will. You and he could talk Jazz all night. But that's neither here nor there. It's Joni that I have the biggest problem with. I am so surprised you don't love her."

"Well, I only know 'Big Yellow Taxi.' It just seemed, I don't know, nice?" I wait for his reaction, he's prepared and barely responds.

"Nice?" he questions me quietly. I can see him holding back.

"You know. It's nice, but it didn't do anything for me," I knowingly provoke him. I can see that deep down he's seething at that word, but he takes it well, very well.

"My dear, your education is sorely wanting," and he bows theatrically, "Joni Mitchell, my sweet girl, is someone you really need to listen to."

"I listened, it just didn't really offer much for me."

"No!" he shouts theatrically and gives out an exaggerated sigh, as if he's nearly, but not quite, lost all hope. "I mean: listen." He turns back to his collection and starts rummaging through it. *"The Hissing of the Summer Lawns*," he states with grandeur, turns around holding the CD case high as if he's found the Holy Grail of music or something that should similarly be regarded as just as important.

"The missing of the what?" I ask joking, not quite sure what he'd just said. He flips the CD out of its case and places it in the player, and returns his attention to me. I watch him, his body taut, his motion fluid, as even though he doesn't play football anymore, he still works out, and my desire for him expands in me.

"*The Hissing of the Summer Lawns*," he says slowly and reverently, and hands the case over to me, two-handed, bowing slightly, and then he flops down beside me. Then reaching his arm around my shoulder, he gently pulls me towards him. "Once you hear this, they'll be no turning back, I promise you."

He had been right, and she smiled at the memory. She'd been happy to wait once the music had started, and their love making that night had had an extra edge of passion. Listening to Joni Mitchell had been a revelation: Folk, Rock, Jazz, African, complex chords and poetry – such poetry. Lyrics the likes of which are rarely heard in Rock music, and in her music she managed to meld them seamlessly like no other. There were layers to Joni which Natalie had never even dreamed of, and Simon had given her that. This was one of the things so special about him: he always gave back as much as he took, and usually more. He loved to give. There were other bands, and she'd given as good as she'd received. He'd never listen to Schubert or Coltrane, never experienced the voices of Ella and Lady Day. Artists he couldn't get enough of once he'd discovered them, but getting to know Joni's music had been special to her. She couldn't thank him enough for that. *The Hissing of the Summer Lawns* is still one of my favorite CDs, but tonight merits another Joni.

She left the stool, eyes dry, tears for the moment gone, and walked over to the only clean area in the room, bereft of art implements and tools. The desk contained a phone extension, a computer with a large hi-def monitor, connected to an equally hi-def printer, and an iPod connected to speakers. Alongside all of that was a picture of her husband holding their newborn daughter. She picked up the picture, admiring its composition, her training seamlessly and subconsciously slipping in to judge the picture and its artistic form from an aesthetic and technical point of view, but here before her eyes was her family, her life, and she kissed it, the last of her men, the first of her children, before returning it to its place. Already thinking about starting the process of another child, a smile came to her face, and for a moment her melancholy receded.

Beside the desk, a little fridge with glasses on top of it hummed. She picked up her iPod lying there, dialed in Blue, and pressed play. She availed herself of some of the fridge's contents and poured herself a vodka from the bottle stored in the freezer compartment and added freshly squeezed orange juice. She took a sip and savored the cold, bright, tangy flavor that only freshly squeezed could achieve, invigorating after the lukewarm drink she had just finished. She raised a glass and silently toasted her friend.

"Cheers, mate," she said out loud, exaggerating her Scouse accent in remembrance, as the cool, somber, and dulcet tones of Joni Mitchell played through the speakers. For a moment she stood there, rocking as the music filtered into her, then she quietly sang along, feeling the emotions inherent in it.

She turned, still singing but now unconsciously as her art started to re-exert itself into her thoughts, and she returned to her stool. She placed the half-filled glass there and stared at the canvas, humming. Inspiration renewed, imagination rekindled, she pressed oil paints onto her palette, instinctively choosing the right colors, and with her palette knife started working the base colors into the tones she wanted for the canvas before her, feeling the sensuous texture of the oil sending its familiar signals up her arm and filling her senses. She watched as her hands worked the paint, studying and still admiring after all these years the colors as they mixed and merged into something new. Time stopped for a moment as her senses, thoughts, and inspiration started to joust in a cooperative battle.

Then, pausing before applying anything to the canvas, she stopped to take in the vision before her. With Joni keeping her company, she allowed what was in front of her eyes to meld with the soothing tones in her ears, until suddenly everything converged in her mind's eye. Now she was ready. Tears gently rolled down her cheeks, her inner vision now opened and clear, and she proceeded to work her friend into the canvas.

A date with the past

Timothy rubbed his fingers and felt the slight sweat of nervousness. Clammy hands, he thought. I can't remember the last time I had clammy hands. He rubbed them again as he tried to think back, but no situation in recent years had bought him to this level of nervousness. Absolutely nothing he could think of came close. Most certainly not at school. He'd been working for the same school, doing the same job for the last twelve years. He loved his job, liked the people he worked with, and the pupils and their parents never gave him any serious problems. It was all very pleasant and stress free, and so he had moseyed on through life without any major mishaps or noteworthy events. He had had various offers from other schools and even some decent colleges, but he liked where he was and didn't want things to change. It's not that he wasn't tempted, but he really didn't like change. He'd accepted the status quo. So, it had been many years since he'd been nervous at work. Ok, there was that crush he'd had on Tina Gershon when she'd started working there two, no, three years ago! He'd agonized about asking her out, but it had all come to naught as she was in a steady relationship and had been married within the year. Apart from Tina, and the very first days as a fledgling teacher, there had been nothing to cause anxiety at work. His social life had been quite uneventful too. In fact, it had most recently been characterized by an accepted solitude and a sense of apathy.

A few dates had caused some mild anxiety. Didn't they always? But he couldn't remember anything like this, and most certainly couldn't pinpoint any specific event that had produced this particular effect. But today he had clammy hands. And a dry throat, he suddenly realized. He coughed to try and clear it unsuccessfully, and he rubbed his hands on his jeans once again in an attempt to dry them. I am so nervous! What am I doing? Why am I so nervous? He felt a little panic rising within him, and he tried to calm himself by taking deep breaths and making fists with his hands. It worked, just.

Apart from the funeral, he hadn't seen Megan in what? Five years? More probably. Stephanie's birthday. When was that? That was six years ago. That must have been the last time. He relaxed a bit and looked around his apartment. It still looks a mess, he thought. He'd attempted to clean and tidy up, but he realized that wasn't his forte. I can't bring her back here! As if that's going to happen. Just calm down. It's just dinner with an old friend. Old friend? It's Megan. Calm yourself. His mind was running riot with nerves and anticipation. He rubbed his fingers again, and then he closed his eyes and slowed his breathing to try to relax. It worked. Somewhat. He opened his eyes, and could still hear his heart thumping.

I'm ready, he thought, mentally checking his angst and his palms again. Yes, I'm ready. I have just over an hour before I need to be there, and I definitely do not want to be late. His mind started racing again as he recalled once being nearly an hour late for one date. He couldn't reach the lady on the phone to tell her of his predicament, and she'd left before he'd arrived. That had been followed by a few days of embarrassing calls and thwarted explanations. Finally, when he had had the opportunity to explain, he had managed to convince her to go on another date; he swore he'd never be late again. He laughed, I haven't been on that many dates recently to be late for. That relationship had lasted two years. I wonder what Stacy's up to these days? I still have her number. He knew he wouldn't call her though.

He went into the bathroom and checked himself in the mirror. A casually dressed man stared back at him, familiar and worried. This is the second time in weeks that I've worn a jacket, he thought. The same question he'd been asking himself these past twenty years returned: Had his feelings for her ever gone away? Or were they just hidden away when she got married? Should I just tell her and risk our friendship? She might feel the same. After all these years? It's just dinner. We're old friends. He rubbed his fingers, they were still sweaty. It's not just any old friend, is it? He sighed. It's Megan.

The taxi seemed to be taking forever. The traffic seemed to be barely moving as he stared out of the window yearning, willing the taxi and other traffic to move more quickly, feeling frustrated as cars passed in alternative lanes. In truth, he was early and could sit in traffic for an extra twenty-five minutes and still not be late, but he was nervous with the anticipation of seeing her, so time and traffic felt unusually slow. He'd misjudged how long it would take to get a taxi. I want to be early, he'd reminded himself. I want to be there before she is. Do the gentlemanly thing, but for Christ-sakes, be cool! Late is not cool. He rubbed his hands again. Still clammy! He touched his forehead, an automatic movement, and felt the dampness of sweat. Oh, dear. I'm in a bit of a state, aren't I? He felt a rush of escalating panic. Opening the window, he leaned towards the rushing breeze to try to cool down and collect his thoughts into some form, any form, of calmness.

When he had suggested that they go out for dinner, he hadn't expected her to say yes. Sure, he had hoped, but he had not really expected her to say yes. Ok, he had expected her to say yes, as a friend, but as more? That's what he'd hoped: more. They had had a fantastically animated and memorable conversation, the years rolling back as if they'd never been apart, but however much he was enjoying talking with her, being with her, he still felt guilty for ignoring her for all those years. Though even as he'd seen her, talked with her on the day of Simon's funeral, it was as if the intervening years had never existed. They'd been talking about favorite restaurants, and feeling he finally had an opportunity, and as his mind was stupidly running through all possible permutations, he'd blurted out the suggestion.

Earlier, she'd made it clear that she was currently single, and his heart beat had increased, his palms got sweaty, that twitch in his right leg started, every sign of nerves and anxiety he felt he could exhibit, but he'd said nothing. He'd wanted to but didn't want to be turned down, rejected. Later, after Angie had left them both basking in the warmth of their conversation, which had now turned more casual and less inhibited, they had turned to enthusing about restaurants. They both lived in New York City. Don't all conversations at some point end up on favorite restaurants? He'd been surprised his voice hadn't come out high pitched and stuttering. Thirty odd years he'd known her, over thirty, and most of those years? He'd loved her, or at least thought he loved her, fantasized about being with her, holding hands, making love, getting married, having children – everything a couple would do together, he had fantasized about, all of that and more. Once he'd had a vivid dream that they were a couple. They'd kissed in the dream, just like they had done once before, that one, single time, and they'd held hands. That had never happened in real life. They said things in his dream that had never been said; dream things, he couldn't remember what. That dream had stayed on his mind for weeks. He chuckled to himself, he would go to bed hoping that the dream would continue. It didn't, but night after night he continued to hope, until it had slowly faded into the background of his memory, diminished in parts and enhanced others, but every now and then he would recall it. And the kiss? He still remembered the kiss! The real one, imitated in the dream, but still alive in his thoughts. It had happened just the once, but what a moment! It had been during a Christmas party at Julian's. Julian's? Yeah, Julian's.

They had been dancing and drinking, everyone had been drinking, he laughed as he remembered Mom scolding him when he'd returned with alcohol on his breath. They'd been dancing to a slow,

R&B number, now who was it? Luther Vandross? Yeah, Luther. He would never forget. He could still feel her breath on his neck, and her hand had rubbed the back of his neck, as he'd gently held her other. She smelled so sweet, her musk familiar but now so close, almost overpowering him. They swayed together in time with the music, and he felt he was in heaven. He squeezed her hand slightly, gently, and pulled away. He looked into her dark and penetrating eyes as she looked back, and all he could think about was kissing her. And he thought about it, and thought about it, and... She leaned in and kissed him. The surprise lasted just a moment, as the barriers of his reticence dissolved, and he had responded in kind. Both now teasing each other's lips and tongue; her arm around his neck held him tighter, and he lifted her to her toes, gently pressing her body against his. He closed his eyes in the moment, and the kiss seemed to last forever. Then the song finished, and the moment was gone. She wandered over to some friends, and he just stood there for a while, suddenly embarrassed and feeling like everyone was watching him. At last he moved, shuffled away from the center of the room, the makeshift dance floor, as Rick James' lively "Can't Touch This" changed the mood. He stood there at the side of the room, feeling slightly dazed, watching her whenever she came into his line of sight, and still lost in the kiss.

He hadn't spoken to her for two weeks after that evening. He hadn't actually avoided her, but he had hidden himself away in his room for most of the holiday, his embarrassment smothering him.

Ignoring company as much as he could, he dabbled in music and programming, his mind preoccupied with the kiss, afraid to face her.

Then at the New Year's Eve party, they had chatted like nothing had happened. The subject hadn't come up. He'd thought about saying something before the party, and was thinking about it as they talked, but he couldn't think of a way to broach the subject or introduce it into the conversation. She said nothing about it either. She didn't appear to be embarrassed, but she never mentioned it, so he assumed she had no interest in pursuing it. It was just something that happens at parties when inhibitions are down. Then, suddenly, too suddenly, the party was over, it was the next year, and everything was back to normal.

Megan had been waiting for Tim to ask her out all evening at the reception. She'd tried to hint earlier, but he hadn't taken the bait. By the time Angie had left them, she'd given up on him and was about to suggest a lovely restaurant for a meal, when he'd blurted? Yes, blurted out his nearly incoherent offer. That will do, she thought to herself, resigned and knowing he wasn't like Simon, didn't have that innate confidence Simon had, and if what Simon had said was true, it really was hardly surprising. He'd obviously been so relieved at her reply, a little embarrassed, a tight smile and eyes averted. She'd smiled, she knew him. Still. Why would he think I would say anything but yes? He hadn't noticed her smile, but relief exuded from him.

Was it going to be awkward? Possibly for the first few minutes.

It had been over five years since they'd last met. Their phone conversation last week had been so awkward. He'd been nervous, that much was obvious, but thoughts of Simon's confession had distracted her, and she'd been unable to concentrate. The phone call had lasted all of three minutes or so, mostly uncomfortable silences, filled with barely audible sentences. Thirty years and more they'd been friends, best friends, and it had finished with stuttering goodbyes and "I'll see you next week." Afterwards, she'd felt terrible. She'd wanted some sort of a sign. Something obvious. She'd hoped that he would sweep her off her feet with some witty repartee that would put her at ease, and then she'd know. But he hadn't, and the confession that Simon had dumped on her had sat with her like the proverbial devil on her shoulder, making her second guess all her thoughts about him. She realized later that it had been a mistake to assume he would resolve it for her, just hand it to her. So, she'd been determined to be proactive, positive, and she would do better at the reception. She'd planned the meeting down to the hug and calling him Timmy to break the tension.

They'd met once after she'd gotten married. At Stephanie's birthday party, so six years then! She was starting to understand just how much her wedding had hurt him. They'd barely spoken at Stephanie's party, where Peter had been with her wherever she went for most of that evening. Even at the time, she thought it a little smothering, but she loved him and loved that he fawned on her. She'd managed a short moment alone with Tim, and she'd really enjoyed his company. It had been great to reminisce, and they easily slipped into banter, talking about whatever they talked about, she couldn't remember what, but it had been so easy and comfortable. They'd both been such good friends with Simon, and outside of Shelly, Tim had been her best friend, and somewhere it had been lost. In those days, he'd always been there for her, and she loved being with him, and apart from the kiss, which she remembered fondly, nothing else romantic had happened between them. She'd thought maybe that he would ask her out on a date or something after that night but then nothing happened. He appeared to just disappeared. But she remembered the kiss, she'd always remembered the kiss.

Julian's parents' place was huge, and the parents were both away on business. Some of the seniors had bought some beer, and Tim's friend Nick was a very good disc jockey.

We're standing at the edge of the makeshift dance floor, looking out over the people dancing, and there's a pause in our conversation. Tim has a beer in hand and I'm drinking a soda, and we're very comfortable in the silence. It's nice. Then Tim starts to sing along with the song, and I'm both surprised and intrigued.

"You like Luther?" I ask him, stopping his little performance.

"Damn straight," he smiles back. He is so cute when he smiles. He usually looks so serious, but he has a great, if rare in public, smile.

I recall that he smiles when we're alone, and he positively beams at the end of a gig.

"Luther?" I reply, shaking my head, still in disbelief.

"Well, apart from the fact he has a great voice," that I knew, "he also has one of the very best bass players playing for him. Actually, one you know very well," he continues, then takes a short sip from his can.

"Really?" I have no clue who he's talking about. I like R&B to dance to and have had a long-time crush on Luther's voice, but mostly I listen to Classical and Jazz, though I must admit, that I miss rocking with Simon and the band, now that he's at college. Tim and I still jam and sometimes we get Karl to play with us, though he's already getting professional gigs around town, building himself a very good reputation. Those were great, fun nights. Karl reckoned we should get a regular gig, but Tim didn't think he was ready to perform Jazz live. The truth was that he missed Simon, because without Simon it just didn't seem the same. I must confess I feel the same.

"Miles," he answers simply.

"Miles?" I shake my head, confused.

"He played with Miles," he states as if I really should know all of this. I'm now finding it a little exasperated.

"Luther Vandross' bass player played with Miles Davis?"

"That's why I started to listen to him. I had been listening avidly to Tutu and found out that Miller also played with Vandross, so I thought I'd listen to him a bit more closely. I mean R&B as a whole is littered with some fantastic bass players." I raise my eyebrows at his mini lecture. I know that, and he knows it. Anyway, I've had enough of the music appreciation lecture.

"I know. Anyway, why are we talking? Let's dance." I grab his arm, and before he can reply, I've dragged him onto the makeshift dance floor, where other couples are already smooching. I wrap one arm around his neck and take his hand, he pulls me close and we slip into the rhythm of the music. I can feel his heart beating against my breast through the rise and fall of our breathing, and I'm savoring the moment, the closeness. In my ear, so close to him, I can just hear his breathing over the music and I can make out that he is singing and humming along quietly. Luther's words of love start to play in my head, and I think of Tim here in my arms, and I think we could make a great couple. The idea pervades my thoughts. It really could work, but I'm conflicted. We have been best friends for so long, what would it do to that? What if we broke up? And the lyrics keep playing in my head. We continue to circle to the music, hips swaying in time, the warmth and pressure of his body feels so comforting. He pulls away slightly and I look him squarely in the face, and he's staring at me as we turn. I'm feeling flush with excitement and an attraction for him I've rarely admitted. I can't resist it. I lean in and kiss him. Why? I don't know, it just seems right in this moment, and he quickly responds. I close my eyes and enjoy the moment, a quick peek tells me that he too has closed his eyes, and then he pulls me passionately closer, lifting me, and I feel like I'm flying. We explore our first kiss. Teeth nipping, tongues exploring, lips massaging each other in mutual satisfaction. He's a good kisser, I tell myself, a really good kisser, and I enjoy the moment, responding to him as he responds to me. Then the music stops, and I pull away slightly embarrassed. I move away from him thinking that I need some space, a bit of breathing space. I've just kissed my best friend. Was that a good idea? The next thing I know I'm surrounded by Shelly and friends and we're talking about stuff I can't even recall, and all I'm thinking is how Tim is such an amazing kisser.

Then he disappeared. She hadn't seen him for weeks after that. Then suddenly, after the New Year's Eve party, everything was apparently back to normal, as if nothing happened, as if there had never been that moment, there had never been a dance and a kiss. That party never came up, and the kiss was never mentioned, and later she'd thought it was better if it just stayed that way, though she felt a twinge of regret. Of course, now, after Simon's confession, she wasn't so sure. Now, there is an overwhelming thought that this guy, my friend, might just be my soulmate. There he was right in front of me, and I didn't even try. I had a moment, a small window, and I missed it. What am I saying? Small window? I've known this guy, and he's been my best friend for over 30 years? I've done nothing, he's as good as any person I've ever known, and he loves me. And I him?

She knew the answer to that question, but she still kept on asking herself.

Megan only lived a few blocks from the restaurant, and Tim walked her home. The evening was cool and pleasant, the traffic suitably noisy for a Manhattan late evening. They walked slowly, drinking in each other's company, chatting but keeping their innermost thoughts private. As far as Tim was concerned, he knew he still loved her, possibly more than he ever had as a teenager. He tried to quantify it. Did his passion for her burn as it did when he was a teenager? Young hormones vs old hormones, flowing differently: which was more or which less? The thought kept coming to him as he watched her, no, just different. He'd known other women since then, and he had had good and bad relationships. He had even fallen in love a few times. Christina? Mary? Yes, but they were all different, his love for them had been real, but deep down there had always been Megan. Is that what had ruined those relationships? Was it his unwavering love for Megan that had stopped him having any lasting relationship with Chris? That had made Mary finally give up on him?

Tonight, it had all seemed the same, familiar, slipping into old patterns with an old friend, but it wasn't the same. They'd had conversations that just weren't possible then, both having grown in knowledge, appreciation, and maturity. He had more experience to compare her too, and she hadn't let him down. But older now, still single, have experienced life's disappointments, he was a little more cautious. He knew he'd have to see her more, be with her more, before he could make any decision. Their rekindled friendship meant so much to him, and he didn't want to lose it or her again. Though deep down the teenager was winning, the teenager had waited and wasted years, and Mature Tim was letting him win, he didn't want to wait, he still wanted her, to be with her. He wanted more than anything for her to be "the one", and nothing except her refusal would stop him from trying. He had to try, he had to tell her, he thought resolutely, and Mature Tim acquiesced and said fine, go for it. Now, just wait for the right time, the right moment. Soon.

"Thanks, Tim, I had a lovely evening." Here, at last, he thought, as he looked up at the looming tower, which contained her apartment, disappointed. He could feel his prior confidence disappearing. He looked at her, his passion overpowering, his skepticism and self-doubt still controlling him, and he could think of nothing to say, his mind racing with responses and questions and answers to the very questions he was currently formulating. She smiled, and he melted.

Megan watched Tim. She had every intention of seeing him again, but he seemed to have stopped talking, seemed a bit at a loss. She chuckled to herself, and again remembered what Simon had told her just those few weeks ago: "Tim loves you, probably more than I do." At first, she'd been confused when he'd dropped that bombshell on her. Then she'd been annoyed. Why would Simon tell her that now? Why not before Peter? Why hadn't Tim tried years ago, when she'd waited for him to ask her out after they'd kissed at the Christmas party? He hadn't spoken to her for weeks after that kiss. Then everything was at it had been before. Just friends. She looked at her life and where it was now. Divorced. No children – something she desperately wished for. Oh, and I've just finished another long term, doomed, pain in the ass, wish I'd never met him, relationship. She felt a brief bitterness from that, but there in front of her was a man she'd known for years and who loved her, fumbling for words because he's shy and afraid to lose her friendship. Then she understood why Simon had told her.

Just a few weeks before the accident they'd met up after a show she was in. Simon had been quiet and subdued, and Megan had a feeling that there was something he wanted to tell her, but he never did. She now knew, of course, that that something was Angela, but she'd been caught up in her own problems and hadn't let him talk. Instead, she'd gone on about being single and alone again. Back living in New York City, and, of course, her divorce, which he'd already known about, and finally, her latest breakup with a guy he'd never met. And Simon? He'd listened patiently through all of it. She had barely let him get a word in edgeways, just the odd encouraging grunt and nod showing he was giving her his full attention and understood what she was going through. He was a better listener now than he'd ever been before, and she'd needed someone to talk to. She had even considered flirting with him, to see how that might go since she was enjoying his company. She couldn't remember the last time she'd felt so relaxed with someone, but that idea had quickly been squashed. With the few words he did manage to get out, he'd mentioned Tim, and now she knew why! Oh, Tim, I am so sorry. Well, this time I'm not waiting, and she did what she'd done those many years ago. She leaned in and pulled him towards her and kissed him. Wrapping her arms around his neck, she pulled him gently but firmly. Luther's words started playing in her mind.

Tim stood there with his mind in turmoil. He had things to say, but couldn't decide on what to say first. So, he just stood there, conflicted and confused, looking at her with his thoughts consuming him and giving him no answers. Come on, just tell her. Tell her how you feel. How you still feel even after all these years. Or at least just ask her out again. Yeah, just ask her out. Okay, where? Anywhere for Christsakes! He was still looking at her, unable to utter a single word, when she leaned in and kissed him. Her arms circled his neck, and he found himself responding. His thoughts were silenced as he let himself be lost in the moment. Everything he felt about her flooded over and through him, and he was transported back to being a teenager. She held him tightly and the kiss continued passionately. He wanted to sing, as at last Mature Tim joined in.

After a few minutes, they disengaged slightly, lips parting but still embracing. She smiled at him, and pecked him gently and quickly on the lips and smiled again, looking intently into his eyes. The teenager in her tried to think of something to say. A woman walked by and smiled at them, a little knowing smile with a nod of the head. Megan, almost burst out laughing with delight, and Tim pulled her closer in response.

The peck on his lips lingered. Momentarily distracted, Tim's gaze followed the passerby for a moment, his thoughts registering her body language, but he wasn't embarrassed, though he knew that in another time, in another place, with another person, he would have been. The touch of Megan's skin and the sound of her breathing brought his attention back to the lady in his arms, the center of his universe, and he could still feel that delicate after-kiss, its inherent romance filling him, and yet the teenager was still dominating, the years difficult to get past.

"So, Megan, err, would you like to, err, go out again?" he asked, indecision controlling his thoughts, as he was still held in the grip of the kiss.

"Well, I was thinking maybe you should come up," she suggested, her eyes twinkling, and laughter lines betraying her thoughts.

"What? Upstairs here?" He knew he'd heard correctly, but still only dared to believe that he had.

"Yes, my dear, upstairs here," and inside she laughed, as she delicately stroked his cheek with the tips of her fingers. He's so sweet, and her mind raced back to her teenage friend.

"Oh, of course, I'd love to," he stammered, but he still didn't move, caught in the grip of her touch and the doubt in his teenage thoughts.

"Well, we could just stand here," she said, seeing his struggle and regarding it as a bit of a compliment, "but I have a better idea," She hooked his arm and steered him towards her front door. He didn't resist.

"Yes, good idea," he muttered, wishing he was less awkward.

"And maybe you can cook me breakfast tomorrow morning," she said brightly. Then she laughed aloud, and he felt the laugh ring through him, relaxing his muscles, removing the tension, as if a huge weight had been lifted, as he let her lead him in.

Part Four: New

Beginnings

Doubts

"Hi, Tim, how's it going?"

"Great, and you?"

"Well, I'm dead," and he smiles. He's standing there bigger than life, his blond hair moving in a breeze. I can't feel anything, but he's smiling that smile I still remember so vividly, and he looks like he's still back in high school. Me? I'm sitting on a really uncomfortable chair looking up at him, and my back is aching.

"Yeah, I know. I miss you," and I start crying.

"Don't cry, everything will be okay," and he's starts crying too, but there's still a big smile on his face.

"Really?" I sniff.

"Really," he laughs, tears rolling down his cheeks.

"I just miss you," I reiterate.

"I know, and I miss you too," he sits beside me and starts singing. There's a microphone in his hand, though it's not connected to any visible amp. "I'm a Monkey," he drones, and the sound comes from everywhere, and I join in with him on the bass, which I now realize has been around my neck the whole time.

"Where's Megan?" he asks as I'm still playing, though there's now no sound coming out.

"Do you want me to play keyboards?" and suddenly I'm in front of Megan's keyboard, and he's standing beside me, and we're both staring at the keys. There's music coming out of the keyboard, and the keys are moving, but we're not doing anything: just staring. He looks up at me, but I don't know how because he's taller, and I'm thinking about the laws of physics, asking myself how is that possible? We're both standing, and he's taller than me. His smile is unwavering.

"No, no need. I just need to talk to her. I miss her too."

"So do I. I always miss her."

"I know you do. You love her, don't you?"

"More than anyone I've ever loved."

"What? Even more than me?" he asks with feigned indignation.

"Even more than you," I answer with a sense of guilt because he's dead, and I truly love and miss my friend.

"Do you think you love her more than I loved her?"

"I don't know," I reply cagily, as I know how much he loved her, but no one can love her more than me, I think, with a hint of a question.

"I mean we dated. She wanted me, came after me."

"I know," I'm starting to worry where this conversation is going. He jumps up and starts dancing. He's wearing his college football kit and is throwing a ball to me. I have no idea where it came from, but the next thing I know it's hurtling towards me. Spinning in that cool spiral that quarterbacks manage, but I could never do. I miss the catch, which reminds me of school. Athletics really wasn't my thing, however much I wanted it to be.

"Come on, Tim, you can do better than that," he says with a hint of disappointment, and he throws another. I try to catch that too, but I can't seem to be able to. Balls are flying at me, and he keeps on throwing them, and I try, but I just can't catch any of them.

"You really are not very good at this, are you?" he taunts me.

"I just can't seem to get hold of any," I answer perplexed. It looks so easy, but they all seem to slip through my hands. I think I'm about to catch one. It's there, right in my hands, but then it isn't.

"Tim? Tim? Tim?" he chides, "can't you keep hold of anything?" the smile is starting to annoy me as I keep on missing the balls.

"I don't know," and I'm still frantically trying to catch the balls; I want to get just one. They are coming thick, but not very fast, and Simon's not even throwing them. He's just watching me with that smile on his face.

"Seriously, my friend, you're not doing very well are you?"

"I'm trying,"

"How are you going to keep Megan?"

"I love her,"

"And she loves you, but she also loves me."

"I know," I answer with gratitude since at last the balls have stopped coming, but the ground is littered with them. I start kicking at them at him, but he ignores them.

"She's always loved me," he smiles at me.

"I know."

"We were going to start dating again," he tells me.

"I know, she told me she'd thought about it."

"If I hadn't died, she'd be with me. You do realize that, don't you?"

"Yes, I do."

"You know what that makes you?"

"What?" I ask knowing.

"You know," he teases.

"Yes, I do. I'm the rebound?"

"Yes, you're the rebound. It would have been all me if I hadn't died," he starts crying again, but he also will not stop smiling.

"But she's with me now."

"But for how long?"

"You told her that I loved her. Why did you do that?"

"I felt sorry for you. I wasn't going to be around so I thought, why not my best friend? You know, to help you out a bit. I mean after thirty years you've not done anything really, just one little kiss, and she's done nothing. You needed a shove, a really big one."

"So, what are you telling me now? That she's really yours?"

"I'm dead, Tim, all she has is a memory of me, a mighty powerful one though."

"I know."

"Are you doubting her now?"

"I don't know, I love her."

"Does she love you?"

"I think so."

"You think so? Hasn't she told you?"

"Not yet, we went out, we kissed, we made love."

"Well, that's a good start: Touchdown for the man with the bass. But she didn't tell you, did she?"

"No."

"She didn't say 'I love you, Tim' did she?"

"No. No. No. Simon. She didn't tell me." I am getting annoyed, and I'm crying again.

"Be careful, Tim, you don't want to get hurt again, do you?"

"I love her," and now the tears won't stop

"I know Tim, but be careful…"

Tim lay in bed, the dream state still upon him as it filtered through his thoughts, the details still raw in his mind. She didn't say she loved me, he thought, but it had been a such a special night. The best. But she didn't say she loved me, he thought, as he drifted back off to sleep again.

Decisions

Angie was now starting to understand how much she missed her father. Thoughts of him pervaded every moment, every sound, every smell, and of course the apartment brought thoughts of him constantly. She wondered what he would say in both real and imagined circumstances. She played with various responses to the same issue. What he might say, if he'd laugh, or if he'd give her that look of disapproval that never possessed anger but left little doubt about his opinion. During the funeral, she'd been preoccupied with that situation but also with being alone in the company of so many strangers. She was angry, uncommonly so, at her loss. Her reaction had been to take it out on his friends who had known and would always know him so much better than she had. Tim had helped, though. With Tim's help, she'd gone to bed that night relaxed and content, glad to feel relief from the days of oppressive depression and numbing grief. It wasn't gone, but it was much less oppressive, staying nicely in the background, present but not dominating her thoughts.

She'd been in this apartment for a couple of weeks now, trying to make it her own, to make it feel like home. She hadn't succeeded. It was still so much his. It felt like his, smelt like his. How was this place ever going to feel like hers? And yet she wanted it to. She'd loved the place when he was here with her. But now? Now she was stuck in some sort of limbo, an emotional and intellectual stasis. Auntie Kay had been up last weekend, and having her here had been a welcomed distraction. Angie had shown her aunt around New York. They'd taken in a show and eaten at a very nice restaurant that Simon had loved, courtesy of Jason the lawyer. Aunt Kay had been suitably impressed. She'd scrutinized the menu, questioning ingredients and techniques. Angie had laughed at the exasperation on the waiter's face, as he'd tried to keep up with questions he didn't know the answers to but which he seemed loathe to admit. Then she'd enjoyed watching her aunt savoring each dish, each flavor, every mouthful, reminding her of Simon's passion for great food as well. Auntie Kay couldn't stop talking about the food after they'd left, reminiscing over every dish, each bite, the combination of the flavors, and how she was going to try and prepare a particular dish in her restaurant when she returned to Boston, but with a West Indian slant. Well, I'm not going to have too much trouble getting Auntie to visit if I can find a restaurant like that for her next visit. Angie had enjoyed acting as the travel guide and New York expert, especially for her aunt, and though her aunt had been a welcomed distraction, the trip had been soured by one thought: New York wasn't the same without him. The galleries were still interesting, the food still very tasty, the sunsets still beautiful, and it was still very noisy, but all in all, it was not the same place anymore without him. Without her dad. She'd only known him for just over three months, and then he was gone, and now she was missing him so very much, painfully so. She tried to understand, to think through why she missed him so much, hoping that maybe understanding would lessen the pain. She hadn't come up with a satisfactory answer, most certainly not one that lessened the pain enough. She just missed him, and that thought brought constant, renewed pain. She would see him in her mind's eye and reiterate the same questions. Was it the smile? Or the way he switched from verbosity, when his passions were lit, to his usual brevity, when it was, how did he put it? Just stuff, he'd say. She smiled at the memory, his face scrunching up when he said "stuff." Hinting at a small level of distaste for the insignificant. She really missed that smile. He was always smiling. Everything she did always produced a smile from him. And he was so passionate about music, sports, his friends, and especially me. She knew she'd never be able to see New York in quite the same light anymore, but on the other hand, it would always remind her of the best of him. Generous, considerate, loving. It was hard to determine if it was just that he was making up for lost time, or if he was so riddled with guilt, and she knew that he was, that he was trying so much harder than he should and that she wasn't really witnessing the real man at all. That's such a facetious argument, she told herself. She could only judge him on how he had treated her. She'd forgiven him for what he'd done as a youth. She'd forgiven Mom and Auntie Kay, though what was there really to forgive? They were all young and stupid. Wasn't that how Auntie Kay had put it? And she was right: don't we all make mistakes? She looked down at her growing belly and chuckled humorlessly. Don't we? Am I any different? It still bothered her though, still grated, and sometimes, though those times were now lessening, it still bought a flood of tears to her eyes. The man she knew, her dad, wasn't a dumb college kid anymore. The man she had gotten to know had most certainly never denied what he'd done, never made excuses for his actions. He'd loved her without question, with honesty and commitment, and that's all I could have asked of him. He treated me as if I was the most important person in the world, and for a while, I was, she thought wistfully. And as for my mistake? He helped me come to terms with it. In many respects more so than Auntie Kay had. He was so enthusiastic about the baby. Auntie Kay just accepted it in her stride, a gift from God she would say, something which we just had to accept. Yes, mistakes had been made, accidents happen, but we accept them and move on, she'd said, but not Simon. He thought the baby was more than just a gift, the child was something to be treasured, my own personal miracle. There was a shame, no blame to be attributed, as far as he was concerned. He thought I was lucky. He would have screamed the news from the rooftops if he could have. I'm still not sure that I totally agreed with him, but the sentiment had been hard to resist. Yes, he might have been making up for his mistake, for lost time, but that was how he had felt, and it had been so infectious, and so gratefully received. Through all this pain she knew that knowing him, even for just those few months, was a gift she would always treasure and how lucky she'd been. Yes, it could have been years, it should have been years, but I'll always cherish the few months we had.

Sometimes she found herself comparing them, lining up the positive and negatives of the two people who loved her most in the world. Auntie Kay and Dad. Both thought the world of her, had given up something, without question and without reward for her. It was an easily made decision: Auntie Kay won hands down. She had time on her side, of course, and considering all that it entails in bringing up a young girl, someone else's little girl, as a single mother, especially since she didn't have to. As if she wouldn't have, she smiled to herself. But Dad, in three months, had offered her something different and valuable. It was a good second place.

She looked around the room, his room. She knew it was hers, though it was not yet official until all the paperwork and taxes were complete, but she still thought of it as his apartment, his room. Though she wasn't actually sad, a melancholy settled on her and the brooding would not go away. It probably didn't help that she had nothing constructive to do. It was hard to start work on any new art when her thoughts and considerations were first and foremost for her coming child, let alone this constant barrage of thoughts about her late father. She really should nip down to Blick, the art store, and get some art materials, she kept telling herself, but she hadn't. She hadn't felt any real desire to paint. She had done some sketching, but just dabbling, nothing of note, and wondered if Natalie ever had that problem. She'd had a child. How did that affect her art? She was also feeling a little intimidated by Natalie's works on display here, even though she enjoyed them. Her baby kicked, reminding her of its presence, him or her, she thought. She seemed to be stuck in a rut. It was either the baby or thoughts of Simon or Auntie Kay; everything else just seemed trivial.

Right now, thoughts of her dad dominated. The last few times she'd been in New York, it had been with him. He had arranged dinners and trips around the boroughs, pointing out their good and bad points, always acquiescing to her requirements, always trying to make up for lost time. He'd known he couldn't roll back the years, that he couldn't be a regular dad, and he didn't try to do that. She felt tears rising up through her, but she held them back. I miss you Dad, I really do. She touched her belly, you'll get to know them both, I promise, she told her child.

And thinking of the child, she was so desperate to have a name for him? Her? It? She hated calling a baby "it," but she didn't know and didn't want to know the sex. She was, of course, curious, but she didn't care one way or the other if it was a boy or a girl. But some sort of name for my son or my daughter would be nice, I don't mind which! She laughed. Though depending on the weather, or my current mood, with whom I am talking, what I'm eating, sometimes I prefer the idea of a girl and then sometimes a boy. She looked down and patted her belly. As long as you're healthy. She left it at that. Right now, she was in a good mood and either was fine.

Earlier that morning, she'd seen her new doctor. He'd been recommended by her usual one in Boston. He was nice. Elderly and fatherly, not my fatherly, she thought, thinking of Simon, but just like grandfathers in movies. Why do we say fatherly when what we really mean is grandfatherly? He hadn't even asked if she'd wanted to know. She'd been tempted to ask, just to see his reaction, but she really didn't want to know, so couldn't really see the point in asking him. It seemed a bit frivolous and futile. He was quite old – really old she admitted to herself – not requiring any politeness in her company. And quirky, definitely grandfatherly. Initially, she'd felt a little awkward having a man as her doctor. She'd always had a woman, even as a child, but he had put her at ease with his comforting banter and his incredibly funny sense of humor. Definitely quirky, she thought, chuckling at the memory of the appointment and a particularly funny anecdote. Auntie has always insisted on female doctors, but she'll approve when she meets him.

She pushed herself into the softness of the sofa – it was an extremely comfortable sofa, so easy to relax in, so easy to doze off in its depths. Right now, though she was wide awake. The TV was on in the background, though she wasn't watching anything in particular. She sat for a moment and let herself relax, basking in the comfort of her new home. Mine! She thought. She remembered her first realization of this. How she had looked around for one minute, then rushed around the kitchen, then splayed out on the bed in her huge bedroom. Just huge, that bed must be three times the size of my bed at home. And the view! The New York skyline with all its lights and shadows at night. Then she was out of the bedroom strolling on the balcony and back to the split level double living room. It's incredible. I could never have dreamed of owning such a place ever, anywhere, let alone in Manhattan! And yet? The question hung over her, she was still waiting for the lawyers and accountants to tell her the final details of Simon's will. She knew much of it was in a Trust, presumably to ensure she didn't spend it all at once, she laughed to herself, but she had no idea how much was available to her and if it would be enough to take care of her and her child, and she so dearly wanted to go to college. It had been her mother's dying wish, extracting a promise literally on her deathbed, and she knew her dad had also wanted her to go as well. Angie had studied hard for it: she'd had great SAT scores, some very good offers, a couple of full scholarships from some okay colleges and some partial ones from some very good colleges. She'd accepted Columbia's offer, she'd considered a few others in New York City, been rejected by a couple, and it was only a partial scholarship, but she loved the program and she knew a few people there from high school. And it was in Manhatten! Mom would have been proud, that's what Auntie Kay always said, and Angie knew it. Her next few years had been all mapped out: college, probably a Masters, then the life of a struggling artist, before discovery and fame. There had been no plan for a baby.

The comfort of the room faded from her thoughts as the memory of what had brought about her current predicament produced some bitterness and regret. Well, that is what was supposed to happen. That's how it was supposed to be, but it isn't, is it? Not now. Just one reckless night – my eighteenth birthday celebration: a bar, a fake id, and a little too much to drink. Now, though, she wondered, would it have made any difference? I knew what I was doing, what I wanted,

I'd even brought some condoms, a lot of good that did, forgetting them at the moment I needed them.

He had been such a charming man; apparently a married, charming man. Dark, near pitch black skin that glistened in the subtle bar lighting. Well dressed, and well spoken, softly spoken. His eyes were always for me. She recalled fantasies of him after she'd first seen him. The reality? She realized later, when sober, that the sex hadn't even been that good: fumbling in the car, lots of scrambling and panting. He wasn't much of a kisser, and there'd been no foreplay, and it hadn't been exactly comfortable. At all! She'd planned this birthday celebration many months ago, and the night had been such a disappointment. Reality can be such a downer. Eyes for her? All he'd wanted was the sex. Period!

It was supposed to have been with Steven, she thought bitterly. He'd broken up with her for another girl; asshole! Two weeks before my birthday. What did I ever see in him? She was still angry with him, but she also knew that she had liked him a lot. So, it hadn't been him, it had been the charming man at the bar. She'd seen him a couple of times before, eyeing her, giving a quick smile, his intentions obvious, though in her fantasies there was more, much more. They'd chatted, just small talk and a lot of flirting, long, searching eye contact, fleeting touching. Every time she'd seen him there, he would offer her and her partner in crime, Jane or Gabby, a drink and they would talk about, well, nothing in particular, and her friend would invariably wander off, leaving them staring into each other's eyes. A quick kiss at the end of the evening, nothing too intimate, but the implication was there, and her fantasies grew. So, it hadn't been too difficult to get his attention that night. She'd dressed up in her sexist black number. It was very short and tight, and she'd paired it with some killer high heels – black with that distinctive red sole. She'd changed at Gabby's. Auntie Kay would never have let her out of the house dressed like that! She looked great, she'd thought then, and he'd positively tripped over himself when she'd hinted to him her intentions; he'd literally coughed into his drink. I'd hinted? I hadn't hinted, she thought, I'd told him what Steve was missing tonight, and that I was considering my alternatives as I batted my eyes at him, leaning over to show my cleavage, touching his leg, holding his hand, smiling coyly, making all the moves. She grimaced at the memory. I would laugh if I'd watched some other girl doing that, be embarrassed for her. She really didn't know whether to laugh or cry at the thought.

It hadn't hurt, even though some had said it would, and some had said that it would be disappointing. They were right about that part, she hadn't even had an orgasm! But later, she had exaggerated, okay lied, and boasted about it to friends. It was so cool, an older man. Making up stories about how he was going to leave his wife, but that she'd had to tell him: No way! I don't need that sort of relationship now, I'm off to college after high school, I'll be in New York in the fall. There'd been such disappointment on his face. Her friends had believed her, and she loved the envy and admiration in their eyes, and the new respect and attention she was getting. However, that hadn't lasted for long.

First, it had been the sickness, followed by the counting, followed by a test, then another test, disbelief and prayer, and then another test. The doctor had confirmed what she now already knew, and her world, her future, came crashing down around her. Auntie Kay had been distraught when head bowed, tears brimming, cheeks red with shame, she'd told her of her predicament. Her aunt was the only one she could tell. Your mother would be so ashamed, she'd said, and had kept on reminding her; as if she needed to be reminded of the obvious, but however mad Auntie Kay was, and she left no doubting she was, she was still there for her niece. She had held her and rocked her to sleep each night for the next few weeks as Angie tried to come to terms with this new reality, this life-changing mistake.

She could have an abortion, her aunt told her, though she knew her aunt's opinion on that subject. She could keep the child, and her aunt promised she would help her in any way possible. She knew her aunt, and had no doubt that she would be supportive, but did she want a child now? So close to college, she had already delayed her entrance and had to make her mind up soon about the baby. She'd be six or seven months pregnant by the time the semester started. A newborn baby and starting college didn't really seem a viable option, and that thought always brought a flood of tears, but she had to decide about her baby and soon. Each day she made her mind up, and later each day she would tell herself that she would sleep on it, and each new day brought indecision.

She recalled the day when she'd finally decided against abortion, when she realized that she had no other option or desire but to keep the child. There was no need to sleep on it anymore, no more need to think about it and the next day and the next the decision was still the same.

"Are you doing all right, my love?" Auntie Kay looks down at me with concern. She is dressed up in one of her favorite dresses, the deep blue one, French Ultramarine to my artist's mind. The cut of it really shows off her ample bosom, as well as one of her handsome legs. She's going out on a date tonight, I conclude, and I'm trying to smile through my current despair, which at this moment is certainly getting the better of me. I'm curled up on the sofa, not really watching anything in particular, the show I was watching had just finished, and I'm flipping the channels and feeling very sorry for myself. I'm thinking about sucking my thumb, but there's my aunt staring down at me with concern etched in her face. I know I will do so when she's gone. I'm still unable to come to terms with this pregnancy, and this stupid mistake. That particular night is playing in my mind again, like a cringeworthy scene in a terrible movie. Tears are welling up, but I keep them at bay, at least for the moment as I look up at my aunt, knowing that if I start to cry she'll start fussing. On the pregnancy I haven't decided; one day I'm pro-choice: my choice, my future. The next day I'm pro-life; the child's life, it's future. Whichever one I choose it's my choice. I do know whatever choice I make, one has to be made very soon if I want to exercise any choice at all.

I notice that she's holding a large ledger. Working? Now? I wish she'd relax and have some fun, someone around here should. Come on Auntie, go out, have some fun, get a life. Apart from me, her restaurant is her life, I tell myself, and I smile a little at the thought of the food, tasty and comforting and spicy, bringing up favorite memories. Auntie, you work hard, too hard, so please, go out and have some fun, I beg in my head. Well, at least she's not working tonight, and there's some leftover curry and rice in the fridge. Chicken? Goat? I can't remember, but that doesn't really make any difference. I'll heat that up after she's gone. The thought of warm spices, countered by the dryness of the rice and peas, start playing in my mind, giving me at least a little comfort.

"Auntie, what's that? Are you working on accounts? Now?" I ask, with an air of nonchalance that I don't really feel, trying to lighten my mood, though not entirely succeeding. After I ask, I realize that I don't care. I just want her to leave. I want to be left alone, so I can be miserable and feel sorry for myself on my own, but I can't show that or she'll start fussing. Go on, off, off, off, please leave me alone, and yes, I know I'm feeling sorry for myself, but what the heck. Can't I?

"What?" She looks at where I'm looking, at the large book in her hand, "Oh this?" she exclaims, as if she'd just realized she was holding it, "This isn't work. This is for you."

"Really?" for me? I'm intrigued, "What is it?" I hope it's not a photo album, I suddenly think with despair, for pictures of the baby. Oh, another hint at what she wants me to do, without actually telling me. I know her opinion on this, but I can't really complain, can I? Because she has kept her opinion to herself all this time, waiting for me to decide, but please, not a photo album. I roll my eyes at the thought, and I let out a small groan at the idea, frustrated again at the decision I need to make.

"It's a photo album," she replies. You've got to be kidding me, I scream in my head, wondering if I should laugh or cry, and I suddenly feel myself deflate at the thought. She sits beside me, and I uncurl into a seated position. She pushes my still hot cup of cocoa to one side to give herself some room. I'm eyeing the cocoa, wishing I could hide behind the mug, but I know my aunt, and she's not finished with me yet, so I turn away from the mug. "It's one of your mom's photo albums." My ears perk up and I'm suddenly a little more awake, a little more attentive.

"Sorry? What was that?" I ask, sure I heard correctly, but just in case I didn't.

"This," and she taps it with a well glossed red fingernail, "is one of your mother's photo albums," she repeats slowly, giving me a look of disapproval, something I'm used to from a woman who doesn't like to repeat herself.

"Really?" I didn't recognize it, but she does have my full attention, and I return a look full of contrition and apology. She's nods, and a wide grin registers her acknowledgement.

"Yes, I found it earlier today, I've been looking for it for days. It's from after college," and she gives me a strange glance, and I know that there is a during college one, and I understand that implication. I let it slide, now eager for more of my mom's past, which is now lying before me on the table. "I thought you'd like to see us in our prime," and she puffs herself out, her large bosom stretching the dress to its limits, and I wonder with a grin if she really should go out wearing it. I laugh with her, and she hugs me, and I enjoy the familiar touch of her body. Her grip tightens, and I revel in the security of her embrace and love. The moment is fleeting, but it serves its purpose, and I feel a little less moody when we separate. I might not be happy, but I'm at least smiling.

"I have to go, sweetheart. I'm already late. Have a look through it, enjoy." She stands up with a bit of a huff, then strokes my hair, "I'll see you later, darling. Don't wait up for me," she gives me a knowing smile and I laugh. She's fiddling with her dress, smoothing it out, ensuring her breasts are fully enclosed, well most of them anyway. The sight makes me smile, and for a moment at least, my woes and worries are behind me.

"See you tomorrow, Auntie," I emphasize, and she laughs back. She leaves me with my cocoa and the photo album, and for a moment I'm both scared and excited about the prospect of viewing this tome.

I sit up and look down at my stomach. Sometimes I think I can notice it, and every day, every now and then, I look in the mirror, front on and in profile, trying to see it. I can't, but I know it's there. The tests said so, the doctor said so, my body? The same. I take a deep breath and open the album, and there's my mother, barely older than I am now. Like mother like daughter, I think with a little disappointment, and I start to cry at the coincidence, and I feel her shame and her forgiveness. The tears are flowing and I've stopped trying to prevent them. I take a gulp of the hot cocoa, which still tastes good and warms me through and through, and as that warmth filters through my body I relax, the tears dry up and I continue to turn pages.

I'm now fully immersed in the book. There are some beautiful photos of Mom and Auntie discovering Boston, places so familiar to me having been born and raised here. The cocoa is ignored and getting cold as I study each photo, immersed in the history I've craved but could never have. Mom looked so young, and I chuckle. She's all smiles and laughter, and barely older than I am now, and she was so pretty. I have some photos of her later in life, after she had me. She was good looking then, but she was really pretty here in these pictures just after college. Then I turn a page and see Mom with Auntie Kay, and time pauses. Mom is noticeably pregnant here, and she's smiling as she dozes on Auntie's lap. She has no makeup on, and her hair is a mess, sticking out all over the place, I can already see myself plating it. It's long like mine, and I would not go out in public like that, I muse, but she looks so peaceful and content, and still so pretty. Aunt Kay has a faraway look, perhaps she was not ready when the photo was taken, perhaps she didn't know, and for a moment I wonder who took the photo, my artistic eye is telling me that that person knew how to frame it. She has one arm over the back of the sofa and the other cradling her sister, my mom, who has one hand resting on her belly as if protecting the child. Protecting me, I realize, and then suddenly, it's obvious. I know my decision. It's all there in one instant. I'm so surprised I haven't asked it before. What if Mom had decided to go through with an abortion? I suddenly ask myself. She was single, at college where she desperately wanted to be, her whole life was ahead of her, and she was with a man she loved. It seems like such an easy option. The repercussions are obvious to me. How could I have missed it? I wouldn't be asking myself this very question, would I? College can wait, my plans can wait. My baby comes first, and life will go on, just differently.

She'd waited up late for her aunt that night, and told her Auntie Kay of her decision before her aunt had barely entered into the house or even had time to remove her jacket. Her aunt had listened quietly, and after her niece had finished she just nodded, and then she held her gently, and talked softly, rocking the girl, as Angie cried herself to sleep.

That decision sparked another, one that temporarily caused a rift between her and her aunt. She had guessed correctly that her aunt would be annoyed, though she hoped the years and a new understanding of her niece, would have opened her mind. It hadn't. She had not been prepared for the level of resentment that her aunt still had for the man, her father. Auntie Kay had been furious when Angie had explained to her that she wanted to meet him, telling her that she didn't want the daughter of her sister being with "that lowlife shit." Angie was shocked at her aunt's use of profanity; she could barely remember her being so angry, and with such language. Livid was most certainly a better word. She'd stomped around the house for a week, few civil words passed between them, both adamant about their views on the matter. Angie was desperate, though. She was dependent on her aunt for everything, especially this piece of information, but she also loved her aunt. She needed to do this, and deep down she knew her aunt understood this, but she also needed to come to terms with it in her own time. Angie had to ask, she couldn't wait, she didn't have the time, and she had to find him before she had the baby. She didn't really know why; she just knew that it was vitally important. To her.

"I need his full name," she stated again, pressuring her aunt.

"Where does he live and work?" she asked.

"Auntie, I need your help," she pleaded.

"Please, Auntie," she begged, but her aunt refused to even broach the subject.

I, Simon...

For a week Aunt Kay had refused to even talk on any matter concerning him. Meals had been quick and quiet, chores suddenly plentiful. Then one morning, curled up in bed, thumb in mouth, the issue returning as she fully woke up, as she tried to decide on a new tactic after a week of failed ones, of begging, of threatening, of pleading and bribing, she found a note folded on her bed stand. She opened it, her heart racing with hope, her mind filled with doubt, and there were his name and address.

She had what she wanted, but that didn't mean Auntie Kay felt any better about her niece's desires and the demands. Her aunt, no less forgiving, was still angry, and Angie kept her distance, did her chores, and apart from a silently mouthed word of thanks, never mentioned the subject.

However, she soon found that wanting this information and having it were not the same thing. She had sat in front of her computer for hours, browsing the web, reading emails, finding new recipes, whilst she struggling over her letter. Now she had the details she needed, now that she now could find him, could talk to him, numerous excuses and doubts had entered her thoughts. What is he like? Will I like him? Will he like me? Will he want to see me? She'd found a picture of him on the web, more recent than those of the young college student she already had, and she had copied it, carefully drawing a detailed charcoal portrait, to get the feel of him, and yet the constant barrage of doubts and questions still assailed her, but it only temporarily delayed the inevitable.

It had been short and to the point. That will do, she thought, and she printed it off, read it, and immediately left the house to go to the post office before she could change her mind, determined that it would be sent. For a while she was pleased with herself, satisfied at the positive decision she'd made and executed.

The next day the doubts and questions returned. What if Auntie's right? What if he has no interest, no desire to see me, to know me? She wished she was back at school. At least there would be some distraction, but she wasn't, and she had very little to distract her during the day. She found it difficult to concentrate on her art or her cooking, and the next day things hadn't changed, hoping and waiting for his reply. He must know I exist, he could easily have found me, couldn't he? The next few days, she'd scanned all the post, before her aunt did, just in case. Wasting hours waiting for its arrival and then even more after, depressed when she found no reply. Until the letter arrived.

Dear Angie

Thank you for your letter. I'm so glad, so happy, yet also so sad. I am so sorry to hear the news of your mother. I know it's been many years, but barely a day goes by that I don't think of her: I have never forgotten her. Hearing of you is a bright light in my day, my week, my year. Of course, I would love to see you. I can think of nothing better.

I know this may be difficult, for both of us, but I will at least try to make up for the lost years and hope you are not disappointed.

Please reply with a date and I will come up and see you. I'm free any weekend you care to choose.

Thank you for reaching out to me.

Your father,

Simon

At first, she didn't arrange to meet up with him. She was afraid to, and the distance of the letters suited her. He never complained, never forced the issue. They communicated with letters for a few weeks, and when phone numbers were exchanged, thinking she was finally ready, she set a date.

"Auntie, I can't do it," there's a hint of panic in my voice.

"You can't do what, sweetheart?" I wonder if she really knows, or if she is just feigning ignorance, or if she really has forgotten.

"You know." She looks up from tidying the room, Swiffer in hand, a deep questioning look, and I can see she's deciding on how to react, "I'm supposed to be meeting my father this afternoon." I state as neutrally as I can, knowing there's going to be an unfavorable reaction, I'm starting to wish I hadn't mentioned it, but I need to talk to someone about it: I need to talk to her. She huffs and shrugs her shoulders, turns away from me, and acts at being even busier.

"And now you don't want to see him?" she suddenly asks while I'm still confused, as if this is a way for me to get out of this new predicament I've put myself into, which she'd always disagreed about, so why bring her in now?

"It's not that," I'm angry, both at her and at myself, but I need some help, some solace, "I really want to see him." She stops dusting, turns to face me, studying me for a moment, then flicks her duster over the table, the nearest object in her reach.

"So, what's the problem? Why ask me?" she asks, her voice rising in both pitch and volume, there is anger in that voice, and I notice that she's now stopped pretending to tidy up, the Swiffer just waving in the air, punctuating her reply.

"I'm scared," I plead.

"Oh, so now you're scared?" She's not letting up, and I can feel my tears coming.

"Auntie, please," there's no holding back and I burst out crying, huge heaving sobs. I stand with head bowed, tears dripping, staring at the floor, unable to face her, and suddenly her arms are around me, her warmth comforting me.

"There, there, my child, don't cry," her voice is soothing and calming.

"I'm so sorry, Auntie. I really want to see him, I do, but I'm so scared. I'm afraid I'll be such a letdown, and what do I say to him?

We've never met. He knows nothing about me, and I know so little about him," I'm babbling, and I know it. I can feel my heart hammering and the blood thumping in my head, overwhelming my thoughts. My arms are frozen to my rigid body, and I know that however much I want too, I won't be able to go.

"You, my sweet, you, will never be a letdown," she whispers, soothingly, "Look, it's simple. If you don't want to see him yet, then don't," she states it as if it's so obvious. I know it's the only way out, but guilt forbids me to admit it, to allow him to think I've chickened out, that I've been playing with him.

"But, Auntie, I really want to see him, I really do. It's just that..." I don't complete the sentence. I really am so scared. I don't even know how to tell her how scared I am.

"And that's natural, darling. Look, you just call him up, tell him you can't make it, tell him the truth or tell him a little lie," I give her a look of shock and skepticism, though inside I'm smiling, she's right, that's all I have to do, and I'll be ok. I can try again later when I have better prepared myself. "You should realize that if he's really worth it, if he really wants to know you, he will understand, he will give you time."

"Are you sure?" knowing that I am now okay. She pulls my head to her chest and hugs me close.

"I'm sure, my sweet."

"I don't want to lose him, but I'm just not ready yet," I say muffled into her breast. The tears have stopped, and I'm now feeling secure in her embrace, and though I'm happy with the decision, I still feel a touch of guilt.

"I'm sure he'll be ok."

It wasn't the only time I cancelled on him, but Auntie Kay was right, if not a little annoyed with her predictions. He kept on coming back. He would drive all the way up from New York, and when I cancelled he told me not to worry, there's no hurry. He never asked why or tried to extract some promise for the next time, and he never appeared to be angry. Though I wouldn't have been surprised if he had been. I would have been, but he didn't appear to be. My guilt lessened, and his patience soon paid off. And Auntie Kay? She's a truly forgiving person, however, she still huffed and puffed at the very mention of his name, but things between us were now back to normal.

It's a shame they never got on, Angie thought, and not for the first time, but it was nice having another person who truly, without question, cared for her, and now she missed him, she missed her dad. Dad? Simon? Sometimes they were one and the same. Sometimes they were two distinct people. She missed them both, and she loved them both. They were, at the end of the day, one and the same person. However, Simon was the guy in the band, the potential NFL player and ex-lover of a now famous artist. Her dad? Well? He was her dad. He wanted to protect her, help her, be there for her, be with her. Simon had wanted to show her the world, he had wanted her to experience all the good things he had and more besides. Now she was here in New York, but he wasn't anymore, neither Simon nor her dad were here now. She loved it here, and she wanted to stay, but they weren't here anymore to share it with her, and so now she wasn't sure. Now New York seemed lonely.

She had originally accepted the offer from Columbia, before the Big Mistake, and then she'd asked for a year off. They'd said it was no problem, that she could take the year off, and a place would be left open for her. She hadn't explained why when she'd made the request since she was so ashamed and worried they might think less of her and reject her request. Just taking a sabbatical, she had told them, before starting her studies. She'd be working at a non-profit, getting some life experience. Well, it really was a new life experience, and having babies doesn't pay! She looked down at her belly and stroked it, definitely an unexpected life experience, and smiled at the irony. I'm going to have to cancel, she knew, and that thought brought a wave of sadness and depression. Auntie Kay will help, of that there was no doubt in her mind. Though if she stayed in New York, Auntie Kay would come down only once a month or so, on her off weekends and vacations, and that just wouldn't be enough, would it? If I'm studying here I'll need a live-in, and will I have to take out a college loan? Is the Trust Fund going to cover any of it? A lot of taxes had to be paid on this apartment, and other properties, she'd been told. These doubts weren't helping her, nothing was. I'm going to have to sell it, she told herself, convinced of the fact, and deep down she suddenly felt anger at the prospect of going back into her old life in Boston and regret at the loss of a new life in New York, and not because she hated the idea, but because she felt that it was being forced on her. I'll have to apply to a college in Boston, that way I'll be close to Auntie Key, but I'm still going to need help. Auntie Kay works long hours, so it's going to be difficult even if I stay in Boston. A good college could really be a problem. She looked around, already missing the apartment. I so love this apartment, but then she looked at her belly: no contest.

The apartment really was amazing, every time she entered the door, it took her breath away, and a tingling ran through her body. I own this? She continually asked herself. It was something that three months ago she wouldn't have even dreamed of. Size-wise it was no larger than her aunt's place just outside Boston, probably smaller square footage, but there was no attic or basement. Auntie Kay's place had a large well-kept garden, but with no view to speak of. This place had a small rooftop garden that overlooked the city in one direction and the East River in the other. At night it was breathtaking, strips of colored lights cutting through a pitch-black sky in symmetric patterns, rising up high and falling down into lines of lights weaving through the gray roads, highlighted by the street lamps and car lamps. The sky was black, but it was never truly dark. During the first few nights after the funeral, she'd been able to fashion a small tent from sheets and sleep outside like she used to when she was younger. It had been comforting and nostalgic, though she'd had to purchase earplugs after the first attempt. The noise of New York City, and especially the garbage trucks on Tuesday morning, which had woken her with their banging and crashing was unbelievably loud, even from up here. Upon waking, she'd thought the world was ending with some sort of disaster! So unlike the gentle tranquility of her home in the Boston suburbs.

The kitchen was her favorite room. Auntie Kay had taught her to cook, and when she applied to college, she had debated between the Art School or Culinary School. She'd made her choice, but improving her culinary skills was still a tempting notion. She believed she could do that on her own, and Auntie Kay had already taught her a lot. One of her chores was to shop and produce dinner on most Saturdays, sometimes even for guests. Sometimes she'd invite a school friend or two over to sample her West Indian cuisine, but this kitchen was something else. Over twice the size of her aunt's, it had every conceivable amenity, and some she had never thought of. She could hardly hold herself back from whipping something up, just to try some new appliance out. Simon had cooked for her the first weekend she'd stayed. She'd been surprised: he wasn't bad. He'd obviously wanted to show off his culinary skills a bit, and to be honest she thought he'd over done it a bit. He'd laid out the table with his best silverware and plates, with multiple knives and forks for each meal on a white starched table cloth and nicely folded napkins with three different wine glasses. The glasses had been a bit superfluous since she wasn't drinking. He had been so apologetic at his thoughtlessness, but she'd taken a sip of one of the wines when he'd gone to the bathroom. It was a golden color the likes of which she'd never seen before, and she'd watched his face when he tasted it. He'd just sipped it, and his eyes had closed for a moment, and she could see his lips moving as he savored its flavors, a small noise of satisfaction escaping. Her curiosity had been piqued, so she'd had a sip, just a small taste. It had been so delicious, the new flavors playing on her tongue, with hints of fruit and nuts and honey. She could easily understand his reaction to the wine. Auntie Kay was fond of wine, though she rarely kept more than a bottle or two in the house, and she would let her have a small glass during Sunday lunch, but this stuff had been heavenly. It was a translucent golden color, and sweet, which had been the biggest surprise. When he'd said he was drinking it with dessert, she'd been surprised. She'd tried drinking some wine with dessert once before and it had been awful, the memory of the bitter aftertaste had sat with her for weeks and she'd been unable to even try any wine for a while. Simon, his eyes bright with excitement and his hands animated, had explained why later.

Her eyes strayed to the taped envelope on the coffee table, it had been there for a few days now. She'd been told that Simon had written it, and it was addressed to her. She couldn't bring herself to read it before the funeral. Jason had given it to her the day before. She looked at it and considered it. His last words. Did he really want me to read it? Her reaction surprised herself. Normally she would have ripped open the envelope and avidly consumed the contents, but the state of the letter confounded her, giving her pause. She picked it up a few times but did not open it, always placing it carefully back the way the lawyer had left it. It had been moved. The cleaner had touched it, she thought as she stared at it. Then she knew. I'm ready, I think I can read it now, she told herself understanding something that had eluded her these past few days. She was ready to hear his voice again. I wonder if Jason read it? Probably. She picked the letter up and turned it over a few times, going through the same motions as before, considering the tape holding it together, there was still nothing on the back and the front still contained simply her name, handwritten in simple careful capitals. It had been found on the floor in this room when Mr. Doherty had been going through Simon's things. Ripped in half, but for some reason, the lawyer had kept it and given it to her, on his last visit. He must have read it, she thought, and for some reason, given its state, he believes I should too. She carefully, with a precise deliberation, pulled the letter from the envelope and compared the placing of the tape. Noticing that it had been crumpled up, she again wondered if she should read it. Her dad had obviously thrown it away, but then again Jason had kept it and must have given it to her for a reason. She took in a deep breath, opened the letter and started to read:

Hi Angela,

My daughter, the new light in my life, the best, the greatest, the most important event to happen to me, and I missed it. I'm writing this letter for you, but you'll probably not see it. I hope not. I really need to write this down, it's just my thoughts roiling around in my head after our argument. I so sorry about what happened. I didn't want to disappoint you, but I failed.

Oh, Dad, you didn't, she thought to herself and continued.

You are more than I could have asked for or ever have dreamed of. Hopefully, in months and years to come, I can again prove myself to you, and this letter will gather dust and fade away. I'm hoping, praying, that I'll be able to tell you these things myself. And I wait patiently. For now, however, I need to put this down as it all weighs so heavily on me. I remember my shrink once telling me it was a good way to order our thoughts.

There is no apology I can make for the mistake I made of not knowing you. Even the fact that I didn't know, doesn't seem justification. I loved your mother deeply, and I believe, no, I know, she loved me, and I knew your mother well enough, and should have realized that she would never have given you up. I feel such shame, at asking, no, pleading for her to give you up, because we were young and at college and not ready, and then she left college and I should have known. It seems so obvious now. No, I can now be honest. I was not ready. I didn't want to ruin my future with a child. I was still at college, and I believed that there would be time for others. What future? A banker, alone, full of regrets: no wife, no children, just work. Ruin my life? I laugh at that thought now. Well, tomorrow that changes.

Angela paused, knowing there would be no opportunity to witness that change, that it was in a future that would never exist. She had only started to get to a glimpse of her father, and so much more time was needed, but now it was gone. The positive memories of the funeral reception came to her, Tim's recollections of her father's high school days and beyond, and she was reminded again how thankful she was for that conversation. Then laughing with Megan, after that first, horribly embarrassing introduction. Tears welling, blurring her vision, she wiped them from her eyes and continued reading.

I can't make up for these past mistakes, and I will take those shameful decisions to my grave, but I want to look forward not back, and whatever I have is yours, my wealth, my time and my love. Everything I am is yours and I will try, if you let me, to make it up to you and Adela.

From what I can tell Adela and Kay did a wonderful job bringing you up. Adela gave up college for you. I wish I could thank her, apologize to her, and I so wish I could have helped her, but I didn't, and now I can't and it might be that you'll never be able to forgive me, or I forgive myself, but I will still try, always try, to prove to you, the light of my life, my worthiness.

She paused again, the tears streaming down her face so that she was unable to see the print, as she remembered her mother and felt the still fresh pain of losing her father. She wiped at her eyes and nose again, partially clearing her sight, and after a few seconds pause gathered herself, and read on:

You've talked about going to college and I can assure you that there will be funds enough to support you and your child, my grandchild, and your education. You should go. You will meet likeminded people, new friends, discover a new world. I know Adela would have wanted you to go.

Angie nodded knowingly. This promise to her mother never far from her thoughts.

If we can't get through this, or even if we do, there are others whom I love and trust who will help you if you ask them, and, of course, you always have Kay. Don't tell her I said so, but through all that we've been through, I actually like her, and I can never repay what she has done for me by bringing you up so well, and I know that she loves you as much as anyone, including me, ever could. She is a rare and very good person, but you, of course, already know this about her.

Angie managed a smile while sniffing and wiping the tears from her eyes.

There's my lawyer Jason, you'll meet him soon. He can seem a bit impersonal, pompous even: he's just shy. See him with his son, and I guarantee you'll be surprised at the transformation. I can assure you that he will set up, and his company will manage, your Trust Fund very well. I've known him for years, from college, and I fully trust him. He looks after and manages all my finances and I honestly would not be as wealthy without him. He truly is an honest lawyer, a very good accountant, and even though he won't admit it, a great friend. He's not cheap! But worth every cent. Just ask and he will help you. Of course, if you want to be a Trust Fund mother, it's your money. I won't judge I assure you.

Finally, I hope you meet my friends, Tim and Megan. After you, they are the best of me and special to me. I haven't seen Tim in a while, but we'll track them down and, hopefully, they can show you a side of me worthy of you. And Megan, well we'll talk about her when the time is right.

Right now, I'm waiting for you to call me. If you do, then you'll probably never see this letter as I will recount all of this to you in person, but if being with me is too painful, if I recall memories in you that you'd rather leave alone, then maybe you may read this, and maybe you might give me a second chance. I can wait. I will always wait.

All my love, your father

Simon

The tears were now uncontrollable, streaming down, her breath heaving in time with her internal beat, unrestrained grief weighing heavily on her. Her mother had never said a bad thing about him, and though she'd never talked about him much, she knew her mom had loved him. Concealed tears throughout the years, hidden but now understood. Pictures that she'd kept private, that she thought her daughter never knew about. So, Angie hadn't really known what to expect of this stranger. She remembered those few months she'd managed to have with him vividly and yearned for more time with him. He had been so good for her. She hadn't made it easy for him. She had asked him to come to see her but had gotten cold feet as fear had gripped her. She'd pretended to be busy those first few weekends, reconciling the argument with Auntie Kay which weighed heavy on her and the nervousness and fear of meeting him: her dad. She had cancelled the meeting, arranging for the next visit, but he never complained, and in the end, his patience won through. Her curiosity got the better of her, her fear faded, and after a couple of cancelled weekend visits, she finally arranged a meeting to get a better sense of him.

I arrive in the coffee shop early, ordering hot cocoa in a real mug, and then I stir in lots of sugar. I cup the mug in my hands, enjoying the heat. It hurts a little, but it's also quite comforting. I quickly survey the room. It's reasonably empty, and I wander over to a quiet corner and sit there waiting, preparing myself.

The place is small and it's early, so the crowd is sparse and a little privacy is still available, but the small flow of people is large enough for me to not feel too awkward with this stranger, my father. I check the time, and it's unlikely he'll be here in the next half an hour or so, so I connect to their Wi-Fi and browse the web, searching for any details of him. It's not the first time, but there's stuff, mostly associated with banking and finance and social networks. He even has a Facebook account. I'd read most of the articles before. It's mostly boring stuff, but I puff up with pride as he appears, from what

I can judge, to be pretty good at what he does. The time flies by, and he arrives a half hour or so later, slightly early then scheduled, but of course after me, which is what I intended. My head goes up every time someone enters, but now I see him at the door. A big guy, still recognizable from the photos I have of the much younger version of him. I watch him scan the cafe, and he quickly picks me out and waves at me as he approaches. He doesn't hurry, his eyes are fixed on me, and he moves with purpose and a beautiful, powerful grace. In my mind, I'm framing the image, painting him. He's wearing a long, expensive looking, black cashmere coat, and as he gets closer, passing others on the way, I notice he's a lot bigger than I had expected. As he gets closer, I see more detail in his eyes, and in those eyes, I see mine – a light and piercing blue. They are so active, looking around at the other patrons with such nervous energy. His nervousness somehow comforts me.

"Hi, Angie," his voice is deep, his speech measured. He sticks out his hand. I'm a bit surprised and I just look at it for a moment. Then refocusing, I reach out and take his fingers and hold them. He squeezes back gently, and I release his hand, possibly a little too quickly, I think guiltily. I continue to stare at him, trying to see something else of myself in him; he looks back at me, and there's a silent void. Then he averts his gaze for just a moment, almost shyly, and then he looks back at me. I still haven't replied to him. I'm nervous, and words, phrases, sentences are spinning out of control in my brain.

"Hi, Simon? Or should I call you Dad?" He visibly winces, as do I on the inside. I hadn't meant to, but I just spat the word out, and it sounds like thinly veiled contempt. I'm as nervous as he.

"Whichever you are more comfortable with." There's no anger in him, just a measured patience. I pause and think for a moment, looking inward, and I try and calm myself, reminding myself that I invited him, that I cancelled the last two weekends, and that he is my father, whatever I call him.

"I think Simon," I tell him, as every time I think of calling him Dad, I start going into a panic, not sure I can say it without an unwanted edge, and I notice a flicker of disappointment in his eyes. "At least for the moment," I try with a smile to take the edge of the situation, and he visibly relaxes.

"Simon's fine," he replies, and I think I can hear disappointment, but the smile stays, and he straightens slightly, "I'm just going to get a coffee, and you? Are you okay?" He nods in the direction of the half full cup of cocoa, still warm, sitting between my hands.

"Yeah, I'm fine," and I continue to stare, rather blankly at him. I realize that I don't want him to read how I feel.

"Ok, I'll be back in a minute." He turns abruptly and heads back to the counter. The motion is captivating; there's still an athlete in there. I consider the situation as I watch him ordering his coffee. This is already awkward, and I'm not helping, I admonish myself. I'm not really trying, but I should give him chance, shouldn't I? He's come all this way again. He's been patient with me. He's trying, so I should at least try and give him a chance, and this is what I want, isn't it? After a few minutes of internal monologue, which is going nowhere, his shadow falls over the table; he's returned. He takes the seat opposite me and sits down, hunching over his coffee and still wearing his coat, even though the room is warm and cozy. The chair looks much too small.

"How is the pregnancy going?" he asks. That's a strange and abrupt way to start a conversation, and I can't tell if he is genuinely interested or just fishing for any sort of conversation. Maybe that was the best he could come up while he was getting his coffee. I decide to go with it, at least for a while. Though if it gets any more boring, I'm out of here!

"The baby's fine, growing, kicking, healthy. As am I," there's little inflection in my voice; I may as well be talking about the weather.

"Boy or a girl?" I forcibly hold an eye roll. I'll be gone very soon at this rate.

"I don't know," I say as evenly as possible, "I told my doctor I wasn't interested in knowing."

"Not even a little?" For the first time a twinkle appears in his gaze, a slight smile on his lips and a shift in his speech pattern, and I momentarily feel that I'm seeing something of the real person. I decide to try and go along with it.

"Well, sometimes I stare at the scans, studying them, trying to see if I can tell," I reply mischievously with just a slight smile. I try a different route. "Simon, tell me about yourself."

"I deserted your mother, thinking I was going to get picked for the NFL. I didn't, I got injured. I ended up on Wall Street, doing well, but don't really enjoy it. Well, I sort of do, but..." it just comes pouring out, no pause, no thought, it just comes out, and it's not what I want to hear.

"You know," I interrupt him, "I get that you feel guilty," I'm so angry and annoyed now, "I have an aunt whom I love, but currently will barely talk to me because I'm here in the city with you. I asked to see you, and I'm sorry it's taken this long to get together, but I didn't come here to have you unburden your guilt on me." He stares at me and looks away shamed, but I'm not finished. I'm not going to let him off the hook that easily, not now! Asshole! I'm sorely tempted just to leave him with his coffee and guilt.

"Mom never said a bad thing about you." His gaze returns, now fixed on me, and I see the pain in his eyes, but I ignore it. "Actually, she never said much about you that would shine any light of any sort on the relationship you two may have had together, but she never said anything bad. And she kept pictures of you, which my aunt has now deigned to give me after all these years. And I know she cried herself to sleep many nights. So, I would like to know why. I'd like to know why she loved you so much, yet you left her or let her leave you or whatever happened." I can feel the prickliness of tears, but I'm not going to stop now. "Because she's dead and my aunt is just angry when it comes to you, and she won't tell me anything. So just tell me something fun about you. Anything. Something that she would have liked about you. Something that will give me an idea, a least a notion of what she saw in you, what she loved about you. We can fill in all the boring details later." The tears are so close now, I breathe in deeply, momentarily hold my breath, and then slowly exhale. The control is just barely working.

"There's a possibility of a later?" His smile returns when he says it, and there's that real person again. I relax a little, and the feeling of tears recede. I can feel that I already like that person.

"If your story is good," I smile back. He leans back in the chair, his fingers interlocked behind his head. I'm looking at him, waiting, but in the back of my mind, I picture that tiny chair toppling over or collapsing and have to hold back a giggle that would probably threaten the moment. He's staring at me, the smile for a moment gone, but this time without such intensity. I can see the cogs whirling as he's thinking of what to say next, but he's taking his time. I like that, but I still hope he hurries up because that vision is ready to burst out as a huge laugh. Which will break this quiet moment first? The chair toppling or me bursting out laughing at the thought that it might? Then some thought suddenly brings a smile to his face. I enjoy the moment, the glow radiating from him, his whole expression changes as he considers what to say to me. Maybe it's a memory of Mom that brings a sudden smile to his face. I wait. Make it good, I plead silently. He learns forward, arms on the table.

"Adela," he said, pausing, presumably for effect, and he has my full attention, "your mother, was a rock groupie," he smiles.

"Sorry?" Okay, I'm confused. What's that got to do with him?

"Your mom was a rock groupie." He leans back, looking satisfied that he has my complete attention, assured that he's given me what I asked for.

"That's it?" he does have my attention, and yet I'm still no less confused, and I'm not totally convinced. I'm fairly sure I wanted to know something about him. I'm fairly sure that's what I asked.

"Ah, it's all in the implications, and that's what makes it interesting," he's laughing quietly, "I hope," he adds with a hint of doubt, though still convinced that this tidbit is worthy of my request. "You see," he continues, "I was a singer in a rock band in college, and she came backstage to meet me. That's how we first met," he finally explains.

"Really? You joking right?" and suddenly I get it.

"Yes, really. No joke."

"You were in a rock band? Oh, that is so cool," I really am impressed.

"It really was. I had one in high school and started another in college. We recorded a few CDs, nothing special, but it was fun and your mother loved us. She turned up to all our gigs. After a few gigs, I started to recognize her in the crowd, and after one gig we ended up in a bar. Illegally," and that smile widens, "and we chatted 'til dawn, and then we just sort of fell into dating, and next thing we knew, we were in love," trailing off a bit at the end. The smile fades slightly, but I'm hooked.

"Oh, that is so so cool. My dad's a rock star," I respond excitedly, and his smile returns with my enthusiasm, and he beams back at me. "What sort of music did you play?" I ask, rapt.

That was the start of many good visits with him. Angie genuinely liked him. He didn't try and force a relationship, and he was polite, but also didn't take any shit from her. Once she tried to get him to buy her a car in a moment of childishness. Aunt Kay most certainly wouldn't have accepted it and would have been shocked at such a request, but she thought she'd try to test the boundaries so to speak.

"I want that car," she'd started, pointing at a fashionably expensive item one day. "Can you buy one like that one for me?" she'd batted her eyelids for further effect. "You can afford it, it'd be really nice. You could teach me to drive." He just looked at her with a raised eyebrow, didn't even bother to answer her, but he did let her drive the Mercedes sometimes. As he started to relax in her company, she discovered that he was interesting and funny. So, after a couple of weekends, her schedule suddenly opened up to more than just cocoa and coffee. Auntie Kay still didn't approve, but she had at least started to talk. She would huff, puff, or snort, sometimes all at the same time, when Angie told her she was meeting her father, but otherwise their relationship had returned to normal, the number of chores decreasing, and silence no long reigning during meal times. More importantly, Auntie Kay was smiling again. That was so important to Angie. She really wanted to get to know her father, but Auntie Kay's opinion of her mattered over everyone else's.

The first few meetings always seemed to end up with stories about her mother. Then she realized that that was what she wanted, that she was driving their conversations in that particular direction, and he was duly obliging, happy to do so, happy to reminisce about a woman he still loved very much, able now to share the past. And he was full of surprises. He was in a rock band, he played football at college, nearly joining the NFL, and he knew her favorite living artist! That had blown her mind.

"Simon," I answer the phone with possibly too much enthusiasm but I can't help it, "are you coming up this weekend?" I blurt out. He hasn't even said hello yet!

"Hi, Angie, I'm very well, and you," we laugh together, and he continues. "Yes, I am. I have tickets to the art exhibition you were interested in." Okay, that doesn't make sense, I'm thinking, just a little confused. Then I remember telling him that I was hoping that my best friend Jane, whose mom works in the museum, would be able to get tickets for the opening night since that was the only night the artist was going to be there. But that wasn't for another week, and I don't recall him responding much to the statement. I told him she was one of my favorite living artists, and all I recall is that he just shrugged, barely seemed to register the fact. I'd actually been a bit disappointed. So how are we suddenly going there this weekend? It hasn't even opened yet.

"Simon, how's that possible?" I'm still running what he just said through my mind, and it's not adding up, "it doesn't open for another week."

"Yeah, I know, but I have some preview tickets. The artist is going to show us around. It should be fun."

"Oh my god, are you being serious? You have preview tickets?" I'm beside myself with happiness. Jane is not going to believe this.

"Yes, my lawyer manages a few people on the board, so I asked him and he got a couple of tickets. He twisted a few arms, called in some favors. He owes me. Apparently, it's a very popular exhibition."

"Of course, it's popular. This is her first major exhibition! She's amazing!"

"I know and a very nice person too."

"What! You know her?"

"We've met," I know that tone of voice, he's hiding something, though he actually wants to tell me.

"And?"

"I met her at college." There was still more I can feel it.

"And?"

"And we dated," he was smiling, I could hear it.

"You dated Natalie Stones?"

"Yes."

"You're kidding me, right."

"No, seriously, we dated for about six months. We've kept in contact, still friends, though I haven't seen or spoken to her in a while. She still lives in Seattle, I believe. Married and she has a little girl. I have some of her artwork."

"You own some of her paintings?" I ask, my voice rising, possibly even a squeal, ignoring all that personal stuff, which I already knew.

"Yes, a few, I own six, or is it seven..." He pauses for a moment. "Nope, it's eight. And some drawings and sketches."

"Really?"

"Really, I'm staring at one right now. I even have a portrait of me sketched by her. Though I'm not too sure it actually looks like me." He's laughing gently down the phone, genuinely pleased with my reaction.

"Oh my god, oh my god, oh my god. She drew you?"

"Long before she was famous." I can hear that he's enjoying this. "So, you like Nat's work?"

"I love her work." My dad knows, no, he dated, Natalie Stones and he refers to her as Nat. That's so unbelievably cool.

"Which paintings do you have?"

"Oh, *Twilight*, that was a present, a few of the others I got at college when she was doing her Masters, and *Waterfall* 2 & 3, a couple of *Windows*. Those I bought. I'm fairly sure she didn't give me much of a discount either," he pauses, "but then again, they're probably worth more now." I can hear him laughing.

"You have *Waterfall 3*! I love that painting. So, you're 'Private Collection'?" I own an art book with this particular painting in it.

"Yes, I'm that 'Private Collection', and you'll see it when you come to New York." He pauses, "when you're ready of course. If you'd like." He sounds a little nervous asking me. I've been looking forward to going to back to New York for a few weeks now and was about to ask anyway. I haven't been there since my college visits.

"It's ok, Dad. I'm hoping to come soon, maybe around the Fourth of July weekend? I know Auntie Kay shuts up the restaurant on that day, and she's thinking about going home to Trinidad for a few days. So, I could come down to New York then, for a long weekend?"

"Of course. That'll be perfect. I'll show you my New York City, and you can enjoy the paintings as well."

"They're not in the exhibition?"

"No, this is mostly her latest work," he knows much more about the exhibition than he'd let on. He loves to surprise, I realize, "it's not a retrospective, I believe." But I'm not waiting for an answer, I'm already overflowing with enthusiasm and anticipation of meeting Natalie Stones.

"Yes, yes, yes," I want to get up and dance.

"So, you're okay for this weekend and the exhibition?" I can hear him chuckling; it's so obvious I am okay.

"Of course! When is it?"

"Sunday afternoon, 4:00 to 5:00-5:30, and I've arranged dinner after. I think there will be around eight of us." Eight people! Now I'm a little nervous, I'm not sure I'm ready for that right now.

"Eight people?"

"Don't worry, you'll be ok. They won't all be old like me."

"Oh, I don't know." No, I'm pretty sure I don't want to be around that many strangers.

"Look, don't worry. You'll meet them at the exhibition. If you don't want to come out later, I'll make sure you get home safely and check in with you after. On the other hand, I can make sure you're sitting between me and Nat if you'd like." Dinner with Natalie Stones?

"I'd like," I respond quickly, and those nerves are suddenly gone.

When we arrive at the exhibition I'm nervous, I'm mentally checking my clothing wondering if it's appropriate or inappropriate, or somewhere in between or… nervous. I stay just behind him, as we enter, my eyes darting around searching for her. I'm barely looking at the art on display here. It's not her work, in the front hall, I assume hers is inside somewhere else, so I'm not bothered. I've seen most of these before, and some are very good, but that's not why I'm here.

"You're very quiet," he smiles at me.

"I'm okay," I try keeping the nervousness out of my voice. "I'm okay," I repeat. I really am so nervous.

"Come on, there she is." He's already moving towards her. My feet are having a problem detaching themselves from the floor.

I quickly pull myself together, scan my clothing, wonder if the pregnancy is that noticeable, but it's a really baggy sweater, and then I propel myself forward, just behind him, sort of hiding.

Natalie moves away from the couple she had been talking to, and her face is all aglow, staring at Simon with a smile that complements his, as I stare at her. It's easy to tell that they were good friends. Very good friends, I smile to myself: Dad dated Natalie Stones. I stand still as they chat, not really listening, just staring at one of my heroes. She's so awesome.

"I'd like to introduce you to Angie, my daughter," Dad says, and I suddenly focus at the sound of my name. I think she looks stunned.

Though when I think about it, it's hardly surprising. I wonder if she thinks I'm his pregnant daughter, I think self-consciously. It takes a lot of control to not rub my belly.

"Adela's daughter?" she replies, in a rather loud voice, or was that just me noticing it, the sound of my mother's name, here, now. I want to turn and run and cry, possibly scream. I don't. I stand there, still. I think I might have flinched at the sound of Mom's name, and now I'm just staring. Standing still. I have no idea what to say.

"I'm sorry," she continues, her voice now soft with compassion, and embarrassment. It's not the first time something like this has happened. It's okay, I tell myself. It's okay. I'm okay.

"Hi, Angie, I'm Natalie," her smile warms me, and I've already forgiven her and her little faux pas. This is Natalie Stones.

"Hello, Ms. Stones. I'm pleased to meet you," I reply in a small polite voice. Oh dear, that was a bit formal, wasn't it? Then it just comes out.

"I just love your work! You're amazing!" Now I'm all smiles. Even my eyes are laughing, and I can't believe I'm here.

"Ms. Stones? Seriously. Call me Natalie, and welcome to my exhibition," she says with a smile, and I just can't stop grinning. I may never stop. I turn to face Dad, and he's smiling at me too.

"Thanks, Dad," I mouth silently, and his smile broadens even more.

They were just starting to be comfortable in each other's company. Embarrassing silences had been replaced by comfortable ones, and conversations didn't feel like they were on eggshells anymore; the relationship was progressing. Moving up from coffee, they had met for lunch a few times, then dinner. They chatted about nothing in particular, most subjects of import skirted. Initially, it hadn't been that easy, but by the time he'd taken her to Natalie's art exhibition, the conversations didn't seem forced, she certainly didn't feel uncomfortable with him, and she really had started looking forward to seeing him. He was boyish and happy just to be with her, and she enjoyed that. Finally, he'd arranged for her to come to New York in a chauffeur driven car. He wouldn't let her fly, which annoyed her, but the car was nice and the driver was good company. He was a struggling artist whose second job was being a chauffeur on the weekends. Angie believed that Simon had arranged this on purpose, though he denied the coincidence with a conspiratorial smile.

She'd stayed here in this apartment, and just couldn't believe the place, couldn't quite believe his version of New York, and she fell madly in love with it.

Everything was going well, but one thing still bothered her, an answer to a question that had plagued her for years. She had believed that she'd never know the answer, that it would always be a question persisting with no one to answer it for her, until Simon came into her life. He knew the answer. He was part of the question. She'd waited for weeks, holding back, gauging when would be an appropriate moment. Her aunt had told her not to, shaking her head with disgust at being so easily ignored, when her advice had been asked, but Angie just had to know. It wouldn't go away, even after trying to convince herself that it was unimportant, that he was here with her now and that it didn't matter anymore. But it did. She would sometimes fall asleep thinking of it, and then she'd wake up still thinking of it. Either way, it wasn't going anywhere, and so she had to know, she had to ask him. For the whole week prior, it had played on her mind, and when they met that Sunday and gone out to explore the city, walking, which was both their choice, it was ringing in her brain. After a while, she'd managed to relax and enjoy the food and the company. He really was good company, and as usual, it was a fun evening, and a very good restaurant. He'd talked about high school and his band and being a jock, and she'd talked about how she didn't get on with jocks and preferred the geeks, and he'd told her about Tim, his best friend and an uber geek, and they'd laughed. They were both relaxed, and as silence reigned for a moment, the question returned, still lying heavily on her. She had to ask.

"Why did you leave Mom?" It was so easy. It sounded so innocuous. She just wanted a straightforward answer to a simple question. He could do that, couldn't he? Apparently not. She didn't like the response. It was all she could do to not scream at him, so she chose the alternative and left. Her mouth was clamped tightly shut, as were her fists, as she tried to control her anger. She glared at him with more contempt than she really meant and left him in the restaurant, the sound of her fallen chair ringing in her ears, as embarrassment and pain and disappointment flushed her cheeks.

After she'd walked out on him, she'd disappeared into her room for two whole days. Thinking. Alone. She didn't want to talk to her aunt about him, how could that be constructive given her aunt's opinion of him, so she was determined to solve the issue on her own. She would nip downstairs after Auntie Kay had left for work, keeping out of her way, so as not to have to broach the subject. She'd cook some food, watch TV, and read the novel she was currently in the middle of, draw or paint to clear her head and think. His response had pissed her off. Why couldn't he just answer the question, properly and honestly? She'd thought he was better than that, and for two days she had deliberated and gotten nowhere. Maybe it wasn't as innocuous as I'd thought, but that answer! Maybe I'm over reacting? That answer, it bothered her. Every time she heard it in her head, she got angry. Why couldn't he just answer the question? She continued to ask herself, and she was convinced she had to solve the problem, his response and her response to it, herself. Somehow, because after two days she seemed no nearer to an answer.

Luckily her aunt wouldn't leave her alone. She could tell something upsetting had happened, and for two days she'd left her niece to her own devices before deciding to intervene.

I'm awakened by the sound of the door opening. I open my eyes and there before me is Auntie Kay.

"Are you alright, Sweetie? Where have you been hiding these last few days?" she sounds concerned but has a warm smile for me.

"I'm okay, Auntie, really." Please leave me, Auntie, I need to be alone, I really do. The concern in her eyes stops me saying this out loud.

"Really?"

"Yes, really." No, not really.

"Are you sure you're okay?" her voice is calm and patient. I'm not okay, all right? I shout in my head. She stands there looking at me, I know she's not going to leave me, not unless I insist or I am rude. I don't want to be rude. I just want the answer to the question. Do you know Auntie? Do you? How has it come to this? I just wanted an answer to a stupid question. I got an answer, I remind myself. I just didn't like it. It was a crap answer. How could he?

And I crack.

"He didn't want me." And I burst out crying. For two days I wasn't even close to crying and now here they come, and I can't control them. "Why didn't he want me?" I wail.

"What did he say?" She comes in, and I sit up as she sits beside me on my bed. I lean into her, our shoulders touching, and she gently holds my hands, rubbing them in a soft massage. Her eyes never wavering, she waits as my tears dry up and I recount the conversation.

"He was a boy," is her gentle, though not totally understandable, response.

"Sorry?"

"He was a boy. Your mom was a young girl and he was a boy. They were young, we were young. Neither had any idea what they were doing. He made a stupid decision. Do you think he knows that now?"

"Yes."

"So?"

"But he didn't want me."

"And I hated him for that, and I still find it hard to forgive him," releasing one hand she quickly crosses herself. "Though I try," she says so quietly and with deep sorrow, "but he wants you now, doesn't he?"

"Yes, very much."

"So?"

"So, you think I should just forget?" and saying it, I know that I can't.

"Can you?"

"No, I don't think I can." How can I forget? It's my history, my life.

"But can you forgive him?"

"I don't know, but that's the problem, isn't it? That's the issue."

"What's important to you now? A boy made a terrible decision nineteen years ago, but now he's trying to do something about it because he paid a terrible price too. He missed you growing up," and there's a fierce love in her voice.

"But what about Mom? He left her. She was pregnant with me, and he left her," and I can feel the pressure of anger rising in me again.

"No, he didn't," she contradicts me. Her voice is calm, but fierce with intention, and I feel like she's also close to exploding. I know she hates talking about him. Now she's supporting him?

"What? Of course, he did." I can see her taking in a deep breath and controlling herself.

"No, she left him." There's anguish in her voice as she says it.

"She left him? Of course not. No, that's not right," I try, now totally confused.

"Sweetheart, this is the truth, your mom left him," there's anguish in her quiet voice, as if she's telling a secret, kept these many years.

"Auntie, how can you say that?"

"Because it's the truth. She left college, she left him, and we came to Boston."

"But I thought she loved him?"

"She did. She loved him very much, but she loved you more, even before you were born, and that love grew as you grew."

"So, it wasn't his fault?"

"Well, I wouldn't go that far; he has a lot of blame to take and he knows it. That's why he is trying so hard now. He made a mistake years ago, and now he's trying to make amends. You should let him."

"I should? You really think that?"

"Yes, you should. I really do."

"What do I do, Auntie?"

"I think you know what to do." She's right. I've known all along; I should have had this conversation with her days ago.

I call him that night. As I'm dialing, I know that this is what I want, and I am glad that my aunt agrees with me. I know how much she detests him, but I also know why. What happened nineteen years ago still drives her thoughts and emotions concerning my father. She can't get past it, and I know she hates that about herself. She wants to forgive him, but it's been so long it is ingrained into her. She has no idea what he's like now, and what I've seen in him, but she knows that he's good for me. I think so too.

I liked him so much, she thinks as she falls asleep happy for having known him and sad at missing him.

The next day Jason, the lawyer, called and arranged to come over again. The last meeting had been short, more of a second introduction, and he'd dropped if The Letter. Anytime, she told him, I'm really not busy. That afternoon was agreed upon. One of the doormen called up when Jason arrived and Angie told him to let him in.

"Hi, Angie. I need to discuss aspects of Simon's last will and testament with you. He left instructions and I need to review them with you before discussing anything with the other beneficiaries. You stated on the phone that you are okay with this?" He was much easier to speak with since the funeral, and he didn't seem so nervous anymore. They were even on a first name basis! She hated being called Miss or Ms. Bridgewater. It sounded so old!

"Of course," she didn't really have much to say. He still sounded a little formal, and once again, she found herself trying to reconcile the incongruity of her father and this man as his friend. She could see her father and Tim, her father and Megan, but Jason? She was baffled, but her father had trusted him, so she was at least going to give him the benefit of the doubt, and he most certainly seemed to be trying.

"First, there are three beneficiaries to his will," he stated with a professionalism that made her internally cringe. Come on, Angie, relax. He's a lawyer. Wait a minute? Three beneficiaries?

"Three? There are two others like me?" He has other children? He never mentioned them. She felt shocked and hurt, it ran through her like a bolt of lightning. Three beneficiaries, two other children!

"Others? No, no, nothing like that!" his smile was bordering on laughter, lines crinkling around his eyes, his face suddenly coming alive, and she was taken aback. He is human after all, she thought with delight and smiled in return as she instantly calmed down, from her mistaken conclusion.

"He left a substantial amount of money after taxes and selling off some properties," he looked around the apartment.

"You've sold this one?" I knew, I just knew it, she thought.

"Here? Oh dear, no, you really need to let me finish."

"I'm sorry." I must stop interrupting, she thought, mentally clamping her mouth shut.

"It's okay, but it's best if I finish first. Then you can ask all the questions you like. Okay?" He sounded a little patronizing, and she was now wishing she'd said nothing and that he would just get on with it.

"Yes, sorry, yes that's okay, sorry," she said, flustered and not a little embarrassed.

"That's okay, no need to be sorry. Now, where was I? Yes, taxes and some properties sold off. Not here," he said reassuringly. "There are still some other properties he owned outright and a few with mortgages. One of the outrights goes to Tim. He stated that this was for services rendered during high school. He believed that he never would have able to achieve any of this without Tim's help back in high school. He is giving some of his art collection, a couple of paintings, to Megan and myself." He coughed and looked embarrassed, but quickly continued, "And he has put aside some funds to pay your Aunt Kay's mortgage off and a small amount for her to live on when she retires," He looked at her, "though through you. He believed that she probably wouldn't accept it directly from him."

"He's probably right," she said nodding her head, "but I'll arrange it." She was pleased that he'd thought of her aunt and pleased that he'd arranged it separately, knowing what her aunt's response would be.

"He has left a reasonable amount of cash to both Megan and Tim as well, and some cash to some charities and non-profits he's chaired over the years," he looked up from the piece of paper in his hand as if finished. "Everything else, which is the substantial part of his estate, is all yours." He paused, "You really will not want for anything unless you have a gambling habit or decide to buy a couple of large yachts." He smiled and started reading again.

"I have set up the funds and distribution as per his request, which is as follows: 1. There is a cash amount for immediate access in a bank account in your name. 2. A Trust Fund managed by my company has been setup. 3. After a year you may review our services and investment portfolio performance, and if you are not satisfied you may, at any time, transfer to another fund manager."

"He trusted you and respected and liked you. I see no reason to do otherwise." And anyway, I would have no idea whom else to trust, she thought.

"Well, one day you may, and I totally understand. Our records are always open to you, and I can introduce you to a few of our clients who will graciously discuss the services they receive from us. Most of them knew Simon."

"4. We have also set up another Trust Fund, to be divided amongst all your children upon reaching their eighteenth birthdays." He continued, "Finally there are the properties..." He paused, noticing her eyes glazing over, "I'm not too sure how much you wish to be involved with the Funds' investments, the buying and selling of shares, bonds, properties etc. I used to put time aside once a month to review them with Simon, and this service is included in our fee. The fee comes in two parts. A small fixed amount, covering basic admin, and a performance amount. If we do well in increasing your total portfolio's value, we benefit from that with a performance bonus. This gives us an incentive to do a good job," he chuckled, "It differs with each client. And finally, I have also adjusted the fund to allow you a reasonable personal income."

"Reasonable?"

"Reasonable." He looked at his notes. "Just under $500,000 per annum, $495,150 to be more precise, after taxes and fees." He looked up.

"Half a million dollars?" A year? What on earth would I do with half a million dollars a year?

"Is that okay? I can adjust for more, but the more you take out now, the less there is in the future as you have no other income going into it."

"Half a million dollars?" Well, I can certainly afford to go to college! Half a million?

"It was a sum I calculated, and Simon and I agreed upon. It will increase annually and over a normal lifetime, given favorable market conditions, the fund will easily sustain it, leaving a reasonable amount for your descendants. But, as I said, I could change it. You can, of course, take money out for major purchases, but I'd advise talking with myself or one of my colleagues, which again is included in the fee, and we can ensure the stability of the fund if we know what you're doing." A recent trust fund kid who gambled and loved boats came to mind.

"Thanks." She was still trying to process the number, put it into some form of real-life context, and she wasn't really listening to the lawyer anymore.

"Okay, that's most of the details. Do you have any questions?"

"Yes, I want you to do me a favor." This is wrong she thought, nearly $500,000 a year?

"A favor?" Here we go she wants more, thought Jason, they always want more. Then, when they ask where has it all gone a few years later, after having ignored all good advice and their spending exceeds the funds to sustain it, you shrug your shoulders and try not to say I told you so. Well, it's their money and their choice. As always, I'll try to advise otherwise, but that does not always work. She wasn't his first Trust-Fund child and was unlikely to be his last.

"Yes, I want you to change the amount of the trust fund." Jason kept his face as straight as possible, but inside sighed sadly, she'd seemed so sensible. Simon had implied that she was sensible, but I suppose it's a lot of money, and money does strange things to good people.

"Considering my going to college next year, possibly living here, the fact I'm going to need a live-in babysitter, helper. I want you to reduce the amount."

"Reduce?" He was surprised and lost for words, his usual professional exterior demeanor failing him. They've never asked him to reduce it.

"Yes, reduce. Whilst I'm at college I want to live as a student, not some rich bimbo, everyone wanting to know me because I have lots of money. I just want to be normal, you know, " she started laughing, "find someone who does want me and my baby, but not for my wealth."

"Reduce? I can do that," the thought brought a smile to his face, which surprised her.

"Jason, after I graduate I might want more, I'll probably want to go to grad school. Hell, I might even want to live in the Bahamas or maybe on a giant yacht," she chuckled knowing this was ridiculous, "but right now? right now, all I want to do is have my baby, then go to college and just be, well, normal."

"Okay, I'll come up with some options we can agree upon. And, thank you."

"Thank you? Why?"

"For not betraying my trust in mankind and especially in Simon. He told me you were sensible, intelligent. He was right, and he would be very proud of you. So, thank you." You have a good smile, Jason, you should do it more often.

Jason left and the hum of New York outside quietly returned, but it was not intrusive. She wandered onto the balcony, the noise now loud but comforting. Shall I make this our new home? she pondered as she felt the baby kicking. She looked out over the city that never sleeps, hardly surprising with all that noise, she chuckled to herself. Amidst the traffic noise, she registered the ringing of the phone. She turned went back to the living room, closing the balcony doors behind her, shutting out most of the noise, reducing it to its previous unobtrusive hum.

"Hello, this is Angie." She didn't recognize the caller id, a New York number, but she answered it anyway.

"Hi Angie, it's Tim." Tim? This was unexpected.

"Hi, Tim. How are you?" She was happily surprised, the meeting at the funeral quickly returning to her mind and bringing a smile to her face.

"I'm fine, great actually," he did sound good, she thought, he paused a little before carried on, "I just thought I'd call to see if everything is all right." His words took a second or two to sink in, and she was intrigued by the fact he felt great.

"Oh, Tim, thank you, that's really kind of you. I'm fine," she looked down stroking her belly, "we're fine, thank you for asking."

"Good, just wanted to check in," he now sounded a little nervous, she knew he was considering, thinking what to say next, possibly lost for the next topic, unable to now sit on her as an icebreaker. She smiled at the memory.

"And how are you?" she asked again, unable to think of what else to say, just a little lost for words.

"I'm fine, just fine, I'm here at home, marking papers, and I thought of you, so I thought I'd just call and check in, see if you're okay, settling in, you know," he said repeating himself. Now you're just fine, you were great a minute ago, she thought, still considering conversation options.

"Yep, I'm great," was all she could think of, the conversation was already drying up and they'd barely gotten past hello.

"Have you decided what you're going to do?" he blurted out quickly. At least it was something, she thought, now having something to work with and considering her reply.

"That's a big question. I'm still not too sure yet." What's happened? She was feeling a little depressed about where the conversation wasn't going. We had such a great conversation last time.

"Are you going to college next year?"

"I haven't had time to think about it much over the last few days, but I think I will. It now appears that I can afford to go to college and also have someone here to look after my baby. And that's what both Mom and Dad wanted. I still have a few months to think about it – where I'm going, what I'm going to do – but yes, I think I'm going to go."

"They would be proud," he stated, sounding a little less frantic. I know, she thought, but thank you. He really is not a good phone conversationalist, is he?

"Yes, they would, Tim, thanks," an idea suddenly entered her head. "Tim, can I ask you a question?"

"Of course, Angie, you can ask me anything."

"Did you know my mom?"

"Well, I did meet her a few times at college. We got on quite well actually." He paused and I could hear him chuckling. "Once when I was staying at Simon's for the weekend, we, your mother and I, spent the whole night chatting. Your dad was playing pool with some of his fraternity buddies."

"What did you chat about?"

"Not surprisingly, mostly Simon. She'd shooed him off and told him that I was hers for the night. He just laughed and left us. She wanted to know everything about his childhood. I couldn't really help since I'd only know him from his last couple years at high school, but that was enough for her."

"But you told her about him?" She was hanging on his every word, for just a glimpse of something new about either of her parents.

"Oh, yes, we just chatted about, well, everything, especially about the band. As you know that's how I got to know him, and funnily enough, thinking about it now, that's how she got to know him too. Adela loved watching him onstage. She was a big Classic Rock fan. She said that when she first saw him on the stage she knew."

"Really?"

"Truly, she loved their music and watching him perform was one of her greatest pleasures." Angie was crying gently, "Look, I'm sorry if I'm upsetting you, Angie, I just thought..." he stopped, feeling guilty for getting carried away with the conversation and forgetting that Adela was also deceased.

"No. No. It's okay, Tim! Carry on. It's just remembering them makes me cry, but I'm really okay. I'd love to hear more, if you can?"

"Of course. Okay, yeah. Where was I? I remember now. We spent an hour or so trying to see who could come up with Simon's greatest flaw."

"His greatest flaw? What did you decide?" she asked eagerly, maybe too eagerly given the circumstances, "if I may ask?"

"Of course, Angie, I can assure you that you never have to be afraid to ask me anything. Anyway, we decided that he was never going to be the rock star he thought he was," Tim laughed again, "but we agreed that we both still loved watching him perform."

"Was he good? Was he a good singer?"

"Not really, he was good at singing, not great, but he had a lot of charisma and could hold a crowd, and he just loved it." She could feel the tears again. I would have dearly loved to have seen him sing, she thought, a sadness floating over her thoughts. Just the once would have been enough, knowing she never would now. "He might not have been a very good singer, but he was a great performer, a very good entertainer."

"Really?"

"Yes, really, he just basked in it, being up on the stage. It was like you were seeing his true self."

"His true self," she whispered, mostly to herself, "What were the bands like?"

"We played mostly cover versions, Classic Rock mostly. He was a huge Stones fan."

"As was Mom."

"Yes, she was. They were her favorite band. Your Auntie Kay could never understand that. She loved Reggae and R&B. She introduced me to Bob Marley when I met her. She sat me down, told me not to move, while she cooked dinner for us," she could hear him chuckling at the memory, "a really good cook, your aunt."

"Yeah, she is. She told me that too," they laughed. "She also told me, just a few days ago, that Mom had said watching Simon performing Stones' songs was one of her greatest pleasures. So, I suppose it must be true."

"I must admit I used to love playing in the band with him," the sadness and loss were thick in his voice.

"I wish I'd been able to see him. That I'd seen you guys."

"Well, I have some old videos of us on stage if you're interested, from high school and from college."

"You do?"

"Yes, I do. Do you want them? They've been transferred to DVD."

"Oh, Tim, I don't know what to say. Oh, yes, please! Thank you so much." Her tears were now flowing freely but with happiness; a wish granted.

"I can drop them off tonight if you wish. If you're around. If that's okay?"

"Of course!" Oh God, thank you. "Why don't you come over and make an evening of it? I can cook for you."

"Well, I was hoping to see Megan tonight."

"Oh!"

"But I'll ask, I'll see if she's happy to change our plans."

"No, no it's okay, don't worry. Just drop them off. That's fine."

"What were you going to cook us?" The enthusiasm in his voice was evident.

"My classic: West Indian chicken curry with rice and peas."

"Count us in, Megan loves that, as do I."

"Really?"

"Yep, it'll have to be a little late though. After her show, if that's ok?"

"Oh, that's fine. Are you and Megan dating?" she blurted out.

"Yes, I think we are," he paused for a moment, "yes, we're dating." she could hear the pleasure in his voice. "Don't tell her I had to think about it though," and he continued to chuckle.

"Oh, Tim, I'm so happy for you both. I won't tell. Please make it work," there was a touch of desperation in her voice.

"Angie, I can assure you I will try with all my heart, with everything in my power, I will try." He laughed out loud, deeply, from his core, the sound reverberating through the phone, and it sounded like all the joy in the world was contained there.

"I'll be checking up on you," Angie laughed back.

"You do that. Anyway, we'll see you tomorrow night?"

"Yep, and dinner will be waiting. You sure it's okay with Megan?"

"I'll check with Megan, but I'm sure, and I'm looking forward to it and I know she will be too."

"Thanks, Tim, bye."

"No problem and thank you. Goodbye, Angie, see you later."

She sat there contemplating the conversation. Nice one, Tim, she thought happily. She was happy for them both and looking forward to seeing them tomorrow. Bob Marley was playing in the background, and she smiled that it was one of the few things Kay and Simon had in common. She had been brought up on Rock, since her mother, to the eternal complaints of Auntie Kay, had loved Rock music. Even before her mom died, Kay felt she had to balance the scales with Reggae and R&B. Marley was easily one of her favorites in any style though. He wasn't the only Reggae she listened to, but she would listen to him regardless of the mood she was in. There was never an occasion that didn't warrant Marley as far as she was concerned. It pleased her that Auntie and Dad had something in common, apart from me and Mom, she reminded herself. She looked around the room, there was *Waterfall 2*, and she realized she may like it even more than *3*. Hard luck; it belongs to Megan now. Tim needs to make that work, she thought. She could definitely see them as a couple. She remembered the look that he'd given Megan, and felt a twinge of jealousy, just for a second, hoping she could find someone someday who would look at her like that. Please make it work, Tim, and give him a chance, Megan, I think you'll find he's worth it.

The night was warm for fall, and Angie lay outside on the balcony, a pillow and a thin sheet to cover her, and let the noise of the city comfort her. The deep black sky of New York showing just the odd few stars through the haze of the city lights. At home in Boston, she could easily find the constellations, the suburban sky filled with stars. Though at this time of the year, she would usually have had to wrap up, she reminded herself. The buildings rose up around her, a symmetric beauty not found in nature, defined by a network of lights, order created in their spaces and different hues, her artist's eye finding and creating patterns, studying the form and symmetries in their midst. She found it comforting and inspiring, and ideas for art began to crystalize in her head. This can be my home. The thought brought a deep pleasure, and she realized it already was home, the home of her heart, created by her father. She could afford to live here now, she could afford a nanny for her child, and she could afford to go to college next year. Simon, Dad, is gone, but he hadn't left her alone. Her future was looking brighter; she had options again and felt a modicum of some control of her life for the first time since The Test, and she stroked her belly at the thought of those early days. But even given her love of the city, she knew, at least for the time being, that she wouldn't be happy here, not yet. In a week or so, maybe a month, the novelty would wear off, then she'd be bringing up a child alone, and still with a nine-month wait before college. She needed more time. And he is gone. Dad's gone. There's no hurry to be here, she thought. I have some friends here, and I know that Tim and Megan will be looking out for me, but I'm not ready. I will be back, I promise, but for now; Auntie I'm coming home, she told herself, and she dozed off, content and ready to find her way back home soon.

Adela, Simon, and Johanna

Kay sat in a rather uncomfortable chair holding Adela. I still hate hospitals, she thought, her previous memories of being in them still strong and very painful. Other than when little Angie was born, she reminded herself. That memory, a bright spot in her mind, still brought a smile to her face. She'd been with her sister when she'd gone into labor. She'd driven her to the hospital in a near panic, her sister panting and swearing in the back of the car. She'd felt every huff, every word, every screamed expletive, as if the pain was her own, while she tried to concentrate on the task of getting her sister to the hospital. All she wanted to do was hug her sister and take her pain away. She'd sat in the hospital waiting room, without a book or distraction, full of strange people and a rather cloying smell, until at last she'd been let in to see her new little niece – a tiny, perfectly formed little child, crying heartily. Adela was smiling with a joy Kay hadn't seen in months. Happy, but exhausted, Kay had thought. It had brought tears to her eyes, and she reveled in her sister's happiness, reciprocating the feeling with a fierce hug and flowing tears. That had been a happy hospital visit, but other visits were associated with pain and death. In her early years, it was both their parents; Adela had been too young to know what was happening, and Kay had never explained it all to her, even when she was old enough to understand. The experience was still painful for her. A few years later, their loving foster parents had died within a year of each other. Adela had taken that very badly. And finally, the worst: Adela, herself, to cancer. After a long period of operations and therapy, she'd succumbed to what they'd known would happen for a few years. Kay had been in near constant tears and a cascading pain, which to this day she still carried, as she'd sat there watching her sister through her final days, hours, minutes. Holding her frail, gaunt hand and praying to a God who didn't seem to be listening. Kay's faith was tested as never before. Adela had already accepted God's grace, and right at the end she had asked and Kay had promised to take care of Angie, the last dying wish of her beautiful sister. In all her adult years she had never needed to enter a hospital for her own purposes, so she carried an unwavering hatred for them. But not today. Angie had asked her to come, and she was here to help with Adela, a task she couldn't resist and that she loved doing. How could she not want to be with Adela? She adored the girl, and being with Adela was simply the next best thing to being with Angie, so being with both of them? Better than cooking for friends, better than... Okay, she corrected herself smiling, equal but different, to being with Christophe. She already missed her new boyfriend. The term rolled around in her mind for a few seconds, giving her pleasure, a joy she'd never experienced before at this level. She wished he'd been able to make the trip, but he was working tonight back in Boston. We'll chat later, she thought with a smile. Everything else was secondary to Adela and Angie, yes even Christophe, she nodded knowingly to herself, and he knew it but appeared to have no issues with the fact. Angie liked him, and so did little Adela. She missed them so much these days.

The baby stirred, shifting position in her arms, but only the light sound of breathing and thumb sucking was discernible. Just like her mother, thought Kay, too tired to actually laugh. The room was quiet now, just three other people were waiting, ensconced in their own worlds. Angie had gone to the restroom, and Kay brooded while her grand-niece slept. It's so quiet here, so peaceful, she thought, struggling to keep her eyes open, feeling the onset of sleep creeping up on her. She shook her head in a vain attempt to hold the drowsiness back. Her eyelids started to slowly close, then suddenly open, as sleep beckoned. It's not like the last time I was in a hospital, the unwanted memory returning. She immediately blocked out the thought and looked at the sleeping baby for solace, thanking the Lord for the beautiful child, and still wishing she'd been able to be here for the girl's birth. The baby had been delivered prematurely here in New York when Angie had been visiting her accountant and gotten away from Boston for a few days. Angie had been going stir crazy since her return from New York to stay with her aunt. Kay had welcomed her with open arms and a flood of happy tears. Though she had only been away for a couple of weeks, it had seemed a lifetime. It was the longest they had been apart since her niece had been born. Kay recalled a conversation here in New York before Angie had made her mind up. Kay was visiting the Big Apple for the first time, and Angie had played the tour guide for her, with an unexpected zeal. On her last day a few hours before returning to Boston, she'd asked Angie the question that been preying on her thoughts before arriving and had been avoiding for the whole weekend.

"Have you made a decision?" I ask, fearing the worst. I don't want her to stay here, a single mother on her own, here in New York. I want her back with me in Boston. I'm using the baby as an excuse, but I just don't want her to leave yet. I know I'm being selfish. I know that it is inevitable. She can't stay with me forever, but I just want to delay that day for as long as I can. And she's going to be a single mother, I remind myself, having already lived through that difficult life choice.

"We've already had this conversation, haven't we, Auntie?" she smiles as she says it. We have, I remind myself. First when she'd applied to colleges, and then when she'd accepted the offer from Columbia. Of course, she would have gone then, would have left me months ago, but for the pregnancy.

"Yes, Sweetheart, but it's different now," I try.

"Oh, this?" she asks with mock surprise. Gently rubbing her hand across her belly. She so large, I think. The baby will be here soon.

"You'll need help. I can help." Am I pleading? I think I am, and I start to feel hot and cold. Not for the first time, I break out in a cold sweat at the thought of her leaving me.

"Oh, Auntie," her face says it all, and I suddenly feel guilty for the discomfort I've brought her with this conflict of interests, from my desire for her to stay with me. "I really have no idea if I'm going to stay here or not. You know I love it here," I blanch, and I see she notices, "and I love being with you," my guilt increases at my not entirely purposeful, but also not subtle, manipulation.

"I know, Sweetheart, and you know I love being with you, but you're going to be a single mother; it's not easy. I should know. I just want to make sure you are okay, that you are happy," I'm not too sure she realizes the amount of work a child can be when you're on your own. I remember days when I wanted to scream, days I cried, believing I couldn't cope with no one there to help me. Forging on, sometimes in desperation, mostly in ignorance, the image and memory of Adela reminding me of my obligation, and now my greatest achievement, pride swelling inside me. Angie the light of my life. Oh Angie, my love, you are my pride and joy.

"I know, Auntie, but I really love it here in New York, and it reminds me of..." she stops, I can feel my nerves tingling. I know what she's thinking, and it still irritates me, heat building slowly as anger surfaces, and I know it shouldn't, but I'm still having a hard time putting it behind me. She knows this too, and her sorrowful look and a small shake of her head tells me all I need to know, and the anger subsides.

"You'll be alone," and my feelings reach out with prayer, but she looks determined. I know it's her decision, but I so want to help her. I don't want her to go through what I went through without real, loving help, having someone there to fall back on. How can that not be good? I'm here for you, Angie.

"Look, Auntie, this discussion, as always, is futile, just like the last time we talked about it. I didn't know then, and I still don't know. It's something I have to work out, and I'm still trying to. So, end of chat, okay?" Her pursed lips and fixed stare cut me off, and the topic was shut down. I respected her decision, what else could I do?

A week later she came back to me.

Kay looked through tired eyes and a small smile at her grand-niece. The baby had decided to come early; that was the way Angie had put it. Not my choice. Not my fault, she'd said, and Kay had still complained, lovingly, and Angie had still defended, likewise.

Yes, my sweet, I would have loved to have been there for you, but I'm here now. She yawned; she felt her jaw stretching and thought it wouldn't stop, her spare hand automatically coming up to cover her mouth. Though I must admit I'd rather be in bed right now, she smiled, her eyes sheepish, as she again shook her head a little in a vain attempt to clear it. She looked around, a little self-consciously, to see if anyone had noticed her wide-mouthed yawn. She was glad to be here, in New York, with her niece, and have a few days away from the kitchen and lunch service. It was getting easier to be away from work these days as Jamie was starting to show the full potential she'd seen in him when she'd hired him – so raw, but so talented. She laughed to herself, giving herself a new bit of energy as she remembered the overcooked roti he'd produced. It had been just bursting with flavors. He had cooked it during his interview, and she remembered his passion when he spoke about food, so reminiscent of her younger self. Theo, the co-owner, was not so convinced, and had thought it was risky.

"This is overcooked," he'd exclaimed.

"We have a good reputation," he'd said.

"Burnt food won't cut it here," he'd exaggerated.

"You know I trust you," he reassured.

"But are you really sure?" he doubted.

She was sure, and he had acquiesced to her decision. They had previously agreed: it was her kitchen, and though he might question, and he did, he actually did trust her, which made for an excellent relationship. She smiled to herself, having now been proven right by hiring Jamie. She had to admit his fried fish was better than hers, and they'd added it to the menu soon after he'd started. There were still people who preferred hers, but she loved his version. Anyway, choice was a good thing. It filled seats, and Theo couldn't be any happier. And his roti? With a little help, it was now perfect.

"Hi, Auntie, everything okay?" Kay jumped, slightly startled. She had started to doze in her reverie, her mind wandering, and now her niece stood before her smiling. "Little Adela not causing you any problems, is she?" Kay hadn't noticed her enter the room, let alone approach her. The baby was still fast asleep, sucking her thumb gently.

"Angie, sweetheart," Kay yawned again, it had come on fast and unexpected, "everything's fine. Adela is as sweet as can be, no problem at all."

"Would you like me to take her?" she looked at her daughter with anxious desire, as she already missed her.

"No, I'm fine. I'm just a little tired." Angie could see how tired her Aunt Kay was, both physically and mentally. Left to her own devices Angie knew that she would doze off immediately. She'd been up all night with Adela, who'd had a particularly rough evening, coughing and crying. She should have woken Angie, but she hadn't, being quite happy at the time to cradle the baby and wait for her to finally fall back to sleep. So, she'd left her niece undisturbed. Then just an hour or so ago, the morning barely started, Fall's light just noticeable in the early hours, they had all rushed to the hospital after receiving the call from Tim. She had hardly slept and the lack of sleep was finally catching up with her.

"That's okay," Angie laughed, "I'll take her." Feeling a little guilty about bringing her already tired aunt here, but glad for the help and company. She bent down and picked up the sleeping baby. Adela barely registered the switch, snuggling immediately into her mother's arm, the gentle sounds of her sleep continuing uninterrupted. Angie stayed standing, slowly walking around the room, rocking her baby and gently cooing to her. Turning towards her aunt, she noticed that her eyes were already closed, her head bowed, and she was breathing softly, oblivious to all around her. Just like little Adela, she smiled. I'm so glad you're here, she thought, beaming at her sleeping loved ones a smile full of affection.

I wonder how Tim is holding up? He looked in such a complete state last time shed seen him, before he'd disappeared back to his wife. You'd think he was the one giving birth, she laughed quietly at the thought. Men! She pictured Tim pacing around, not knowing what to do with his hands. One moment they would be in his pockets, then they'd be wrangling with themselves, then occasionally behind his back, then crossed in front, it was a veritable display of arm gestures. Megan, on the other hand, would be completely in control even as labor continued. She would be in pain, but still somehow so relaxed and focused. And she would still look gorgeous, thought Angie. I wouldn't be surprised if it had been Megan who asked us here to keep Tim company. Though I had begged them to let me be here if it happened when I wasn't in class.

She recalled the last time Megan and Tim had been over, a few weeks ago for dinner. Megan looked great; her back straight, well as straight as can be expected given her condition. Shoulders back, baby belly out, just so proud to be pregnant. Not like I had been, she remembered. She'd bought extra baggy clothing to hide the fact until the obvious couldn't be hidden, and then it had been long coats, hats, and sunglasses coupled with an undercurrent of smoldering panic every time she stepped out of the house. Only Simon's enthusiasm for the coming child had enabled her to cope in public, to understand that there was no shame to be had in having the baby. Now though, everything was different. Having Adela was the greatest thing she could think of. Sure, it made college tough, but she'd had eleven months or so to just be with her baby, and time to adjust to being a mother. Her nanny, a distant relation from Jamaica, was fantastic, and she took much needed pressure off of her. Simon's bequest obviously helped, and at that thought she prayed for both her mother and father, believing them now to be together, in Heaven.

Megan was exhausted. Apparently, the birth had been quick and easy. She'd hate to think what a bad one was like. The pain, still a close memory, was now gone. Her hair was a tangled mess. She was wondering if she stank from all the sweating she'd done, and she knew that she must look awful without any makeup, and where did the hospital get these unflattering gowns? She laughed at these truly silly thoughts. Wondering why, at this moment, the best in her life, such nonsense was running through her head. None of those things really mattered. All that matters is that I have a son and a daughter and Tim. We are a family! Her joy was overflowing. The nurse in the room looked at her when she heard her laughter, but Megan shrugged and continued smiling. She was ecstatic. I'm a mom and soon I'll be the wife of the man of my dreams. What's not to be happy about?

She'd been so nervous when she'd kissed him outside of the apartment that night. Near trembling when she invited him up, though she'd given the impression of confidence and control. The air of bravado and calm was completely fake, but she didn't want him to know that then. She knew what he was like, how shy he was, how he would be thinking and over thinking the situation as they stood there, as she waited for him. Waited! Again! Not this time! However, if Tim had been shy in company, he surprised her by showing none of that shyness in bed. She didn't really know what to expect, though she already knew he was a great kisser. The same could now be said for his foreplay, she reminisced with a smile, recalling her orgasms. He was knowledgeable, considerate and fun, showing none of the desperation she'd anticipated and admittedly dreaded. The next day he'd gotten out of bed quietly so as not to disturb her, though she was already awake and was laughing into her pillow, even before he'd tiptoed out of the room wearing just his colorful boxer shorts. He'd cooked her breakfast. He must have slipped out to the shops, because there was nothing in the fridge, and he'd brought her breakfast in with a flower in a champagne glass. She smiled at the memory. They'd enjoyed the meal together, and then they'd chatted, light conversation, feeling each other out after so many years apart, the intimacy of the moment highlighting their emotions, enhanced by the new physical intimacy. Her iPod played some quiet jazz in the background. Evans, a phase she was currently going through, as she rediscovered her jazz piano roots, forgotten over the years of trying to keep her failed marriage alive, and then so much work required to get back on the stage, honing her acting chops, reading scripts, practicing day and night in front of the mirror, her previously learned skills so long unused. Though honestly, they'd hardly noticed the music, as they'd touched and kissed and held hands all morning.

Then, with a nod and a smile, it was back to bed before the afternoon had even arrived.

She continued to smile as she reminisced, but a question returned, haunting her: Why? Why had it taken so long? Why hadn't she seen it? How could she not have noticed? And though she kept on asking, she could find no satisfactory answers. I probably never will, she sighed, the questions coming back nonetheless, and they will probably continue to do so, she concluded. She could hardly describe how happy she was, and so glad that Simon had questioned it, seen beyond his own desires to tell her, regardless of how long he'd actually gotten around to do it. What if he'd never mentioned it? The thought had also saddened her, as still slightly conflicted, she'd once hoped, just prior to his death, mere weeks before she and Tim had finally got together, that she and Simon might have worked out as a couple, had another go at it, even after their first failed attempt. Now she knew otherwise. She'd loved Simon dearly, but she knew now that her relationship with him, wonderful as it was, was never on the same level as what she had with Tim. But both relationships were beautiful. I'm so lucky and so privileged to have had both, and her smile and newfound joy overshadowed any melancholy of loss.

Tim had stayed the whole day; they'd made love throughout the rest of that afternoon, and in a rush of changed clothes and a quick snack masquerading as a late lunch or an early dinner, he'd escorted her to the theater for her show that evening. They'd kissed outside, just a quick one, but they had still been caught by a couple of her co-actors. There had been plenty of winks and back-patting prior to and after the show and then during drinks later. The incident had made its journey around to all of the company gathered there. They all seemed as happy about the new relationship as she was, and they radiated their feelings, washing over her with warmth and love. She hadn't realized that they cared how she was, how she felt, but they did, and she'd cried that night as much for her newfound re-acquaintance with Tim as for the loving and joyful responses from her fellow actors and friends.

The next morning as she woke and as consciousness returned, she knew she was missing Tim already. They hadn't agreed to meet up the next day, and after a morning pottering around doing nothing, she realized she was waiting for him to call. She decided to take the matter into her own hands, as the memory of the old Christmas kiss returned, and its unsatisfactory aftermath. Now, there in the forefront of her memories, she was determined that such a mistake was not to be repeated.

"Hi, Megan. How are you?" He answered, and she could hear the pleasure in his voice, but it seemed tempered with doubt, even after the day they'd experienced together, so reminiscent of that time many years ago. She had no doubts, she knew, but? How are you?

"Hi, Tim, how are you?" she responded with heavy sarcasm.

"I'm fine," he stuttered with a slight pause, and in her mind, she stopped her train of thought that was hinting at anger. I'm not doing this, she thought, I'm not going to play around with him. This is Tim, I've known him since I was in kindergarten. I know him too well. So, he didn't call. He's shy. He is truly awful at phone conversation. He wants what I want, but he doesn't think he knows what I want. He does know. I want him. He's just being too careful not to hurt my feelings. He lacks confidence, I know this, I've always known it. I need to tell him, or at least give him a hint; a big hint. She smiled with the certainty that this was what she wanted.

"Come on over."

"Now?"

"Now!"

"Okay." She could hear the laughter in his voice.

After she'd put the phone down, Megan decided she wanted to make sure that Tim would have no doubts about how she felt, and she proceeded to plan for his arrival with a playful mischievousness. First, she had to prepare herself, so she hurried to the bathroom. She didn't want to be halfway through her preparations when the doorbell rang. That just wouldn't do, as an anticlimactic vision hit her of him standing there with her half-dressed and still applying makeup. She chuckled to herself.

He arrived about thirty minutes after she'd finished showering, applying her makeup, and deciding what to wear. She'd tried playing some piano to pass the time, but she could barely concentrate, and after starting through a opening few bars of several pieces she that would normally flash through, she quit with a sigh of disappointment. She flipped through TV channels for ten minutes or so, and when she'd at last settled on something, the door buzzer sounded his arrival. She was glad to turn it off and let him in and shivered in anticipation of her plan.

The knock on the door announced his arrival. She took a quick and final look in the mirror, satisfied with her appearance, which she'd already spent considerable time preparing to perfection, and she let him in.

"Hi, Megan, I'm here," and he kissed her on the cheek. What I'd hoped for was at least a peck on the lips, she thought, not totally surprised at his action, but a little disappointed that he'd been so predictable. She was still visualizing him grabbing hold of her, and kissing her passionately before she'd even had a chance to reply. It's Tim, she reminded herself, with a hint of disappointment, at the lost fantasy. Then she realized that Plan A was definitely going to happen, bringing an inner tingle and she knew she was looking forward to it.

"Hi!" Hello, Plan A, she screamed internally with delight to herself.

"Oh my god. You look," he struggled for a second, "fantastic!" his eyes admiring her.

"Thanks," she responded, slightly distracted with the idea of putting Plan A into action, though accepting the compliment with some pleasure. His eyes quickly dropped and he walked into the living room, then turned when he realized that she hadn't followed him.

"Tim, where do you think this relationship is going to go?" she asked him, her voice neutral, her gaze steadily focused on his, but her heart was racing at the sight of him and the anticipation of Plan A.

"Well, I was hoping we'd get to know each other," he replied cautiously.

"Get to know each other? Again?"

"Yeah, sort of," she could hear the quiver in his voice showing how nervous he was, and she knew he'd thought about it, most certainly over-thought it, and was still unsure. She didn't know why, but then again, she was not surprised. He's probably had this playing on his mind all day, probably last night, and certainly on the journey over, and has thought and thought, and over-thought it, letting little doubts creep in and turn into large doubts. I want him fully committed and totally sure, she thought, I haven't got time to play around. I'm already sure. I'm already committed. All I want is you, darling.

"Okay, hold on a minute." She walked past him, appearing to ignore him, which certainly wasn't the case, the thought of him, and anticipation of Plan A tingling through her.

"Yes, of course," he replied quietly to her back, he turned and watched her as she'd made her way to her iPhone. Her hips swinging, the tight dress accentuating her moves, he felt the tension that registered arousal, and his eyes moved up and down her form, his passion for her increasing, wondering where this was all going. She stood at her desk, her back to him, and dialed in the songs she'd just downloaded and prepared just for this moment, and pressed play. Tim's face turned from yearning to quizzical as Luther's voice came over the speakers. Megan turned with one hand on a jutting hip, and smiled.

"I'd like to dance, how about you?" she asked suggestively.

"Of course," he stammered, watching her hips now swaying to the song, and she then started mouthing the lyrics "...you're the sweetest one..." and her fingers, made a come-hither gesture that he just could not resist. He relaxed and tightened up at the same time, the anticipation gripping him, but at last, he smiled as the doubts caused by his dream fled. He was fully committed to the woman he'd loved for so long, and he fell in rhythm to her actions and desire. He walked towards her slowly, in time to the music, as her body swayed and her fingers pulled him. His eyes were fixed on hers, occasionally straying over her body, her tight dress flowing over her body, accentuating: the curve of her hips, the line of her thighs. The cut was low and showed her ample bosom, and the fit hinted at no knickers or bra he surmised, but her dark eyes, so alive and holding such passion, dominated, called him, beckoning him irresistibly towards her.

They stood inches apart, not touching, apart from a single finger, he gently stroked her soft skin, as they swayed in time, together, with the song. She was in control, and he knew and wanted it, waiting for her as she continued singing to him along with Luther's voice. She reached out and held his hand, intertwining her fingers with his, and a shiver ran through his arm at the contact. He pulled her towards him with his other hand. Their bodies pressed together, and she knew he was aroused. Their faces were now just inches apart, and she pecked his lips, "... you are the one..." she sang out as a whisper, very quietly, but loud enough for him to hear. They continued to dance through the song, as she sang with Luther to him.

The next song slowed down and she put her head on his shoulder and he held her closer, and never losing their timing, they danced as one. For a moment she enjoyed the peace, the previous weeks' troubles disappeared and the only person that mattered was Tim. She lifted her head and looked into his eyes. He didn't need prompting anymore. He bent forward and kissed her, teasing her, playing with her, and she joined in. As the song was coming to an end, she released his hand and wrapped her arms around his neck, and crushed her lips to his, her tongue probing. He followed her lead, complementing her, offering his own directions for her to follow, as he followed hers. After a few minutes, and through another song, he suddenly stopped, pulling back slightly, and laughed out loud. A huge and hearty laugh that rang off the walls. Sweeping his arms underneath her, he easily lifted her and carried her to the bedroom as she's kicked her bare feet in the air and laughed along with him.

Those days ran into weeks, in a continuous flow of pleasure and emotions as she and he were now both fully committed to their new relationship with no questions or doubts. She had to admit that it was the easiest relationship she'd started, but then reminded herself, with a smile, that it had been nearly thirty years in the making. It was worth it, but all of that was nothing compared to what came next. After the first sickness bout, she knew, or at least guessed, hoped? Then after she'd returned from the doctor, she'd danced around her apartment performing delicate ballet moves she hadn't practiced in years, giggling like she hadn't done since high school. She'd pulled all her clothes off, stared at and then stroked her stomach, which of course was the same as always, but it wasn't, was it? And then she'd danced and danced and danced. She hadn't thought she could be happier than she had been just a few days earlier, after their quick weekend trip to Boston, when all they'd done was make love and eat at Kay's restaurant every night; she was wrong. And so, she danced naked and alone, and then… She had to tell him. Now! But first…She practiced telling Tim. Nothing quite seemed right, each version felt inadequate, each becoming more exaggerated than the next, as if she was in an old fairy tale or preparing for a part on the stage, every line causing her to start laughing at the thought of seeing his reaction. It was truly comforting to know that her new partner in crime would have no issues with this news. There was no need for tentative questions to gauge his feelings; they were obvious already. No having to prepare a statement or some sort of apology, no attribution of blame to be made, no questions or decisions to be asked about an unplanned pregnancy. However she told Tim, she knew he would be thrilled with the news, just as she was ecstatic about it. However, just tell him? How? She wanted to tell him her way, so she thought and planned her way through it. It had to be right. It had to be perfect. More than perfect. This was the best news, ever!

And so she spent the day preparing.

She laughed at the thought of all that preparation. It had been worth it though.

I'm snuggled up on the sofa. I have my head on the lap of the man I love, and I'm bursting with the news that only my doctor and I know. We are listening to some early Miles, having just finished eating our late dinner. I have been patient all day. I've been planning this all day. I've come up with some elaborate ideas, but I've realized that simple is best. I nearly told him on the phone, but I stopped myself just in time as the news nearly slipped out. I nearly told him when I arrived back home after the evening's show. He was already in my, my? our kitchen, cooking dinner, singing along to Michael Jackson. He loves to cook. I don't, but I love to eat, and I really love to eat good food, and he's very good, so that works out very well. He'd prepared a delicious pasta with pesto and tomatoes, followed by some chocolate brownies and raspberries, but I still waited. I want him relaxed and unprepared. I keep wondering if he's guessed, since I didn't enjoy a glass of wine with dinner, and though I don't always, I'm just a little self-conscious about it, feeling that it might be noticeably unusual. Well, I don't notice any questioning looks from him, and he doesn't hide his emotions well when he's excited, so right now I'm assuming he has no idea, not even an inkling. And I'm bursting to tell him, but I wait. I have a plan. It's simple, but it's going to be fun.

He's relaxed now, stroking my hair with his fingertips, like a light breeze, then gently ruffling it, all in time with the music, I notice. The sound of the bass line or Miles' trumpet escaping as an intermittent humming or buzzing in my ear, not totally unpleasant, but let's be honest, I smile to myself, neither Holland nor Miles needs the help.

I'm ready.

"Tim, do you want kids?" I ask him, already knowing the answer to the question since the subject has come up a few times, but I just need to get his attention, to have a little fun with this.

Miles' impromptu accompaniment stops. "Huh?" Yes, he's unprepared. My smile is hidden with my head facing away from him, and I still feel his fingers in my hair.

"Do you want kids?" I ask again, with a seriousness I'm not feeling, knowing he heard me the first time, wanting to jump up and down and laugh the news out.

"Of course I do. You know I do," he answers with the offhandedness of someone relaxed, believing they are ready for wherever the conversation is going. My smile broadens with a childishness I should be ashamed of but am not. I know, I can't be. "Why? Would you like to try now?" he offers with a snort and a laugh. I can see his smile in my mind, as he now lightly jostles my hair, with his humor. Wrong direction darling, though I find the idea very appealing, and for a second, I'm distracted and find myself already starting to plan later into the evening, but, no, not yet. I have something to do first, I remind myself, pulling away from that pleasantly distracting thought.

"Well, I really can't see the point," I say with as serious a voice as I can muster, without sounding too weighty. And inside? I'm laughing, dancing again, as I was yesterday, earlier today, and probably tomorrow.

"Really? Why?" and now he's confused, and the stroking has stopped. And I know he knows, but it hasn't registered in his brain yet. I can be such a child sometimes, I think, smirking, enjoying the moment. Oh, Tim, I love you so much.

"It really is a little late to try now," I twist around, turning my head and look up at him to see his reaction, and still he's thinking, I can see it in his eyes, the lines in his face, I know. Today he's being a bit slow, and I just want to laugh out loud. Maybe he was a little too relaxed; Miles can do that to him, I surmise with some satisfaction. He looks down at me questioning, not really believing what he'd just heard. Tim, Tim, Tim, come on.

"Too late? You mean? You're? We're?" he's just a little afraid to ask, without full confirmation, just in case. I let him off the hook, I acquiesce, I nod. It's hard to describe the transformation of the look on his face, but I can feel it light up the whole room and me – the whole world.

"Yes, I do. Yes, I am, and yes, we are," I smile back at him. His spontaneous smile is a thing of beauty.

"Really?" his voice goes up a few decimals and an octave, and I'm holding back my true feelings, I'm trying to seem nonchalant, but it's really hard. Really, really.

"I confirmed it with the doctor yesterday and have been dying to tell you. I assume you're okay with it?" I ask with feigned indifference, positively dying to leap up and hug him. I give him a sly wink and a beaming smile bordering on a laugh. He confirms my previous assumption with a whoop and nonstop tears of joy, lifting me off my feet and swinging me around, followed by a stream of profuse apologies, due to his misconception of my now supposedly delicate state, and through all of that? All I can do is laugh out loud, as I hug him tightly and kiss him with total joy.

He moved in with me within the month, subletting his apartment to a fellow teacher; giving it away, was how I had described it, his bequeathed apartment already rented out, and after over thirty years we now, at last, started to get to know one another.

There were endless things to like about Tim. As a friend, she already knew most of them. As a lover, he exhibited the standard stuff in spades, she smiled to herself. And the rest: it had been a great first day, an unforgettable second, and as far as Megan was concerned, it just kept getting better. Though to be honest, she reminded herself, he needed to be seriously housetrained, chuckling at the thought with a little sigh of despair. He'd obviously been living alone for too long. This could be easily resolved, she believed, but the clincher for her was that he never seemed to take her for granted.

Simon had taken her for granted. Football or the band always seemed to take precedence. Maybe it was just their age, as they had been so young, but being in a relationship with him had been so competitive. When they were together it could be great fun; unless you disagreed with him, then it was constant questioning and debate. Why do you prefer that band? How can you not like this? Do you really think so? Seriously? When he was in that mood, there was a constant barrage of questions to which there were no satisfactory answers. She realized later that it was just his way of finding out about things, teasing his lovers and testing his friends, but mostly testing himself. The questions were really for him. They were his way of resolving the dichotomies of opinion. It was years before she understood and appreciated this about him. Then sometimes, when they were alone, he could shut out everything else, and it would just be the two of them. He was a hopeless romantic, considerate and funny, really funny, a dry humor that he could switch on at will, and later after when they'd become such good friends, and when he wanted to be, he was a great listener. And he was always smiling, what was not to like about his smile? It would be possible to believe that he was never miserable, though she knew this not to be true. Even when he wasn't at his best, that smile always seemed to turn up. Even when he felt a bit down, he always found some humor in any situation. The problem was that sometimes just getting together, just the two of them, was a chore. She had to compete with everything else for his attention – sports, the band, his friends, and he appeared to have a lot of friends back then. It was exhausting. After she'd broken up with him, when they'd become better friends, and later when they were older and supposedly more mature, the timing and any real chance of getting back together just never seemed to be right. He'd definitely changed over the years, was more considerate and a very good listener, but the timing was always wrong. There was Adela, his college sweetheart, the girl who was Angie's mother. Then later he dated that artist. Then I meet Peter and left Manhattan. There just never seemed to be a right time again. To be honest, she thought, I don't think it could have been this good, this deep, as beautiful as it is with Tim. She could understand more so now, how Simon and Tim, seemingly opposites at school, had become such close friends. Both smiled a lot, both were terribly romantic, and both were crazy about music, but everything was so much easier with Tim. About her exes, the less said the better, she thought bitterly. But she soon brightened again as she thought of Tim, her future husband. Yes, there have been many wasted years, too many, but now he's mine, and I'm his. She looked lovingly at her two babies in their cots beside her. Where is he? I want him here with me, with us.

"Hi, nurse? I'm sorry, I don't remember your name?" The girl next to her focused her attention on Megan.

"Yes, Mrs. Seaman? It's Mandy," replied the nurse. Megan didn't flinch anymore. I'll be dumping that name in just a couple of months, she thought with some satisfaction.

"Hi, Mandy," the girl smiled, "could you call my husband back please?" Okay, a little poetic license, but it sounds so good, she told herself. I think I'm used to it already. "He should be with some of our friends in the waiting room."

"Of course, Mrs. Seaman, I'll be back in a moment with him."

"Thank you, Mandy."

"You're welcome, Miss." Megan watched her as the girl carefully checked the sleeping babies in their cots, her heart soaring at the thought of them. Her eyes followed Mandy as she left the room. Her mind now fully occupied with her newborns and her husband-to-be. He'll be here soon, back with me, with us. She giggled at the thought. She'd kicked him out just a while ago, as he'd been fussing and crying, and laughing and fussing, and he had completely forgotten our guests waiting in the waiting room.

Thoughts of her newly born babies returned with added pleasure. Simon and Johanna, her grandmother's name and a name she particularly liked thanks to so many wonderful childhood memories associated with it. He'll come around. Actually, Sarah's a very nice name, but two S's didn't quite sit right with her. She didn't really mind either way, but he'll come around. Tim's smiling face came to mind, and with her babies now starting to cry heartily, she realized that this was going to be a totally new experience for both of them. Now, will he actually return with our guests? She asked herself, a slight smile accompanying her doubt, as she started to feed her children.

"It's a boy and a girl," Tim rushed in, face flushed and obviously excited. Kay jumped up at the sudden noise, woken, disoriented, and facing the wrong way.

"Boy? Girl? What?" She flustered, getting her bearings and finally facing the grinning man, staring at him, still a little unfocused. His eyes were wide and his mouth agape, and she was feeling disoriented from sleep.

"Oh my God! I'm a dad. I'm a dad," shouted Tim to no one in particular and to everyone in the room. He still wore the hospital gown he'd worn at the birth hours ago, too excited to remove it, and now oblivious to the fact that he was still wearing it, even though Megan had reminded him several times before she had just given up. A couple of strangers looked up at the commotion, smiled and nodded in some sort of agreement, before returning to their books, tablets, and waiting.

"So, why are you here?" asked Angie in a controlled voice, gently rocking and cooing her child, though inside she was jumping up and down and dancing with joy that they'd allowed her to come. I did beg a lot, she smiled to herself.

"What?" he asked perplexed.

"Here. You. Why are you here?" She asked the confused man, smiling. And why are you still wearing that awful looking hospital gown? she thought with a quizzical look of distaste.

"Oh, and Tim?" she quickly got in before he could reply, having decided that subtlety was not in order here, "Why are you wearing that hideous looking gown?" He looked down at it and nodded.

"Yeah, this? I can't seem to get out of it at the moment," he laughed.

"It's pretty hideous," she reminded him.

"Yes, it is, but..."

"Seriously, you should remove it, everyone will think you an idiot."

"Really?"

"Really."

"It's not kind of cool then?" he asked hopefully.

"Cool? Seriously? Seriously? No. It's just hideous," she said screwing up her face to emphasize the point.

"Ok," he replied and promptly removed the offending item, dumping it on a nearby chair.

"And again? Why are you here?" she reminded him.

"Oh, Megan kicked me out," he replied laughing, "I kept fussing, and shouting and... I'm a dad!" and tears of happiness rolled down his face. "Oh, Angie, Kay, I'm so happy. Is there anything better?" He stopped moving at last, and Adela woke up at the commotion and started to cry. Tim stared horrified at her, an apology written all over his face. Angie just laughed and started to rock her child back to silence with gentle murmurs.

"Well, are you going to get married now?" asked Kay, now fully awake, the nap having taken the edge of her previous tiredness.

"What? Married? Oh, yes," he laughed, "we really weren't expecting her to get pregnant so soon," not that we weren't, unofficially trying, he thought. And he laughed even louder inside at the thought. I'm a dad!

"Tell me about it," laughed Angie, still trying to control her restless child. They both laughed with her, once again disturbing the few others in the room. Tim had calculated, they had calculated, and agreed on a couple of months after they'd started dating. The possibility had been an unspoken agreement, accepted after the first few nights, so neither had worried about any forms of prevention, and both were ecstatic when the news had been confirmed. Marriage, though implied, hadn't even been discussed in earnest until after the news. They'd agreed on something small after the birth and maybe a reception later in the year, possibly soon. Well, Megan wanted soon, like, very soon, like next month. So...

"We've decided to have the wedding during the Christmas break, now I've just started my new position. Just a small ceremony with a few friends." He looked at them assuring them that they were considered to be part of this select group. "So, in just a few months?" he raised an eyebrow with the question. Angie laughed, struggling a bit with her child as she squirmed for some freedom, babbling now to her mother with mostly incoherent baby words, but which Angie appeared to understand.

"Oh, are we invited then?" she asked rhetorically. Tim laughed, relaxing a bit but still flushed with excitement.

"Yes, you're both invited," he answered a little more seriously as if implying a hidden apology.

"Both?" She nodded at her child with a sly smile, giving a not so subtle hint that maybe Tim had missed someone?

"You're all invited," he laughed. "I'm a dad!" he repeated and burst into another round of smiling tears. Angie and Kay look at each other and burst into laughter. Adela looked at each of them and laughed and babbled with them, reaching out as if she wanted to be part of the happy celebration. Angie hugged her, and Adela wrapped her sweet little arms around her mother's neck, laughing with the abandon that only babies, and possibly new fathers, can have.

"So, a boy and a girl. Names?" Kay asked breathlessly.

"Well, we always said if we had a boy, he would be named Simon," he looked at them, his smile still there but his eyes more serious. Kay nodded her approval, and Angie laughed and started to cry. Adela continued laughing still caught in the moment, "or if a girl, Simone. So, Simon it's going to be, but we still haven't agreed on the girl's name. I'm partial to Sarah, but Megan's more than partial to Johanna, and she'll probably win. I'm just happy we have healthy babies." He beamed at them both, all seriousness now gone.

"Of course, you could call the girl Simone and the boy something else. I don't know, Joe?" offered Kay teasingly, now fully awake and full of mischief.

"Yes, we could," Tim replied warily, "and I could have another naming argument with my fiancée. I think not," he laughed back.

"There is that," she agreed.

"Twins!" He shouted to no one in particular, and ignoring present company for the moment, proceeded to strut his funky stuff.

A nurse entered.

"Ah, um, excuse me." Tim didn't notice and didn't hear, all the rest of the eyes in the room were going back and forth between the nurse and him as he continued dancing with his arms flailing, legs twisting, buttocks swinging, all moving in time to an internal beat that could just be heard coming out of mouth, while everyone tried not to burst out laughing, friends and strangers alike.

"Excuse me. Mr. Seaman?" She asked a little louder. On hearing her, Tim winced realizing she meant him and he stopped mid-gyration. He looked at the nurse and gave a slight shrug, then gulped to get some air. His face glistened with a soft sheen from the minor exertion, and he panted slightly, his smile seeming fixed permanently to his face. It most certainly wasn't going anywhere soon.

"That's my fiancée's name. I'm Tim," he corrected her, still panting, he recognized her from earlier when she'd helped Megan with the children after the birth.

"Sorry. Tim," the nurse was still staring at him as though he had lost his mind. Hadn't she seen any other happy fathers act as such, thought Tim still too elated to be embarrassed, "Your wife, sorry, fiancée, is asking after you." Tim's already wide smile, turned into a huge teeth-baring grin. He returned his attention to his guests.

"Gotta go, ladies," he bowed theatrically to first Kay and then Angie and her child, "my lady wants me, and I must away. I must leave you three lovely ladies," he then turned, and veritably skipped towards the door and started to leave the room, following the already departing nurse. He stopped at the opened door, paused and turned back to face them, remembering his original task, just before he walked through it.

"How stupid of me. I'd completely forgotten," he apologized, "Come with me. Come and see Megan and our babies?" he offered excited, they looked at one and other smiling. "Please?" They didn't need to be asked twice and quickly gathering up bags and Adela's toys they left the waiting room, following Tim and the nurse.

"Hi, sorry I'm a little late." Everyone turned towards the voice, and breathing rather heavily, clutching and mostly dragging a little boy beside him, Jason had arrived, a sheen of sweat visible on his forehead. He appeared to be fighting for more words as well as his breath.

"Dad got lost," said the much calmer boy. He was smiling and didn't appear to be in any sort of distress at all.

"Well," Jason paused for another breath, looking down at his son, "I didn't get lost, Timmy," he tried to explain, although it was sounding more like the justification of an excuse about to be formed.

"Well, what were we doing halfway across town then? At the other hospital?" the boy, still smiling, asked with feigned innocence. "I know you only came because I wanted to, but…"

"I'm very happy to be here," and he was, but even more so because Timmy had begged him. He couldn't refuse him, "I'd just gotten the name wrong, my young padawan?" and both laughed, with the familiar banter.

"So, lost then," his son persisted, the smile telling everyone how much he was enjoying the moment.

"Not so much lost, as..." he fumbled for the right phrase, as his son continued smiling, just a little too cockily for Jason's taste, "misdirected." I've lost this one he thought but smiled back at his son, resigned to whatever his son was about to say.

"Semantics," the boy stated with the confidence of a child getting one up on a parent. Jason looked at his son, proudly and with only a little exasperation. Semantics? He's too smart for his own good, he thought, his pride easily outweighing any annoyance. He laughed again as he ruffled the boy's hair, accepting defeat. Everyone else looked amongst themselves, understanding what had happened, but still feeling a little lost at the interplay.

"Hi, Jason. Hi, Tim," said Tim, interrupting the father and son's obvious fun. The boy turned and smiled at Tim with acknowledgement, "You're just in time. I'm just about to introduce my children to the rest of the world," Tim beamed, looking around at his companions. "Come and join us. Megan will be pleased to see you," and without waiting for a response he turned and continued towards his family, expecting the others to follow him. He quickly disappeared around the corner. Little Timmy was the first to respond, letting go of his dad's hand as he raced after his friend and music teacher. The others had barely moved when he popped his head back around the corner.

"Come on, you slow coaches, catch up," the boy laughed and disappeared around the corner again.

Printed in Great Britain
by Amazon